STILL LIFE WITH BADGE

DAVID W. KANNAS

ISBN: 1484819926
ISBN-13: 9781484819920

Library of Congress Control Number: 2013908487
CreateSpace Independent Publishing Platform
North Charleston, South Carolina

Contact can be made at northadmiral@hotmail.com

PROLOGUE

Yvonne Gillespie's last glimpse of her bleak world was of the cigarette-smoke-yellowed ceiling of a has-been room in one of Seattle's fringe hotels and that of her killer's contorted face. She was on her back on the worn linoleum floor, naked and sweating, gasping for one more breath, a breath that wouldn't come. The brutal rape that she endured was no longer of any concern. The ligature that her killer had wrapped around her neck cut into her flesh, turning her face red and causing the vessels in her eyes to rupture. The only mercy shown Yvonne came when she lapsed into unconsciousness as blood stopped flowing to her brain. Her killer's face was little more than a snarl as it dripped sweat on Yvonne's exposed breasts. His eyes bore into her like knives. His hands, two over-sized pieces of meat, gripped the length of leather lace with both hands. He was trying to cut through her neck; he was succeeding. Then Yvonne died.

Her killer, naked and breathing like an enraged bull, let go of the leather lace, leaving it in place. He got up, wiped his matted chest hair with his T-shirt, and then pulled it over his head. He put on the remainder of his wrinkled clothes, clothes that had taken on the odor of the room, and glanced around the room. He heard a noise in the dim hallway, stopped what he was doing, and listened, nose in the air like a rat. This was a hotel, at least its owner called it a hotel; there were other people living here. He had been quiet in his task. She hadn't screamed; she didn't have time to scream before he had control of her.

The man slowly opened the door of Yvonne's room just enough to check the hallway. There was no one there; he didn't expect that there would be.

It was four thirty in the morning; most residents would be in bed or passed out drunk in an alley. He heard a click like a door closing. He looked toward the sound and saw only a mop bucket and mops sitting at the end of the hall near a door that had a sign attached: "ROOF."

Yvonne Gillespie hadn't experienced many of life's joys, but she had a firm grip on what a living hell was. From the time she was raped in a shed in Iowa by a neighbor at age twelve to this night, when she sold herself to her killer, life was one long struggle to survive—except for the periodic dream she had of finding a better life around the next corner or at the end of the next road. Like a lot of end-of-the-roaders, Yvonne had ended up in Seattle. It was about as far as a person could go without falling into the Pacific Ocean. Alaska was the next stop, but that was too depressing for even Yvonne to contemplate. Yvonne Gillespie died having no memory of anything but the crap that life threw her way and in quantities that could ruin a battalion of lives just like hers.

CHAPTER ONE

Across Elliot Bay from downtown Seattle and a world away from the room where Yvonne Gillespie lay, still warm but very dead, Don Lake startled fully awake as he swung his legs from his Swedish modern bed and onto the polished wood floor of his bedroom, overlooking Elliot Bay and the Seattle skyline.

As he sat there clearing his head, Don saw some evidence of the events that had gone on the night before. There, on his very polished and dust-free birch floor, was a pair of panties. From their appearance, he knew that they had been thrown there with some abandon.

Don got up slowly, gazed at the clock, and then sat back down. The hands of the retro alarm clock from Lands' End said 6:37. A soft light came through the room's curtains. The sun's glow was just beginning to illuminate the tops of the Cascade Mountains and bring the city to life.

Maybe it would be a stretch to call it an actual sunrise. Seattle in April rarely saw the sun burst from behind the Cascades. More often than not, a wet blanket of clouds, producing their usual duck nibbling mist, shrouded it as it tried its best to illuminate the day. Nor did the city ever completely sleep. This wasn't Fergus Falls, Minnesota, or Mendocino, California; this was Seattle, well on its way to becoming a "world-class city," or so the movers and shakers proclaimed every time they proposed a new and expensive project that the public would pay for.

The sound of water running in his shower brought more clarity. Since Don had neither a wife nor a roommate, this could only be the owner of the free-range panties standing in his shower. Then it all came back. Man, did it come back.

The water stopped and the door to the master bath that adjoined his bedroom opened, letting more light filter into the bedroom, adding to the glow through the windows. Roseanne Vargas walked into the room, towel working vigorously on her long black hair. The view was stunning.

Roseanne Vargas had Mexican blood running through her veins. She was five foot ten, which was tall if a man was threatened by a woman his height or taller. Don wasn't one of them. She was also perfectly proportioned. She could have made it through the day braless without anyone knowing, unless she wore something tight, which she usually did. The water that dripped from the curves of her muscled and naturally tanned body was forming water spots on Don's polished wood floor. He'd attend to that later.

Roseanne was Don's neighbor, a neighbor outside the usual definition, but a neighbor none-the-less. She owned a townhouse across from Don's and in the same complex of expensive townhouses. From the first casual conversation Don had with her shortly after moving in, Roseanne gave the impression that she could be more than just a neighbor if he pursued the matter. She smoldered as she talked, something that Don found more than attractive; the smolder extended to her body. Not that he was a sexist jerk; he wasn't. At least he tried his best to deny it if he was. He just liked women, especially women who didn't play games and let it be known that they were available under the right circumstances for more than passing the time of day in idle chitchat. They had engaged in a lot more than idle chitchat last night. At least Don couldn't recall any chitchat.

"Howdy, neighbor," Roseanne said in her best smolder as she sat next to Don on the edge of the bed, the towel covering her damp hair but nothing else.

"Howdy yourself," Don whispered in her right ear as he took the towel from around her head and threw it in the direction of the clothes hamper, missing. He gazed back at her breasts now on full display, the remaining water droplets dripping from her erect nipples. "Did you lose something last night?"

"If you're talking about my virginity, I lost that many years ago."

"To an attorney?"

"You've got to be kidding."

One of Roseanne's many attributes that Don found appealing was her humor and bluntness where sex was concerned. She knew what she liked and didn't mind that others knew it, especially Don. "No, I mean your panties, the pair over there," Don whispered in his best imitation of Humphrey Bogart. "The ones that seem to have been thrown there last night, those panties."

"Oh, those panties. I wondered about those panties. They might come in handy later, but now I'd rather we worry about your obvious problem." Thus, the saga of Don's life as a very happy bachelor resumed.

CHAPTER TWO

D on Lake found his way into his pleasant, although at times troubling, circumstance by way of a few of life's nonlethal ambushes. He considered himself one of the luckiest SOBs on earth. Although his life was littered with hairpin curves that most men of his age didn't have to negotiate, he had managed to not go off a cliff... yet. It seemed that no matter what he got himself into, he was rewarded in one way or another. Even an early marriage and divorce had a way of honing his life to a fine edge. The reward of that marriage was a teacher of techniques in bed that would likely find their way into *The Joy of Sex Volume Who Knows What* some day. Too bad the teacher hadn't been a great wife in other respects. It seems she believed that the world would benefit if she spread her skills around. Come to think of it, so did Don, just so long as she spread them well away from him.

Then there was that national *faux pas* known as the Vietnam War. While it was not the war to end all wars, it was a war that could be used to one's advantage if approached just right. Some of the war's veterans used it for endless sympathy over things like posttraumatic stress disorder (PTSD). Don looked back on it with both nostalgia for the friendships he made and disgust for some of the things he had done, but he mostly tried to forget it.

He'd had all the things that money could buy when he was growing up. The one thing he didn't have was blindness to the unfair hand that life often dealt. All around him he saw that most of his male classmates in high school would have the military or the iron mines as choices once they graduated, if they graduated. If they ended up in the mines, they might just get lucky enough to buy a fishing boat to haul behind their pickup as a means of getting away from what was waiting after the weekend. Then there were the girls, who mostly looked forward to marriage, pregnancy, and getting fat before they knew that their lives were over before they started.

Don could have weaseled his way out of the draft by wasting a few years in college. That injustice was Don's reason for enlisting in the army, knowing that, in the eyes of his family, he was wasting time. If the army and Vietnam were good enough for the poor and sometimes just plain dumb fucks that lived in his hometown, it was good enough for him. His parents and grandparents thought that he must have lost his mind. Maybe he had.

After the indignity of basic training and infantry school, followed by a hellish nine weeks of ranger training, Don found himself in what he thought was a respectable little unit in Vietnam, one that engaged in actual combat. The commonly held idea among those with similar skills was that if you had it, you should use it. It wasn't made up of your average PTSD assholes, as Don liked to call them. However, even that potentially life-changing experience managed to produce roses in the patchwork of a garden Don called life.

He still harbored some guilt for taking an active and willing part in the Vietnam War, a war fabricated on the lies of chicken-hawk warmongers and military "heroes" who wanted a few more medals to hang on their chests. The guilt was all about what he and the war had done to that country and to the good old USA, a war that would definitely not end all wars.

For his honorable service in that less than honorable war, Don found that he was given preference in some things like public service jobs and enough GI Bill benefits to get through not only a BA degree but an MA as well. While the PTSD assholes were sitting in therapy circles, performing mental masturbation, singing "Kumbaya," and whining, Don was attending classes at a reputable university and loving every minute of it. He not only liked the academics, he liked the supply of females who paraded past him.

To his delight, he discovered that foregoing the PTSD route placed him in good stead with some of the female students and a small number of female faculty members. Being perceived as a tough guy had its advantages. There were times in Don's memory when he thought that he should seek the attention of a shrink to find out why he had this almost overwhelming interest in women, but he decided that his interest was normal, so he forgot about that.

He gave very little credit for his success with women to his appearance. Don was of Finnish and Lutheran heritage, so his stoicism was exceeded only by his feelings of guilt and inadequacy, and, at five foot ten and 170 pounds, he wasn't the biggest guy around. His Nordic features were somewhat flat; his Nordic hair was blond and thin; and his Nordic sense of humor was dry and sardonic. All gave him an inexplicable manner that women found appealing. Roseanne was no exception.

When he and Roseanne Vargas had finished playing the games both enjoyed and Roseanne was on her way home and then to her office where she would try to pull one more of Seattle's crooks from the clutches of an unfair criminal injustice system, Don got on with the day waiting for him. While showering off the pleasant aroma of Roseanne, Don gave some thought to his moral standing in the world. He was a productive person, no doubt. He performed a job that not many could or were willing to do but found fascinating enough to spend most of their waking hours watching it on television or reading about it in paperback novels, poor bastards. But what was this thing he had for women? He loved the female of the species. Was that so wrong? And he found Roseanne Vargas especially attractive, even though she was a public defender. Or maybe it was because she was a public defender that Don found her so attractive, almost forbidden fruit. Then there was the simple truth that Roseanne made it clear she was into sex and not relationships. Truth, Don thought, was a rare characteristic among attorneys, especially defense attorneys, so he did nothing to discourage her.

Every time Don got ready to meet the day, he gave thanks for his "job." He was a Seattle Police Department homicide detective. This was no small thing, given that most assignments to the unit were made based on whom one was drinking or golfing with or whom one was slipping into bed along side or all three. Don didn't golf. He felt that it was for wimps who didn't know how to run, hike, kayak, or ride a bicycle. He didn't drink much, although he enjoyed a glass or two of so-so red wine every day. Trader Joe's Two-Buck Chuck was his wine of choice. But he did like the bed qualification. He just didn't know anyone he wanted to take to bed who also happened to be connected to the Homicide Unit. At least that was the case before he was assigned to it.

Three years had passed all too quickly since Don became a part of the Seattle Police Department Homicide Unit. Finding that there might actually be a day when retirement reared its head and he was left wondering where his life had gone, he made a decision to follow what he liked most in life: wringing all of the juice from it that he could without killing himself along the way.

When he learned that the Seattle Police Department was hiring, he was living off his significant inheritance and a few odd jobs. The *Seattle Post-Intelligencer* announced in bold print that the Seattle Police Department was looking for a few good men and women, but mostly men. He completed the preliminaries and received a date and place to start the testing process. He found the strength and agility tests to be unimpressive at best, thinking that if someone couldn't pass them, they shouldn't be on the street. He was surprised at how many failed, the sorry bastards. The written test was about as challenging.

Apparently the people in the department who decide such things were impressed enough to call and tell him to come in for more tests. The only test that gave Don some concern was the polygraph. He had attended San Francisco State where it was practically a requirement that the student body and most of the faculty enjoy the benefits of marijuana.

To its credit, the Seattle Police Department valued honesty above purity. He told the polygrapher that he had indeed used the noxious weed. Nothing more was made of the character flaw, and Don never again used the substance.

He was hired and assigned a slot in the state police academy. During the next three months, he learned the basics of how to be a cop in Washington. What followed were three months of fun as a student officer on the street. What Don had a hard time believing was that he was paid for having fun.

Work for Don wasn't a job per se; it was more accurately a game, much like baseball, but he didn't play baseball. Baseball was just another wimp sport that required only that one be able to chew snuff, scratch, and look bored, all at the same time. He liked his work, he liked getting to the bottom of things, and he liked fucking with people who needed a healthy dose of being fucked with.

Getting to work, that is, the physical process of transporting his ass from house to office, started with a choice of transportation. The townhouse that Don owned was on a bluff overlooking Elliot Bay. It provided a great view of downtown Seattle, the Flatlands—also known as South of the Dome, or SODO—and on a clear day, the Cascade Mountains. Today was not clear.

Like most days in April, a mist blanketed what was potentially a view of the mountains and most of downtown. With the memory of his early morning romp with Roseanne fresh in his mind, Don chose not to take his bike off the rack. He would instead take the water taxi. After getting into his work "uniform" of slacks, shirt with tie, sport coat, and trench coat, he walked to the closest bus stop and rode to West Crest Park where the water taxi docked.

There was the usual unhappy lot getting on the boat. Most didn't fully appreciate that they might have been getting on a hot and smelly bus in New York City instead of a boat that smelled only of salt air. The dock bounced with the wave action created by the boat's arrival mixed with a southwesterly wind. The waves didn't know which way to form and ended up being nothing more than a confused chaos of chop.

This would not be a good morning to be in his kayak on Elliot Bay. Not that Don kayaked to work; he found the whole idea slightly stupid. While it might play well in a novel or movie, it was stupid. Where to stow the boat on the other side was a question Don had asked himself and hadn't yet found an answer. One of the low-life pricks who made a living breaking into cars parked under the Alaska Way Viaduct would drag it to God knows where and sell it for twenty-five dollars five minutes after Don pulled it ashore. He did not like making the lives of this scum any more comfortable.

When the taxi quietly slipped away from the pier, Don noted with more than passing delight that his favorite fellow passenger was aboard. She sat on the opposite side of the boat with her Starbucks coffee in hand, reading *The Seattle Times*, the right-wing rag that competed with the *Post-Intelligencer*. This he could overlook since she was such a vision. About thirty-two was his guess. She always dressed in a Northwest stylish fashion with a knit cap pulled over and around a face that could only be described as cute with a hint of beautiful thrown in. The fleece jacket she wore said that she wasn't going to an executive's office to take dictation. Her slacks were tasteful and snug across the butt. Don was reminded of Roseanne Vargas's bicycle butt; it was round and very firm. It got that way because she exercised it, probably on a bicycle, a serious plus in Don's opinion. On more than one occasion she had acknowledged Don's presence. He couldn't be sure if it was a smile or grimace that crossed her face when she did. He'd have to work on that when he had the time and the courage, that's if he could get past his Finnish Lutheran self-doubt.

The trip across Elliot Bay wasn't just eyeballs and imagination. Don's love of the city grew with each trip. There was the whole seaside village shtick of West Crest Park complete with seagulls, sea lions, and the smell of salt water, the things that made tourists from Topeka want to stay, and who could blame the poor saps? Ships lined the two waterways to the south, ships from various world ports. Orange cranes that resembled praying mantises were attacking each ship, loading and unloading the stuff that America loved to spend its money on, most of it cheap and cheaply made in China.

Then there was the skyline of the city. The taller buildings disappeared into the low-level cloud layer, forming a watercolor against the gray sky to the east. Smith Tower tried to maintain its status among the giants that were doing their best to hide it and were mostly succeeding, except from this water-side view.

Smith Tower was once the tallest building west of the Mississippi River. It was now struggling to hold its head up, but it was, in Don's opinion, still the most beautiful piece of architecture in the city. It was hard for Don to believe that the Foshay Tower in Minneapolis was in contention for the honor of tallest building at one point. Don didn't know where that argument ended or if it did. From what he knew about Minnesotans, they were still fighting the battle, the single-minded pricks.

The short but bumpy ride across Elliot Bay ended near Coleman Ferry Dock. From the dock it was about a five-block walk to the Public Safety Building (PSB) where the Seattle Police Department Homicide Unit and Don's very modest cubicle were located. The walk took him under the Alaska Way Viaduct on an elevated walkway that formed a tunnel under the viaduct's southbound lanes.

The tunnel smelled of stale urine from the bums—the mayor preferred that they be called "homeless"—who called this spot home. Don could only imagine the horror the Bainbridge Island commuters experienced every morning on their walk from a Washington State ferry to their cubicles in one of the high-rise office buildings. The Bremerton blue collars would take it in stride; God bless them. They carried a lunch pail or sack lunch to work or knew someone who did. They knew what the noon whistle at the Bremerton shipyard meant. The Bainbridge crowd still remembered the angst of their sixteenth birthdays when daddy hadn't produced the BMW as expected. Don thought that they could all benefit from a thorough ass kicking in one of the urine-saturated alleys that defined and defiled this part of town.

Maybe Don was just being himself. He often transferred a little of his past onto these, no doubt, fine people who wanted nothing more than to get through another day in the evil city and then escape back to their island, an island awash in the fragrance of fir trees that would erase the smell of the urine left by sub humans and the general deviant air of the city. *Screw them,* thought Don as he stepped under the viaduct, doing his best to hold his breath.

The Public Safety Building at 610 Third Avenue was one of Seattle's great eyesores and clear evidence in support of the death penalty. It had every feature of architecture that any Fascist dictator would love: cold, gray, straight, brooding, functional, and dusty, and over the years it had acquired a certain smell that was hard for Don to put his finger on. It lingered among cigarette smoke, urine, and car exhaust with dust thrown in. In Don's opinion, the architect responsible for its design should have been drowned in Elliot Bay and then eaten by crabs. However, this is where the wheels of justice turned, where the Seattle municipal courtrooms were located and where most of the inner workings of the Seattle Police Department resided. The chief of all police had his office on the tenth floor overlooking Elliot Bay. And there was rumor afoot that plans were being made in high places to replace it with something more appealing.

Don's work cubicle was on the fifth floor with the rest of Homicide, Robbery, Special Assault, and a few other units, all of which were viewed as seriously flawed by most homicide detectives. It provided no view unless you considered the drunks and derelicts on Third Avenue somehow aesthetically pleasing; Don did not. It was truly a rat's maze of cubicles and offices. If the PSB had one redeeming feature, it was, despite its many flaws, "the fifth floor." The fifth floor was the fount of greatness, the floor on which most aspiring detectives longed to practice their trade and some who aspired to just screw the system and collect a check. Don had made it to the fifth floor. He wasn't sure how this had happened, but it did.

Security on the fifth floor wasn't up to Fort Knox standards, but it did require a key to get in. After getting off one of the five elevators that served the building, Don said good morning to the unit secretary, Marjorie Manford. Marjorie was her usual cheerful self and dressed in her usual but not exactly Seattle-like fashion. Marjorie didn't think that polar fleece, pants, and comfortable shoes fit the image she tried very hard to effect. Don quietly thanked her every day for her taste in dress as well as her hairstyle and extremes in makeup. Marjorie dripped sex from every pore and she knew it. Every male on the fifth floor was in love with her. Don was certain that some of the women were as well.

"Hi, Marjorie, how's it hanging?" Don said as he opened the door to admire her latest fashion statement. Today she went for the Marilyn Monroe look. Lacking Marilyn's chest, Marjorie made up for it by wearing a bra that enhanced her natural charms with either water or gel; it would be difficult, thought Don, to really determine which unless he used his hands, and he wasn't about to go there, so to speak. Whichever was doing the job, it pushed her breasts up and out the top of her very low-cut pullover blouse. Don had to catch his breath before continuing. He again wondered why she didn't just spring for a boob job. If she couldn't afford it, she could take a collection among the detectives on the floor. She would have more than enough for the procedure with some left over for a new and more revealing dress and under garments from Frederick's of Hollywood.

"See anything you like, Don?" was Marjorie's breathy reply.

"Great blouse, Marjorie." What he wanted to say, and would have if he had let his mouth precede his brain, was "nice tits." But he thought that this would have caused further delay in his trip to his desk, although she would have no doubt taken it as a complement.

As he continued the stroll to his cubicle, Don's mind wandered to an evening shortly after his arrival on the unit. His squad was working the night shift, four to midnight. The night squad had a tradition of going to dinner as a group at least once a week and often went to a dive that was within walking distance. The dive was the Crazy 8 on Fourth Avenue. The Crazy 4 wouldn't have the ring that the Crazy 8 had, was Don's guess. Marjorie rotated shifts with his squad, so she came along on some evenings when she wasn't deluged with transcribing tape-recorded statements.

The Crazy 8 was smoky, smelled of stale beer, and was in serious need of a lighting consultant. For that matter, it could have benefited from a once-over by the Seattle Health Department. Don's guess was that the health department inspectors were living a little more comfortably because of dives like the Crazy 8. When the squad walked in, all five of them plus Marjorie, they went to their usual booth near the back. The booth was horseshoe shaped and covered in a worn blue plastic that had suffered many abuses over the years. There was just enough room to accommodate the squad. The booth's final assault was a subtle whiff of the nearby men's room. *Classy* was Don's sardonic thought.

Marjorie sat directly across from Don, squeezed between Sergeant Wilton Sherman and Detective Bill Grimes. Both had been in the squad for many years. They dressed alike and looked alike, as old married couples did after spending years together. Don's guess was that they could end each other's sentences.

After everyone had ordered, Marjorie began to give Don a look that he could only assume was a come-on: she licked her lips while staring directly at him; she pulled her already overly expressive blouse lower, exposing more cleavage than was necessary to make her point; and she smoldered. Don hoped that she didn't spill something hot down her front. The rest of the squad was exchanging the usual small talk: whose wife was screwing which officer or detective, the incompetence of the chief and his minions, the usual.

Then Don felt a foot on his right calf. The foot was naked and very dexterous, as if its owner could type with it should the need arise. The foot was slowly making its way up his leg to end at who knew where. Don hoped that the foot was attached to Marjorie's leg. She was very good with her toes. She knew how to manipulate a man while appearing to be doing nothing but being the good dinner companion. If this continued, Don was going to be too distracted to eat without choking. He decided that he could sacrifice dinner for the current ministrations, provided the others at the booth didn't notice what was going on, but come to think of it, they had probably enjoyed the same over the years. The waitress arrived with their orders, and Marjorie withdrew her foot. Life went on.

Don's image of Marjorie was cast in granite on that night. She was available and not very subtle about making it known. He would try his best to ignore his inclination to give in to his true self. Mixing business and pleasure never worked was Don's maxim. He could, however, be persuaded otherwise given enough evidence to the contrary, and he often was.

The walk back to the area that the Homicide Unit called home took Don along a dark hallway that smelled as if it hadn't experienced fresh air since the day it was built. The color of the walls didn't matter; it would have looked the same in any color. The walk took him past the entrance to the lineup room, which was right out of the era of film noir. When the lights were off, it was like being in a cave. The chairs were old and made of wood, probably salvaged from a long since demolished movie theater of the X-rated variety. Near the back of the room was a cardboard box filled with various pieces of clothing that were used to give the men—they were usually men—in a lineup a similar appearance. The clothes had been in the box for years and had never seen the inside of a washing machine.

On the way to his cubicle, he met the night janitor who tried to keep the fifth floor somewhat presentable. He mostly failed for two reasons: he was lazy and the detectives whose work areas he tried to keep clean were, by nature, slobs. Wally Fox had stopped caring about his work a long time ago. This morning he was out of place because he should have been off duty. He was pushing an unplugged vacuum cleaner toward a janitor's closet, a closet Don had never laid eyes on and didn't want to.

"Good morning, Wally. Working a little late, aren't you?"

Wally grunted and continued on his way, his clothes hanging on him as if they too hadn't seen a washer for a while. Don noticed that Wally had developed a limp and hoped that it wouldn't hinder his work, not that it mattered. Wally's face, like his clothes, hung on his facial bones. The word *slob* entered Don's mind.

"Hurt yourself, Wally?"

Wally grunted again and continued on his way.

Chuck Weinstein was exercising his two typing fingers when Don reached his cubicle.

"Morning, Chuck," Don said as he sat down at his desk.

"Morning, Don. Did you bring coffee and donuts?" Chuck responded, not looking up from the paper in his typewriter for fear that he would hit a wrong key and have to correct it with his ever-present correction tape. Don could only imagine what Chuck was costing the city in correction tape.

Don recalled the first time he met Chuck Weinstein. They were new patrol officers in the South Precinct, working second watch. Chuck had been in the department a little longer but was younger than Don by a few years. His first impression of Chuck was that he was homosexual, not that Don had a problem with that. Chuck kept a very low profile, not acting out the bullshit that could get an officer's ass kicked unnecessarily.

Over the five years that Don and Chuck had worked on the same patrol squad, Don found that Chuck, no matter his sexual orientation, was one of the best and toughest guys he had ever known. He would walk into any blind alley with him, and that was saying a lot given Don's general opinion of his fellow man and woman: they could not and should not be trusted until they proved themselves in the heat of battle.

"No, I brought my exalted self and thought that that should satisfy even you," Don chuckled.

"Sorry, no donuts, no ass-kissing for your holiness," Chuck harrumphed.

The office was quiet. Most of the remainder of Don's squad and the other day squad hadn't arrived. They straggled in until the last one arrived at about nine. Some would arrive smelling of last night's drinking binge, others with attitudes that screamed, "When can I retire from this bullshit?" Don, Chuck, and Sergeant Wilton Sherman were the general exceptions, although Sergeant Sherman had lapses. They, for the most part, appeared to like their jobs and were anxious to get to it. Don hadn't quite figured out the sergeant, though. He seemed to be nothing more than a babysitter to a couple of other guys on the squad while expressing an apparent fear of Chuck and Don. *What gives?* was Don's thought.

Before Don had a chance to settle in with his morning cup of so-so coffee and a quick look at the *Seattle Post-Intelligencer*—Seattle's liberal-leaning paper—Sergeant Sherman stuck his head into the cubicle and said, "We got a callout, guys. Manager found a body in a room at the Fairview Hotel in Chinatown. Patrol wants us there posthaste. Take the van and meet me there."

Don thought that Sergeant Sherman wasn't his usual self this morning. He hadn't bothered to shave and his clothes looked slept in.

"OK, Sergeant," both responded.

"Is it a stinker, Sergeant?" Don asked.

"You'll find out when you get there, won't you?"

Don did not like stinkers: bodies that had assumed room temperature and started to move with the help of the maggots that had taken up residence just under now putrefied skin. He took action, preventing the inevitable puking and retching. One had to maintain a certain level of decorum around patrol officers and other detectives was Don's thought. If they found the stinker mask unmanly, fuck them.

Chuck and Don took one of the painfully slow elevators to the parking deck where the homicide van was parked. The van was a GMC delivery painted department blue, complete with lights and siren, although one would have a hell of a time getting the van to move along at anything above the speed limit. Its function dictated its form: it supplied detectives with enough stuff to process almost any crime scene. What it lacked, like cameras, the unit kept in the office. Anything extra, like neck-snapping acceleration, wasn't part of the van's function. The van had seen pretty much everything that Seattle had to offer in the way of mayhem.

Chuck had the keys, so he got behind the wheel and maneuvered out of the Public Safety Building from its spot just inside the James Street entrance. The door that blocked the entrance from the street rolled up as the front bumper broke a motion-activated switch. They drove out onto James, turning left and heading up to Fifth Avenue where they turned right and drove to Chinatown, which started at Yesler Street, and continued south to Dearborn. The Fairview Hotel was on Jackson Street, just south of Yesler. They turned left onto Jackson and stopped in front of the hotel. A Seattle Fire Department unit was leaving as they drove up. "Looks like Fire has completed its job of crime scene destruction," Don said. "Now they're on their way to be detraumatized after being subjected to man's inhumanity to man."

"Uh-huh," Chuck responded in agreement.

There were two marked patrol cars parked in front, both unoccupied. A bored-looking officer was standing in front of the hotel, probably because the patrol sergeant told him to deflect any press from the building—a good call, not that the press would care about a stiff at the Fairview. They were probably too busy checking out a fender bender on Interstate 5 or a lost dog in Baltimore that Seattle would find interesting with morning coffee.

Neither Don nor Chuck recognized the officer. He was apparently newer to the department. His name tag identified him as Henderson. He looked like a Henderson: tall, stocky, and blond, clearly a Swede, in Don's opinion.

Don never quite forgave the Swedes for subjugating the Finns for centuries. Even during the Winter War in 1939 when Russia attacked Finland, the Swedes sat on their asses and claimed neutrality. That was, in Don's opinion, nothing more than an excuse to exercise their right to be chickenshit. *Screw them, and fuck the blond Swede who didn't have the guts to look at a dead body.* Maybe Don was being overly judgmental as usual, but he still had problems with Swedes.

"Your zero one zero (the code for a homicide) is in room number sixty-one. You better take the stairs because the elevator has been acting squirrely according to the desk guy," said Henderson with more deference than was called for.

Your zero one zero? Why not call it what it was: murder. The clearance code for a homicide was 010, but the officer wasn't clearing anything. Don thought that he might be sucking up for future consideration. He knew that that's what he had done as a younger troop, and it might have worked.

16

But he still didn't know how he made it to homicide, so maybe it didn't. Don and Chuck grabbed their briefcases and walked into the hotel.

The Fairview was one of several single-occupancy hotels in the seedier parts of the city. It wasn't a hotel that you would recommend to a relative who happened to be visiting from Minnesota unless you disliked the relative. Don could think of one or two who would fit that bill. In its earlier days, the Fairview had been an OK place to stay for a night or two. Those days were long gone. The foyer was once resplendent with a checkered tile floor and marble half wall. The two entry doors were heavy oak with beveled glass. The door hardware, once polished brass, was now dull and pitted. The registration desk was small but well built. There were cubbyholes behind the desk. The place could have been used as a set in any noir film out of the forties or fifties. Alan Ladd in a fedora, sitting in the lobby, looking over the top of a newspaper, would have fit right in. Veronica Lake in her white, wide-brimmed hat sliding sexily from the backseat of a black 1948 Buick with wide whitewalls would have made the scene complete. But this wasn't the forties or fifties, and Alan Ladd's ghost wouldn't be seen dead in the place; then again, maybe it would.

A man of an undetermined age, wearing a wrinkled white dress shirt complete with pocket protector and yellowed collar and in serious need of a haircut, sat behind the desk. There was a J. A. Jance novel facedown on the counter in front of him. Don asked if he was the manager and when he came on duty. The man said that he was just the deskman and had been on since six. Don made a note of his name and told him that he would be back to talk to him. He also asked the man to hand him the guest register.

"Is that necessary?"

"Yes, it is."

"OK," said the deskman, satisfied that he had stood his ground for a second.

"Did you report this?"

"Yeah, but the guy who cleans rooms and empties garbage told me. He found the door partway open and saw what he thought was a body or at least a very sick woman without clothes lying on the floor of sixty-one. He reported it to me and I called nine-one-one."

"We'll need to talk to that guy when we come down."

"OK, I'll see if he's still around."

Don took the dog-eared register, and then he and Chuck walked to the elevator. Don was pleased with things so far. He hadn't made the poor sap who manned the desk feel like a lesser being, and he had the register in hand. Win, win situation in Don's mind.

Contrary to Officer Henderson's advice, Don and Chuck elected to try the elevator instead of wasting time and energy climbing to the sixth floor. The elevator had the smell of the mostly unwashed bodies that occupied the hotel and the years of cigarette smoke that yellowed the once white ceiling. To add to the unpleasant atmosphere, the elevator's dull walls were scratched and dented and a slight odor of urine drifted up from the carpeted floor. Why anyone would find the need to piss in an elevator was a question that went unanswered in Don's mind. The light was the lowest wattage that the building's maintenance man could find. It did its job, just. Don made a quick estimate of the elevator's capacity and whether it would accommodate a body on a gurney. He thought that it might with some effort.

When the elevator reached the sixth floor with nothing more than the usual complaints of machinery of its vintage, Don and Chuck stepped out and walked into a dimly lit and narrow hallway. A patrol sergeant was standing in the hall outside room sixty-one. Don recognized him as Sergeant Bill Warner, one of West Precinct's first-watch sergeants. He was not one of the many sergeants who thought that detectives were unnecessary and lazy assholes who got where they were because they knew somebody or were too gutless to work the street where the real work of the department happened. Sergeant Warner had been around long enough to know that there was deadwood in patrol and investigations and that detectives were a valuable and necessary arm that made his job easier. But there was no denying that there was a lot of deadwood in the department.

"Morning, Sergeant," Don and Chuck said in unison.

"Good morning, guys. Where's the coffee and donuts?"

"I was about to ask you the same question," said Don. "You've had more time than us to round them up."

"I'll send the newbie to get some while we figure this thing out."

The "newbie" came out of the room where she had been standing just out of sight. The "newbie" was a female officer about twenty-five years old with blonde hair that didn't come from a bottle and was curled into a regulation bun just above her uniform collar. Don glanced at the nameplate attached to her jacket: "Morris."

His first thought was that it was a good thing she had a nameplate pinned on her jacket. He might otherwise have been found guilty of staring and giving the impression that he was just another in a long list of sexist pigs in the department. At the moment, however, he was exactly that, although the terms were redundant in his profession. Officer Morris had no right to be so attractive and still be in uniform. She should have been in a silk blouse with her hair allowed to unfurl over her shoulders. The body armor she was wearing did a great injustice.

Breathe, thought Don. *Let's keep this professional and let this vision jet off to the nearest coffee shop for coffee and donuts.* His next thought was w*hat a sexist fuck you are for thinking that she should be going for coffee.* But hadn't he been relegated to coffee detail as a young troop? Yes, he had, and it had nothing to do with his sex. On the other hand, had it? There was the time when a female sergeant had sent him off to fetch coffee for the gang because he was the newest among them. He didn't recall being that upset or traumatized by the task. Then he recalled that the sergeant who had sent him on the mission was gorgeous both in and out of uniform, mostly out. He'd have to check on her current assignment one of these days. There was no redemption.

"Detectives, this is Officer Morris. She's new to the department and new to my squad. Officer Henderson is her field training officer for the day," said Sergeant Warner."

Don couldn't help but note a slight smile on Sergeant Warner's face as he spoke. Sergeant Warner, rumor had it, had been through several wives and several female officers during his career. Officer Morris may have been on his radar, but he didn't stand a chance.

"Would you be so kind as to go to the nearest Starbucks and get us coffee and pastries of your choosing?" Sergeant Warner asked Officer Morris in his most fatherly tone. He then gave the young officer a twenty-dollar bill that she took without any expression and left. Don interpreted her manner to mean: *Fuck you, Sergeant; I've got your number, and I'll be taking some notes when I get to the patrol car.* The good sergeant didn't seem to get that he was now living in modern times. Then Sergeant Warner turned back to Don and Chuck and described what was waiting in room sixty-one.

CHAPTER THREE

Yvonne Gillespie, aka Gloria Chapman. aka Kitty Carmichael, aka Shirley Wonder, had been new to Seattle. She had a past that would rival the seediest sex novel. She was born in Iowa to a no-good and never-will-be father and a mother who didn't have sense enough to get out of the rain let alone raise a child. Yvonne was fortunate to have the name given her by her parents because she had little else. She had a few more IQ points than her parents, but not many. Yvonne did have one thing to thank her parents for: her looks. Yvonne could always fall back on her looks. Men fell all over her for no other reason than the simple fact that they couldn't bed a woman like her without paying, and if they were paying, why not get someone they could only go to bed with in their dreams. She wasn't especially smart. She couldn't cook or clean house. She had never had a house to keep clean. Yvonne Gillespie was smart enough to know that her appearance was valuable and would keep her alive as long as it lasted. She tried her best to keep this valuable commodity in shape. Given her life, it wasn't easy.

Yvonne escaped Iowa as soon as she found out that there were better places, places that weren't covered with cornfields and sky and men who thought they were free to take from her that one thing of value she possessed without giving back what she wanted: money. Her one regret in leaving was her younger sister. Who would watch out for her when she left? Yvonne went to Seattle, via Las Vegas, Los Angeles. and San Francisco to seek her fortune, and she found it. That is, she found it until it took her to the Fairview Hotel.

Sergeant Warner led Don and Chuck into room sixty-one where the body was slowly assuming room temperature. She had become a piece of evidence in a murder instead of the warm and very attractive woman she had been. They saw the body lying on its back on the floor, her arms stretched out to the side forming a crucifix. She stared at the ceiling through half-closed eyes that were dried and dull.

The woman was naked except for a leather ligature clinging to her neck. *Why would a murderer leave such a critical piece of evidence?* was Don's first thought. It dug into her flesh in such a way that it appeared whoever did this had tried to decapitate her. Her tongue extended slightly from the right side of her mouth. There was still a look of terror on her face. Her beauty hadn't saved her this time. In fact, it had led her to this.

Her body had retained a horrible perfection. Prostitution was her chosen profession, or it was what was available to a woman from Shit City, Iowa, lucky enough to have a body like hers. This time, however, she had met the wrong person. The man who killed her apparently didn't care that she was beautiful or that she only wanted to capture part of the American dream by the only means she saw available to her. He had used her in the most violent way he could. *What a waste,* Don thought, and he meant it in the best sense.

What was she doing in the Fairview was what Don wanted to know. She could at least have been making porn flicks in the San Fernando Valley where she could be certain that she wasn't going to freeze in the cold rains of Seattle. Her greatest threat there would have been AIDS or premature aging from the sun.

Don opened the desk register that he still grasped in his hand. He saw that the person registered to room sixty-one was Kitty Carmichael. At least she was using that name when she rented the room. You could never be sure about the names of the occupants at the Fairview, or any other hotel for that matter. She had been there for a week and paid daily, which told Don that she wasn't sure when she was going to leave. She used an Iowa driver's license to register, probably fake.

"Well, Chuck, how do you want to handle this?" Don asked with as much deference as he could muster. Don still tried his best to give Chuck the lead in investigations because Chuck had been around longer, but both Don and Chuck knew that Don was better at the business and the natural leader.

"How about we wait for the sergeant and see what he thinks."

"OK, sounds good, but how about we start by knocking on some doors and seeing if anybody heard or saw anything before he gets here? It might pay to catch these folks before they get out of bed. But first let's find who she really is."

"OK, sounds good," said Chuck.

Chuck Weinstein may have been gay, but it didn't necessarily show by his demeanor if the stereotypes were true. He did, however, have an endearing quality of modesty that Don found appealing in a partner since he possessed enough arrogance for both of them. At an even six feet tall and weight in proportion, Chuck was Don's superior in many ways. For example, Don knew that Chuck could, if he was so inclined, kick his ass. Chuck's black belt in karate was the real thing. He also had it all over Don in dress. Chuck pressed his jeans, something that Don found excessive and usually only practiced by prison inmates with little else to do but press their pants and pump iron. Don liked that Chuck knew his business but didn't flaunt it like several others that he could name. Then Don returned to the matter at hand.

They found a suitcase in the closet that had some official-looking papers in an envelope tucked into a side pocket. In the envelope were documents from Iowa's Department of Corrections addressed to one Yvonne Gillespie. Kitty Carmichael was in fact Yvonne Gillespie, who happened to be under parole supervision in Iowa. The crime for which Gillespie had done time wasn't on the forms. They took the letter and the suitcase.

Sergeant Warner agreed to watch the room and the body while Don and Chuck went to the nearest rooms to talk to whoever occupied them. The rooms were furnished with just the essentials: bed, dresser, closet, and sink. A bare bulb hung from every room's ceiling. A communal bathroom was down the hall. None of the rooms came complete with a piece of "art" hung on a wall at an angle like most cheap motels that dotted the country's highways. There were ten rooms on each floor; they would need to canvass every one of them. They started with the closest one and worked out.

It took a few minutes for the occupant of the closest room to answer the door. He looked like he had seen better days, needing a haircut and a shave, not to mention a potent mouthwash. This would fit the basic description of every occupant of the hotel. He hadn't seen or heard anything, not unusual; people who occupied the Fairview made a career of not seeing or hearing much of anything. He had seen Yvonne, however, aka Kitty. He was very impressed with her and wondered what she was doing at the Fairview. *Perceptive man,* thought Don.

As they continued from door to door like a couple of Mormon missionaries without the white shirts, black ties, and pasted-on smiles, Don realized that they wouldn't learn a hell of a lot. He had been to hotels like this on investigations. One recent investigation of a shooting came to mind in which the two shooters had a gun battle that took them along a hallway and down a stairwell to a lower floor where the shootout continued. Each combatant hit the other several times, and when they could no longer hold their guns, were taken to Harborview Medical Center. None of the other occupants of the hotel saw or heard anything. Both suspects/victims lived to duel another day.

Don and Chuck took the names and contact information of everyone they talked to on the floor, not that it meant squat. They also left their cards with everyone in case they recalled something at a later time, like over a beer at the Red Door Tavern down the block. The murder would give the morons something to talk about while sucking Rainier from a bottle, but it wouldn't translate into helping "the man." It would, however, be a diversion from the usual subjects of conversation, like when the next supplemental social security check would arrive or "like that time in Vietnam."

By the time Don and Chuck were done with the canvass, Sergeant Sherman had shown up and was talking to Sergeant Warner as if it was old home week. Don noticed that Sherman had shaved and changed clothes for the occasion. Don also noticed that the ligature around the body's neck had been moved. He suspected that Sergeant Sherman was guilty of this crime scene no-no.

Sherman and Warner had been at many crime scenes together over the years and found it nothing more than an opportunity to catch up on the usual. As they covered who was sleeping with whom in the department part of the exchange, it was clear that Officer Morris, who had returned from her assigned task, was taking it all in stride. Don thought that things were looking up for Officer Morris's police career. So did Sergeant Warner, who glanced over at her from time to time to see how she reacted to being in the presence of two old farts who still wondered at the wisdom of taking women out of the kitchen, bedroom, and nursery and putting them in a man's uniform. Little did they know.

"You two might as well take this case," said Sergeant Sherman. "You've already got a good start on it, and it looks like it probably won't go anywhere since she was obviously a prostitute who just ran out of luck. Did you find any witnesses?"

Don noticed that Sergeant Sherman made decisions like this pretty quickly and without much information to support them. He was old school and thought that certain professions didn't deserve the full measure of the "serve" part of "to protect and serve." Prostitutes got the least amount of service from Sergeant Sherman. His attitude rubbed off on the other two detectives on the squad. Detectives Bill Grimes and Jack Martin were next up for a murder, but they would be passed over for the time being. Don and Chuck were of another school. They would give Yvonne Gillespie the service part even though they weren't around to protect her when she was raped and killed.

"No, we haven't found any witnesses, but we have some residents of the hotel identified that have to be talked at," Don said.

Deoxyribonucleic acid, better known as DNA to the cops and citizens who couldn't quite manage the longer version, was a relatively new tool in the kit box of murder investigators. It was slow, but it was certain. It was almost as good as fingerprints. Identical twins could fool the DNA geniuses; fingerprints could not. Even identical twins had unique fingerprints. But DNA was now the go-to technology when fingerprints weren't working. Having both to take to trial was the best of all worlds.

Chuck and Don were up on all the latest investigative technology, and they used it. This gave Sergeant Sherman heartburn. He thought that a real detective relied on shoe leather and talking mixed with copious amounts of liquor; he also thought that detectives like Don and Chuck were threats to his way of life. Sergeant Sherman and the other two detectives on his squad, Grimes and Martin, knew that it was only a matter of time before things would return to how they were and how they should be.

To make Sherman's life even more tense, the new chief of police was destroying a way of life that he had perfected over the years. The new chief was into bullshit voodoo policing. He forced the idea on everybody that "community policing" was the future. What the fuck did the "community" know about policing? Fuck a bunch of "broken windows" crap. Broken jaws and hard drinking got the job done in the past; it would continue to do the job in the future. Sergeant Sherman sweated over these thoughts every day that he was on duty and when he was wandering around his empty house, drink in hand, when he was off.

Sherman hung around the scene longer than he did at most of those Don had experienced. Don also noticed that Sherman showed more interest in the body, but who could blame him there? Even in death, she was attractive. Don caught himself; he wasn't, after all, into necrophilia, but was Sergeant Sherman? He'd have to put that on a list for later consideration.

When Don and Chuck were finished processing the scene, they called for someone from the medical examiner's office to come by, do their work, and take the body away for autopsy. The short trip from Harborview Medical Center to the Fairview Hotel took Dr. J. Wyman Mills and technician Mike Griswold about ten minutes. Dr. Mills knew both Don and Chuck and liked to work with them. Don also liked to work with Dr. Mills for more reasons than her professionalism at scenes and autopsies. She was a vision to observe, even when inserting a thermometer into a stiff's liver or sawing off the top a skull.

While Don and Chuck looked on, Dr. Mills bent over the body and, using a scalpel, made an incision in the skin over the liver. *A serious case of bicycle butt* was Don's knee-jerk thought. She then inserted a thermometer to get the body core temperature. She might have been checking a turkey just out of the oven. This would give an approximate time of death since the body's temperature decreased at a standard rate under different conditions. This was a normal condition for a room since the room wasn't cold or overly warm. She also put a thermometer on the nightstand when she first walked into the room. This would give ambient temperature, which made her estimate of time of death more accurate. "Eighty-two degrees," said Dr. Mills. "Probably died at three or four this morning. Just an estimate, though." She did not like to tie herself to a precise time because that might come back to bite her at trial. Assuming there ever was a trial.

In her examination of the body, Dr. Mills pulled its half-open eyelids up with forceps, exposing the whites. Both eyeballs were a spider web of broken capillaries or *petechiae* in medical terminology, evidence of strangulation. She would most likely find a broken hyoid bone in her neck as well.

"Would you mind scraping her fingernails before bagging her hands?" Don asked Dr. Mills. "She probably scratched the guy before she died. She has fingernails that would almost certainly pick up some skin."

"Sure, we can do that. You might get a jump-start on things at the lab that way."

"I'm guessing she was raped," said Chuck.

"Do you think?"

"Screw you, Detective."

"Point taken," said Don with his usual smirk when he was fucking with Chuck.

"That's my guess, too," said Dr. Mills, not paying attention to the verbal jousting between Don and Chuck. "She has some trauma around the vagina; we'll know at autopsy. Do you guys smell that? There's a disinfectant odor coming from her. It's almost like that stuff you smell in public restrooms just after they've been cleaned."

"Yeah, I thought it was from the room. These rooms are subject to some serious germ exposure," Don added.

"Are you planning to attend the autopsy, Detective Lake?"

Don was always happy when he made points with Dr. Mills. He hated autopsies, but he put on his best detective face when she was doing the cutting. Retching was not an option when she sliced a body from pubic bone to sternum and cut out human organs to comment on, weigh, and probe. He didn't even wear the available mask that reduced some of the odors associated with opening body cavities. If she hadn't been cutting, Don would have told Chuck that it was his turn, which it was.

CHAPTER FOUR

Sergeant Sherman returned to the office after Don and Chuck were well under way with processing the scene. He was anxious to go to breakfast with two other members of the squad, which was his usual practice on day shift. Detectives Bill Grimes and his partner, Jack Martin, were late as usual. They spent a lot of time running bars or trolling for whores after work. This hobby took them past midnight on most nights and later on some, which meant that getting to work at a reasonable hour suffered.

Shortly after reaching his desk, Sergeant Sherman's phone rang; it was Detective Grimes. He wasn't feeling well and would be taking a sick day if the sergeant didn't mind. The sergeant didn't mind. He knew that Grimes's sickness had something to do with a bottle; he could empathize.

Jack Martin arrived at his desk promptly at 9:30 a.m., early by his standard. He was a little hung over but would be an acceptable breakfast mate, thought Sergeant Sherman. Martin had time to take a quick piss and check out Marjorie one more time before he and Sergeant Sherman left for the local dive where they usually ate.

"Where are the faggot and his college boy partner?" asked Detective Martin as they walked to Rose's Cafe at Second Avenue and James Street.

"They caught a murder at the Fairview this morning. Some hooker got her neck squeezed by a john," Sergeant Sherman said. "I know you and Bill were up for the next one, but they were here, so they took it. Besides, I know how you guys feel about hookers, so I thought I'd save you the aggravation."

"Thanks, Sarge," said Detective Martin. "What's good this morning?" he asked as they slid into their usual booth near the kitchen. "I feel like chicken fried steak, hash browns and two over easy."

"You look like chicken fried steak this morning. And your eyes could pass for two over easy."

"Fuck you" was the best Detective Martin could come up with on such short notice; he wasn't the brightest conversationalist. He usually left that to his partner who happened to be recovering from the previous night's sins.

"Want to get a tee time for Saturday morning?" asked Sergeant Sherman. "I thought we'd go to West Seattle this time. I like the greens there, and the hills might give us a workout."

"Sure thing, I haven't got anything going, and it might do Bill some good to get some air and exercise. Did you tell Bill about Saturday when you talked to him?"

"No, he sounded a little under the weather, so I thought I'd call him later."

Bill Grimes had been in Homicide as long as anyone could recall. What he lacked in the skills required to conduct a murder investigation, he made up for with his overbearing, arrogant nature, not to mention his appearance. Grimes had once been a good-looking man who dressed the part of a detective that one might see in a movie: tasteful suit, matching tie, polished shoes, and good haircut. No more. Grimes wore the same blue Sears sport coat every day. It had lost its shape, assuming it ever had one given its pedigree. It definitely needed a trip to the cleaners, but it would probably fall apart if subjected to the rigors of a dry cleaner. His once toned body had turned to fat. A double chin had formed to hide part of the knot of his greasy and tasteless tie. Bill Grimes had seen better days. It was a mystery why he remained on a job he no longer liked and at which he was a complete failure. The only cases he solved with his equally incompetent partner were the smoking gun variety: man shoots wife and sticks around to tell about it with the age-worn excuse, "the bitch needed killing." Grimes had once been an OK detective, not good, just OK. Grimes was failing at the husband business as well.

Clorice Grimes disliked her husband for what he had become and for the way he treated her. She was a piece of meat in a pinch when there was nothing else available, and then he was rarely able to perform. She had been a beautiful woman and still retained some of that. She took care of herself for the simple reason that she knew Bill probably wouldn't live to retirement and, if he did, would die soon after with his mouth wrapped around either a bottle or a hooker's breast. She wanted a life after Bill and the opportunity to spend his retirement money, which she had earned by staying with him through thick and thin, mostly thin.

Detective Grimes and Clorice had no children, not that they wanted any. This was mostly Bill's choice since he thought that kids would get in the way of their lifestyle; they were swingers, or had been. They had found new partners on a fairly regular basis and enjoyed it a lot. Clorice wanted nothing more than to experience more than Bill, a desire that began in high school and continued. Bill still loved chasing after the illusive high that accompanied sex with a new woman, provided he could manage to get it up. Most of the other women were now prostitutes. Clorice was more selective but just barely. She enjoyed the periodic partner that Bill didn't know about. At least she thought he didn't. Bill's partner, Detective Martin, was only one of her occasional bedmates. They knew that it was only sex and that nothing would come of it, other than an enjoyable break from the boredom of day-to-day life. Bill never let on that he knew that his partner was back-dooring him. Clorice and Detective Martin had been together part of the previous night, calculating that Bill wouldn't be coming home. They were right.

Don and Chuck left room sixty-one of the Fairview Hotel after collecting everything of evidentiary value and using up all the film they had. They put an evidence sticker on the door and screwed a police lock into the age-hardened doorframe and clear oak door. They never knew when they might want to come back and give it another once-over. The lock would keep the curious and lowlifes out; there was no shortage of both at the Fairview.

They followed Dr. Mills and Mike Griswold as they maneuvered the gurney carrying the body of Yvonne Gillespie, aka Kitty Carmichael, toward the elevator. Don was right about the elevator; it was almost too small to shoehorn the gurney into. Thankfully, the gurney tilted at about a forty-five degree angle so the door could slide shut. Don and Chuck, along with Sergeant Warner and Officer Morris, took the stairs. When they reached the main floor, the medical examiner and gurney had already arrived.

"When are you doing the autopsy?" Don asked Dr. Mills.

"How does two this afternoon sound?"

"OK, I'll be there." He could hardly wait for another opportunity to work with Dr. Mills. Chuck didn't like autopsies, but he willingly attended those conducted by an especially attractive male pathologist.

Before they left, Don returned the hotel register to the deskman. "Thanks, man, I appreciate the cooperation." He gave the man his card and asked that he call if he thought of anything that might help find the killer. "One other thing," Don said. "When does the maintenance guy start work and what kind of shoes does he wear?"

"He starts before I do because he lives here. The only time he goes out is to eat and stuff like that. He wears some kind of work shoes, I think. I don't spend much time checking out his feet."

"What's his name and date of birth?"

"John Barber, we call him Jack. He's about forty-five years old, but I don't know his date of birth."

"And your name and date of birth?"

"What's that for? Do I look like a murderer?"

"If you can tell me what a murderer looks like, let me know. I'll publish it in some high-powered journal and start teaching at some East Coast university," said Don.

"Right. I'm Wilbur Olson, and I was born on October tenth, 1935, about the same year as you."

"Are you taking lessons from my partner, Wilbur? Not good. Don't forget to have him call."

"No problem," replied Wilbur, who gave Don a slight smile. "When can we have the room back?"

"It shouldn't be more than a week or so; we'll have to run it past the prosecutor first," said Don. He knew that if there was ever any help to be gained from Joe citizen in cases like this one, it was by treating him like part of the human race. That was sometimes hard to do.

As Don and Chuck turned to walk away from the desk, Don turned back and asked, "Did your night guy see the dead woman come in with anyone last night?"

"We don't have a night deskman. After ten, our residents open the front door with their room key."

"One more thing. Did you know that she was doing business out of her room?"

"What kind of business?"

"Come on, Wilbur, you have to know that she was a hooker."

"No, I didn't; we don't allow that here."

"Oh, of course. Forgive me for thinking such a thing," Don said with a knowing smile.

Before Chuck and Don released the patrol officers, they asked Officer Morris to do some quick and very preliminary computer work on John Barber, white male, age about fifty. She used the desk phone and called Data. A man matching those unverified descriptors was a registered sex offender. He was keeping up with the requirements of his legal status, so he wasn't wanted by anyone except Don and Chuck, and they wanted to talk to him in a major way.

After they passed around the requisite thank-yous to the two patrol officers, with a special thank-you to young and unimpressed Officer Morris and a little attention to the Swede from Chuck, Don and Chuck loaded the evidence and processing equipment into the van. They then drove back to the Public Safety Building where they unloaded everything, took the evidence to the homicide processing room, and locked it in for later bagging and delivery to the Evidence Unit.

The route to their cubicle once again took them past Marjorie Manford's desk. After spending time around a stiff, it was always nice to return to a somewhat healthy perspective on the human race with a once-over of Marjorie Manford. Marjorie was delighted to see them. She seemed to be delighted to see almost anyone. *God bless her* was Don's thought.

"So, want to catch a little breakfast before the festivities at the ME's office begin?" asked Chuck. ·

"Let's do that; I could eat a horse, so long as it was on a tofu diet."

"Fucking vegetarians, you'll bring democracy as we know it to its knees" was Chuck's sarcastic response.

"You must know by now that I'm a part-time vegetarian. If some animal looks good, I'll try it."

Seattle was nothing if not well stocked with sources of vegetarian or vegetarian-leaning restaurants with a few vegan places thrown in. This was, after all, the center of liberal social mores and politics, fleece and furry-legged women; why not add tofu to the mix?

They took Dexter Avenue to Fremont, just north of the Ship Canal and across the blue-and-orange lift bridge from Queen Anne. Fremont was home to a statue of Lenin that rested in a stop-and-rob convenience store parking lot next to a major arterial. Lenin had come a long way from the Russian Revolution of 1917. On summer nights, it was even possible to catch an outdoor movie projected on the side of a white brick building. Customers had to bring their own chairs if they wanted to sit on something other than an asphalt parking lot. The movies were generally of the dated and often English-subtitled variety that most who attended didn't understand but weren't about to admit it.

Of more notoriety was the Fremont Summer Solstice Parade, the only parade in the known universe where nude bicyclists took part with the blessings of the local constabulary. It drew a crowd, mostly of curious middle-class conservatives from Bellevue and other cities east of Lake Washington where family values were vigorously guarded.

Police officers volunteered for the overtime duty in droves. Both Don and Chuck had volunteered when they were in patrol, but neither was lucky enough to make the cut. Don thought, and still expounded, that the only fair way of handling volunteers for such a significant cultural event was via lottery; fat chance of that happening. He now had to attend it on his own time.

They found an empty space on the street that Don paralleled into with one try. Chuck congratulated him, and they went into one of the many restaurants that served the dietary needs of both vegetarians and carnivores with the odd vegan thrown in. Although he was a part-time vegetarian, Don considered vegans truly odd. But, then, they probably wouldn't be strangling anyone with a leather bootlace. A fabric lace, perhaps, but not leather.

There were no right-wing restaurants in Fremont, the kind that served breakfast all day, a breakfast consisting of a half pound of hash browns; choice of ham, bacon, or sausage, or all three; two or three eggs; and biscuits or toast on the side. Those were the restaurants found on Aurora Avenue and downtown with a notorious one in Georgetown at the north end of Boeing Field. It surprised Don that people crossing the Fremont Bridge weren't checked for their liberal credentials. He would have passed with flying colors.

They walked into a place that smelled faintly of patchouli oil. A sign at the register directed them to please find a place and sit. They followed the directions and sat at a table with a view of the sidewalk, where they could watch the strange life forms that passed. A young woman, smelling as if she was the source of the patchouli ambiance, asked what they were having.

Chuck requested—one did not order in Freemont— the ham-and-egg scramble for which he was rewarded with a cold stare from the waitperson. "Waitress" was not a term that she would have accepted without serious consequences. Don ordered the tofu scramble, which was received with a sweet smile from the same server. Don could only imagine what an order from the vegan menu would have resulted in. The server appeared to have issues with shaving her legs, however, a serious liability in Don's opinion.

"I think it's your turn to write the scene," Don said after both had ordered breakfast and nothing of interest was happening on the sidewalk. "I did the last two."

"The reason you did the last two was because I was on vacation during one of them."

"Just saying."

"Well, say it to somebody who looks like he gives a shit."

"OK, since that's out of the way, why are we doing this case anyway? Martin and Grimes were next up for one."

"We're newer on the block than those two wastes of breathable air, and we aren't in the golf and booze club with the sergeant in case you hadn't noticed, Detective. You probably also noted, being the astute detective that you are, that both of those guys come in and leave whenever they choose. The sergeant doesn't seem to have any control where they're concerned."

"Point taken, Detective; now let's eat," said Don. "But one more thing, As soon as we get back to the office, let's call Wilbur Olson and see if John Barber has shown up. We need to let the crime lab know that they can attempt a match of the body's scrapings with the DNA of Barber if they have any on file. While we're at it, let's get going on producing a bulletin on Barber for patrol in case he's decided he doesn't want to make himself available for a chat."

"Don't you mean that I should get going on that along with the scene write-up while you whisper sweet nothings in Dr. Mills' ear?" said Chuck.

"That's true. You're a lot sharper than people give you credit for, Detective."

"Does 'screw you' ring any bells?" smirked Chuck.

CHAPTER FIVE

Detective Bill Grimes hadn't had a serious job after high school until he joined the department. He joined as a way of getting around the draft and Vietnam; he did not want to go to some fucking sewer like Vietnam, a place he couldn't find on the map, and get his ass shot off when the poor black slobs from Rainier Valley would better fill that bill. He didn't think of himself as a draft dodger but as an astute observer of the facts of life. Some people were meant to go to war for their country; he wasn't one of them. Besides, young guys like him were really meant for one thing: fucking all the broads they could get their hands on. That long list didn't include some slant-eyed bitches in Vietnam. Bill Grimes had had a great life while his female-magnet looks lasted; they were long gone. Nowadays, Bill Grimes primarily paid for sex, some of it with Vietnamese women.

Grimes hadn't made it home until nine o'clock on this particular morning. He was hung over and smelled of bad booze and cheap perfume. His clothes were even more disheveled than usual. The blue blazer with tarnished, gold-colored buttons was wrinkled and stained. He had to send it to a dry cleaner one of these days. He'd have Clorice do that as soon as he had her make him some breakfast.

"Did Sherman call this morning?"

"No, should he have?"

"I called him earlier and told him I wouldn't be coming in. I don't think he always trusts that I'm telling him the truth about being sick."

"Where were you last night?"

"None of your fucking business," said Grimes in his most mocking tone. "You know that some nights I have some follow-up to do that keeps me out."

"Sure, I know that you follow your hand up some whore's leg whenever the opportunity comes along. That's the only follow-up you're capable of these days, and I don't think you're capable of taking care of what you find at the end of that leg."

"Who'd you fuck last night that made you such a fountain of wisdom?"

"Wouldn't you like to know. Maybe you could take lessons from him."

The conversation wasn't going well for Grimes. His wife was smarter and always had been, even before the booze pickled his brain. He sat and ate the breakfast that Clorice had reluctantly made for him. The use of a subtle poison occurred to her every time she relented and made a meal for him even though she knew that he had just come from a hooker. At least she had that thought, and his pension.

Bill Grimes was born in Ballard, a community in Seattle north of the Ship Canal and west of Fremont. He still lived there with Clorice. It was the best part of Seattle in Grimes's opinion, filled with Scandinavians, although he wasn't one. Norwegians were the main stock, but there were also a fair supply of Swedes and Finns. Olson's Foods on Market Street was a testament that the population took their heritage very seriously. One could find most foods that you might find in Oslo, Stockholm, or Helsinki at Olson's. What Grimes found to be the best attribute of Ballard was that few if any blacks found their way across its border. They were in their place in Rainier Valley and Capitol Hill. Some made their way to West Seattle's High Point. Grimes knew that Don Lake lived in West Seattle, so that was OK with him. Screw Lake, who thought the sun rose and set on his ass.

The phone rang as Grimes was eating; it was Sergeant Sherman.

"How you feeling, Bill?"

"I'm feeling better now that I had some breakfast. I'm going to sleep for a while longer and maybe come in when I wake up."

"Lake and Weinstein picked up a case this morning, so you don't have to come in unless you want to."

"What case was that?" asked Grimes.

"Some hooker got choked at the Fairview Hotel. They don't have any suspects yet."

"Better them than us."

"You want to play eighteen on Saturday?"

"Sure, sounds good. Where?"

"West Seattle," said Sergeant Sherman.

"Isn't that where Lake, the boy wonder, lives?"

"Yeah, but he lives with the high-class assholes in the north end of the Admiral District near Duwamish Head."

"See you later, if I feel like coming in."

"OK, we already had breakfast, so you don't have that to look forward to," said Sergeant Sherman. "And one more thing: your caseload is getting a little out of control; you might want to give that some attention. The lieutenant is giving me some grief about old cases, and your list of open cases is longer than any detective's in the unit. There are some domestic violence assaults that should have been filed a long time ago. You know that the victims and City Hall can get a little impatient when they appear to have been forgotten."

"Why the sensitivity lecture, Sergeant?" asked Grimes. "I've always come through. It's just that some of those fucking women needed what they got. Most of them could benefit from having their teeth rearranged once in a while. Taking the old man to court takes him away from a job, and where does that leave the wife and kiddies?"

"Yeah, I know, it's tough being you, but you have to do the job, or I'm afraid the lieutenant is going to start looking for a replacement," said Sherman. "That leaves us without a golf partner. Neither of the college boys plays golf, and who knows if a replacement would. Looks like we can't ask what a guy's handicap is in any future interviews. For that matter, we might get a fucking broad to satisfy the fucking chief's quota. First a queer, next a broad," he said with a sigh. "Next thing we'll be getting rid of misdemeanor murders around here."

"I'll be there in a while after I get myself together."

What the hell's happening to my life? Grimes thought after hanging up. It was working OK for a long time. Work was fun even if the actual stuff that went with solving cases wasn't. Dealing with prosecutors had become nothing but a pain in the ass. But the social stuff, the part of "being" a homicide detective was good. It impressed a lot of people who could benefit him. Carrying that card instead of one that told the world that he was a low-life burglary detective was sweet. It impressed most of the women who hung out at the bars he haunted, all lowlifes. As time progressed and he became less exciting to look at, even they paid less attention to him and his card. He found that he had started to pay for the pussy that was once thrown at him; *not good, not good at all.*

CHAPTER SIX

When they left the restaurant, their clothing smelling vaguely of patchouli, Don and Chuck walked back toward their car, passing by some of the funky shops that lined Fremont's compact shopping district. Both felt at home here among the people who voted Democratic or Green and smoked the occasional joint, not that either of them did the latter any longer. The people who lived and hung out here were the same people that Don had gone to college with. The one difference between then and now is that the people Don went to college with weren't hippie wannabes. Most of the people populating Fremont today were.

"I could live here if I didn't already live in the best place Seattle has to offer," said Don.

"Agreed, although North Capitol Hill is in fact the best place in Seattle to call home," said Chuck. "It's easier to get to work from, the night life is better, people are more accepting of alternative lifestyles, and I can even buy a Tibetan prayer flag there if the need arises. Name me a place in West Seattle where you can do that."

"What the hell would a Finnish boy like me want with a Tibetan prayer flag?"

"Finnish, you're Finnish?" asked Chuck. "You don't look Finnish, and your name doesn't sound Finnish."

"I don't look Finnish because there's a little Norwegian thrown in on my mother's side, and what the fuck does a Finn look like anyway? As for the name, you can blame my grandpa for that. In the early part of this century, my grandpa and most of the Finns living in northern Minnesota were iron miners, or they did work that depended on the iron mines. Some were loggers, but most were miners who worked underground. The working conditions were so bad that in about 1916 the Finns decided to strike. They came from a country that had some serious Socialist leanings, and they brought those along when they came to this country. When they went on strike, they were locked out of jobs. Anybody with a Finnish name wasn't allowed to work in the mines and were discriminated against if they worked in other jobs. Some, like my grandpa, decided that one way of staying solvent was to change their names. His name had been Jarvi. If you translate Jarvi into English, you get Lake. That's why I'm Lake. I've thought of changing it back to Jarvi but haven't quite worked up to it. Some day…"

"Interesting, now let me tell you about why I'm Chuck and not Charles or Chucky."

"Save it for a time when I'm thinking about killing myself from boredom."

Not one to leave such things lie, Chuck had to get one more question answered while the subject was at hand. "Since you're Finnish, you're also Lutheran, right?"

"Finnish Lutheran, if you must know."

"How does the 'thou shall not kill' thing work in your chosen profession? And I'm guessing that you were a Finnish Lutheran in Vietnam."

"We Lutherans had the good sense to change that particular commandment to 'thou shall not murder' a while back. That opens up all manner of possibilities without breaking the commandment."

"Great. I can see where that would make all the difference. How about the one that says that 'thou shall not covet thy neighbor's wife?"

"If you recall, I'm not coveting my neighbor's wife."

"Then there's the one covering the coveting of thy neighbor's ass. Does that also cover coveting thy neighbor wife's ass?"

"I see your point, Chuck. It gets pretty confusing when you think about it. That's why I don't think about it. How about you? You must be Southern Baptist, right?"

"That's why I'm calling Seattle home."

"Enough said."

As Don and Chuck made the drive back to the Public Safety Building, they confirmed that Don would attend the autopsy alone and Chuck would start putting the evidence into some order and type up the scene notes. Chuck didn't like autopsies and didn't have a romantic interest in Dr. J. Wyman Mills. Don didn't like autopsies, but he was quite fond of Dr. J. Wyman Mills. They also decided that one day they would find out what the J. stood for and why the Wyman. Don might even start on that today.

Chuck dropped Don off at the south end of Harborview Medical Center, or HMC as it was known by most cops and all of the people who worked there. It was also "Harbor Zoo" to anyone who saw its emergency department on a weekend night. HMC was a great gray monster that loomed over the city from its perch at Ninth Avenue and Jefferson Street. It sat on four blocks of land and had a reputation as the best place to go if you were circling life's drain or the worst place to go if your life was sucked out of the drain and you had to spend time on a floor to recover. The truth was somewhere between those extremes, although most cops would say that if shot, stabbed, or bludgeoned, they wanted to land at HMC.

The medical examiner's office was in the basement on the south end of HMC. It was more secure than the fifth floor of the Public Safety Building, which was hard to understand given that no one was attempting to escape from it and few wanted in. Once a body got out of the ME's office, it went straight to a funeral home, no stops at the local bar. That is unless there was no family to pay for a funeral, in which case the stiff was placed in cold storage until other arrangements could be made, like a potter's field burial.

Don walked in, signed the register, and hung a visitor's badge around his neck. The receptionist said he could go back to the autopsy area if he wished, or he could wait until Dr. Mills called and said that she was going to start. He went to the autopsy area in hopes that he could exchange small talk before the cutting began.

"Hi, Doc," said Don, when he arrived at the floor where the cutting would commence. The floor was one below the reception area. Doctor Mills was putting on an apron that covered her from neck to knees as Don stepped onto the floor.

"Hello, Detective Lake, are you ready for this? You can have an apron and mask if you like or you can stand behind the glass," said Dr. Mills.

"I'll wear the apron, but the mask isn't necessary," said Don in his best detective's voice. Why the fuck Don was trying to impress her was a mystery. The business at hand was the autopsy and the means by which Yvonne Gillespie met her end, not whether Dr. Mill's pants were vulnerable. Don, however, was never without his ulterior motives where an attractive woman was concerned. He only hoped that Dr. Mills was not so single-minded that she didn't notice.

Dr. Mills, with Don following close behind, went to a table where Yvonne lay. Her body had turned a sickening gray while retaining the beauty that Don saw at the Fairview. He had to remind himself that he would have to be one sick bastard if he still found her sexually attractive.

A technician had prepared the body but hadn't washed it. Dr. Mills removed the bags from Yvonne's hands and again scraped under her finger-nails. There was still the odor of sweat and death on her. She hadn't decom-posed like some of the bodies Don had observed being dissected. *Thank the stars for that*, Don thought.

Dr. Mills started a recorder and began a dialogue about what she was doing and what she saw before her as she did it. She described Yvonne in clinical terms that made her the piece of evidence she had become. She was a "well-formed female," which Don had to agree with, although he didn't say so for the tape. She was still the sexually attractive woman she was last night before she was killed, just not warm.

Dr. Mills swabbed Yvonne's vagina, placing the swabs into plastic vials. She took combings of her pubic hair and then placed them in an envelope. She swabbed the inside of Yvonne's cheeks and placed those in another vile. She was meticulous and fiercely professional. She spoke while she worked, describing every detail of her work. Don tried valiantly to keep his break-fast down. Then Dr. Mills started cutting.

She started at Yvonne's pubic bone and continued to her sternum. One clean cut with a very sharp scalpel. She made incisions from the area of each of Yvonne's collarbones and met the incision up her middle. Both incisions were in the shape of a Y. Don had to flinch slightly when she made the cuts. Yvonne's breasts were still spectacular. They lost a little of that spectacle after the cutting she was undergoing. There was no bleeding; there was no heart beating to pump blood out of the cut veins and capillaries. Yvonne's blood had pooled around her back where it displayed itself through the skin like a huge, rose-colored bruise. Dr. Mills cut until she had access to Yvonne's abdominal and chest areas. She used a tool that most people use for trimming branches in their yards to cut her ribs and sternum. She took samples of urine from Yvonne's bladder and then dipped the entire contents of the bladder, with what appeared to be a gravy ladle, into a plastic bag. Don would never again see Thanksgiving dinner in the same light. Dr.

Mills continued this procedure until she reached the neck area, the area of primary interest to her and Don.

Yvonne's neck bore the marks of a brutal attack with a ligature at the hands of her killer. This was no mystery to either Don or Dr. Mills; they had the ligature in evidence. What was of interest was what the ligature did and how it killed Yvonne. Dr. Mills began to dissect Yvonne's neck.

The neck structure of the human female is fragile; it doesn't take much to destroy it and make breathing impossible. The same is true of the male. The difference is that males are rarely raped with such violence, and if they are, they tend to fight a lot harder to prevent it from happening.

Yvonne's trachea was crushed; she could not have breathed through it even with the ligature removed. The blood supply to her brain via her carotid arteries had been cut off, probably long enough to cause brain damage even if she could breathe. Yvonne would not have done well if she had survived the strangulation. She would have been taken to the Trauma Intensive Care Unit at HMC where she would have ended up on a ventilator until she died of pneumonia. For all of her other sins, Yvonne had "donor" on her driver's license. If she had died from some manner other than homicidal violence, she would have been parted out and her organs placed into some other poor soul's body. Don had to wonder if her killer had been as thoughtful when he last renewed his license, probably not. Don also wondered if her organs might have found their way into the body of some Bible thumper who looked down his or her nose at people like her. Ah, the irony of it all.

The next part of Yvonne's body that was of serious interest was her genitalia. Her vagina was badly bruised. As Dr. Mills began to dissect, she found something that caused her to produce a "hmm."

"What did you find?"

"I don't think she was raped with the usual tool. It looks like what caused the external soft tissue damage was pushed into her with a lot of force and then continued too far into her vagina. I would have to guess that it was a hard, round object that had nothing to do with a man's penis."

"Any idea what it might have been?" asked Don, thinking back to when he was eighteen and was still capable of a steel-like erection.

"Not yet, but I'll take some tissue samples and see if there's anything there that doesn't belong."

When Dr. Mills finished the autopsy and had put all the organs that Yvonne no longer needed back inside her body cavity and stitched her up, she turned to Don and said, "That was the most brutal attack I've ever seen. I hope you and Chuck find the motherfucker who did it."

Motherfucker? Did that word just come out of the mouth of this very refined, highly educated, and more than attractive woman? Yes it had. Don felt that this was a breakthrough in their relationship. What had been only professional had now become more, a relationship based on a shared vocabulary. On the other hand, maybe that was the only word that was sufficient to describe the motherfucker who killed Yvonne Gillespie. Don was as angry as Dr. Mills about what they had witnessed. Maybe this shared experience would somehow draw them together or maybe not. Don would have to do a little analysis.

"We have a person who lives at the Fairview who is of some interest. Seems he's the guy who found the body, and he's a registered sex offender. We're going to lay hands on him as soon as we can," said Don.

"Great! I hope he's your guy."

"Would you like to join me for a cup of the cafeteria's finest coffee?" asked Don after they had taken off their protective gear and walked to the floor above. "I'd like to talk to you about what we just saw here."

"Sure, give me a minute to do a couple of things and I'll join you."

Don had to shake himself when she agreed. He didn't expect that she would agree to have coffee with a lowly detective like him. Nevertheless, she had.

They walked along the basement corridor toward the central part of the hospital. The cafeteria was on the same floor as that of the medical examiner. Both were hard to find if you were new to the building. Once they found their way to the cafeteria, they both got coffee and sat down at a corner table.

"Would it be too personal if I asked what the J stands for?" asked Don. He thought that if he didn't get right to it, the autopsy would take over the conversation.

"Well, yes, it is personal, but I'll tell you anyway. It's Janet. I never liked that name, so I stopped using it when I became a big person. That was when I turned fifteen. I thought that since men seem to get away with using only the initial of their first names, so could I. No one has ever asked me about it before you did just now. I suspect that since I'm a doctor they've been afraid to ask. Thanks for asking."

Dr. Mills smiled when she said it. Don was glad that he had. He also noticed that she didn't wear a wedding or engagement ring. Maybe she just didn't wear them at work because they didn't fit under latex gloves. She was also very fit and tanned. Don suspected that the tanned part didn't come from a tanning bed and that the fit part came from working out in some fashion.

"You can call me Wyman, though. It's the name I chose when I became a big person. I stole it from Jane Wyman. I had great respect for her because she divorced that asshole she was married to: Ronald Reagan. I have nothing but contempt for him given all that he did to us," she said with scorn dripping from every word.

"OK, Doctor, er, Wyman, you've gained a foot or two in stature with that last statement. I have a serious issue with his politics, too."

"Great! Now let's talk about murder, shall we?"

"OK, let's," said Don.

"This guy didn't rape her with the usual tool. At least I don't think he did. That means he is probably unable to get it up; he is a serious psycho who only wanted to kill her while inflicting as much pain as possible, or the former led to the latter. I'm guessing that this guy is likely to do it again. He also knew that the body would be found fairly soon after he killed her. He didn't even attempt to secure the room's door."

"You think that he's a first-timer, not your Green River type," said Don.

"If I knew that, I'd be doing your job. It probably wouldn't hurt to look at cases around the state and in Oregon and Idaho. People who find their way into places like the Fairview seem to be transient, not that I'm suggesting the guy who did this is or was staying at the Fairview. He did find his way there, however."

"You're really up on the things we use to help us solve murders, aren't you?"

"Sure, my interest in pathology doesn't end with a trip to the scene of a murder and then dissecting the body. I want to see justice done as much as you do, maybe more since the mystery of human life is what drew me to pathology in the first place. It's gratifying to talk for the dead person when I'm on the stand during trial," said Dr. Mills.

"Pretty passionate about your work, aren't you?"

"Sure, but so are you. If I didn't think that you were, I wouldn't take the time to talk over coffee. I know some things about you that tell me that you're a smart and dedicated detective, not one of the jerks that pollute your office. There are very few in Homicide that I'd give the time of day to except where it made a difference in solving a murder. That may come off as unprofessional, but I'm nothing if not professional, and I see a lot in your office that's not. Someday it will bite the whole unit in a major way."

"Thanks for the compliment; I needed that since I don't have a wife to fill my head with 'attaboys,' and my boss is pretty shy when it comes to pointing out good work. My partner and I are a mutual admiration society of two although you'd never guess; he's pretty verbally abusive at times, but it's his way of saying he loves me like a brother. And you're right, I think that keeping our focus on speaking for the dead has a humbling effect." With that, Don stopped and hoped that Dr. Mills would reveal a little more personal information: married or unmarried, straight or lesbian, bicyclist or runner or both.

"So, smart, dedicated, and sensitive." said Dr. Mills. "I may have to have coffee with you more often. But until then, how about we make a date for dinner at my place on Friday?"

Single.

This was new territory, territory Don could get used to. It took some of the pressure off to not risk being reduced to a flyspeck in the presence of a woman who, moments before, was a picture of perfection. In the current instance, Don was almost speechless but not quite. "Yeah, that would be great! I was thinking the same thing, but I didn't know quite how to get there."

"I don't have the time or the patience to beat around the subject without getting to the point; maybe that's why I'm not married. I'm just too forward," said Dr. Mills. "Then there's the doctor thing. You'd be amazed how much of a threat that is to most men."

"It's like the detective thing. Being a cop isn't the magnet you might think it is. It threatens a lot of people in not-so-good ways. It works on the job, but it can get in the way of personal stuff."

"I'll think about the magnet part of the attraction, but until then, here's my address. How about seven?" said Dr. Mills. She slid a napkin with her address and phone number across the table, touching Don's fingertips with hers. They stayed there for longer than was necessary to pass the note.

Don walked from Harborview back to the Public Safety Building, all down very steep James Street. He probably wouldn't have noticed if it had been all up hill. He was thinking that this had been, for the most part, a good day. There was the Roseanne Vargas wake-up call. There was the water-taxi mystery woman, complete with bicycle butt and possible smile, maybe grimace. There was the tragedy of Yvonne Gillespie to darken the otherwise bright day, but when Dr. Mills. touched his fingertips, things changed. I guess this meant that she was now Wyman or J. He'd have to get some clarification on that. However, life was good, better than the alternative.

CHAPTER SEVEN

Saturday morning was unusually bright with no hint of the usually threatening clouds as Grimes and Martin drove across the West Seattle Bridge. Even Mount Rainier, or "the mountain" to locals, was standing proudly to the south. Martin was driving his 1980 full-size Dodge four-door with paint the same color as most of the plain pool cars the detectives usually drove on the job. The only thing that was missing was a roof antenna, and Martin would have had one of those installed if he didn't think he'd catch heat for it from the other detectives in the unit.

Martin loved looking and acting the part of a homicide detective; he wore the right clothes and he had the demeanor down, or so he thought. He liked having the card with "Homicide" printed on it to pass out to witnesses and victims and whoever else might be impressed. But he didn't exactly like the stuff that went with the job. The bodies, the blood, the hours, the court appearances, and the paperwork were all more than Martin could stomach. Nevertheless, the title "Homicide Detective" made him stay. He would die if he were sent back to Burglary/Theft where nobody gave a shit about you and there was more work than he could manage. No, he would do what it took to stay where he was.

Martin even had the added benefit of Grimes's wife who was available to him with a phone call. As long as he could screw her without Grimes's knowledge, he would do it. From time to time, he thought that Grimes knew that he and Clorice were getting together but didn't care, but he couldn't be sure.

Martin and his wife, Martha, had met at West Seattle High School. When they were seniors, Martha became pregnant. Martha's parents made it clear that a back-alley abortion wasn't in the cards, leaving one alternative short of enlisting in the army and going off to Vietnam to get his ass shot. That screwed up his plans in a major way. He now had three kids who ignored him and a wife who had little time for him except on payday and when the garbage needed to be taken out. They stayed together for the kids and because Martha didn't want to have to move out of the house that she couldn't afford to keep on a teacher's salary.

Martha and Jack hadn't had sex in over a year. They found their sexual gratification elsewhere. Martha had a "friend" at work with whom she had work-related "meetings" on a regular basis. She was happy with the arrangement. As long as Jack had Clorice, things progressed nicely.

"Lake lives up in North Admiral; let's go check out his place," said Grimes.

"OK."

Martin took the Harbor Avenue exit off the West Seattle Bridge and then turned north onto Harbor. They drove past houses that had seen much better days and businesses that got away with all manner of environmental sins, mostly because they were passing along some hefty checks to the right people. There was a tow company that towed some of the SPD impounds. A plant at the end of Florida Street impregnated poles and timbers with creosote, producing an odor that made living in the vicinity a challenge. There was a lot of land just waiting for developers who hadn't yet recognized the gold mine that it was. For now, it was property to drive through on the way to Don Armeni Boat Ramp or Alki Beach where Seattle residents and those from surrounding towns came to languish in the sand during the summer and ignore during the winter.

When Martin and Grimes reached California Way, they turned left up a steep climb to where California Way became California Avenue as it made a sharp turn to the south. This was where the world changed. Here was where the moneyed and tasteful lived. If you weren't moneyed, you could still live here if you were tasteful. It was a far cry from Ballard. It was where Grimes and Martin rarely came on the job except on the investigation of the rare domestic assault. Domestic assaults were handled differently in the rarified environs where Don Lake lived. And the murders committed in West Seattle took place in High Point or Delridge Valley. There were a few on the Seattle side of White Center or "Rat City," as the locals called it with a certain amount of pride. They had little else to be proud of.

Martin and Grimes passed Hamilton Viewpoint and then turned left onto Palm Avenue. They had been at the viewpoint to watch the Ivar's Fourth of July fireworks along with the other thousand or so revelers. Palm Avenue was where Lake lived.

Lake's townhouse wasn't really a townhouse. The houses were separated by walkways and shrubbery. They didn't share walls. They were obviously expensive and definitely tasteful. Each one had a view of downtown Seattle and the Cascades. Some had views of Mount Rainier. They were all two stories high with a garage on the first floor. They cost the owners a bundle.

Grimes and Martin parked a half block away from Lake's house.

"How the fuck does he afford that?" said Grimes. "He must be on somebody's payroll."

Just then the garage door of Lake's house began to open. When it was completely open, Lake walked out to pick up his newspaper. Following him was none other than Dr. J. Wyman Mills. They were both dressed in a fashion that would lead one to think that they had spent the night snuggling. Then there was the way that they touched each other. It spoke volumes about a budding romance. They didn't look around to see if they were being watched. This was North Admiral after all, not Ballard.

"What the fuck" was the best Grimes could come up with on such short notice. "That's Dr. what's her name from the ME's office. I thought she was a dyke."

"That's Dr. J. Wyman Mills," said Martin. "I didn't think doctors fucked cops."

"This is good, too fucking good," said Grimes.

Grimes had already filed this bit of information for future reference. He wasn't sure if it was unprofessional or unethical to fuck an assistant medical examiner, but it was good to know, just in case

They waited until Lake picked up his newspaper, went back into his garage beside Dr. Mills, and closed the door; then they drove away. Golfing and sharing this new bit of gossip with the sergeant made the day a little brighter.

The previous Friday had come way too slow for Don. He and Chuck accomplished a lot on the case, but his mind was on Dr. Mills. They took the nail scrapings to the state crime lab and reviewed what they had so far.

John Barber, the maintenance man who wore boots at the Fairview, hadn't called. He would be Monday's focus. And they had done some victimology. Yvonne's past, both personal and criminal, might tell them something about her that would help to identify her murderer. But Dr. Mills was foremost on Don's mind.

On Friday evening, Don drove his Subaru station wagon to Queen Anne where Dr. Mills lived. Queen Anne Hill was one of the seven or so hills on which Seattle was built. It was due north of downtown Seattle and home to more of the folks who valued taste. At one time in Seattle's history there was a cable car that traveled up Queen Anne Avenue. It was as steep as any of San Francisco's cable car routes. The cable car was long gone, but the hill remained. During the rare winter snowstorm, Queen Anne Avenue required an all-wheel-drive car with chains to get up it. That's why Don owned a Subaru. Seattle's hills were not two-wheel drive friendly during a snowstorm.

Dr. Mills's house was one of the most tasteful that Don had seen, and he considered himself a better-than-average judge of architecture. It was a small two-story home built in the early twentieth century. The garden was well maintained, and a paint job that might be found on the best San Francisco Queen Anne made the house stand out.

As Don walked to the front door, he heard music playing. The front door had a frosted glass window with a doorbell located in the center. A twist of the lever sounded the bell, no electricity required. Don twisted the lever. Wyman opened the door as though she had been watching him come up the walk; she had. When she opened the door, the music that Don had heard flooded out. It was a piano concerto by Mozart. *How did she know I like Mozart?* Don wondered. Wyman extended her hand and kissed Don lightly on the cheek before welcoming him in. *Life is good and getting better*, thought Don.

The hallway that J. Wyman Mills led him into could have been from an Agatha Christie movie set. The hall was lined with dark wood wainscoting above which the walls were a muted green plaster. Prints and artworks in heavy frames hung on both walls. An Oriental rug lay on the hardwood floor. *Perfect*, thought Don. *Could it get any better?* Indeed it could.

Don noticed that Wyman—he decided to go with Wyman—wore only socks on her feet. Since the rug he was about to step on must have cost as much as his car, he decided to go with bare feet as well. His socks were matching and colorful, so he left them on. Wyman then led him into the kitchen.

"Classy" was the only word Don could come up with to describe it. It had stainless steel appliances and white cabinetry with stone countertops. The cabinet doors were glass through which he could see an orderly display of dishes, glasses, and food. He was impressed. The cabinets were backlit, giving the antique china a glow that turned them into museum pieces rather than mere plates from which to eat. *This set her back a small fortune* was Don's thought. The whole house set her back a fortune.

"I know what you're thinking," said Wyman. "You like the décor."

"Yes, very much; I was thinking that you must spend your entire salary on your house."

"It's about all I have to spend it on. I don't have a husband, kids, or pets, and my college loans are paid off. This is my escape from the world. I decided that I would indulge in my nest. When I found this house, it wasn't so beautiful. The woman who lived here hadn't taken very good care of it. Toward the end of her life, she stopped all maintenance and collected junk. The yard looked like it hadn't seen a mower or shrub trimmer for ten years. When the woman died, her family didn't want to deal with it, so I got it at a pretty reasonable price. The next five years I spent remodeling, cleaning, and gardening. It was good therapy, though."

"You done good," said Don. "This has to be the all-time greatest house I've been in, except for mine, that is."

"I'll have to see yours sometime," said Wyman. "Now let me take you on a tour, and then we'll start the salmon."

Don immediately shifted to his all too pervasive pig state and thought, *You show me yours and I'll show you mine. Hmm, getting better.*

The rest of the house and garden were no less impressive. Wyman hadn't missed a beat. The garden was a work of art, literally. She had hung and placed small works of art in the form of canvas, ceramic, and metal throughout. She placed plants and shrubs in ways that would suggest that nature put them there. Chairs were located where it would feel right to sit and read or just be.

As Wyman led him from house to garden and back, Don couldn't help but notice once again her very impressive butt, definitely a bicycle butt, encased in well-tailored pants. Her butt looked good in scrubs, too, thought Don, but it looked spectacular in these.

By the end of the tour, Don had to wonder why anyone would ever leave it to take bodies apart. However, that was the reason for its being: it provided a haven from that job. He knew the need. Then they reached the laundry room where Don saw the reason, or one of the reasons, for Wyman's sculpted butt.

A green Klein road bike was hanging from a hook on the wall. It looked like it was more than decoration. There was a seat bag attached to the saddle, an indication that Wyman paid attention to such things as the necessity to fix a flat now and then.

I might have to marry this woman, thought Don.

"Let's do this thing," Wyman said when they returned to her kitchen. She took two salmon steaks from the refrigerator, setting them on the work island where she sprinkled them with herbs and olive oil. Then she placed them on the stove's grill. "Would you open the wine?" she asked Don.

Don had brought a bottle of a so-so white wine from Trader Joe's. "Do you mind drinking my swill, or do you want something a little more refined?" asked Don.

"Trader Joe's is my wine merchant of choice, and Two Buck Chuck is one of my favorites," said Wyman.

"Swill it is then," said Don. It wasn't Two Buck Chuck, but close.

When the salmon was done and Wyman had produced a picturesque salad, a brown rice dish of some sort, and French bread, they sat down to eat. The food was as great as the house was beautiful. Don was starting to feel a little subpar. He was a good cook, and his house was great, but neither quite compared to this. Then he remembered that they had shared the experience of rooting around in the body of more than one murder victim. That meant that they had bonded in a way few others did. In addition, she was so damned attractive.

"At the risk of being snoopy, would you mind if I ask what brings you to Seattle and to forensic pathology?" asked Don after they finished eating.

"No, I don't mind. I came here by way of Minneapolis and San Francisco," said Wyman.

"You've got to be kidding," said Don. "I'm from Minnesota and went to college in San Francisco. "

"Small world," said Wyman. "I knew from a fairly early age that Minnesota was not where I would be spending my life. The winters suck and most of the summers. Only parts of fall are bearable. Minneapolis is a great city to visit but...you know. As for the forensic pathology, it sort of chose me. I've always wondered about how the body works, but how the body stops working is even more intriguing. Forensics adds another dimension to that. Now I get to tell a jury how someone made another person's body stop working. I get to see some asshole get his or hers. The one downside to pathology is the relationship thing. Most men don't find women who root around dead bodies all that attractive, or they at least suspect that they aren't completely balanced. I had a fairly serious thing going with another almost doc while we were in medical school, but he thought that having a pathologist wife would be a serious bummer. It's been like that ever since. That's why I went off the reservation and asked you to join me for dinner. You don't seem all that concerned that I root around dead bodies for a living."

"I guess that's a compliment," said Don. "Although, rooting around a dead body together doesn't make that great a basis for a relationship. It is a unique start, though."

"It was meant as a compliment," said Wyman. "I've had my eye on you for a while. I like the way you go about your business. And you aren't full of yourself like a lot of the other guys in your unit. The homicide thing hasn't gone to your head as far as I've seen."

"I am guilty of having an ego. I like who I am and what I do. The department and the unit are better places because I'm there. But I think that you have to work at getting to that ego state and staying there. There are a few guys in the unit who have forgotten why they're there. The title is more important than the job. When I get to that point, I want someone to sink me in Elliot Bay."

"OK, it's a deal. A cement block tied to your ankle should do the trick," said Wyman. "How about dessert and coffee? Then let's go look at that castle of yours in West Seattle. I've shown you mine; now you have to show me yours."

Smart, beautiful, and a mind reader, thought Don. "It's a deal. Let's take your bike in case a ride is in our future."

"OK, that's also an important part of my life, as you saw," said Wyman.

The coffee was good, shade-grown French roast, whatever that meant, and the dessert was a homemade cake. Don was beginning to suspect the CEO of Starbucks of wanting to take over the world, so he was pleased to see that Wyman wasn't serving it. He liked the coffee. The cake was outstanding. As Don had discovered, life was good and getting better.

CHAPTER EIGHT

The next Monday found Don and Chuck in the office before any of the others in the squad arrived, which was almost always the case. Marjorie told them about Saturday's golf game, so they didn't expect anyone until at least ten; golf tended to extend well into Sunday and Sunday night. Grimes, Martin, and Sherman had played in West Seattle. Two other members of the unit, Detectives Roland Hase and Brian Monson, had worked the weekend. Maybe worked was a poor choice of words to describe what they usually did.

On Saturday, Hase and Monson came in late and went to breakfast at a dive in Georgetown where they started consuming their first alcohol of the day. Then they went back to the office where they sorted the reports that came in overnight. After that exhausting morning's work, they went shopping at Home Depot where there was a sale on power tools. Neither one bought anything, but they enjoyed looking at the tools and dreaming about the great things they could do with them if they had the time or talent. Then it was back to the office.

At about one, the office phone rang. Both prayed that it wasn't a callout. Neither one was in any condition to handle a crime scene. Hase answered the phone; it was a man who identified himself as John Barber. He said that he had Detective Lake's card and that he was supposed to call him. Hase asked what it was about. Barber told him about being the maintenance man at the Fairview Hotel and having found the body of a woman. He had gone away for a few days and now wanted to talk to Detective Lake.

"What do you want to talk to Lake about?" asked Hase. "Did you see something that might help in the investigation?"

"Maybe, I don't know," said Barber.

"I'll tell Lake you called and he'll get back to you."

"OK," said Barber and then hung up.

Barber thought the conversation was a little strange since he might have seen the person who killed the woman in sixty-one, but what did he know since he wasn't a homicide detective.

"Who was that?" Monson asked after Hase got off the phone.

"Some lowlife at the Fairview who wanted to talk to Lake about last week's murder," Hase slurred. "That place is a nest of crooks and drunks who wouldn't give you a straight story if their mother's lives were at stake. Fuck him."

"Lake and his pansy partner are pretty boys who got here because they know somebody or are screwing the right person. Don't tell them shit," said Monson.

"You got anything going this morning that would keep us from going down to the Fairview to visit Barber?" asked Don. "It looks like he isn't too excited about calling us."

"Yeah, I need to go talk to an assault victim on the Hill if you have time. How about we talk to her and then catch Barber on the way back," said Chuck.

They took a pool car and drove up to the Central District where the assault victim lived. Daytime was the best time to catch her because her business took her out at night. She was a hooker who had been assaulted by a john. He thought that if he didn't want to pay her, he didn't have to. And maybe he was like a lot of johns who just got off on beating up hookers, thinking that they had to take it. After all, prostitution was illegal. The thing he forgot was that soliciting was also illegal and assault was sure as hell illegal. She was lucky that Chuck had been assigned the case. Grimes or Martin would have blown it off, but since Chuck knew something about discrimination, he didn't.

They drove to the address the victim gave the officer. It actually existed, no small thing. They knocked on the door to the apartment. A very attractive black woman answered. This was a miracle. Hookers rarely gave accurate information about where they lived. Hookers didn't usually report crimes committed against them either.

Although the woman was attractive, it was clear that she had been around the block, ridden hard and put away wet on many occasions.

However, she retained her beauty. She was milk-chocolate brown with sad eyes. Her figure was perfect in a voluptuous sort of way. Don had a hard time concentrating on anything but her very impressive cleavage and lips that he thought screamed to be kissed.

"Hi, ma'am, I'm Detective Weinstein; this is Detective Lake. We're here to talk to you about the assault you reported. Can we come in?"

The woman opened the door farther and stood aside. Don just managed to brush her with his left arm as he passed; the touch was electrifying, and she smelled as good as she looked. They were a little surprised to find a clean and fairly well-furnished apartment once they were inside. What they didn't expect was a young boy. He was about five years old and sitting in front of a television. When they came in, the boy got up from the couch, walked over to where they stood, and looked up at Don in an accusing manner. Don didn't pay much attention to him. Then he felt a slight pain in his right shin where the boy had kicked him as hard as he could.

"Raymond, that was not nice. Now apologize to the man," said the woman.

"No!" said the boy, who then stalked off into the kitchen.

The woman said, "I'm sorry, he hasn't done that before."

"That's OK, ma'am," said Don. "I know how little boys can be. I used to be one."

"But now you're a big one," the woman said with a sexy smile.

Chuck asked the woman for any identification she might have to verify her name. She produced a Washington State driver's license: Shondra Wilson, black female, five foot five, 130 pounds, black hair, and brown eyes is what was stated about her without asking any questions. Her date of birth put her at just under Don's age. Her hair was now a reddish black, but the rest of the information was accurate except for the address and the fact that it was inadequate in describing her.

Chuck got all the information that the woman had to offer. The description of the man was detailed right down to the pattern of his necktie: a diagonal stripe in maroon, gray, and royal blue. He had hit her repeatedly with his fists as he raped her, something that was left out of the report. When the suspect was finished with her, he told her that she was lucky he didn't kill her and that he would not be paying her. She said that she felt lucky to be alive. She had been beaten by johns in the past but never like that.

"Do you think you could describe the suspect to a sketch artist?" asked Chuck.

"Sure. He was pretty close to me as you might guess, and we were face-to-face for quite a while. The son of a bitch didn't even wear a condom. That's the strange part. My customers are mostly afraid of AIDS. He didn't seem to have any fear. I'm HIV negative, but I'm not so sure about him. I'm going for testing tomorrow."

"I'll arrange for an artist," said Chuck. "I'll call you so we can meet, OK?"

"Make it after noon. I don't get off work until late, if you know what I mean," she said.

"OK, we can make a time that works for everybody. How about your boy, does he have a place to go when you're at work and when you come down to the office?" asked Chuck.

"My mother watches him when I'm working," said the woman. "He's really a good boy. I don't know what got into him."

"That's OK, it really is," said Don.

"Do you still have the panties or other clothing you were wearing at the time of the rape?" asked Chuck.

"Yeah, I didn't wash them yet. I was planning to do the wash today."

"I'll need to take them," said Chuck. "And would you tell us where you pick up your customers?"

"Is this going to cause problems in getting this guy's ass off the street?" asked Shondra.

"No, we just need to know how and where this guy picks up women," said Chuck.

"OK. I have this guy who manages my work, but I work out of bars mostly. Sometimes I walk the street, but I do that on Fridays and Saturdays and when there are conventions in town. Mornings are sometimes good where guys pass on their way to work at Boeing. I get a customer coming from Mercer Island or the East Side sometimes."

"Where did this guy pick you up?" asked Don.

"Like I told the officer, I was at the bar at Twenty-three and Union. He came in and spotted me. We went to his car and he drove to a motel on Aurora where I pretty much have a running account. After I did the usual, he started to hit me and didn't stop until I was able to kick him in the crotch, pick up my clothes, and run out the door. I ran to the office, where I got dressed. I'm thinking of firing the guy who manages my activities for not being around the corner. That is, if he'll let me."

"What motel were you at?" Chuck asked.

"The Cascade Motor Inn. It's really nothing but a place for people like me to bring their customers."

"That's a long way from Twenty-third and Union," Chuck said. "Why didn't you get a place a little closer?"

"He was a white guy. He said he didn't want to hang around the Hill and get mugged."

"Did you get his license number?"

"No, I was running too fast. I thought the asshole was going to kill me."

As they drove away from the woman's apartment house, Chuck asked Don why he thought the boy kicked him.

"What would you do if you were five years old and the only time you saw police was when they were coming to cart Mom off to jail?" said Don.

"Yeah, I see what you mean. Poor little shit thought Mom was going away again, and that was the only response he could come up with. He was just protecting Mom. I don't have much hope for his future, though. He's pretty light for a black kid. Why do you suppose that is? You don't suppose that Mom was knocked up by a john, do you?"

"Stranger things have happened," Don said. "But what I wonder is why the officer who took the report didn't classify it as a rape and take her to Harborview for rape screening. This was a rape with a beating thrown in for good measure. Motherfucker who did that wasn't some drunken asshole who just had a hard-on to take care of. He knew something about how police generally view prostitutes and their complaints of assault and rape. You plan to do this up right, right?"

"What do you think?" said Chuck, sounding more than a little pissed. "You think I might not because she's a prostitute? You forget that I'm one of those people who has been discriminated against his entire adult life. She's one, too. Too bad about the kid, though. Maybe I'll call the Department of Social and Health Services and see if they can give her some help."

"Good idea. The kid's going to end up like Mom if he doesn't see that there's more to life than television and a mom who sells her ass to the highest bidder. Before we go to the Fairview, how about we stop for a snack at Uwajimaya?" Don said, keeping things in perspective.

"OK, you buying?" asked Chuck.

"No, but nice try. First you get me assaulted by a rug rat and then you want me to pay. Let some fresh air into your wallet for a change."

Uwajimaya was the central business in Chinatown and about two blocks south of the Fairview Hotel. It was a Japanese market in the best sense. There were the usual grocery items with emphasis on Japanese foods and fish. The fish market was the best south of Pike Place Market, which was second only to Fisherman's Terminal. It also stocked kitchen appliances and lottery tickets, lots of lottery tickets. Don had made one observation about the Japanese and Chinese population since arriving in Seattle: they liked to gamble. Playing the ponies, buying lotto tickets and pull-tabs, or any other form of gambling seemed to have a big appeal.

They found a place to park on the street and went in. The smell of Asian foods, both cooking and raw, hit them before they walked in. The food court in the back of the store was Don's favorite fast-food place. The salt and MSG in the fast foods were killers if consumed on a regular basis, but Don didn't eat there often enough to worry about it. Chuck didn't either; he was on a fairly strict diet, one that complied with his workout regime. Don knew that Chuck didn't bicycle, so he couldn't figure out how he stayed in shape other than the so-called workouts he got practicing karate.

Don ordered tofu in a sauce of some sort with steamed rice, vegetables, and green tea. Chuck went with two-pork hum bow, plain brown rice, and steamed broccoli. He also had green tea.

"How's a boy like you going to grow eating like that?" asked Don.

"It doesn't include tofu, in case you hadn't noticed. I get my protein from things that aren't made of soy. That shit'll kill you over time. You know that, don't you?" Chuck responded.

"Yeah, I suppose you're right, but so would boredom. If I ate like you, I'd die of food boredom. Over half the world consumes soy and are healthier for it."

"Over half the world consumes soy because Iowa farmers have sold them on the idea that it's good for them. The farmers are getting rich and the consumers are getting skinny," said Chuck. "Now they've sold us on the idea that they should grow lots of corn and turn it into ethanol to burn in our cars. Sneaky fucks, I'd say."

"You might have something there. I don't exactly have the highest regard for Iowa farmers. When I was a kid, every summer they would invade northern Minnesota in their pinstriped coveralls and white shirts to fish for blue gills and crappies. There they were in the land of walleye, bass, and northern pike, not to mention the monster muskie, and they were hot for blue gills and crappies. I never could figure that out. Those farmers' daughters weren't so bad, though," said Don.

"Did they have any sons?" asked Chuck.

"I didn't notice, why?"

"Just wondering."

When they finished eating and discussing the demise of the Western Hemisphere at the hands of the Iowa farmer, Don and Chuck drove the short distance to the Fairview Hotel. Wilbur Olson was still at the desk, his shirt unchanged, his nose in a paperback novel. J. A. Jance had been replaced by a Rex Stout.

"Don't you ever get out from behind that desk?" asked Don.

"No, I don't. I like it here. I've seen everything there is to see outside, and the clients here aren't my type, so I don't feel the need to socialize. So I sit here and read and listen to KIXI," said Wilbur.

"You have great taste in music. It gets no better than a Lawrence Welk polka in my opinion. Unless it's a Frank Sinatra ballad," said Don.

Not sure whether Don was messing with him or just being complimentary, Wilbur smiled.

"Is Barber in?" asked Don.

"Yup, he's in room seven just down the hall on the right. I saw him come in about a half hour ago. I suppose he's taking a nap before he does the afternoon garbage run and mops the lobby."

Before they left the office, Don and Chuck ran all of the names that had been in the Fairview at the time of the murder. They found the usual misdemeanor warrants for drinking, failure to appear, and other antisocial behaviors that brought lesser beings to Seattle Municipal Court. There were a few under Department of Corrections supervision. No one was wanted for a felony. They decided to forget the minor warrants and let patrol and other follow-up units use them as leverage in the future.

They had confirmed the identification of John Barber. He was a registered sex offender, convicted of second-degree rape twelve years earlier. He served five years on McNeil Island and remained in compliance with his reporting requirements. He had been employed during most of the time since he got out of prison.

Don knocked on the door of room seven. They listened for any activity inside and heard only the squeak of an old, worn bed and the shuffle of feet as they approached the door. The door opened slowly and John Barber stood before them. He was about six feet tall, stocky going to fat, his larger-than-necessary face needing a shave. He needed a haircut, too. He didn't appear to be a man who gave two shits about his appearance or what others thought of it. He had a scowl on his face when he said, "What do you want?"

Don said, "We want to talk to you, John."

"Here I am, talk."

"We're detectives from SPD Homicide," said Don, producing his identification. "We want to talk to you about what you saw and did on the morning that you reported finding the body in room sixty-one."

"I didn't say I found a body. I said that I saw a woman who wasn't moving and had no clothes on in room sixty-one."

"What did you think you found that morning?" asked Don.

"I thought I found what I said I found: a woman who was naked and wasn't moving."

Don looked at Chuck who was standing to his right where he could jump on John Barber should the need arise. Chuck rolled his eyes and smiled ever so slightly.

"Do you mind if we come in and talk so the whole world doesn't hear us?" said Don.

John Barber stood aside and held the door open for them. Being the ever-suspicious detectives that they were, Don and Chuck motioned John Barber to go in first. There was one chair and a bed, sink, and closet. It was a duplicate of the room in which Yvonne Gillespie died. Barber sat on the unmade bed and Don sat on the chair. Chuck stood, waiting to spring should the need arise.

"Let's start again, John," said Don. "We're kind of curious why you haven't gotten back to us after we asked Wilbur to give you our card."

"I did," said Barber.

"You did." It didn't come off as a question; it was more of a *You're a fucking liar, John* statement.

"When did you make this call to us, John?" Don asked.

"Last Saturday morning. I talked to some guy who said he'd tell you that I'd called. He didn't give his name. Didn't sound too interested, if you know what I mean."

Chuck was taking notes of the conversation. Barber either didn't notice or didn't care. Chuck noted the part about the call that Barber said he made. He looked skeptical.

"Tell us what you saw the morning that you found the naked woman who wasn't moving, John," said Don.

"You didn't ask me if I wanted a lawyer," said Barber.

"Do you want a lawyer, John?"

"No, those fuckers are who landed me in prison."

"Is there anything else we can do before we talk, then?" Don asked. "Coffee? A warm cinnamon roll? Clean socks? Just let us know. If not, can we get into why we're here."

"OK, I was up about three-thirty that morning; I couldn't sleep. I thought I'd get a jump on the day and start collecting garbage. The garbage accumulates in the bathrooms and in the lobby. If I don't keep on top of it, it's all over the floor. I was on the sixth floor working my way down. As I walked past sixty-one, I heard what sounded like a gagging sound and then a thump like something heavy hitting the floor. I looked at the door and saw that there was a light on. The doors don't fit all that tight and the light comes through the cracks. I kept on going to the bathroom and didn't pay any more attention until I started to come out. I saw the door to room sixty-one just start to open, so I closed the bathroom door and turned the light off. Then I opened the door just a crack. I saw this guy, a big guy, walk out of the room and close the door, but the door didn't latch. The guy walked past the bathroom and on down the hall. I thought he might come in, but he didn't. He went out the fire exit and down the stairs. Those are the stairs that go down to the alley alongside the hotel."

"How good a look did you get of this guy?" asked Don.

"Pretty good; it was quick, but I saw his face pretty good," said Barber. "His clothes were another thing. The hall lighting isn't all that good, and the clothing was dark, so I couldn't say much about them except that he was dressed."

"If the lighting wasn't that good, how did you get such a good look at his face?" asked Chuck.

"It was like he was all sweaty and lit up. The light in the hall must have magnified his sweaty face," said Barber. "It was weird and spooky."

"If you saw this man again, do you think you could identify him?" asked Don.

"I think so," said Barber. "But, like I said, the lighting wasn't all that great. The owner of this dump thinks that forty-watt bulbs in the 1940 light fixtures will pretty much make due."

"How about describing him for a sketch artist; could you do that?" asked Don.

"I can try."

"We're going to arrange for you to sit with the artist later this week," said Don.

"OK, that'll work so long as it's not too early; I have to get this dump cleaned in the morning."

"We'll see what we can do. You know where the Public Safety Building is, right?" asked Don.

"What do you think?" said Barber.

"Before you describe the guy to the artist, tell us what he looked like," said Don.

Barber gave a complete description including the dark clothing.

"I'd also like to get a cheek swab from you for DNA purposes. You don't have to do this without a warrant, which I will get if you refuse," said Don. "You already have DNA on file somewhere from your rape conviction. This will just make things quicker. We only want to eliminate you as a suspect in this. To be on the safe side, we're going to ask you to sign a consent to search form."

"OK," said Barber. "How did you know I had a rape conviction?"

"You don't really think we're complete dummies, do you?" Don shot back.

"Not complete."

Don took an envelope and two swabs from his briefcase and swabbed the inside of both of Barber's cheeks.

Before they left, Don noted that Barber was wearing ankle-length work boots with leather laces. Both laces were in place and well worn.

"Do you mind if we look in your closet before we leave?" asked Don.

"Do I have a choice?"

"Sure, it's just that if you refuse, we will ask ourselves why and call your DOC supervisor who will come and search the whole room with us present," said Don. "Why put both of us through that for a simple thing like satisfying our curiosity about what's in your closet?"

"Go ahead," said Barber.

Don opened the closet door and found a very neatly arranged rack of clothes. On the floor was one pair of athletic shoes. Except for the ones in his boots, there were no leather laces in sight.

"One more thing," said Don. "When was the last time you were in room sixty-one?"

"The day before the woman who died there moved in. I cleaned it and changed the sheets. There's one more thing you should know; I didn't rape that woman I went to prison for. She said I raped her because she was afraid of her husband. I had a shitty lawyer, and the detective didn't do what he could have to prove that she wasn't telling the truth."

"Shit happens, John," said Don.

"You're right there."

"One last thing, John," Chuck said as they were walking away. He half turned and looked over his shoulder at John. "Do you think the man saw you?"

"I don't think so; the bathroom was dark."

"OK, thanks."

Don and Chuck went down to the lobby where Wilbur still sat behind the desk.

"Wilbur, you're going to die at that desk if you don't get out and get some exercise," said Don.

"Probably true, but everybody has to die sometime and someplace," Wilbur said with some resignation as he closed the book he had been reading.

They drove back to the Public Safety Building and walked up to the fifth floor for the exercise; Wilbur was still on both of their minds. Given the state of the air in the building, the exercise was probably more damaging than beneficial. When they opened the door to the unit, Marjorie was at her desk typing away at something, probably the transcription of a taped statement, something that occupied most of her time when she wasn't checking herself in a mirror or reading a glamour magazine

Marjorie looked up as Don and Chuck walked in. She was decked out in one of her most revealing tops to date. It was a wraparound thing that separated her breasts in a way that gave each its full measure of perfection. Her cleavage was on display in such a way that Don felt he really needed to comment on it, but then thought better of it. Even Chuck, usually the picture of decorum, was impressed.

"How was your morning?" asked Marjorie.

"Never better," said Don. "It only improved by seeing you after a long weekend away."

"Don, you are a flatterer. One of these days I'll have to show you my appreciation."

"I look forward to it, Marjorie," said Don, only half jokingly.

Don and Chuck walked back to the squad area and found that the entire squad was there, a rare occurrence. They walked to Sergeant Sherman's cubicle where he was doing a crossword puzzle in pencil. He looked up as they came in.

"Sergeant, who was working this weekend?" asked Don. He knew who was working, but he wanted to get Sherman's attention and that of anyone else who was listening.

"Monson and Hase. Why?"

"The guy who reported the murder at the Fairview said he called here on Saturday and talked to some detective who said he'd tell us he called."

"He talked to me," said Hase from over the wall of his cubicle. "I forgot to leave you a note."

"You know this is the guy who might have seen the killer at the Fairview, right?"

"No, I didn't know that; I thought that he was just some fucking drunk."

"Well, he wasn't, so maybe next time you leave us a message, or better yet, give me a call," said Don.

Don didn't like Hase or Monson. Both were about as useless as tits on a male hog. On top of that, they both had attitudes, and, from what Don knew about them, both were draft dodgers who talked as if they were battlefield heroes. Chicken hawks drove Don around the edge. They were worse than PTSD assholes.

As Don and Chuck turned toward their cubicle, Hase said in a voice just loud enough for them to hear, "Fucking asshole and his pansy partner think they're hot shit just because they're college boys."

Don turned back toward Hase and Monson's cubicle and walked to its opening.

"Do you have a problem with my pansy partner and me doing our jobs?" Don asked in the calmest yet most threatening tone he could muster.

Chuck stood beside Don with both fists clenched. He didn't like to be called a pansy, although he was one. That and the fact that he held a black belt in karate gave Chuck an edge to his demeanor. He liked to fuck but not be fucked with.

"No, I just don't like you telling me what I should do. I've been around a lot longer than you."

"That's true, you have, and you're still not worth a shit when it comes to the job. In the future, pass along messages and we might get along just fine."

Don and Chuck then went back to their cubicle where Sergeant Sherman met them.

"What was that all about, Don?" asked Sherman.

"Hase and Monson took an important call for us this weekend and didn't think it was important enough to pass along. The guy who found the body at the Fairview called. We talked to him this morning. He said the guy he talked to blew him off. This guy said he probably saw the killer and can probably identify him. He's coming in this week to do a sketch."

"You really need to try to get along with the other guys in the squad," said Sergeant Sherman.

"That's a two-way street," said Don. "Ever since I got here, those guys have done almost everything they can come up with to make my presence seem somehow unwelcome. That goes double for Chuck. What gives? I'm not going to kiss anybody's ass just to be able to do my job. If that's what's required, let me know, and I'll see what I can do about it."

"That's not some kind of threat is it, Don?" asked Sherman. "If it is, I think we need to take it up with the lieutenant."

"That wasn't a threat. That was a statement of how I see Chuck and me treated by the rest of the squad. Both of us know that there is a thing like discrimination at work here. We both also know that Grimes and Martin were due for the next murder when we got this one. Are they somehow exempt when they don't feel like coming in?"

"You guys started the investigation, so I thought you would have a better handle on it, that's all. Besides, you guys will do a better job on a hooker murder than those guys would," said Sherman.

"Thanks," said Don, his voice dripping with sarcasm. "We try."

"I know you and Chuck try and mostly succeed. Bottom line is that you're our best detectives at the moment. We need some clearances or we're going to have a major shake-up around here," said Sherman.

"I'm sorry to cause you grief, Sergeant," said Don. "You know that I don't really take too much shit from inferiors or anybody else for that matter, don't you?"

"Easy, now you and Chuck go back to work on this. Let's just hope the shit doesn't hit the fan and you get another one before you close this one," said Sherman.

Chuck was standing with Don during the exchange with Sergeant Sherman. He and Don walked to their cubicle together. On the way they passed the cubicles occupied by Grimes, Martin, Hase, and Monson. Both teams of detectives gave them cold stares as they passed. *Fuck them*, thought Don. *We can fuck up all of these assholes without too much sweat.* Then there was the issue of having to work around them.

Grimes gave a special glare at Don and Chuck. If Don was right, he saw a slight pallor to Grime's face, but he could have been wrong. It was probably just another rough night with his bottle. If the rumors were accurate, Martin probably had a rough night with some back-alley whore.

When Don and Chuck were settled in their cubicle, Chuck typed the follow-up notes and Don called a sketch artist to arrange a date for the two sketches he wanted done as soon as possible. They agreed on Wednesday afternoon.

While Don was on the phone and Chuck was typing away with both fingers, Grimes got up from his desk and walked out of the office. He took the elevator up to the sixth floor where the Evidence Unit was located. He walked over to the window where one of the evidence warehousemen was sitting.

"How's it going, Grimes?"

"Pretty good, Smitty," said Grimes. "I'd like to see the evidence sheet on the murder of that hooker at the Fairview Hotel last week. I don't have the case number, but you probably have it since it was the last murder we had."

"I thought that was Lake and Weinstein's case."

"Yeah, it is, but they're asking that we do some stuff on it, so I need to see what there is in evidence."

"Don't they have the sheets in their file?"

"Look, are you going to show me the sheet, or do I have to ask your sergeant?" growled Grimes.

"Don't get your shorts in a knot there, Detective. I'll get it for you."

Smitty had been with the department for thirty-five years and was close to retirement. He didn't take too much shit from anybody but was good at handing it out. He knew that he had certain powers over sworn personnel that they didn't have over him. He always thought that Grimes was a self-important asshole and didn't like taking the current ration of shit, but he had more important things to do than spar with this prick.

"Here you go," said Smitty as he handed Grimes the evidence sheets. "You can make copies over there."

Grimes made copies within sight of Smitty and then brought the originals back.

"Thanks, Smitty, I appreciate it."

"Right," Smitty mumbled, turned, and walked away, insincerity dripping from his mouth.

After Grimes left the Evidence Unit, Smitty picked up the phone in the empty sergeant's office and called Don Lake.

"Just thought you might like to know that Grimes just came up and asked to see the evidence sheets on the Fairview Hotel murder case. Said he was giving you guys a hand on it. Does that sound familiar? He didn't know the case number, so I thought there was something strange going on."

"Thanks for the call, Smitty. They are giving us a hand, so it's OK that you gave him the sheets."

"It's just that the bullshit meter went off the charts when he came up, and I thought you should know."

"Thanks again, Smitty," said Don.

When Don hung up the phone, he looked at Chuck who was still typing in his pathetic and tortured two-fingered style. He thought that this was turning into something very strange.

"Hey, Chuck, how about we take a break and get a little exercise?" said Don.

"Anything you say, boss. My fingertips are getting sore anyway."

Don and Chuck walked out of the office and past Marjorie.

"Can we bring you anything?" Don asked Marjorie as they reached her desk.

"No, I've already been to lunch, but thanks anyway," she said with her usual killer smile.

What a gem, thought Don. *Why isn't she married?*

When they reached Third Avenue and started walking north, Don turned to Chuck and said, "We have a little problem, partner."

"What?" asked Chuck.

Don explained what Smitty had told him and started wondering aloud what it might mean.

"Wait a second," said Chuck. "Grimes asked for our evidence sheets in a case he has nothing to do with. He doesn't even like hooker cases and does everything he can to not be assigned cases involving them. He even steers around hooker assaults. What the fuck does he want with our evidence sheets? Do you think we should go to the sergeant with this?"

"What do you think? You've been in the unit longer than I have."

"But you've got a better handle on the inner workings of the minds of assholes than I do," said Chuck.

"That's true, but it's only true because I've dealt with more of them than you have. You've been sheltered, and you have to admit that by virtue of your alternative status, you tend to be a little more sensitive and trusting than most," said Don in his best sardonic voice.

"Fuck you," said Chuck.

"No thanks, but I appreciate the thought."

"Fuck you," Chuck repeated.

"I don't think we should go to the sergeant," said Don. "I don't know if we can trust him to not tell Grimes and the other guys what we know. I'd like to know what Grimes is up to before we take this anywhere up the chain. I think there might be a few kinks in the chain."

They continued walking north on Third Avenue toward the downtown area and Pike Place Market. The weather was perfect for a spring day. There was always a lot of pedestrian traffic at this time of year, and today was no exception. They both walked with their own thoughts for a while until they reached Pike Street.

"How about you buy me a coffee someplace other than Starbucks," said Chuck.

"OK," said Don without the usual chat about who owes whom.

They turned toward the water and Pike Place Market where the original Starbucks was located. There was a Starbucks on just about every block in Seattle, but this was the original and the one where tourists insisted on having their pictures taken in front of, like it was Mount Rushmore or the Grand Canyon. Don guessed that if he was from Bum Fuck, Kansas, he'd think that being photographed there was a big deal, too. He had to admit, however, that he had had his picture taken in front of some questionable places. There was that pile of dead Vietcong in good old South Vietnam...

"Where were you born?" Don asked Chuck.

"That's a strange question," said Chuck. "You've never asked me that before, why now?"

"Just wondering if you would have your picture taken in front of the original Starbucks if you were a tourist here."

"Probably," said Chuck.

"OK, thanks. That explains a lot."

"I'll just leave that for the time being, but I'll need to know where that came from at some point," said Chuck. "Now let's have coffee on your dime and talk about what's going on. And, in answer to your question, I was born in Kansas. But haven't we had this conversation already?"

"You have my sincerest sympathy. And yes we have."

They walked past the tourists taking pictures in front of Starbucks and turned into a little dive just north of it where they had coffee. Don paid.

CHAPTER NINE

Detective Grimes was nothing if not devious and, well, devious. If there was a mission, he would complete it at any cost so long as it benefited him. His somewhat pickled brain still worked well enough that he could formulate plans and make the plans become reality. His partner, however, was stupid. This was something that Grimes was burdened with from the beginning of their partnership. That's one of the reasons that he greased the skids to get Martin into the unit, that and Martin's wife.

Grimes once thought that Martha would be a great sex partner. Sadly, he found that she wasn't interested in him or the unit. Jack Martin, however, was a lapdog. He'd go along with anything that Grimes suggested and some things that Martin came up with on his own. For example, Grimes knew that Martin was fucking Clorice; he didn't care. So long as Martin was his loyal lapdog, he could fuck Clorice and whomever else he wanted. Grimes just hoped that they would keep it to themselves. That is unless Martin's wife started getting into the act, in which case a foursome was something he could get into.

"Hey, Wil, got a minute?" asked Grimes.

"Sure, come in," said Sherman. "Sit down. What's on your mind?"

"Jack and I were talking and thought that we've been kind of hard on Don and Chuck and that we should get off the dime and give them a hand with their case at the Fairview. Jack and I were up for a case when they got it, so we should work on it with them. What do you think?" said Grimes, his voice dripping with insincerity.

"I'll ask them," said Sherman. "They could probably handle some help with something. You and Jack don't have much going, right?"

"No, we have that body pulled out of the Ship Canal, but we don't know what killed him yet. Probably some drunk who fell off a pier."

"OK, I'll talk to them," said Sherman.

"Thanks, Sarge," Grimes said over his shoulder as he walked away.

Don and Chuck sipped their coffees and ate scones at an independent coffee shop in Pike Place Market. Chuck talked Don into scones since Don was paying. They both ate the scones knowing that they shouldn't since they were men who valued their physical condition and that scones weren't part of their usual diets. Both thought, *Fuck it*.

"Why do you think Grimes would have any interest in our evidence?" asked Chuck.

"Knowing Grimes, he might be trying to sabotage our case," Don said through a mouth half full of blueberry scone.

"Isn't it a little obvious? I mean, how could he know that Smitty wouldn't call us?"

"I don't think he was thinking. I think he might have been on panic mode for some reason. Do you suppose he might think he knows who did it?"

"I know that he's an arrogant ass who thinks he doesn't have to adhere to the same laws that he is sworn to uphold, but that's going a little far even for him," said Chuck. "You have a crumb on your chin."

"I suppose you're right," Don replied, wagging a finger over his chin. "Let's not start looking for commies behind every bush just yet."

When they finished, Don and Chuck walked out onto the cobblestones in front of the coffee shop and north along Post Alley, over to Steinbrueck Park overlooking Elliot Bay, and across to Bainbridge Island, Kitsap County, and the Olympic Mountains. Two state ferries left crossing wakes behind on their routes to Bremerton and Bainbridge Island. A passenger-only ferry on a catamaran hull sped on a plane to Vashon Island to the southwest. Standing at the railing separating them from traffic that flowed below on the Alaska Way Viaduct and ignoring the array of troubled humanity with tourists behind them, both contemplated what lay before them.

People who lived on Vashon Island were a breed apart from those in Bremerton and Bainbridge. Most people from Bremerton were the salt of the earth and hard workers, accustomed to hardship; some were navy. Those from Bainbridge Island were, for the most part, new Volvo, BMW, and Mercedes-driving twits, steeped in the notion that they were the chosen people who came to Seattle only to replenish their bank accounts to better supply themselves with lattes and fresh cilantro. *Fuck them*, thought Don. *Ditto*, thought Chuck. Those who called Vashon Island home were indeed a cut above, with the exception of the recent arrivals from California who thought that they would escape and raise goats while bringing along their taste for fine wine and Brie cheese. The majority of Vashonites—or was it Vashonians or maybe Vashonistas?—were stuck in the sixties. They drove Volvos, but Volvos that were built in 1970 or earlier. They smelled of goat feed with a hint of patchouli oil. Come to think of it, some of the people smelled like goats as well. If they came to Seattle, it was to do an honest day's work, knowing that they were going home to God's country or some other deity's at the end of the day. On the other hand, they may have come to supply themselves with those things needed to make rugs, macramé, clothes, or beer. These were people whose clocks were set according to demands made by a dimension other than the ones driving those on Bainbridge and Bremerton. *Great people*, thought Don.

On every visit to Vashon Island, Don left with the thought that he should move there. Then he came out of his dream state and remembered that it took a huge effort just to get to and from the place. He had to be satisfied with the periodic bike trip to and around the island with a weekend at an inn, accompanied by a willing partner thrown in for good measure.

Don finally broke away from his thoughts about the various tribes that populated Puget Sound. By tribes he meant the people who were separated by water, thus having differing views of the world that a discerning person could point out. Don prided himself on his ability to point out these differences.

Living in western Washington, especially around the island-dotted Puget Sound part of it, brought that out in a person, provided that he didn't have shit for brains. Don didn't have shit for brains, nor did Chuck. Chuck's just hadn't developed as thoroughly because he hadn't lived as long and in the strange places that Don had: Vietnam, San Francisco, and the strangest place of all, Minnesota's Iron Range.

"Where do we go from here?" asked Chuck.

"We just need to be very careful around these guys. We can figure out what gives if we just do our jobs. Then there's the old trick of bringing them into this to some degree without letting them fuck us over. We could ask for minor help like bringing the witnesses in for the sketch sessions, stuff like that."

"OK, let's ask the sergeant if he'll ask one of the teams to bring them in on Wednesday."

"Sounds like a plan."

By the time Don and Chuck got back to the office, they noticed that all the other detectives were gone, not unusual. Their clearance rates were not the stuff on which cop shows were based. After lunch, the other detectives were generally found in one of many dives in Seattle, solving the age-old question of how many detectives it takes to screw up a case. Depends on whether it's a case of Scotch or a criminal case.

Don called Barber via the desk at the Fairview and left a message about the sketch appointment on Wednesday. Chuck called his hooker who wasn't home; he left a message on her machine. Then they went up to the Identification Unit to check on the prints they'd lifted from room sixty-one.

The Identification Unit consisted of a half-dozen technicians who were skilled in finding, lifting, classifying, and comparing fingerprints with those on record. They examined print cards lifted by officers and detectives as well. If there were named suspects or others who were known to be at a crime scene to compare with, it made their jobs a little easier. Don and Chuck had done a fingerprint search of room sixty-one and lifted some prints. They submitted these with the names of people they knew to have been in the room. Among them were Barber's. The unit was very good at what it did. Their testimony in court could make a case for a prosecutor. It paid big dividends to treat them well. Don and Chuck did just that.

They talked with technician Jim Schuller. Jim had been in the unit for as many years as Don could remember. Even as a patrol officer, Don submitted more print cards from scenes than almost any other officer. The technicians recognized this and worked with him to solve cases where they could. Jim Schuller was one of the technicians with whom Don and Chuck had developed a close working relationship.

"So what have you got?" asked Don.

"Looks like we have a match with Barber on the print you lifted from the bed frame," said Schuller. "It's a good match, at least twelve points."

The "points" Schuller mentioned were the points of comparison between a known subject and latent prints lifted from a scene. Twelve points were enough to be a positive match. They might even persuade a jury if the jurors weren't all eighty years old and hard of hearing.

"Great," said Don. "That was the print that was in a place that would have probably put him on the bed and not just standing and facing it like he was making it. It was at the head of the bed, too."

"But he's the guy who changed sheets on the bed by his own admission," said Chuck. "Then there's the fact that the rape and murder took place on the floor."

"You are a serious spoilsport, aren't you?"

"Just a realist is all. Somebody around here has to be. When we talk to the prosecutor, that's the first thing he'll point out."

"Right, but it gives us a little more leverage on the guy," said Don.

"Right," said Chuck. "Are there any others that might be of interest?"

Schuller showed them another card that Chuck had lifted from the Formica tabletop that was the room's answer to a desk and dining/general-purpose table. "This is Sergeant Sherman's palm print. He was there with you, right?"

"Right," Don responded.

Don and Chuck thanked Jim for his work and went back to the unit. On the way, they passed Sergeant Sherman's cubicle.

"Don, Chuck, come here a second, would you?" said Sherman.

"What's up, Sergeant?" asked Don.

"Grimes and Martin said that they feel kind of guilty about you guys getting this case and would like to give a hand where they can. It might pay to let them do a little work, you know, for the sake of peace in the squad."

"What do you think, Chuck?" said Don.

"Sounds good to me, but it might be just grunt work."

"Why don't you go over and tell them what you need when they get back."

"We'll do that, but any idea when that'll be?" asked Don.

"No idea."

"Oh, I almost forgot," said Don. "Turns out we lifted your palm print from the table in the room."

"Sorry about that. I guess I'm getting careless."

Now that Don and Chuck had a print match on Barber, although it was of questionable use since he cleaned the room and changed sheets, they had a little more ammunition. It was time to flesh out his character a bit. One way of doing that was talking to people who had a history with him.

Don called the detective who had investigated the rape that put Barber away. Detective Nick Corson was still working the Special Assault Unit (SAU), the unit that did all manner of sex crimes. What they didn't do were Vice cases like prostitution, human trafficking, etc. SAU did your everyday rape, statutory rape, incest, and other cases that had a sexual motivation behind them as long as the victim didn't die in the process; Homicide did those. Sometimes there existed a thin line between case responsibility that led to another unit doing a sex case. In the rape that Corson investigated, there was no thin line; a woman was raped pure and simple, and Barber committed the rape.

"Hello, Nick, this is Don Lake; how's she hanging?" said Don when Corson answered.

"Just sitting here biding my time until I can walk away from this fucking sewer and get on with life in Arizona."

"In other words, you love your job," said Don.

"Yes indeed. If I was any happier doing what I'm doing, I'd have to be committed. There comes a point when you would like to see every male of the species neutered—and some of the females. When you reach that point, a man shouldn't be doing what I'm doing. There's the whole objectivity thing to consider, and I'm way beyond that. But enough of this bullshit, what's up that you called a lowly sex crimes puke like me?"

"Do you remember a rape that you investigated about twelve or so years ago on Capitol Hill? A young teacher just moved from Idaho and into an apartment where she was raped by a guy named John Barber. I pulled the case and saw your name as lead detective. It looked pretty solid that Barber did it," said Don.

"Let me rummage through my steel-trap brain and see if I can put a face on that. Yeah, I have a vague recollection of the case only because of the obvious nature of it. Barber was a tenant in the building that the victim had moved into a short time before. That was the Debauch Arms on Tenth Avenue just off Madison, as I recall. She had just gotten married, so maybe it was all they could afford. I recall that Barber was the maintenance man there in exchange for his rent."

"That's the one. I looked at the place and can't quite understand why the victim would have chosen that dump. Maybe she was naïve, dumb, or poor or a combination of all three."

"You have to remember that it was a while back and the dump wasn't quite the dump it is today," said Corson.

"Sure, probably not quite as bad but still a dump. Anyway, Barber is now a person of interest in a case Chuck and I are doing at the Fairview Hotel; now that's a dump. He's the clean-up guy around there; he lives there and is staying pretty up to date with reporting as a sex offender and staying in touch with his probation officer. He's the guy who reported the murder. He found the body in a room he had cleaned before the victim moved in. The victim was a hooker who was there for a couple of days before she was raped and killed. The killer almost decapitated her with a leather bootlace. Sound familiar? Oh, and one more thing, Barber says that he and the woman whom he raped in your case were having an affair and that her husband got suspicious. He said that he didn't do a rape, that it was consensual. When she was afraid that the husband was on to them, she reported him as a rapist. He's adamant that he didn't rape her."

"We both know that there aren't any guilty pricks behind bars. Every one of them has been framed by the victim, the police, or the gods," said Corson. "Barber was as guilty as anyone I have ever put away. He should have stayed in prison a hell of a lot longer than he did. He's also a pathological liar. But I guess that's no surprise either. The victim in my case was twenty-six years old and had been married for two months. She and her husband moved here from some small town in northern Idaho. He was a new teacher in one of the local schools, and she was looking for a teaching job but hadn't found one. They didn't have a lot of money; that's why they moved into the Debauch Arms. She was doing laundry in the basement on the day she was raped. Barber found her there and started playing grab ass. He wasn't such a bad-looking guy then. She didn't want any part of it, so he took her to the floor and raped her. It was pretty brutal. There was a lot of tearing and bruising. She was a great witness, and there was no doubt about who did the rape and that it was a rape. Then there was the unfortunate piece of evidence that Barber left behind: his semen. The dumb fuck didn't use a condom. He was toast. I think the jury took about thirty minutes to come back with a guilty verdict. Do any of those facts fit your case?"

"Pretty much all of them except for the innocent nature of the victim and the marriage parts, and Barber isn't so attractive these days. I'm guessing that the pathological liar part might still be accurate, and he's still a maintenance man who probably still fucks people against their wishes. But I have some doubt about his guilt in this case," said Don. "When you talked to him back then, did he come off as somebody who had the capacity to kill his victim?"

"No, I didn't get that, but if the circumstances are right, any rapist is capable of killing his victim," said Corson. "I don't feel real good about him living in Seattle again. I wish he had chosen Vancouver or Portland. We don't need him here."

"Thanks, Nick. You've been a big help. I feel better about steering things toward Barber."

"Anytime, so long as it's not after about the first of next year, because I'm making good my escape about then. I'm on my way to Arizona along with about half of the retirees."

With a certain amount of envy, Don hung up and returned to the life of a detective who had a long way to go before he went to Arizona. Arizona? Why the fuck would anyone want to move to that dry, snake-infested desert where you would suffer second-degree burns just by sitting on your car seat in the summer? Don always thought that it was the haven of people who had given up and had no more imagination than a gopher. Golfing would carry a person only so far, and that was impossible for all but about three months of the year. The rest of the time you were subject to either sunstroke or snakebite on the ninth hole. A major part of the year was spent looking for the latest early bird special at Denny's, watching some inane fuck on television talking about where to put your retirement funds, and attending the latest mega church where Pastor Screaming Jones was all about getting his parishioners off their wallets. Don thought that suicide would be the better option. It made staying put in Seattle with the periodic trip to foreign lands look good. The foreign lands would be places like San Francisco or Vancouver, British Columbia, places that forbid pastors like Screaming Jones.

"Don, you out there somewhere in never land, or do you want to talk?" asked Chuck.

"It looks like we should look at Barber a little closer."

Before the end of the shift, Grimes and Martin had returned to their desks. Both smelled of an intoxicating beverage, had bloodshot eyes, and were slurring their words—*the stuff of a solid DUI arrest*, thought Don. He set aside the patrol officer observations and got to the point at hand.

"The sergeant tells us that you guys want to give us a hand with the Fairview Hotel case in any way you can," said Don.

"Maybe not in any way, but we can pitch in as time permits," said Grimes.

"How about picking up the witness from the Fairview on Wednesday afternoon and bringing him here for the sketch artist?" said Don.

"Yeah, we should be able to do that if nothing happens between then and now," said Grimes.

Martin sat like a mannequin while Grimes did the talking. He didn't express anything by his demeanor. This wasn't unusual for Martin, thought Don. He was, after all, brain dead, in Don's and Chuck's humble opinions.

"Plan on picking him up at about noon. His name is John Barber. He's in room seven at the Fairview. It's on the first floor. We'll let him know that you're coming. He thought that he'd walk, but I don't want him changing his mind on the way. He thinks he can identify the guy he saw the morning of the murder."

Don and Chuck then walked back to their cubicle where they exchanged skeptical glances. Both cleared the clutter from their desks, what there was of it, and left for the day.

The trip past Marjorie's desk didn't go unrewarded, as usual. She had decided to give the guys and some of the gals on the fifth floor a sample of her latest purchase from Victoria's Secret. The cleavage she displayed was, in a word, sinful, but who was complaining? Even Chuck was dazzled by her choice of dress.

Don wondered once again how she had escaped the clutches of some lecher in the Violent Crimes Section. She was a great gal with everything situated exactly where it belonged and in the appropriate proportions, although there was room to grow in the breast area. There was no explaining why she was unmarried and apparently unattached in any way with any member of either sex. *Go figure* was the best Don could come up with.

CHAPTER TEN

The ride back to West Seattle on the water taxi was uneventful. The smile, maybe grimace, woman with the serious case of bicycle butt was on board, as usual. Was she timing her trips to coincide with Don's? Entertaining that possibility was more pleasant than thinking about where to take the murder of Yvonne Gillespie from here.

Don's talk with Corson had brought him around to giving Barber a closer look, yet he had his doubts. Why not give it all a rest and concentrate on the business at hand: smile or grimace?

Ms. bicycle butt was sitting alone as usual, reading *The Seattle Times*. Don concluded that now was the time to approach her and make small talk. He was still fearful that the smile was actually a grimace and that he would be dismissed in a way that his ego might not survive.

"Hi, anything interesting there that we could waste a few minutes talking about?" asked Don as he sat down across from her.

"Sure, we could talk about tomorrow's weather. Since we both ride this tub, we should keep an eye on that," said the woman.

Holy shit, she knows who I am. It's a start.

"Are you by any chance a bicyclist?" asked Don.

"Yes, I am; why do you ask?" said the woman.

"I have this innate ability to identify people who bicycle for some reason," said Don.

"And what about me suggests that I'm a bicyclist?" asked the woman, a perfectly groomed right eyebrow raised as she asked.

Don had to do some quick thinking and come up with something other than her perfect butt.

"Your tan and your muscle tone are dead giveaways," said Don. "We bicyclists are like farmers. Our tans start early in the year."

"I see what you mean. Are you in the habit of noticing the muscle tone of women you encounter or just of women you find attractive? And as for muscle tone, the weather hasn't really encouraged me to wear my more revealing clothes. Muscle tone is pretty much hidden from view this time of year, unless it's the kind of muscle tone only a man would notice," said the woman.

"Guilty," said Don.

"My name is Tiffany, and I've noticed that we seem to ride the same boat on a regular basis. What brings you downtown from God's country?"

"I work for the City of Seattle. How about you, what do you do?"

"I work at the Seattle Art Museum, but back to you. City government is pretty big. Could you narrow it down a bit? Like do you mow grass at Myrtle Edwards Park, fix sewer lines, get the mayor his coffee?"

"I suppose you could say that I'm in the sewage business to a certain degree. I guess you could say that I deal with toxic waste from time to time. By the way, does the sense of humor come naturally or did you develop it over time? Not that there's anything demeaning in mowing grass and cleaning sewers. I just don't do either. See the hands? If I did those things and actually worked for a living, I'd have a few calluses. What I do is generally the conversation killer in cases like this. I'm a cop. My name is Don."

"Hmm, a cop. Yes, I see what you mean; that would kill conversation but only if you were a creep or I was a crook, and I haven't sensed any creepiness in you, yet. How about me? Do you have that creepy feeling about me? I am, after all, working at an art museum, a real conversation killer."

"What do you do at the SAM?"

"In a nutshell, I assist in acquiring and hanging new exhibits. It's kind of a curator job without the curator status or pay. But I love what I do and feel fortunate to have been hired to do it. I'm one of those rare art history majors who is not asking if you want fries with that," said Tiffany. "Not that there's anything wrong with asking that. How would one know whether you want fries if one didn't ask?"

"Now that we've established our liberal and egalitarian credentials, where in West Seattle do you call home?" asked Don.

"Wait a minute there. 'Egalitarian' smacks just a little of someone who doesn't write parking tickets for the police department. What is it you do, or would you have to kill me if you told me?"

"If I had to kill you, I'd also have to investigate the murder. I'm a homicide detective," said Don.

"You're kidding. You don't look like a homicide detective."

"Thank you, I think. But what does a homicide detective look like?"

"He's a little older than you, dresses badly, and isn't in very good shape," said Tiffany. "And he smokes stogies, eats at greasy spoons, and has left several marriages behind."

"You don't exactly fit the image of an art curator either," said Don.

"And that image is what?"

"They're older than you, single, graying hair that's wrapped in a bun, dark plastic-framed glasses, very skinny, awkward around strangers, wear over-the-knee dresses, and have a pencil pushed behind one ear," said Don. "Oh, and they carry a shopping bag full of books on art. And cats. They have cats."

"I am single," said Tiffany.

"Good," said Don. "One thing I've noticed about you, and I hope you'll forgive me for noticing things about you, is that you read *The Seattle Times* and not the *Post-Intelligencer.* What's that all about? I thought that we just established our liberal credentials, and I see you reading the *Times.*"

"My parents gave me a subscription for Christmas, so that's what I read. I try not to let the editorial page influence me. I read *The New York Times* at work. There's always a copy lying around. You wouldn't believe how liberal the people there are. My parents wanted to pull me back from the brink of debauchery that being a liberal leads to, according to them. It almost drove them over the edge when they found that I was majoring in art history at the U. If they knew I was reading *The New York Times*, they would concede that they've lost the battle. Luckily, I'm an only child and unlikely to be disinherited," said Tiffany. "Don't get me wrong, I love my parents; they just think that FDR was the devil incarnate and that Reagan walks on water."

The water taxi was arriving at the dock while Don and Tiffany were still covering the high spots of who and what they were. They had a lot of ground to cover since they had been putting off acknowledging each other for so long. Don was feeling a little guilty and didn't know if this conversation with Tiffany would lead anywhere and further muddy his already muddy romantic life. However, she had that great butt, was single, and didn't wear her hair in a bun.

"Here we are," said Don. "You haven't told me where you live in West Seattle."

"I'm just at the top of California Way and to the west toward the water."

"I'm at the top of California and in the other direction," said Don. "I haven't noticed you on the bus from here. How do you get up the hill?"

"I walk," said Tiffany.

"'Mind if I walk with you?"

"No, I'd like that. Maybe on the way you could tell me how a real homicide detective lives."

"For starters, didn't your parents tell you to never go anywhere with strangers?"

"You are strange but in a good way. I'll take my chances," said Tiffany.

As they walked up California Way, they went further into the banter that had a way of getting at the truth about a person. Tiffany divulged her age as thirty-two, several years younger than Don; and that she had been married but had no children; her parents were near panic about the whole progeny thing; and she liked smart and physically fit men. She also found men who liked art in any form to be especially sexy.

"I have a minor collection of minor art in my house," said Don. "Does that qualify?"

"I'd have to do a survey to determine whether it does or not," said Tiffany through what had become a fixed grin.

"Done. How about we turn east instead of west at the top of the hill?" Don said with more hope in his voice than he intended.

"I'm afraid that I have to get home to my cats before they think I've abandoned them. George and Martha are extremely time conscious. They expect me at a certain time and panic if I'm not there to feed and walk them."

"Cats, you have cats? Of course you have cats. That's one of the characteristics of an art curator. Hair in a bun and cats."

"Screw you."

"That might be a bit premature, but it could be arranged," said Don.

"How about tomorrow after work you and I stop at my house and I'll introduce you to George and Martha, and we'll see what happens after that? A walk with the cats has a way of separating the poseurs from the real deal."

"That sounds like a deal, provided I'm not called to do the chief's bidding. Here, take my card and give me your number in case I'm not able to make the cat walk. Include your number at the SAM."

Tiffany wrote her name, address, and telephone numbers on a piece of paper and handed it to Don, who noticed the artistic script. He also noticed the address. It was on a bluff overlooking Puget Sound, a very high-class address. What was she doing by befriending a lowly detective? Granted he was a detective with a master's degree and a certain amount of class, a lot of cash, and a townhouse in a better part of town, but a detective nonetheless. *Go figure* was the best he could come up with.

At the top of California Way, Don and Tiffany parted ways but not before Tiffany planted a light kiss on Don's cheek. *This has progressed nicely*, thought Don. *This has potential*, thought Tiffany.

As Tiffany walked away to the west, Don again glanced at the name and address she gave him. Tiffany Winslow was her complete name. She must be pulling his leg. Either that or she was testing his artistic gravitas. On the other hand, maybe she was just giving him her name.

CHAPTER ELEVEN

It was six o'clock the next morning; Don had just crawled out of bed and was drinking his first cup of coffee and reading the *Post-Intelligencer* when the phone rang. It was never good news coming from the other end of a phone at this time of day. It was usually work-related and usually had something to do with someone's day ending badly. *I should answer this*, thought Don. *It might be the Publishers Clearing House people telling me that I have come into a lot of money.* It was Don's guess that it was not.

"Good morning, Detective, this is Police Radio. Sorry to interrupt your beauty rest at this beastly hour, but a patrol officer has asked that you call her," said the cheerful voice at the other end.

"Is this a recording, or are you for real?" asked Don.

"For real; this is Sergeant Grant. There's an Officer Morris at a suicide at the Fairview Hotel who insists that you be disturbed, so give her a call at this number." Sergeant Grant gave Don the number; it was to the front desk of the Fairview.

Officer Morris, thought Don, *the very attractive officer who greeted Chuck and him at room sixty-one at the Fairview. He had no right to be twice blessed in this way.*

Wilbur Olson answered the phone at the Fairview with a tone that would definitely not attract business: "Fairview Hotel."

"Good morning, Wilbur, this is Detective Lake. Is there a patrol officer there who wants to talk to me?"

"Yes, she's been waiting for you, but it's been no hardship for me. She's quite attractive," said Wilbur. "She's the same one who was here the other day."

"Good of you to notice, Wilbur. Now let me talk to her if you'd be so kind."

"Hi, Detective, this is Officer Morris. I don't know if you remember me from the other morning, but I have something here that I thought you should be informed of."

Not recall you from the other morning? thought Don. *What was she thinking?*

"Of course I remember you. You were very professional at that scene, even with the sexist crap you endured from two of the oldest dinosaurs in the department. I should have apologized for them before I left."

"That's not why I called, and you don't have to apologize for anybody in the department. I can take care of myself. I had no illusions about what I might experience. I know that I can be a magnet for sexist behavior from some older men and most young ones. Anyway, I got a call to a suicide here this morning. A man jumped from the hotel's roof. He just happened to be the guy who reported the murder in room sixty-one. He landed in an enclosed area on the west side of the building where garbage is collected. He's a mess, but I think you should look at him."

Don was appropriately admonished by a brand-spanking-new officer and wondered why that was. But that was beside the point; she was telling him something that she thought was important, and it probably was since the guy was the only potential witness in the murder of Yvonne Gillespie.

"What is it about the body that makes you suspicious?"

"That he was your witness, for one. Then there's the fact that he's not wearing shoes and it's raining. He also seems to have some marks on his wrists that don't look right," said Officer Morris.

"Have you called the medical examiner?"

"Not yet. I thought I'd call you first. I talked with Sergeant Warner and he said that I should just call the ME, but I didn't. Is this something you want to look at?"

"Yes. You did the right thing. Your sergeant might not agree, but your judgment rules the day on this one. I'll call my partner, and we'll be there within an hour or so. You might want to call your sergeant and tell him what's going on. It might save you some grief later."

"OK, I'll be out with the body on the west side of the building."

"If you have a tarp or plastic sheet, would you cover the body?"

"I think there's one in the trunk of my car."

Coffee cup in hand, Don called Chuck who was about to climb into the shower. Chuck said, none too enthusiastically, that he'd go directly to the hotel from home. Don agreed to go to the office to get the van.

After a quick shower, Don drove his Subaru out of the garage and into the rain over the West Seattle Bridge to First Avenue where he got off and then drove north to the Public Safety Building. Detectives weren't permitted to park in the building on day shift, but Don thought that an exception could be made under the circumstances. He went to the office to get his briefcase, the van's keys, and the unit's 35mm camera. There was no one in the unit this early. He placed a note explaining what had happened on Sergeant Sherman's desk and left. The van was parked in its usual place. The drive to the hotel was wet but quiet. There wasn't much radio traffic. Don added to what little there was by logging on with Police Radio before arriving at the hotel.

When Don arrived, Chuck was already there and waiting with Officer Morris.

"Good morning, troops," said Don. "You too, Chuck."

"Screw you, boot," said Chuck.

"Boot? I didn't know that you were up on military jargon," said Don.

"He may not be, but I am," said Officer Morris. "I also told him that it meant a new troop in the military."

"So he snitched to you that he has time on me while he was waiting to be directed in how to go about his job."

"Yes he did, and I told him about the term. I was in the army before joining the department," said Officer Morris. "We're also on a first-name basis now. My name is Victoria, Vickie for short."

"I thought there was something a little more professional about you than other FNGs."

"Let's see, FNG is short for fucking new guy, as I recall. It was a term that was used in Vietnam for guys fresh off the plane from the world, guys whose life expectancy was that of a fart," Victoria stated.

"Good," said Don.

"I was military police. It gave me a leg up on this job."

"OK, let's get a leg up on this scene. Show us where the body is."

Officer Morris led them out a door that opened onto the garbage collection area. There was a large, green Dumpster on a concrete patio that was blocked from view from the street by a gate. Don was appreciative of the gate since it blocked the scene from people on the sidewalk. It was never a good thing to shock the good Asian citizens of Chinatown as they went about their day selling overripe fruit and ginseng root while doing their best to look like the world was about to end.

The people who inhabited Chinatown were accustomed to police cars at the Fairview. Don wasn't so sure about the van. Most people in town knew that when that particular van showed up, it meant that some poor fuck's day had come to a bad end. John Barber's day had definitely come to a bad end. They walked to the body, now covered by a blue tarp. Don pulled it back.

When Barber's body left the roof of the Fairview, it managed a trajectory that took it about ten feet from the building. Unfortunately, it hit the corner of a Dumpster. The solid and heavy container didn't give much, but Barber's head did. It was partially torn away by the impact, and his arms were obviously broken in several places as though he was trying to stop himself from the inevitable. Don imagined that his internal parts were displaced as well. Barber lay on his face with both legs bent in a grotesque pose; they, too, would have multiple fractures.

"What did you see on his wrists that was interesting?" asked Don.

Officer Morris walked to the body and pointed to bruises on both wrists. The bruises didn't result from the fall or impact. They looked almost like those that resulted from handcuffs that are applied with too much force. Don knew the drill: complete assholes often get the tight handcuff treatment.

"Good eye," said Don. "I think you'll go places as a cop if you keep this up."

"Thanks, but isn't that what officers are supposed to do: find things, investigate, note facts that might solve a crime? Otherwise I think you might call us report takers or secretaries."

"I know that you don't need kudos from me or anybody else, but you really are going to go places here if you want to," said Don. "But you might want to back off on the defensiveness."

"Thanks, for starters do you mind if I help process the scene? And I'm sorry about being defensive. You see, I have been on the defensive so long because of my appearance that it's hard not to be."

"Understood, but please help wherever you can. Chuck is slow in the morning so isn't of much help. And I know the feeling, having been born handsome."

"Screw you," said Chuck with little or no enthusiasm.

They all pitched in with the measurements, pictures, and note-taking. Don and Officer Morris—Vickie—went to the roof to take more photographs and look for anything of interest.

Access to the roof was up a stairway off the sixth-floor hallway; it was identified by a placard that read ROOF. The door to the roof was unlocked from the inside, making it inaccessible from the outside when closed. Don put his flashlight in the jam to keep it open when they walked onto the roof.

The roof was the usual tarred surface with vents scattered around. It wasn't a place where one might go to get a tan on a sunny day even if one was an SSI drunk. There were puddles of water in various places. Immediately outside the door, Don started looking at the roof surface for things out of the ordinary. He was immediately struck by two skid marks, as though someone or something might have been dragged across it. The marks weren't sharp like they would be if they were made by the heels of shoes. *Check his heels,* thought Don.

"Did you see the drag marks?" asked Officer Morris.

"Yes I did." Was she trying to piss him off, impress him, or just be a good cop? Don's guess was that she was just doing what she did: investigate.

"I didn't look at his heels, sorry."

"We'll do all that when the ME gets here."

They went to the spot where the body would have left the roof. Don thought that if he were going to jump from this particular roof, he wouldn't have done it at that spot. Hitting the Dumpster was an almost certainty, and that would have made an open-casket funeral questionable at best. He would have gone off the front onto the sidewalk.

"If you were intent on doing yourself in, would you have jumped from this spot?" Don asked.

"No, I'd have jumped onto the sidewalk. Hitting that Dumpster would make an open casket almost out of the question," said Officer Morris.

Christ, she is good, thought Don. *I'll have to start calling her Victoria. I wonder what secrets she has up her sleeve.*

After Don photographed the objects he thought significant on the roof as well as several of the body where it lay, they went to Barber's room, which they opened with the key that Wilbur had provided them on the way up. Barber was no longer concerned with his right to privacy, so a warrant wasn't required.

Don didn't notice that any big changes had occurred since the day that Chuck and he had talked to Barber. His boots were still lined up under his neatly made bed, although it looked like someone had sat on it after it was made. His wallet was on the table. It contained twenty-seven dollars in cash and a check from the owner of the building for $150. Beside the wallet was a checkbook for an account at Washington Mutual. He had $492.36 in the account. In a drawer under the table were various papers. Among these was a savings account book from a different bank showing a balance of $17,564.78. The last entry was made on the day that Yvonne Gillespie was murdered. Don wondered where this guy was getting the money. He didn't make much at the hotel.

Officer Morris opened the closet door and looked up at the shelf above the few clothes that hung neatly on a wooden dowel. Travel brochures were neatly stacked on the shelf. All were for the Pacific coast of southern Mexico. She took them down and laid them on the table.

"Detective, do you think a guy who might have been planning a trip to Mexico would kill himself? And it looks like he had the money to pay for it," said Officer Morris.

"You're right, people who have a future don't usually kill themselves," said Don. "And would you call me Don?" The graying hairs showing at his temples gave Don a moment's doubt about his chances with this gorgeous and younger woman; then it was gone.

"Of course, I've been hoping you would ask. After all, we've been to-gether at two death scenes. That calls for first-name basis in my book," said Officer Morris.

"OK, Victoria, you're right. That's one of the ways you differentiate a suicide from a murder. No future: suicide. Future: murder. Simple as that in my experience," said Don.

"And another thing," said Officer Morris, "do you smell that disinfectant?"

"Yes, but the guy was a janitor, so that isn't out of place."

Don knew that when a very attractive female officer was first encoun-tered on the job, there was a lot that wasn't revealed. Officers wore body armor, which, on women, was very unflattering. The armor flattened every-thing it came in contact with. Officer Morris may have been flat chested or well endowed and Don wouldn't know. Body armor was a cruel life-saver. Then there was the jacket that most officers wore at this time of year, especially on first watch. It covered the midsection of an officer and most of the butt. Don couldn't make a valid assessment of Officer Morris's butt under the jacket. He would have to remedy that in some way before he decided to pursue this any further.

Then there was the ethical issue with which Don struggled. He had too many relationships and potential relationships going at one time. He had to start discriminating a little. Life, however, was short, and he loved the life he was leading. The life he was leading was woman focused. All of them were potentially great permanent partners. Don would have to go with what he currently knew about Officer Morris: she was very attractive, she was smart, she cared about the job, and she seemed to be interested in being more than "Officer" Morris. Then it occurred to him just what a sick, conceited fuck he was.

When they walked back into the alley after leaving the roof, Chuck was still taking notes. Don took more pictures of the alley and body and then called the medical examiner's office.

While they waited for the ME, Vickie went for coffee and Don and Chuck started analyzing what this "suicide" meant.

"This is too coincidental to be a suicide, don't you think, Don?" said Chuck. "Barber was our only witness that we were aware of and he kills himself? I don't think so. I think the guy who killed Gillespie killed Barber because he knew that he saw him. What does this tell us?"

"Wilbur Olson did the Gillespie murder and then killed Barber?" asked Don.

"That could be, but Barber outweighs Olson by about fifty pounds and Olson hasn't gotten up from that desk for several years," said Chuck. "His muscle tone must be near nonexistent. And on top of that, he probably couldn't work up the hard-on to rape anyone."

"Maybe we should lean on Wilbur a little, take a DNA sample, that sort of thing. That might rattle his memory a little," said Don.

"Let's do that today before we leave. We'll at least give Wilbur something to think about while he sits behind that desk."

Vickie returned with the coffee at about the same time as the ME's van drove up and parked in front of the gate to the garbage area where the body lay. Dr. J. Wyman Mills and a technician got out of the van and walked into the hotel where Don and Chuck waited.

"Good morning, Dr. Mills, we have to stop meeting like this," said Don.

"Yes, we can do better than the Fairview Hotel. Something in a bed-and-breakfast, for example," said Dr. Mills.

Chuck and the ME technician rolled their eyes and smiled. They sensed that there was more to this than attempting to find a killer. Vickie didn't appear to be all that amused.

When they reached the body, Dr. Mills started her routine. She took notes and then found a place to cut a hole to insert the thermometer that would tell her his body temperature. With latex gloves, she felt around Barber's head, now ruined from its impact against the unmoving Dumpster.

"There's a slight indent on the back of his skull. It appears that contact with the Dumpster was face on. Bleeding from the facial wounds appears to be less than I would expect given their severity."

"Are you suggesting that he may have been dead when he hit the Dumpster?" asked Don.

"Could be. As you know, head wounds bleed a lot and these didn't. Maybe he was killed somewhere else and dropped off the roof in an attempt to make it look like a suicide."

"Actually, that's what we were thinking before you arrived," said Don. "We found what looked like skid marks on the roof that could have been made by the heels of his feet. Let's look at them."

Both of Barber's heels were black. They appeared to have been dragged across a dirty surface. Don got a swab and sterile water and swabbed Barber's heels. He also reminded himself to go back to the roof and get a sample of the tar.

"This gets more and more curious."." said Don.

"Well put, Detective," said Dr. Mills. "You may now be dealing with a budding serial murderer."

"It'll take one more to reach that, but we're moving in on it," said Don. "When do you want to do the autopsy on this one?"

"How about same time, same place this afternoon?"

"Sounds good," said Don.

After the body was bagged and taken to the van, Don and Chuck went to the lobby of the hotel where Wilbur Olson sat behind the desk, immersed in a book that had the appearance of something other than a mystery novel.

"What are you reading, Wilbur?" asked Chuck.

"It's a history of the United States by Howard Zinn," Wilbur answered, his eyes not leaving the page. "He's the only historian who has got our history right. The rest or most of the rest have bought the lies of the ruling class."

"I've read it," said Don. "You're right about the ruling class; they have written our history for too long, but I'm not supposed to get political on the job."

"You reported the suicide to nine-one-one, right?" said Chuck.

"Yeah, I came in this morning at about five thirty and opened the gate on the west side of the building. That's where I park my car, except on garbage pickup days when I park it on the street until the garbage truck has gone. When I opened the gate, I saw Jack. That is, I thought it was Jack lying on the ground. He was a mess, so I didn't look too close. I then went in and called nine-one-one. You guys know the rest."

"Where were you last night?" asked Chuck.

"At home where I am most nights; I don't have an exciting night life."

"Where is home?" asked Don.

"The Debauch Arms on Capitol Hill. I've been there for years."

"Did you know Barber when he lived there?" asked Don.

"Yeah, I knew him then. That's why he works, or worked, here. He did maintenance, so when he got out of prison, he came here. You see, we communicated while he was in prison."

"Did you get involved in the rape investigation that landed Barber in prison?" asked Don.

"Yeah, the police asked me some questions about it, but I couldn't give them much help."

"Were you and Barber friends or what at that time?" asked Don.

"I owned the Debauch Arms then, so he was my tenant and employee."

"Do you own it now?"

"No, I lost it in a legal judgment. The victim of the rape brought legal action against me and my property for the crime committed by an employee. I lost and the ownership of the Debauch Arms went to the victim of the rape. She still owns it and rents to me. She is a great landlord, although it's still the Debauch Arms. You'd think that she would at least change the name. By the way, she never did get a teaching job; she didn't have to. The property is now worth millions. At some point she will sell the place, which will, no doubt, be torn down and replaced by a condo tower. Getting raped can be profitable, if you know what I mean."

"Wilbur, you are a major piece of work," said Don. "But you can redeem yourself by doing something for us. We need a cheek swab from you to eliminate you as a suspect in this case."

"Suspect? The guy jumped off the roof! Why would I be a suspect in a suicide?"

"We think he was helped off the roof, Wilbur," said Chuck, "so we need some DNA to help us find who helped him."

Wilbur went along with the request. Don took swabs from both cheeks after Wilbur signed a consent to search form.

"We would be very disappointed if you decided to leave town unexpectedly, Wilbur," said Don. "That would give us a serious reason to expect you were the guy who assisted Barber off the roof."

"By the way, Wilbur, what side of the building would you jump from if you were going to commit suicide?" asked Officer Morris.

"I'd sure as hell not jump off the west side and land on the Dumpster," said Wilbur. "That would hurt like hell."

"Go back to Howard Zinn," said Don," and let us know how our history turns out."

"Will do, but do I look like somebody who could throw anything heavier than a Mars candy bar from the roof?"

On the street Don asked Vickie if she had updated her sergeant on the case; she had. It was policy that a supervisor respond to the scene of any suicide. Sergeant Warner decided against coming since Don and Chuck were there and had processed the scene. Vickie's ass was no longer hanging out. Don hoped that sometime in the near future he could get a better assessment of her ass. *Get a fucking grip*, he thought.

CHAPTER TWELVE

Clorice Grimes and Jack Martin had spent the better part of the previous night at her house. Clorice was still pretty in a slightly over-the-hill sort of way, and she still had the sexual prowess that Martin was attracted to when his partner first introduced them: she filled out a pair of jeans in a way that still caused men to turn around and stare.

On one of the first days after Martin and Grimes had become partners, they stopped by Grimes's house. It was on a slow afternoon following a long lunch that included several martinis. Clorice had come home early from her job as a part-time clerk at a Ballard bookstore because she had a dental appointment. When Martin shook Clorice's hand, he felt a certain sexual spark that he rarely felt. He certainly hadn't felt it from his wife in a long time. Clorice gave him a look that suggested she might be interested in him. It was mutual.

About a week after that first meeting, Clorice called Martin at his desk and asked if Grimes was there; he wasn't. She asked if he would meet her at a coffee shop in Ballard; he would. Martin left Grimes a note that he had some business and left. He drove to the coffee shop where Clorice was waiting.

"Why do you suppose I called you?" asked Clorice.

"I have no idea." He did have some idea, but he thought that the idea might have been a dream.

"Sure you do. You must know that Bill and I are swingers and that we don't have much going on between us that is sexual in nature anymore."

Martin acted surprised, although he had heard that they were swingers. "But doesn't swapping require the consent of both partners?" asked Martin.

"It's supposed to, but Bill no longer does the actual swapping part. Now he goes out and screws whatever crosses his path, and I find my own partners. It's a variation on swapping."

"Why are you telling me this?" asked Martin, as though he didn't know.

"Surely you aren't that naïve; it's because I'd like to screw you."

Martin put on his best shocked look; it wasn't convincing. "When do you want to do this?"

"Now, of course; let's go back to my house."

Martin and Clorice drove to her house in her car, leaving the pool car on the street. By the time they arrived, Martin was ready to tear her clothes off and screw her in the front seat, but she suggested that they save it until she got the garage door closed and they were in her bedroom.

Once in the house, Martin began to fondle Clorice who was more than willing. By the time they reached her bedroom, Clorice was nearly naked, only her bra and panties remaining in place. Martin couldn't quite believe his good fortune. He was about to screw his partner's wife, and he was going to do it in his partner's bed. *Screw him,* thought Martin.

Clorice was a true expert in the use of her body. Martin's wife, Martha, wouldn't dream of doing some of the things that Clorice was doing. Martha thought that blow jobs were unclean. Clorice seemed to think otherwise. By the time they had completed the afternoon's sexual gymnastics, Martin and Clorise were exhausted.

"Does Bill know that you bring guys home?" asked Martin.

"I suspect he does, but I don't think he cares. He spends most nights on the prowl, so I've stopped being concerned about what he thinks."

"How about the AIDS thing? Are either of you worried about that?"

"If he wants to screw me, he wears a condom or he doesn't do it. It doesn't come to that very often, though, and when it does he usually doesn't do such a good job. You may not be as big in stature, Jack, but you're bigger where it counts."

Before Clorice drove Martin back to his car, they took a shower together where they practiced a sexual technique that could easily have put Martin in traction. By the time they got to Martin's car, they agreed that they would meet on a regular basis to practice and perfect what they had started.

As Martin drove back to the office, he couldn't help but reflect on his good fortune. Every time he looked at his partner in the future, he would see Clorice and the things she had waiting for him. Grimes had treated him like a gofer from the start. That might continue, but now he was getting a little payback.

That was several years ago, but nothing had changed except their technique. They were practicing again on this particular night. They had just about reached perfection.

While Martin and Clorice were engaged in more technique honing on this particular night, Martin's wife, Martha, was in a "meeting" with the assistant principal at the school where she taught. Her kids were old enough to watch themselves. Martha's "meeting" took place at the assistant principal's apartment in Bellevue overlooking the I-405 freeway. The view wasn't all that great, but the sex was outstanding. Martha thought that her future at the school was a little more secure with each visit, which it was.

The next morning Grimes walked into the house just as the sun was coming up. He walked into the bedroom where Clorice was asleep. Martin had left about an hour before, and she was exhausted from the workout she and Martin had put in. Grimes undressed, put his clothes into a hamper, and climbed into the shower where he washed off a night's worth of sex.

He had started the night by picking up a hooker at one of the local bars. They went to her room at a low-life motel on Aurora Avenue. The hooker had managed to keep him partially functional with her mouth and then screwed him. He managed to finish the process before losing his erection, so he didn't succumb to his usual rage following a failure to perform. The hooker was more fortunate than she knew; he had beaten others in frustration.

When he was done with the hooker, he drove around thinking about what his life had become. He knew that Clorice wasn't with him out of love any longer and hadn't been since the time they started their life of swinging. It was his idea to swap partners, but it was Clorice who kept it going. She seemed to like it, a lot.

Clorice, who grew up in a very straight and religious household, loved to screw. She loved to screw a lot and a lot of different men. Grimes had a problem keeping up the pace. Clorice would arrange the swaps and he would go along. Sometimes Grimes would just watch without taking part. Clorice liked this as well.

When he drove past his house the previous evening, he saw that there was someone in the house with Clorice. He didn't see who it was, but he knew that it was a man who was there for one reason. He drove away, giving Clorice time to take care of business and the man to leave before going in. Then he went in search of a hooker.

Grimes also thought about what he was becoming.. He was no longer a detective in any real sense, just on a card. He knew that he no longer deserved to have a badge or carry a gun. He knew that his partner deserved better, although his partner was also screwing Clorice. But he also knew that he had to keep on or end up sleeping in seedy motels and drinking himself to death. He had to cover himself in any way he could. It was that or swallow the barrel of his gun.

CHAPTER THIRTEEN

The autopsy on John Barber was not quite as gruesome as the one Don had witnessed performed on Yvonne Gillespie. This was partially because Barber wasn't anywhere near as attractive as Yvonne, but it was also because he hadn't been raped. Don barely gagged during the entire procedure.

Dr. Mills did the usual incisions and bone cutting, but her main interest was his head. She confirmed that he had been hit with something substantial on the back of his head. The object was probably rounded like a baseball bat but probably not that big. His face was destroyed, but that was easily explainable by its impact with the Dumpster at a high rate of speed. In Don's experience, the face always lost in these matters.

When she arrived at Barber's wrists, Dr. Mills examined them with a magnifying glass and let Don do the same. The bruises on both wrists were a dark purple. Don had seen them on people who had the cuffs put on too tight in retaliation for acting like a jerk. Don took more photos of the wrists now that they were clean. Dr. Mills did the same.

"What do you think happened, Don?" asked Dr. Mills after she had put the body parts back in Barber's chest cavity like so many giblets and sewed him up.

"I think what I already thought," said Don. "I think he was killed somewhere other than the roof and then carried up to the roof to make it look like a suicide. But there's one thing about this that makes that open to some question: his size. Whoever did this is big and strong. It's my guess that the killer first subdued him with the cuffs by telling him some story and then hit him. Wherever he was killed, there might be some blood, but

I didn't see any on the stairs leading onto the roof. We'll have to go back and look a little closer."

"I think you're right, Don. And another thing, have you considered why this guy was killed? He was your only possible witness in Yvonne's murder, wasn't he?" asked Dr. Mills.

"Yes I have." Both Chuck and I seized on that thought from the beginning. Another thing to consider is who would know that he was the only witness? That's a little spooky. It'll mean less work for the sketch artist. Barber was coming in on Wednesday to describe the man he saw to the artist. We have another person coming in on Wednesday. She's Chuck's victim in a rape and assault. She's a prostitute who was pretty badly beat up by a john. She thinks she can do a good job of describing him for the artist."

"It sounds like you have your work cut out for you for a few days. How about we make plans for the weekend?" said Wyman. "The weather is supposed to be nice, so how about a bike ride on Vashon?"

"Sounds great; I haven't been out there for a while. It's a butt kicker of a ride if we go around the island, but it's worth the effort," said Don. "How about we start from my place where we can have breakfast. I'll nudge you when the coffee is done."

"Pretty presumptive aren't we, Detective?"

"Yes I am, but in a good way," said Don. "Now I have to get some work done before people start drawing accurate conclusions about us."

Don returned to the office where Chuck was hard at work on the new follow-up report. He looked up when Don walked in.

"It's almost certain that Barber was killed at another location and dragged to the roof. There's a crease in the back of his scull that was made by something rounded like a baseball bat but probably not a baseball bat. This is getting a little weird and too coincidental to be coincidental," said Don.

"I think that whoever did this didn't want Barber to describe Gillespie's killer to the artist. But that brings us to another question: who knew about Barber?" said Chuck. "Maybe we need to start looking closer to home or at the tenants of the Fairview. There's always Wilbur, but he's such a physical wreck he has a hard time getting up from behind his desk. I don't think he has it in him to drag Barber up to the roof. Besides, he's not the type who would go around strangling prostitutes. But that brings up another question. What's the type that goes around strangling prostitutes? Which brings up another question: Why the fuck am I writing this scene and follow-up while you're playing grab ass with the ME over an autopsy?"

"You know that autopsies make you sick, Chuck," said Don. "I'm just being sensitive to your feelings."

"You're a real prince, and I think we need to go to Barber's room tomorrow and look for blood. Then we need to go over the route from his room to the roof."

"Right."

Don and Chuck briefed Sergeant Sherman before they left for the day. Sherman seemed a little more interested than normal. It looked as if this may be the start of a serial case, and serial murders were real press magnets. They also screamed for quick closure. The Violent Crimes commander and the chief of police would want to know about any progress. Then there was the issue of the two worthless detectives: Grimes and Martin. They could be less than helpful and possibly screw things up. Sherman seemed pleased that Don and Chuck had both cases. At least, that was the impression he was attempting to give them.

"One more thing, Sergeant," said Don as he turned to walk away, "did you know that Grimes went to the Evidence Unit to look at what we collected at the Fairview after Gillespie was killed?"

Don detected just a moment's hesitation and confusion on Sherman's face before he answered.

"Yeah, I suggested that he go look at it so he and Martin could get a better idea about what we're working on."

"Oh, OK," said Don. He was glad that he asked the question now and not immediately after Chuck got the call from Smitty in Evidence. He had been pissed then. Now he and Chuck had time to think and talk about it. They still hadn't come to any conclusion. He didn't believe what Sergeant Sherman had just told him.

Don was sorry he had driven to the office although he had no real alternative. It got in the way of the conversation with Tiffany that he was looking forward to. He thought that he had her schedule down, not that he was stalking her, although you could call it that. Or maybe she was stalking him. No, that would be unusual for a woman and a sure indication of self-flattery.

Don drove to the water taxi dock in West Seattle in hopes that he might catch Tiffany either getting off the taxi or walking up California Way. *Holy shit,* thought Don, this does have all the characteristics of stalking.

When he arrived on Harbor Avenue and parked in front of the dock, Don noticed that the taxi had arrived and was backing away from the pier on its return to the downtown side of Elliot Bay. "Shit" was all Don could come up with. Then he saw Tiffany come out of the café that was located near the dock. She had a cup of coffee in one hand and a bag filled with stuff of some kind in the other. The bag looked heavy.

"Hi there, want a lift?" said Don as Tiffany walked toward the sidewalk and California Way.

"Thank you, I was just thinking about taking the bus. This bag of books is a bit more than I'm used to carrying up the hill," replied Tiffany with a smile.

Don opened the rear door so Tiffany could put the bag in. He couldn't help but notice the subject matter.

"You do fit one more of the characteristics of an art curator. You carry bags of books on art. Now I'm waiting for the hair done in a bun," said Don.

"I'm saving that for a special day," said Tiffany. "I do appreciate the ride."

"How about you introduce me to George and Martha today?"

"OK, go to the top of the hill and turn right on Massachusetts, then left onto Sunset."

Sunset Avenue was one of the premiere addresses in West Seattle. Its residents didn't land there unless money was not an issue, or they were in hock up to their asses. There were a few poseurs on Sunset, but most had either arrived financially sound or were well on their way. Don wasn't doing too badly in the address category, but Tiffany was one step ahead, not that he was keeping score.

When they arrived at Tiffany's house, she pointed it out and told Don to park in the drive off the alley. Don was momentarily disappointed when he saw that her house was across the street from those on the bluff overlooking Alki Avenue, Puget Sound, and the Olympic Mountains.

"This is great," said Don. "You just have to wait for the next rainy winter or earthquake and you'll have bluff property."

"What do you mean?" asked Tiffany.

"The houses across the street will fall off and you'll be on the bluff with a better view and higher property value."

"Good thinking, I'll have to remember that during the next long, saturated winter. Now let's go in and meet the cats."

Don could take or leave most cats, and this was a case in point. "Let me get your books, and I'll follow you in."

The house was one of the oldest on the block. It was a two-story red brick with a slate roof. The trees and garden surrounding it were mature and well kept. This was a house that might have been in the family for a long time and was well loved. Don could appreciate that.

When they walked through the front door and into a long hallway that divided the house down the middle, two cats came running from some hiding place.

"Hi, guys," said Tiffany. "I want you to meet Detective Lake. He's a homicide detective. Aren't you impressed?"

The cats wrapped themselves around Tiffany's legs and purred. They seemed to like her but didn't give a shit whether Don was a detective or a snake charmer. Cats could be incredibly indifferent at times. Don could be indifferent, too, but his indifference stopped at the legs the cats were wrapped around.

"I'll just put this stuff away, and then we'll go on our test walk."

With both cats outfitted in their harnesses and on leashes, Don and Tiffany walked north on Sunset. Don had Martha, at least he thought it was Martha, on his leash, and Tiffany had George. The cats walked ahead on the leashes as if they thought they were dogs. Unlike dogs, however, the cats didn't stop to sniff at and piss on every object that came along. They also didn't require constant attention like dogs, which allowed Don and Tiffany to talk undistracted.

"How's my cat presence working so far?" asked Don.

"They don't seem to mind you being around, at least not yet. They both sleep on my bed, you know."

"No, I didn't know that. But it's good to know. I hear they make great watchdogs, I mean watch cats. One can't be too cautious when sleeping."

"That's my take on it."

"You mentioned that you were married in a former life," said Don. "What brought that to an end, if I may ask?"

"You may. It all came crashing when we found that I was French Impressionist and he was American Modern. There is no way we could be in the same house with that gaping chasm between us. Seriously, that may sound flip, but it says a lot. If two people can't agree on what genre best fulfills what the meaning of great is in the art world, and those two people eat and breathe art, they must not live together. To do so will ultimately lead to a new art form cast in blood. We are still speaking but only about matters involving the cats. We got the cats during our marriage and custody of them was a big deal in our divorce. We first thought that we should each take one. Can you imagine George and Martha separated? So now he takes them on a periodic weekend, and I get them the rest of the time."

"What are the cats' tastes in art?"

"I haven't quite figured that out, but they do look at some of the books I bring home and show an interest in Pi*cat*so," Tiffany replied.

When the cats were apparently satisfied with the walk, they turned around and walked back to Tiffany's house. Tiffany asked Don if he would like to join her and the cats for dinner. Don thought that was the best idea of the day.

"We'll have either kitty treats with a side of catnip, or we can have a leftover stew that I made a few days ago and a salad," said Tiffany.

"I'll go with the stew, although the kitty treats sound tempting."

What Don was really thinking was *stew?* Is this another French Impressionist/American Modern chasm? Of course, "stew" didn't have to be beef stew. It could be carrot stew or tofu stew or vegetable of some sort of stew without the other stuff that makes it not vegetarian. Don had to remind himself that he did eat the odd piece of meat if circumstances warranted, and this might be one of those. But he'd rather not kick his principles to the curb every time these choices came up just because a beautiful woman's approval was at stake.

"I hope you don't mind if it's vegetable stew," said Tiffany.

Don't mind? thought Don. That's like not minding that she had the greatest butt he'd seen in a while or that she lived close at hand, although Roseanne Vargas lived closer, or that he was the luckiest guy in the world without deserving it.

"I love vegetable stew," said Don.

Dinner was pleasant. The dining table was in the kitchen that overlooked a lush backyard. Tiffany served a meal that was elegant in its simplicity. The wine was from a local grocery and set her back about seven dollars. She was clearly a woman who could interest Don in ways beyond her culinary skills. But what to do about his increasingly complicated love life? Not that this relationship had reached into the love-life category.

"What are you hoping for in life?" asked Tiffany, without much warning, as they worked on cups of coffee.

He had to think about that for a few seconds before diving in. "Hope can be a slippery thing. You hope for something and it slips away like an eel. But my hope is to live life in a way that I won't regret on my last day. You know how sometimes something just happens in your life that seems to have come out of nowhere with no effort on your part and that thing is just right? I've been very fortunate in life. Things have happened to me that I don't seem to have played any part in, and most of these things have been good. My job sometimes appears to be the pits. The people I deal with can be pathetic and the victims overwhelming, but that just shows me how lucky I am that I'm not them. I'd be a sorry SOB if I didn't acknowledge that; how about you?"

"Compared to that, I've got nothing. Deciphering what piece of art is good enough to be exhibited and which is to be rejected seems small time in comparison," said Tiffany, "and it seems sort of an egotistical exercise."

"I disagree. What you do separates us from our dark side. Without art, there would be nothing to aspire to beyond the commonplace stuff of survival, so we might as well cash in now. We hang art on our walls and read good books because we seek a meaning greater than ourselves and our continued existence. Art is the glue that holds us together. Some might say it's religion or family, but they pale in comparison to art. It's unfortunate that most of our leaders don't get that. Most of them find meaning in power, and the greatest expression of power to them is war. They don't get that war is the ultimate failure, the greatest perversion that man has devised. You notice that I said 'man.' There haven't been many women in history who have used war as the greatest expression of power. So what you do is the ultimate in good. I hope you don't think that this little speech is nothing more than a slick way of getting into your pants; it's not. I believe it with my whole being. But getting into your pants wouldn't be such bad thing."

"Bad thing?" said Tiffany with a certain amount of breathiness. "Let's skip dessert for now and take this to the bedroom where we can discuss the meaning of life in more detail. The cats can stay here."

Don and his mouth got him into it again. Tiffany Winslow was all that he had imagined and a little more. It wasn't a cliché in this case. The bicycle butt that Don had been admiring was in reality what he saw in his imagination through her tailored pants. The rest of her body matched her brain: it was well endowed and responsive. She gave in a way that only a very smart person gives. Smart people tend to understand that sex is one of the great gifts, and it keeps on giving. He also discovered that she was a natural strawberry blonde.

By the time Don and Tiffany came up for air, they had explored most of each other's bodies. They also found what pleased the other on more than one occasion. *Fuck, life is good,* thought Don. *Yes, it is,* thought Tiffany.

For the second dessert course, Tiffany brought out some strawberries and cream. She also made fresh coffee that, to Don's trained palate, didn't come from Starbucks or any of the other big-named coffee roasters. *So she isn't contributing to the world's domination by the oligarchs. Good for her,* thought Don.

"Where do we go from here, Detective Lake?" asked Tiffany.

"We could try out your couch or the floor in front of the fireplace."

"That's a thought, but I mean, where do we go from here? You know, this thing we seem to have started a long time ago with you ogling my behind and me acting all school girlish and smiling demurely and then leading up to you finally getting off the dime and talking to me like a bashful ninth grader. Where does that sort of thing lead us after the first romp, or second or third, soon to be fourth romp, I hope. Where does all that lead?"

"Since we seem to be neighbors, although you live in a high-rent district and I in the working class, and we travel to and from work on the same conveyance, I think we should make this a regular thing and see where it takes us. We've both been married and divorced, so we're both damaged goods, so there isn't that chasm between us. I don't know your religion and you don't know mine, so there isn't that, and we both like cats. But there is the French Impressionist thing. I actually have high regard for the Fauvists."

"I took you for someone who is fond of the Wild Beasts, and I find that attractive in a man, just no American Moderns."

"I hope that doesn't include Jackson Pollock."

"Jackson Pollock I can live with. There's so much going on in his paintings that their meaning still isn't fully understood."

"I'm relieved to hear that."

"I'd have to see the piece before making any judgment. If you're trying to tell me that you own a Jackson Pollock, I will be so impressed that I may have to include Abstract Expressionist in the styles I like."

"Deal, now how about we try out that rug in front of the fireplace," said Don.

"How about we save that for a time when the cats are with their dad and won't be subjected to any perverse stuff," said Tiffany.

"Sounds fair; I wouldn't want to be party to the perversion of anyone's cats," said Don.

The sun had long since dropped behind the Olympics when Don left Tiffany's house. He walked to his car with a plastic bowl of strawberries in one hand and a rolled print of an Henri Matisse in the other. The plastic bowl was Tiffany's way of saying that she expected a return visit. Theirs was the start of a relationship that was building on more than sex; it was Tupperware based. It did not get much more committed than that.

Don drove to his townhouse with a new perspective on life. He liked his life before today, but after his stop at Tiffany's and his bonding with her cats, he was rejuvenated. It was like coming away from a massage administered by a real masseuse, not a half masseuse/half hooker. Don had experienced both. He really liked Tiffany, her cats, and her way of viewing the world. She hadn't been jaded by life, by the ugly crap that got in the way of living it to its fullest. She didn't seem at all concerned about having to fix a broken world except in an unconscious way. She gave those who took the time to see, a bit of the beauty that man and woman are capable of creating when they aren't out maiming and killing each other. This was a rare gift that not many had the ability to pull off. This could go beyond the return of Tupperware and delve into the return of Tupperware full of Don's fresh potato salad. The possibilities were endless.

When Don drove into his garage and closed the door behind him, he heard his telephone ringing. By the time he got out of his car and into the kitchen, the phone had gone silent. He checked his calls and found that Roseanne Vargas had called. She hadn't left a message. He considered not calling her back but thought that she might have seen him arrive and wonder why she was being stiffed. Don called her.

"Hi, Roseanne, I noticed that you just called. I couldn't make it to the phone fast enough without the risk of breaking something on the way. What's up?"

"Yeah, I just saw you drive in, so I thought I'd check to see what's new in your life. I have a great bottle of wine from T. J.'s that I thought you might like to sample with me," said Roseanne.

Don was in a quandary. Should he put all his eggs in the Tiffany basket or keep his options open? There was the need to make neighbors happy after all. And he did like Roseanne and found her very, very sexy.

"Sure, give me a few minutes to shower the day's grime off, and I'll come over," said Don.

"How about if I help you scrub the day's grime off?" asked Roseanne.

"That's very neighborly of you," said Don.

"Be right over. Don't start without me."

"I wouldn't dream of it," Don said without giving a second's thought.

CHAPTER FOURTEEN

The next morning Don awoke alone. The view from his bedroom overlooking Elliot Bay was clear, bright, and uncluttered by rain or fog. The bay was calm with only slight wave action from the frequent ferry traffic. It was a rare spring day in Seattle. Don reflected for a moment on the previous day's events and smiled. If he could just keep all of the balls that life had thrown his way in the air at the same time, everything would be OK. Did he feel like he was using his good fortune with more than one very attractive woman unfairly? That was something he would have to ponder in the coming days. Until he came to a conclusive answer, he knew that he continued to be luckier than he had any right to be. There was also work to be done and cases to be solved and a bad guy or guys to put away. This was the stuff that kept him energized.

The ride across Elliot Bay on the water taxi was uneventful. Tiffany hadn't made this run, which was a major disappointment to Don. He was happy, however, to just have a few minutes to reflect on the previous day and to organize the day that lay ahead.

The first cloud of the day formed when Don walked to the door that separated the Homicide Unit from the rest of the world. Through the small window in the door, he saw Marjorie sitting at her desk, as was usually the case. Someone was standing behind her; it was Grimes. Don saw that Grimes had put his hands on Marjorie's shoulders and then slid them down her chest and into the low-cut blouse that barely covered her breasts. Grimes held his hands inside Marjorie's blouse, cupping her breasts while talking into her ear. Marjorie appeared to be less than her cheerful self.

Don made as much noise as he could in opening the door with his keys. By the time he arrived at Marjorie's desk, Grimes had removed his hands and was standing a few feet from Marjorie with a slightly guilty look on his face.

"Good morning, Marjorie, how's it hanging?" asked Don while looking directly into Grime's eyes with a clearly menacing gaze.

"Fine," said Marjorie. She wasn't convincing.

Still staring into Grime's eyes, Don said, "Do you and Martin have any plans this morning? You agreed to pick up a witness for the sketch artist."

"Maybe."

"OK," said Don, still staring a hole into Grime's eyes. "We still need you to do that."

"I have some stuff to do today, so I can't help you."

"Of course you do," Don said in his most sarcastic voice.

As Grimes walked away, Don walked next to Marjorie. "I saw what he was doing. What do you want me to do about it?"

"Nothing would be the best thing. You know that I've got a reputation around here, don't you?"

"I know that you have an aura that would make a eunuch horny," said Don.

"There's that, but there's more. A few years ago I had a thing going with Grimes and his wife. We got along real well until Grimes sort of stopped being up to the task, if you know what I mean. Clorice and I continued the fun and games without him. He would sometimes watch, but that was all. Now he thinks I'm still his whenever he wants."

"Let me know if there is anything I can do."

"Thanks, I will. By the way, I still think you're very attractive."

Holy shit, thought Don as he walked toward his cubicle. *This is getting way out of hand. But she bounced back. That's a good sign.*

Don was at his desk before Chuck for a change; he must have had a late night. In Don's opinion, Chuck had an even more challenging love life than his. Chuck wasn't bashful about telling Don all about his partner or partners. Don was getting an education in the complete spectrum of the gay "lifestyle," as if there was such a thing. It wasn't all about sex, although that was a big part of it. Chuck told Don about weekends spent with a partner shopping for the week's groceries and then morphed into a trip they may have taken to Vancouver or one of the nearby mountains to ski. Except for the grocery shopping part, Don didn't see much difference between his life and Chuck's. He'd have to have Chuck and his latest partner over for dinner some night. Of course, Chuck could cook Don under the table, so he would have to plan this carefully.

As Don was going over the plan for the day and rereading the case file, Chuck walked in without the usual shit-eating grin on his face. "What gives with Marjorie this morning? She doesn't seem her usual self," Chuck said. "When I asked her how it was hanging, she didn't even smile or make the usual comment about my tasteful attire."

Don described what he had witnessed when he came in, and Chuck nearly came unglued.

"How about we go over and practice on Grimes's face. I'll do a few kicks and you can do the O'Neil method shit on his neck. That's what they taught you heroes in ranger school, right?" said Chuck.

Don knew that Grimes was a short distance away and was the only other detective currently at work in the unit. If Grimes was the scumbag that Don thought him to be, he was listening to everything being said.

"No, let's leave it be for the time being. When the time is right, we can set Grimes right about a lot of things," said Don.

Just then the office phone rang. Marjorie usually picked it up, but she wasn't doing it this time. Don finally picked it up, answering, "Homicide, Detective Lake."

At the other end was a man's voice. "Detective Lake? Is Detective Weinstein there?" He pronounced Weinstein as "Winestine" instead of "Winesteen." "I need to talk to him."

Don told the man to wait just a second and then told Chuck to pick it up.

"Detective Weinstein, how can I help you?" said Chuck.

As the man started talking, Chuck signaled Don to listen in.

"Hey, man, are you the guy who came to Shondra Wilson's apartment a few days ago?"

"Yes, Detective Lake and I stopped by there."

"You asked her to come in and describe the guy who beat her up, right?" said the man in a slightly threatening tone.

"That would have been us, too."

"Why you want to do that to her? To get her killed?" said the man.

"No, that wasn't our reason for asking her to come in. We want to catch the guy who beat her up," said Chuck.

"You know what she does, right?"

"Sure, we know that Shondra's a prostitute, but she got beat up, and that's what we do when even prostitutes get beat up. We investigate and hope that we can identify and prosecute the guy who did it," said Chuck.

"Well, the guy who did this called Shondra this morning and told her that if she identified him, he would kill her. How's that helping Shondra?"

"How would the caller know Shondra's number?"

"Damned if I know, man, but he did. And Shondra's scared. She wants to leave town for a while. She sure as hell ain't coming to identify anybody today or any other day. If I find the fucking cracker who called her, I'll do a hell of a lot more than just mess up his face."

"What time did Shondra get the call?" asked Chuck.

"It was early this morning. She was in bed. She said the man's voice sounded just like the man's who beat her up."

"What exactly did Shondra say the man said to her?"

"He said that if she thought he had hit her before, she didn't know what hitting was. She wouldn't wake up from the next one. Something like that."

"Can I talk to Shondra?"

"She's done talking to you guys. She ain't at her apartment anymore, so don't go looking for her there."

"You mind telling me who you are?" asked Chuck, knowing that he wasn't going to get an answer.

"Yeah, I'm the cracker killer if that fuck comes anywhere near Shondra." Then he hung up.

"We seem to be striking out, Chuck," said Don.

"Yes we do. Who do you think that guy was?"

"My guess is that Shondra is his meal ticket and he doesn't want to miss any meals just yet."

"Her pimp, right?"

"You catch on faster than the average resident of Capitol Hill," said Don.

"Screw you."

"I think we need to go for another walk there, Chuck boy." In a lowered voice, Don told Chuck that he should probably lock up his files before they left. Don did the same.

When they got onto Third Avenue and began walking south past the King County Courthouse, they felt secure enough to talk at a normal volume.

"I can think of only two ways that the guy who called Shondra could have got her number," said Don. "He either got it from her as a loyal customer or he got it from your case file. I doubt that the guy was a loyal customer otherwise he wouldn't have assaulted her. That leaves the file. If the number came from your file, who in the office lifted it? And the bigger question is why would the guy threaten to kill her? That sounds like a desperation move from someone who has a lot to lose."

They continued past "Muscatel Meadows" as the south lawn of the King County Courthouse was known. What had at one time been a pleasant park with shade trees and benches was now a camp during the night for derelicts and during the day for the same derelicts. The daytime hours found them sitting, drinking, and contemplating how "the man" had fucked them over. It had about it a slight smell of the open sewers Don recalled from his time in Asia. If they ended at a breakfast stop, Don would have to get the image out of his mind.

"I didn't tell you this, but I noticed that the file had been moved a few days ago. I have a way of arranging them by date, and it was out of date sequence," said Chuck.

Don knew that Chuck kept the neatest desk of anyone in the unit. His files were always precise and even color coded: assaults in blue folders, murders in red, and gun cases in green. There was almost never a kidnap to investigate, but Don was waiting for the color Chuck would choose if he got one. Don hadn't yet been in Chuck's apartment but suspected that it would make his look like a dump when in fact it was very neat and tastefully decorated, and he wasn't even gay. Although Don didn't much care for some of the stereotyping that followed gays, he saw a few of them in Chuck. There was one serious advantage to Chuck's fastidiousness at work: he knew when something on his desk was out of place, and Don could always find one of his files should the need arise. Chuck, Don had come to realize, was the perfect partner. He didn't even compete with him for women.

"We're going to have to permanently relocate our files to our desk drawers," said Don. "I know it's going to throw your color scheme off, but if someone is going through them for reasons that seem to be real serious, it has to be done."

"Agreed, except for the color scheme thing; I don't do it for aesthetic reasons. It's easier to lay my hands on the one I need if they're classified by color," said Chuck. "Speaking of narrowing down, how do you propose we identify who in the office is looking at our files? The Gillespie file may also have been gone through. It wasn't out of place, but it seemed a little off the day after I put it together."

"I think you seem a little off," said Don.

"Sometimes I don't think you take me very seriously," said Chuck, with a smile.

"You are very wrong there, my good man. You're the best detective in the unit and, therefore, the department, except for me. You recall the great work we did as patrol grunts? Well, we do even better work here, and it's because we work together like a finely tuned Volkswagen, 1960 vintage. Without you on the team, there would only be me—while perfectly adequate, not fully functional."

"A 1960s Volkswagen? If memory serves, that was a piece of machinery that needed constant attention and sucked gas like there was no environment problem. If we work together like that piece of crap, God save us," said Chuck.

"Don't you see the beauty of the image?" said Don. "We're that imperfect machine, constantly working at getting it right but never quite achieving our goal. That's our job; we never achieve perfection and never will. We get lucky through hard work and put some crook where he or she belongs some of the time, but we never do it perfectly, nor do we get all the crooks. Like that 1960s VW, we putt along in spite of our flaws, and we do it in a rather classy manner, don't you think?"

"You should have been a fucking poet, man."

"How do you know I'm not?"

"Enough of this, let's find some breakfast and talk about nailing the spy. If you suggest a tofu place, I'll have to shoot you in the right knee," said Chuck.

"How about vegetable hum bow? I know this little…"

"I hope you have your running shoes on," said Chuck, "'cause if you don't, I'm going to cripple you."

"OK, let's go down to that dive on Second and James with the roaches."

"Sounds good; I have a bottle of ipecac in my desk," said Chuck.

Don and Chuck walked into the dive that came with roaches at no additional cost and greeted one of the owners who was at the register. They walked toward the back where they could keep an eye on everyone who came in. The place welcomed every type of clientele known to Seattle.

Some had had run-ins with the law. It was just good defensive policy to not give anyone unfair advantage in such a place.

They sat at the booth nearest the kitchen and uncomfortably close to the restrooms that probably hadn't been cleaned for a while, if ever. Don did his best to get the visual image of an Asian open sewer out of his mind as he scanned the menu. Chuck ordered the Nasty Scramble that came with ham, sausage, potatoes, eggs, onions, lots of onions, and toast. Don ordered oatmeal with a side of whole wheat English muffins. Both had coffee. This was no Seattle oligarch's coffee. This was Midwest weak-in-the-knees stuff. It took several cups to get the sense that this was actually coffee you were drinking. This was dive coffee.

"You know that you're gonna die of a massive coronary at your desk, don't you?" said Don.

"Yes, and you're going to die of boredom."

"Now that we have that out of the way, what do we do about the office spy?" Don asked. "We already know that Grimes went to the Evidence Unit and looked at our stuff there. We also know that Sherman told us that he told Grimes to do exactly that, although I don't believe him. There remains the question why he wouldn't just tell Grimes to come and see us so we could show him our evidence sheets on Gillespie. We know that Grimes declined to pick up Shondra after first agreeing to do it. Do you think that Grimes might have something to do with the assault on Shondra? He had a swap deal going between his wife and Marjorie, and I saw him fondling Marjorie this morning. He is one guy I wouldn't trust any farther than I could throw a 1960s VW. Maybe he has gone to prostitutes for solace and failed there as well, so he beats them up in frustration."

"As you already know, I hate Grimes with a passion I usually reserve for conservative Republicans," said Chuck. "He's probably capable of anything if he's threatened. If he's shown the door before his planned retirement, I think you'd see a very bitter and dangerous man, and a dangerous man with a gun. Not a pretty picture."

Their food arrived accompanied by some great aromas. Don had to admit that Chuck's scramble smelled better than his oatmeal. He wasn't about to let Chuck know that and went about sprinkling brown sugar and pouring a little milk on top. He splurged on the muffins and applied a layer of peanut butter topped with preserves from a plastic container that had an expiration date that was probably well into the twenty-first century.

Then he watched with envy as Chuck upended the hot sauce bottle on his scramble, a slight smirk crossing his face.

Just as he was about to put a spoon full of oatmeal in his mouth, Don stopped and let the spoon hover under his nose as if to savor its aroma, staring in the direction of the door.

"You'll never guess what just walked in."

"The ghost of Jimmie Hendrix from the look on your face," Chuck responded through a mouth full of scramble.

"Close but no cigar. Sergeant Sherman, Grimes, and Martin."

Sergeant Sherman acknowledged Don and Chuck with a nod, and then all three walked to a distant booth. Don noticed a periodic gesture from one of the three that told him they were the subject of their conversation.

Don and Chuck made short work of breakfast, asked for the check and then got up. The trip to the cashier took them past the booth where Sherman, Grimes, and Martin were consuming their heart-stopping meals. No one spoke as they passed by.

"After we get back to the office, how about we check out a car and see if we can find Shondra," said Chuck as they walked back up the hill to the PSB.

"Good idea," said Don. "Finding her might lead us to Gillespie's murderer."

"I think you're onto something," said Chuck. "Why would someone threaten to kill a hooker if she helped us identify him? Beating up a hooker seems like pretty small stuff next to a murder of another hooker unless the same person did both or knows who did."

"Then there's Barber, who might have been able to identify Gillespie's killer or thought he could. He's killed so he can't help us, or so it appears," said Don. "Too much coincidence for my taste."

Sergeant Sherman and Detectives Grimes and Martin talked about what Don and Chuck might be doing on their two murder cases as they ate. They referred to Don and Chuck as "the college boys." None of the three had attended college and were slightly envious of those few in the department who had. They let it be known that they were envious by berating them.

"How are the college boys doing on the Fairview murder?" Grimes asked Sherman.

"They seem to be giving it a lot of attention but getting few results yet. The witness at the Fairview is no longer among the living, so that puts a big dent in the case," said Sherman.

"You'd think that the victims were actual people instead of a hooker and a convicted rapist," said Grimes. "We should be putting our efforts into solving real murder cases not some misdemeanor homicides."

"Like you've been solving any real cases lately, murder or otherwise," said Sherman.

"It might be a good thing that we aren't solving too many cases, if you know what I mean," said Grimes with a knowing look on his face.

Martin sat and ate, not understanding what was going on. He was slow on the uptake in most things unless they were spelled out for him. He hadn't yet figured out that Grimes was aware of his affair with Clorice and that Grimes let it go on for his own purposes, waiting for a time when bringing it to Martin's attention could best serve his needs.

"Let's cut to the chase here, guys," said Sherman. "I'm going to call a squad meeting for later today where we'll talk about our open cases and how we can get a handle on them before the lieutenant gets a handle on them for us. I suppose you're aware that there's talk about us getting a new captain assigned to the section. There's even rumor that it may be a woman. That's all we fucking need is some woman coming in and fucking us over. I've been around longer than anybody here, and I know where all the skeletons are buried. I'd rather not go through anybody's inquisition. If I'm right, the captain that will take Black's place is Wildwood at the East Precinct. She's a serious climber and won't hesitate running over anyone to get where she's going. We have to at least put on a good show of working around here, otherwise we're all going to be in patrol."

Sergeant Wilton Sherman had been in Homicide longer than anyone currently assigned; he had been in the department longer than any except for one guy who worked Patrol South. He thought that he was God's gift to investigations. He liked to suck up to younger officers, especially younger patrol officers who tended to worship at his feet. They didn't realize that he would screw over them in a heartbeat if it served his purpose. The same was true of the detectives under him. Some thought he walked on water, like Martin. Others, like Grimes, knew him for what he was and kept him in check with that knowledge.

Sherman was a native Seattleite. He grew up in the north end, the son of a Boeing worker and a stay-at-home mother. He was spoiled rotten like most only children. He was kept out of harm's way by being sent to private schools and attending church on a regular basis. He was too young to have served in the Second World War but was just the right age for Korea. His parents didn't think it was fitting for him to be subjected to such violence and instead talked to their congressman about getting a deferment. They were successful, and Sherman continued to enjoy the life of a spoiled brat and bully. When his parents thought he should be considering college, Sherman was having second thoughts. The Seattle Police Department was hiring, and he thought that would be a great place to continue his bullying lifestyle. As was the case up to this point in his life, Sherman was hired and started what he found to be a very satisfying life.

He never married. There was a rumor around for a while that he was gay, but he had broken the teeth of more than one officer in order to dispel that rumor. Through the years, Sherman found that there were certain ways of getting ahead in the department. One of these was sucking up to the right people. These weren't necessarily high-ranking people but people with influence both inside and outside the department. He achieved the rank of sergeant by these means and gained a certain amount of wealth as well. He still lived in North Seattle, near the home where he grew up. He wasn't going to give up what he'd worked toward, although what that thing was he wasn't sure. Arizona always sounded like a righteous goal. He'd never been to Arizona, but a lot of his cronies had retired there and seemed to think that they'd arrived. He'd have to go there one of these days.

Don and Chuck walked back to the office, noticing as they passed her desk that Marjorie was back to her old self. Her smile was in place like a mask, and she was dressed in her usual come-hither manner: blouse as low on her chest as was legal and skirt riding too near her panty line for any man's comfort, including Chuck's.

"How's it hanging, Marjorie?" Don and Chuck said in unison as they passed by her desk.

"You would know better than I since you have the advantage of a better view," said Marjorie.

"Put your tongue away and let's do some computer work and see where Shondra might be staying," said Chuck as they continued to their cubicle.

"My guess is that she's at her mother's place, and that shouldn't be too hard to find."

"You're probably right," said Chuck.

Don called the motor pool and reserved a car with plain plates so it wouldn't be too obvious when they parked it near Shondra's mother's house.

Shondra's mother lived in a well-kept bungalow in Madison Valley on the east side of Seattle, a short distance from the swells of Washington Park where a new BMW was the minimum requirement for entry; a Mercedes was preferred. When Don and Chuck drove past, they didn't see any cars parked outside, but they did see the little critter who had kicked Don. He was playing on a swing at the side of the house. Don wondered if they'd find a Beware of Child sign on the gate. They had Shondra's mother's telephone number from information that Shondra had given officers in previous arrests for prostitution. There had been several.

"Do you ever wonder how a beautiful woman like Shondra who was raised in a fairly nice place ends up a prostitute?" asked Chuck. "I mean, look at this; I didn't grow up in a place as nice as this."

"Maybe it's the beautiful part that got her into it. There are all kinds of guys out there who are on the prowl for women like her. They talk to them real nice and give them nice things when they're young and then spring the trap. Once in the life, it's hard to get out, especially if there's a guy around the corner who told you that he will fuck you up if you step out of line. She ends up with a kid and very little else. He ends up with an endless supply of money with almost no work. Come to think of it, that describes a few detectives I know."

"Let's call Mom and see what gives."

Don grabbed his radio and got out of the car. He went down the block where he could see if anyone came out of the house. Chuck found a pay phone a few blocks away on Martin Luther King Way.

The phone rang several times before a woman answered it. Chuck identified himself and then asked for Shondra.

"She isn't here, and I don't know where she is," answered the woman.

"Are you sure you don't know? This is very important. We think that her life may be in danger, and it's important that we talk to her."

"She brought Raymond here earlier and left with a friend. That's all I know."

"Did she say when she'd be back for Raymond?" asked Chuck.

"No, she usually doesn't say exactly when she'll be back."

"If we were to come over to your house, would you talk to us?" asked Chuck.

"Come on, I've got nothing to hide."

Don and Chuck waited about ten minutes after the call and then drove up to the house. Raymond, the mini pit bull, was still playing at the side of the house. They opened the gate and walked to the front door. Don watched for an attack from Raymond while Chuck knocked. An older Shondra opened the door. She was obviously Shondra's mother. Shondra clearly had several more years in the business provided her pimp or a john didn't ruin her face.

"That didn't take long. Come in," said the woman. "What's this about?"

"We think Shondra's in danger from a guy who would rather she not talk to us," said Chuck. "She doesn't want to talk to us now out of fear. That might work against her in a very serious way. Now we want you to help us find her."

"Her friend, the guy she left with, said that they were going away for a few days and that I should take Raymond until they get back. That's not all that unusual in Shondra's life. I know she goes to Las Vegas sometimes for her work, but she always comes back. The guy goes with her. He gives me money for taking care of Raymond. They might have gone there this time. I like watching Raymond; he's a good boy. We go to the arboretum and the lake to play. He likes that."

"Does Raymond have any brothers or sisters?" asked Don.

"No, it's just him. He goes into kindergarten next year. He already knows his alphabet and can count to one hundred. We're working on reading now. He's a smart little boy. He doesn't know what his mom does, but he will soon enough. I'm trying to protect him from that."

"You're doing a great job," said Don. "He seems like a good little guy."

Chuck gave the woman his card and asked that she call them if Shondra called and told her where she was. She said that she would. They believed her.

Don and Chuck walked out and onto the walk leading to the gate. Raymond walked up to them and stared for a short time. Don waited for the blow. It didn't come.

"I'm sorry," said Raymond.

"Thank you for that, Raymond. You know that it takes a big person to apologize, don't you?" said Don."

"Yeah, I know, but I'm not very big," said Raymond.

"You're bigger than you realize, Raymond. Let me shake your hand."

Raymond put his hand out and Don grasped it, giving it a couple of shakes, and let go.

"Can I have a card?" asked Raymond.

"Sure, here you go."

Don and Chuck gave Raymond their cards and told him to call them if he ever ran into a problem that he couldn't solve. He said that he would. He then looked at both cards.

"Chuck? You're Chuck?" asked Raymond.

"Yes I am."

"I like that name."

"Thank you, Raymond. I like Raymond, so I guess we're even."

Don and Chuck turned and slowly walked to their car, neither one saying anything.

As they drove back toward the Public Safety Building, Don and Chuck began a conversation they rarely had; this one was serious. It wasn't cloaked in the usual humor that they and most cops used to mask some of the sorrow that followed them around. This was about a small boy who would probably become one of society's throwaways. His mother was doing the only thing she knew how to do to provide for him. But it wasn't enough. He was going to end up in prison like the inordinate number of black males in the city who would pave the way for him. It was only a matter of time.

"What can we do with this situation with Raymond?" asked Don. "Should we go to Child Protection Services and see if they can take him away from Shondra and maybe put him in foster care or under court-ordered care of Grandma?"

"Then he'd really have something to kick you for, and when he turns sixteen he'll have something to shoot you or someone else for. No, that's not what he needs. How about if you and I step up to the plate and take some direct action. I've been thinking about this since the day he kicked you. We could spend some time with him on days off. We could show him some stuff he wouldn't otherwise experience. I'll bet he hasn't been to Seattle Center or on a ferryboat. He probably hasn't seen the inside of a library or a restaurant. That kind of stuff leaves an impression on a kid. Then just being with him would mean something; I know it would mean something to me. I know I'm not likely to ever have a kid, given the attitude of society toward my kind. We aren't really to be trusted around kids if you're to believe the righteous do-gooder Christians. So maybe I can help with somebody else's kid. How about it?"

"Life right now is complicated enough without you feeling your mothering instincts on top of it. Do you know that I'm currently involved with more women than is really healthy for me or them, and we have two murders that need some attention?" said Don.

"There are weekends when we aren't doing weekend duty. We could trade off spending time with him. All of this will need the approval of Shondra and Grandma, so I could be dreaming about nothing."

"OK, you do the legwork and get the approvals, and I'll go along," said Don. "But you've got to understand that I'm not agreeing for any reason other than I like the little guy even though he assaulted me."

"Thanks, I knew you weren't as big an asshole as you put on," said Chuck.

"Screw you."

"Likewise."

CHAPTER FIFTEEN

The rest of the week was a blur as Don and Chuck did the secretarial things that accompany a murder investigation. The state crime lab hadn't completed DNA analysis on any of the evidence. The department's Identification Unit didn't have anything else to work with, although they were still working on what they had.

Don and Chuck worked on the Barber case with the same enthusiasm as Gillespie's because they were now convinced that the same person responsible for his collision with the Dumpster had killed Yvonne Gillespie. They still needed to find where Barber was killed. It was possible he was killed on the roof, but they had found no evidence of a struggle anywhere up there or on the stairway leading to it. They were almost certain that Barber must have bled quite a bit from the blow to the back of his head, but they couldn't be sure. It rained the night he was killed, so if he was killed on the roof, his blood may have washed away. If he was killed somewhere else, he would have to have been carried onto the roof, but there was no blood on the stairs leading to the roof from the sixth floor of the Fairview. Barber was not a small man, so his killer would have to have been strong. Then there was the phone threat. Shondra was a prostitute who was beaten. Gillespie was a prostitute who was beaten and killed. Coincidence? Don and Chuck thought not.

As Friday rolled around, Don was ready for a bike ride with Wyman. It had been too long since he had his bike off the hook where it hung in his garage. The weather was supposed to be good with no rain on the horizon, unusual for western Washington at this time of year.

Before leaving for the day, Don called Wyman at her office to confirm the ride. "I was just about to leave the office and wanted to confirm our date on the bikes," said Don after Wyman picked up on the first ring.

"Your timing is impeccable," said Wyman. "I was just finishing up; I don't have standby this weekend and my bike needs a workout. I'll pick you up in front of the Public Safety Building in about twenty minutes? We can pick up my bike and then go to your place," said Wyman with more enthusiasm than Don had heard from anyone all week, except maybe from Chuck and his ideas for Raymond.

"I'll be at the Third Avenue entrance. I'll be the guy who doesn't need a shave and is not holding a Will Work for Beer sign."

"And I'll be the woman in the red VW Jetta with Make Love, Not War and Share the Road bumper stickers on the rear. I'll also be in scrubs," said Wyman with more mirth than Don had heard from her.

"I like the love thing and the war thing; I've done it and found it to suck in a major way. See ya."

They hung up, and Don went about straightening his desk and locking his files in his desk. Chuck had already left. His desk was spotless, smelling of the stuff he used to clean the surface; toxic, no doubt. His files, too, were locked neatly away in his desk, by date and color coded for easy retrieval. They should be safe until Monday.

When Don left the floor, he said good-bye to Marjorie and wished her a pleasant weekend. "I hope you have plans for the weekend that don't include Grimes or his wife," said Don.

"What do you have planned? Maybe we could get together and explore the possibilities," Marjorie said with her come-hither smile.

"I'm afraid the weekend is spoken for but maybe some other time," said Don.

"Something tells me you're afraid of me," said Marjorie.

"I just don't like to mix business and pleasure, and you would be a serious pleasure," Don replied, hoping that Marjorie didn't think that he thought he was too good for her. Also, he didn't want her to think that because Grimes had been there, he was no longer all that interested, and that seemed to be the only way a man could express interest in her. Don didn't tell her that he was going to spend the weekend mixing business and pleasure with Dr. J. Wyman Mills, forensic pathologist.

Don had his right hand out and his thumb extended as a red VW sedan turned right onto Third Avenue from James Street. Wyman had a smile on her face that may have meant she was happy to see him, but could have meant that she was happy to be away from slicing and dicing cadavers for a few days.

"You must be Detective Lake since I don't see the Will Work for Beer sign," said Wyman as Don slid into the passenger seat. He leaned over and kissed Wyman on the cheek as she steered into traffic.

"Yes I am, but I will work for a beer. I like dark ale best, but anything will do as long as it's not a light from Denver or Milwaukee."

"I have some Guinness in the refrigerator if that will do."

"I can taste it already. It's been a long week and I'm parched," said Don.

"I hate to mix business into this, but I have something that we need to discuss," said Wyman.

Don had a sinking feeling. Maybe she had learned about his female juggling act, but that wasn't business. He looked over at her; she looked back with a serious look on her face.

"We've been trying to find Gillespie's next of kin and are striking out. We need to release the body to someone. We can give it a month or so, and then we'll have to find somewhere else to put her."

"Is that something you deal with a lot?" asked Don.

"Yes, all too frequently. People like Gillespie tend to fall off the edge of the earth as far as family is concerned. That is, if there ever was a family in any real sense. We have to bury them somewhere, so they go into the modern-day version of Potter's Field. That has always bothered me. Gillespie was a sad case who deserves a little more than that, don't you agree?"

Don hadn't given the problem much thought, but here was a woman whom he liked a lot presenting it to him. He had to respond in a way that wasn't going to paint him into a corner.

"You know, I didn't really know that that was a problem the ME had to confront. I agree, though, it doesn't seem like a very humane thing to put her in an anonymous hole after the life she led. What do you plan to do if her family can't be found or doesn't want to be found?"

"I've taken collections in the past for a headstone and decent casket. Some of us have had a small service at graveside. Your department chaplain has taken part."

"Count me in if you want to do that for her," said Don. He meant it; it wasn't just a way of remaining on her good side.

Wyman drove her VW into the alley behind her house then into the driveway, stopping at the garage door. She left the car outside and they walked to the house and in through the back door. She walked to the kitchen and opened the refrigerator. Setting neatly in a row were several bottles of Guinness, cold and waiting to be lovingly fondled.

"I've had room-temperature Guinness on tap," said Don. "It lacked something. I don't quite understand the British preference for warm beer."

"I tried it in Ireland and didn't care for it. It's probably one of those acquired tastes like blood sausage and ripe cheese."

Wyman opened two bottles and took down two glasses. She poured them in a practiced way that gave Don the impression that she knew her beer.

The beer was perfect. The place was perfect. And the woman was pretty much as near perfect as Don had experienced in a long time, although Tiffany Winslow was in serious contention. Then there was Roseanne Vargas.

Let's not think about Tiffany or Roseanne now. That would just muddle the weekend, thought Don.

"I'm going to take a quick shower, and then we can load the bike and go," said Wyman.

"OK, I'll go out and wait in the garden," said Don.

"You wouldn't consider joining me?" said Wyman.

"I was waiting for an invitation. It's not polite to barge in on a lady's bath where I come from."

"The place you come from must be pretty tight assed. Where I come from, they shower together on a regular basis."

"As I recall, we come from the same place," said Don.

"Yeah, but I'm from Minneapolis and you're from the Iron Range; they're light-years apart. You rangers even speak in a different dialect. The first ranger I talked to wasn't understandable."

"Did that ranger like to shower together?" asked Don.

"After I introduced him to the idea, he learned to like it."

"There you have it. We Iron Rangers are quick learners, especially when the reward is a beautiful woman."

When the "shower" was over and the Guinness consumed, Don and Wyman took her bike from its rack and put it in the VW's trunk. Wyman loaded her bag of weekend clothes and riding gear, and locked the house, and they drove off toward West Seattle.

Rather than risk the jam that the Alaska Way Viaduct can present during rush hour, Wyman turned onto the waterfront and took Alaska Way to

East Marginal Way and then to Spokane Street. Spokane took them across Harbor Island to Harbor Avenue. It was a clear day, so there was a more-than-average number of sailboats on Elliot Bay and the Sound.

"This is what brought me to Seattle," said Wyman. "It was the water and mountains. Then there were the people who are for the most part capable of a reasoned thought. At one time I was thinking about trying for a residency in Dallas. They have a great hospital there. You know, the one where Kennedy died. Then I thought, that's where Kennedy died; why would I want to live and work in such a place?"

"I know what you mean. This is partially what brought me to Seattle. The other part is the weather. Minnesota was out of the question. Every season but fall pretty much sucks. And there is the female part. There is such an incredible number of beautiful women here. A case in point is sitting next to me, of course."

"Of course, it goes without saying. I'm not only beautiful but smart and witty, too."

"And humble, you missed humble," said Don.

"Yes, and humble, and I have great taste in men."

"Yes, yes you do," said Don.

With it firmly established that they were both smart-asses, they drove up California Way to Don's place.

The previous evening Don had gone to a local market and picked up stuff for tonight's dinner. He wasn't in competition with Wyman in the kitchen, but he did want to show her a thing or two, or three.

Salmon was the old Seattle standby, but that's what she served at the debut dinner at her house. He decided on meat loaf. If that wasn't Midwest fare, he didn't know what was. He mixed it up the night before. It just needed to go into the oven. Then there were baked potatoes and creamed corn. He thought he'd go with sliced white bread, but thought better of it. He made rolls from mix. There was no salad. But there was dessert: tapioca pudding with blueberry sauce served with coffee, of course.

"You've been true to your Minnesota heritage," said Wyman. "It was great, and it took a lot of courage to pull off. All that was lacking was Jell-O with fruit cocktail and whipped cream on top. But I'll have to say that you done good."

"Thanks, it was my intent to give you a taste of what you left behind in Minnesota. You noticed that there wasn't a hint of vegetarian in it, right? I would have starved as a kid if I'd decided that I was going to be a vegetarian."

"You strike me as someone who isn't all that concerned about what others might think about any choice you make," said Wyman.

"That's true to a certain degree, but my mother made the menu decisions, and I ate what was there or I didn't eat. It was that simple."

"Tell me about that time in your life. I know that the Iron Range was a world apart from Minneapolis. How did it make you what you are?"

"There were limited ways to earn a living there; that was primary in forming life's choices, and it had a huge impact on my life, I know. My dad was an iron miner, but an iron miner with a twist. Iron mining was hot and dirty in summer and cold and dirty in winter. Then there was the winter shutdown when Lake Superior was frozen and the ore boats couldn't move. During those months, my dad was lucky because he was in management, so he could still work at something like doing watchman duty at the mine. Then there was that little thing called inheritance. My grandpa was rich and my dad inherited that, but he still worked. For the less fortunate, it was layoff time. The whole community was hit every winter by that. The pay of a miner wasn't all that great anyway, and unemployment money was much worse. So they lived on less during the toughest time of year.

"I was a town kid. The town was big by northern Minnesota standards: about five thousand population at that time. It was complete with a paper mill that employed most of the people in town, but a lot were employed by the iron mines. It was there that I managed to develop the attitude about human nature that I've carried around my entire life. It's where class structure was clear. There were the 'town kids' and the 'country kids.' It was clear who sat in the place of preference. I never forgot that class structure bullshit and how it affects us as a people.

"People who haven't known hardship or don't have any empathy are beneath contempt. Then there are the whiners who can't manage to get out of bed without pissing and moaning about how tough they have it. There are a lot of people who never had much in the way of opportunity for one reason or another but who have managed to live life as though it was the gift that it is. Where I'm from, people made it one way or another without too much complaining. Some would log during the winter when laid off to bring in more money. They would get together and hunt a deer when meat was short just because that's what they always did, even out of season. The local game warden knew this but understood. They fished, and they smoked fish. They had big gardens that they canned and put it in the cellar. They picked wild berries that became jams and sauce. They did OK, and we helped those who didn't.

"When time came for me to make a decision about what to do after graduation from high school, there was a clear choice: follow my dad to the mines or go to college. What I knew, though, was that I was not going to the mines and I wasn't going to live off anybody else's money. I also knew that I wasn't going to college. The mines or the military were the only alternative for guys with less than me. If it was good enough for them, it was good enough for me.

"Then there was Vietnam, and that changed my take on our foreign policy and how I would go on with life. College followed when I could really appreciate it. I wasn't using it as a way to dodge the draft like a lot of the fucks I work around, so there was no guilt involved. I accepted what the government gave me, knowing that I gave them their money's worth and a lot more.

"But growing up on the range, eating venison meatloaf, potatoes from the garden, corn from a quart jar that my mother canned followed with pudding covered in sauce from berries that I helped pick is partially to blame for what I am today. We didn't have to do those things just to survive, but we did them anyway. Maybe that's what's at the heart of who I am.

"Forgive the mini-lecture. Now that I've shown you mine, you have to show me yours," said Don.

"There is no way I could come close to it, so I won't try."

It was understood that Wyman would spend the night and that they would leave for their ride in the morning. After talking about what they wanted in life until midnight, they went to Don's bedroom overlooking Elliot Bay and the skyline of Seattle. The last of the ferries was crossing the bay, lit like party boats, their reflections on the water creating pieces of art worthy of the SAM. Don tried to put Tiffany out of his mind as he snuggled with Wyman.

On the street outside Don's townhouse sat a car with one occupant. The car had been there for over an hour, just out of the soft glow cast by a streetlight. The occupant was concerned that someone might call the police to check on him, but he had a scanner with him, so he would know if that happened. The man was slightly overweight with short greasy hair and dressed in disheveled pants and a sport coat in need of a cleaner's attention. His white shirt was stained around the collar. He wore no tie. The man watched the lights go out in Don's townhouse. He got out of the car and walked across the street and down the block to the entrance of the townhouse garage. From there the man walked slowly through the opening that separated the townhouses. He continued to the waterside where there was a paved patio enclosed by a low fence. He had a 35mm camera with a telephoto lens and low-light setting in one hand. Two French doors connected Don's townhouse to the patio. The man took some photos, turned around, and walked to the stairs leading to a second balcony. He slowly made his way to the top of these and gazed through a window that covered the wall. He took more pictures of two people engaged in some serious snuggling and went back to his car. The man then drove slowly away in search of any available hooker.

On Saturday morning, Don and Wyman awoke to sun shining through Don's bedroom window. It was a better day than they could have hoped for. Vashon was a tough ride. Vashon in the rain was a tougher ride. They dressed in their biker garb: Lycra shorts, bicycle jerseys of various bright colors, and jackets. Helmets, shoes, and gloves would go into the car with water bottles and snacks.

They had a quick breakfast and then loaded both bikes on the roof racks that Don had permanently affixed to his Subaru. He left room for a ski rack that would go on during the winter months. However, bicycles were the focus of his outdoor activity.

The drive to the Fauntleroy Ferry Dock took about fifteen minutes along the Sound and through one of Seattle's nicer and pricier residential areas. Don always thought that it was too high priced given that a good winter storm could launch a floating log into your living room. He'd stick with his place, high above the water. They parked in Lincoln Park and rode their bicycles to the ferry. It took about twenty minutes to cross the Sound. Once on Vashon Island, they were immediately confronted by a mile-long climb to the island's backbone. Don was impressed with Wyman's climbing ability. He rode behind her so he wouldn't ride faster than she was capable of. From that vantage he had a great view of her Lycra-covered butt. Don found very quickly that he was having a problem staying on Wyman's rear wheel. Thankfully, today wasn't about determining who the better rider was; it was just a nice ride on a nice day.

Riding completely around the island was too much of a hardnosed biker exercise. Don liked to do it on those days when he was feeling like the professional bike racer that he thought he could have been. Today they would go partway around, stop in Vashon Village for lunch, and then ride back to the ferry. The route took them along a very hilly route that kept them quiet and concentrating on the work at hand. It also allowed them to look at what Vashon had to offer. There were views of Mount Rainier from various points, views of neat farms from others. They rode along beaches strewn with driftwood and smelling of rotting seaweed. It was a meditative ride in the truest sense. Formal religion had nothing on a bike ride around Vashon on a beautiful day.

Being in Vashon Village was like stepping back in time. There was a feeling to the place that transported Don to his days in San Francisco and surrounding counties. The clock slowed. The food tasted better, like it was made by hippies. White bread was forbidden on Vashon; at least Don thought that it should be. Certain people probably secreted it onto the island in hidden compartments built into their Volvos, but they risked censure and being exposed in the local newspaper.

Don and Wyman had lunch in a brightly painted restaurant with walls covered in the work of local artists. The subtle smell of patchouli oil hung in the air, or maybe it was Don's imagination in overdrive. The food didn't exist in his imagination, though. His vegetarian side was pampered. Last night's meat loaf was diluted to near nonexistence. Wyman didn't have any complaints either. She seemed enchanted by the island and the village. This was her first time under Vashon's influence.

The ride back to Fauntleroy aboard the ferry was icing on the day. They had coffee from the galley and sat in one of the many comfortable bench seats. Mount Rainier was standing to the south like a white-capped sentinel. The water of the Sound glistened in the sun. Don and Wyman, both Midwesterners, were accustomed to the view of a neighbor's garage roof from their second-story window. This was luxurious.

When they reached the Fauntleroy Ferry Dock, Don and Wyman rode off the ferry and to Don's car. They put the bikes on the car's roof and drove to Don's townhouse. The rest of the weekend was spent in bed, eating or thinking about returning to bed. Bicycling had that effect on the body. It had something to do with endorphins, in Wyman's informed opinion. It had only to do with horniness in Don's.

CHAPTER SIXTEEN

Don didn't exactly welcome Monday as he looked out over an almost invisible Elliot Bay from his bedroom. Rain was sweeping against the window as if it was coming from a carwash wand. The trees just below the lip of the bluff on which his townhouse sat were whipped by the wind. Don's one thought was what a great weekend it had been. Dr. J. Wyman Mills had set a new standard for him. The rain and wind, however, brought his focus back to the task of getting to work without being swept overboard. Then he thought of Tiffany Winslow.

"Good morning, Tiffany, this is Don, your neighbor on the poorer part of North Admiral."

"It's good to hear your voice. I was worried that your bluff had broken loose and fallen onto Harbor Avenue. How's life on the poor side of town?"

"I hoped that I could persuade you to let me pick you up this morning and take you to the water taxi. Walking might lead to a bad cold at the minimum."

"Thank you, that sounds great. What time can I expect you?"

"How about thirty minutes? I'll just do a quick shower then be over."

"See you then," said Tiffany.

Don and Tiffany walked across the pier toward the water taxi holding onto the floating pier's rail. If it had been any longer, the pier would have caused seasickness among the few passengers who showed up this morning. The taxi was bouncing around on its mooring lines, making getting aboard a further challenge. It was only another day in the life of Seattleites who traveled by boat to work. The motion of the boat had a way of forcing

STILL LIFE WITH BADGE

people to make bodily contact. In the case of Don and Tiffany, it wasn't unwelcome.

Once they found seats on the lower deck and out of the rain and wind, Don and Tiffany compared weekend notes. Don gave a partial report of his activities. He described the ride on Vashon. Tiffany was a biker, too, so she appreciated the ride around Vashon. They agreed to do it in the near future. Don couldn't keep the *life is getting way too complicated* thought from his mind as they got off the taxi on the Seattle side.

The walk from Coleman Dock to the Public Safety Building was wet and windy. An umbrella was of less than no use; it would have turned inside out in the first block. Wearing a waterproof coat was the better choice. From mid-thigh down was another matter entirely. *Ah, Seattle*, thought Don.

Tiffany gave Don a quick kiss as they parted ways at Second Avenue and Seneca Street. Tiffany turned north toward SAM and Don south toward the Public Safety Building. What a contrast. SAM was a center of beauty and culture in Seattle. The work of some of the world's great artists hung there. The Public Safety Building hung heavy on the hearts of the people who worked there and those who were taken there against their will to answer for various sins. The gulf would never be bridged.

Marjorie was sitting at her desk as usual. After Tiffany's kiss, her smile was the only sun that Don had seen today. In deference to the rain and chill in the air, Marjorie had gone with slightly more conservative attire. There was a distinct cleavage that Don admired, but the cleavage was accented with a high collar and long sleeves. Neither hid the charms under her blouse.

"Good morning, Marjorie. How's it hanging?" said Don.

"You look like your weekend was a hit," said Marjorie.

"Yes, yes it was," said Don as he walked toward his cubicle.

"Did you hear what's happening?" asked Marjorie.

Marjorie was always the first to know what was happening in the unit. It was as if she had a direct line to the top.

"No, what?" asked Don as he turned and started back for her desk.

"We're getting a new captain. She's coming from Internal Investigations."

"She? Who's she?" asked Don. Don wasn't familiar with anybody from Internal Investigations since he was never the subject of an investigation that he was aware of.

"Captain Mitchell. You must know who she is."

Of course Don knew Captain Mitchell. She came to the department about two years before he did. She went up the chain quickly. He had met her on her way up. She was once his sergeant at the South Precinct. He liked her no-nonsense approach to the job. She had never been married and had been rumored to be interested in women. That was always the rumor when an unmarried woman joined the department. Don did know that there was no doubt that she was great to look at, even in uniform.

"When's the blessed day?" asked Don.

"Today, she's starting her move-in today. Captain Black moved his stuff over the weekend. Rumor has it that he's retiring. Sounds like retirement short of getting the ax."

"Thanks for the update. How do you know all this anyway?"

"I have my sources," said Marjorie with a wink and smile.

Don walked back to his cubicle and found that Chuck hadn't beaten him to it as was usually the case. But given the weather, it wasn't a surprise, or maybe he had had a good weekend as well. The second thing Don noticed was that his phone was blinking at him, telling him that he had messages waiting. This new message innovation on phones in the department was both a blessing and a curse. He spent a lot of time just listening to messages left by people with whom he wanted to talk and a lot whom he didn't. He didn't have the magic method of knowing which was which.

He dialed his voice mail and listened to the first message. It was a man who didn't identify himself. The voice sounded like it was either coming through a piece of insulation or he was speaking with a mouth full of shit. The voice was just understandable but needed a couple of replays to be sure. It was fortunate that Don was sitting when he listened to the message, because having a firm base let him concentrate and not go with his first impulse, which was to throw his phone.

"Detective Lake, you don't know me, but I know you. I also know your partner. I'm the guy you're looking for. There's no value in any attempt to look for the source of this call. I'm at a street pay phone, and it's three in the morning. There's no one around except me. I know where the hooker is, and I'll be handling that little problem before you can find her. She won't be helping you with your little problem if you know what I mean. There, you see, I tied up all the loose ends for you. Now you and your faggot partner can spin your wheels, but it won't do much good. Good-bye."

Don took his tape recorder out of his desk and recorded the message so it wouldn't be lost. He then made a copy of the recording and ran it up to the Evidence Unit so that it couldn't be tampered with. He knew that this was getting out of control and that the person he and Chuck were dealing with had information that only a cop or someone in the department would have, or at least would likely have. It gave Don the shakes knowing that it was probably a cop who was killing people and beating hookers. They had a serial killer in the making on their hands.

When Chuck came in, Don told him about the call and then played the message for him.

"Holy fuck," said Chuck. "This is getting serious."

"Like murder isn't serious," Don said.

"You know what I mean. We already thought that we might have a problem when Grimes looked at our evidence without telling us, now this. Do you think that Grimes might be behind this?"

"Grimes is my person of choice. He's sneaky, he doesn't like either one of us apparently because we don't belong to the good-old-boys club, and we do our jobs. But let's not get fixated on him until all the evidence is in. That could lead us down a path to failure," said Don. "By the way, did Marjorie tell you the news this morning?"

"Yeah, we're getting a new captain and it's Captain Mitchell from IIS. That's a good thing; old Captain Black should have been put out to pasture long ago. He hasn't been here in a while, and when he is here, he plays with his toy soldiers like he was actually a soldier or actually saw a war. She'll shake up the works. Maybe a few of the emptier heads will roll as a result," said Chuck.

"We can hope. Since she's coming from IIS, maybe she's been sent on a mission to get rid of anybody who might embarrass the department. We have some history with her. It was positive history, so we probably aren't in her crosshairs," said Don.

Don had just finished his sentence when Captain Christine Mitchell walked into the Homicide Unit. Her duties were to command not only Homicide but also all of Violent Crimes including Sex Crimes and Robbery. But her primary concern would be Homicide since that's where the most attention was directed from the public, the press, and the mayor's office.

Captain Mitchell was about Chuck's age, a few years younger than Don. She went from college to the department while Don went from military to college to the department with some stops along the way. She was driven by her work and had never married, apparently because it might get in the way of her plan to rise to the highest rank possible. Don had no problem with that goal since she was also very good at what she did. Don also had no problem with her as a person and a female. She was, in a word, drop-dead beautiful. That was three words, but you get the idea.

There were the usual rumors about Captain Mitchell: she was a lesbian, she screwed her way to the rank of captain, her daddy made certain political contributions, etc., etc. None of them was true as far as Don could tell. He knew her only as a hardworking cop who got where she was by work and smarts. But still, she was so damn good looking.

Captain Mitchell walked around the unit before fixing on Don and Chuck's cubicle.

"So where is everybody? Are you guys the first ones here in the morning?"

"Yes, ma'am, we usually get here first because it's quiet and we can get a jump on the day," said Don.

"That's encouraging; at least somebody believes in earning their pay around here. We'll be having a meeting soon to address that issue. Do you have anything interesting going on?" she asked.

"Well, strange you should ask," said Don.

Don and Chuck briefed Captain Mitchell on the three cases they were working that they now thought were connected and the call that Don received via voice mail. She listened throughout the briefing with no interruptions. As the briefing progressed, she became more and more focused. It was as though she was drilling a hole into whichever detective was talking. She intimidated neither Don nor Chuck for two reasons: they knew her from the past, and they knew their cases and how to work them.

"So you have the impression that the man who left the message may be connected in some way with the department? That's quite an impression and one that you may have a hell of a time proving. Later today bring all of the files attached to these cases into my office, and we'll go over them together. You already know that I don't believe in micromanagement, but if your impression is correct, we will have a serious mess on our hands. At some point the chief will have to know about this, but we haven't reached that point just yet. How much does Sergeant Sherman know about your thoughts?"

"We haven't told him about the message yet, so he doesn't know unless he has put two and two together and saw what we saw," said Chuck.

"Don't get me wrong here, guys, but I don't know about Sergeant Sherman's ability to see anything anymore. His best days are behind him. He seems to be living on a reputation that was built during a former age, but I'd appreciate it if you didn't noise that thought around. Let's keep Sergeant Sherman uninformed for the time being."

Both Don and Chuck nodded in agreement. Deep down, both were gratified that they were now working for a person who was in the present and who didn't believe in the good-old-boy world or even the good-old-girl world. Strange how the arrival of a new brain on the block could change everything.

Before Don and Chuck started their search for Shondra, they whipped out a boilerplate search warrant that they would fax to the phone company so they could get the number and location of the phone from which the call was made. They should have that before noon if they could corner a judge to sign it. They walked across the street to the King County Courthouse where they were fortunate enough to find a judge who had a minute to look at the warrant. He signed it and wished them luck. As they walked back against the almost horizontal wind, they talked about what Sergeant Sherman already knew. On the one hand, it was always good policy to keep the sergeant informed, but this was different. They couldn't be sure about who knew what and who might be feeding information to whom. The debate was made moot when they arrived at the unit to find that they and Captain Mitchell were still its only occupants. This was not going to be one of Sergeant Sherman's best days.

After Don faxed the warrant off to the phone company, they checked a plain plate car out of the motor pool and drove to Shondra's mother's place. James Street was a river from the Public Safety Building up to the crest of the street at Ninth Avenue. It was going to be a great day not to be a pedestrian, unless you were into surfing.

They continued on James to Martin Luther King Way where they turned north toward their destination. Madison Valley collected water from three sides. Today it was catching hell from all of them. The streets were filled from curb to curb, hiding any defects in the surface; there were many.

Don found a spot near the house, and they watched it for about ten minutes. There was no movement, which meant nothing on a day like this. If the occupants had any sense, they were sitting tight and riding out the storm. Although they didn't look forward to getting any wetter than they already were, Don and Chuck got out of the car and ran to the house. Both stood to the side of the door under the overhang while Chuck knocked. There was a long pause before someone inside answered.

"Who's there?" It was Shondra's mother's voice.

"It's Detectives Weinstein and Lake again. Can we talk to you?" said Chuck.

The door opened slightly and Shondra's mother looked out. Raymond was standing behind her.

"You better come in before we all catch our deaths."

Don and Chuck stood just inside the door, both dripping onto a rug. The television was on in the living room, and all the drapes were closed. It was warm and dry, a welcome refuge from what was going on outside.

"Good morning, Raymond," said Chuck. "What have you been doing lately?"

"Oh, just doin' stuff around here. We went to the park yesterday after church."

"Your grandmother takes you to church. That's very nice of her, don't you think?" asked Chuck.

"Yeah, it's fun. We do some fun stuff while the big people are prayin' and singin.'"

Shondra's mother asked them to sit on the couch. She had an expectant look on her face, as if she was expecting bad news. "Did you find her?"

"Not yet, but we're looking, but we need some information from you, and it's very important that you be completely truthful with us," said Chuck. "Maybe you should find something for Raymond to do while we talk."

Raymond was happy with a movie he'd already seen many times. He stayed in the living room while Chuck, Don, and Shondra's mother went to the kitchen.

"Shondra is probably in quite a bit of danger, so it's very important that we find her as soon as possible," said Chuck. "We need the name of her pimp for starters, and I'm sorry about the bluntness, but we all know what she does for a living. We don't care about that. What we care about is his name and where we can find him. We also need to know where Shondra hangs out when she's not here or at her apartment."

"All I know is his first name; it's Maurice, and he's called 'Mo.' He hangs in the south end somewhere. He drives a purple Cadillac. He's a pimp all right. I tried to keep Shondra from that life, but he was too good. Her father and I went to college; she could have, too, and should have. She got pregnant with Raymond while she was still in high school. She wouldn't tell us who the father was. Maybe she didn't know since I think she was already into prostitution. My husband and I were happy about Raymond; he's the sweetest little guy you can imagine. He loves his mother, but her life isn't very healthy for him, so he spends most of his time here."

"You obviously do a great job parenting him," said Chuck, who was a little more impacted by the story than his cop side should have allowed. "Does Maurice ever come here?"

"Yes, he comes by and picks up Shondra from time to time. But he isn't very open about himself."

Chuck asked when the last time was that he was there.

"Just before she disappeared. He came, picked her up, and told her to bring some extra clothes. They had to go to her place to get them."

"Did he touch anything that would have left fingerprints when he was last here?" asked Don.

"Yes, he smokes, and even though I asked that he not smoke in my house, he does anyway. I still have a big glass ashtray that my husband used; he died of lung cancer two years ago. He used that, and when I gave it to him, he took it with his right hand and carried it with him while he was here. When he left, I put it away without washing it. It probably has my fingerprints on it as well."

"We'll need to take that with us and also take your prints to eliminate them when the examiner looks at any prints on the ashtray," said Don.

Don opened his briefcase and took out a booklet of print cards and an inkless pad. He directed Shondra's mother how to stand and what to do while he rolled her prints.

"Your print card will be destroyed after it's no longer needed. Even though there is no ink visible in this process, you should probably wash your hands."

"We're going to take the ashtray back to our lab and do some computer work to see if we can figure out who Maurice is," said Don. "We'll let you know if anything comes up."

"There's one thing that you should know about Maurice," Shondra's mother said. "He's not black like you probably think. He's white, but he sure tries to act black, right down to the purple Cadillac."

Don and Chuck left the house and walked into the rain and wind that didn't look like it had any plans of letting up anytime soon.

"Do you ever wish you lived in Arizona at times like this?" asked Chuck.

"You mean with the right-wing freaks and snakes, or is that redundant?" asked Don.

"I see what you mean," said Chuck. "Sun doesn't make up for everything, does it?"

They left the pool car in the garage but kept the keys and walked to the unit. When they opened the door to the unit, the first thing they saw was Marjorie with her usual smile and cheerful greeting. She was dressed a little differently than she had been earlier in the day when Don first saw her. She had changed, for unknown reasons, into a tight and very low-necked pullover. There was almost nothing left to the imagination. She was obviously not wearing a bra. Maybe she had the pullover under the blouse she was wearing earlier and decided that it was now show time.

"So, Marjorie, how's it hanging?" asked Don, as if he needed to ask. Anyone could see how it was hanging. It was hanging very nicely.

"There's a unit meeting at about ten thirty, in case you didn't know. Everybody is expected. There will be no refreshments served," said Marjorie.

"You are the queen of good news, Marjorie," said Chuck.

Don and Chuck didn't have much time before the meeting, so they went to the processing room where they packaged the ashtray, took it to the Evidence Unit, entered it there, and immediately checked it out so they could take it to the Identification Unit. They briefed the supervisor about what was going on and asked that the ashtray be handled expeditiously. They were assured that it would be processed within the hour.

They made it back to the unit just as the meeting was starting. Captain Mitchell was sitting at the head of the long conference table that was in the center of the unit between the rows of cubicles. All detectives assigned to the unit except those on the evening shift were sitting around the table. There was not a smile in sight. Don and Chuck found chairs and sat down.

"I know that this reassignment of command is a surprise to everyone. I just learned of it on Friday myself," said Captain Mitchell with a friendly demeanor. "I spent the weekend moving. Since this was such a quick thing, I thought that it would be best if I introduced myself in this setting as soon as we could all get together. You all know that I came from IIS. That plays no part in my having been picked to come here. Captain Black decided rather quickly to retire for personal reasons."

Don was looking around the table and noticed eyes roll at that last comment. Everyone knew that Black's days had been numbered.

"I've worked with a few of you in the past, so we aren't complete strangers. Some of you I'm seeing essentially for the first time since I've never been in the Investigations Bureau."

Don saw more eyes roll with that one. He thought that Captain Mitchell was not making much headway with most of the old hands in Homicide; she didn't appear to give a shit.

"I hope that we can work well together even without my having much investigation experience. But there is one thing that I want to make very clear." Captain Mitchell's demeanor changed from the conciliatory new guy on the block to commander of the unit who wasn't about to take any shit from anybody. "I expect that everyone from this day forward will pull his weight. I will schedule a meeting with each of you over the next few days. At those meetings, we'll go over your open cases and where you stand in each investigation. I've already gone over the unit cases and found that some of you have a serious backlog of open cases. You'll need to explain why that is. Don't take this as any sort of threat. I don't make threats; I only want results, and if it appears that anyone in the unit isn't willing or able to achieve results, then we need to discuss that detective's future in the unit. Are there any questions?"

There were no questions. There were a few sweaty brows and worried looks, however. Clearly, Captain Mitchell came with a mission from on high, and she was the person for that mission.

Don and Chuck both gave sighs of relief. They knew Captain Mitchell. They knew why she was here before she said anything. Her presence was meant as a threat although she said otherwise. Sergeant Sherman could now make some serious choices. Would he save his ass, or would he continue to enable the deadwood in the unit? Most left the new captain's office with frowns and a little more sweat on their brows.

"Let's get on the computer, Chuck boy, and see if we can find out who Maurice is, shall we?" Don said as they walked into their cubicle.

"OK, how about you jump on the terminal before somebody else gets it. Check for accomplices of Shondra for starters. I'll do a quick bulletin on Shondra for all the precincts. Maybe some patrol officer will get lucky and stop Maurice's purple Caddie and find Shondra on board."

No sooner had Chuck finished the sentence than his phone rang. It was the phone company in Colorado. He spoke for a very short time while taking notes. He finished the conversation by asking that the information be faxed to him.

"The caller was telling the truth about the pay phone," said Chuck. "It's a phone at First and Virginia."

"Let's check that out just for the hell of it and see if there might be any prints, although it's unlikely after the storm," said Don. "And, who knows, there might have been somebody out and about who saw something."

They gathered their briefcases and a fingerprint kit and started to walk out when Sergeant Sherman called them over.

"I want you guys to get with the rest of the squad as soon as you get back. We're going to talk about how we should handle this Captain Mitchell thing."

Don and Chuck looked at each other as if to ask: *What Captain Mitchell thing?* It was clear from his tone that Sergeant Sherman was feeling the heat.

"OK, we probably won't be too long, but we're pretty busy with the three cases we've got going," said Don.

"Three? I thought you had two murders open," said Sergeant Sherman.

"Yeah, but then there's Shondra Wilson who seems to have gone missing," said Chuck.

Don thought that he detected a worried look on Sergeant Sherman's face as they left; he was right.

Marjorie beamed her brightest smile as they walked off the floor and toward the elevators. Her life would probably improve under Captain Mitchell, although she might have to revise her dress just a little. Don would learn to live with it if he must.

CHAPTER SEVENTEEN

Following the meeting with Captain Mitchell, Sergeant Sherman walked into Grimes and Martin's cubicle. It was its usual mess with files piled on both desks. This was going to have to change. "For starters, guys, get those desks cleaned up before the captain jumps in my shit. But, first, let's go have some breakfast."

They walked out of the building and down the hill to Rose's for the usual grease. When they walked in, they noted that their usual booth was occupied by some lesser detectives from Auto Theft; this was not a good sign. There was a pecking order among detectives that had always been observed. Auto theft hovered down below Burglary. Did these guys know something?

Sergeant Sherman walked slowly past "his" booth and glared at the detectives. They clearly didn't know who they were fucking with. They didn't seem to notice, and if they did, they didn't appear to care.

When they found another booth nearby, Sergeant Sherman, Grimes, and Martin sat for a short time without saying anything, letting the insult thrown at them by the low-life pukes from Auto Theft sink in. Then Grimes started the conversation by stating the obvious. "We seem to have a slight problem here, don't we? It looks like the old status quo is no longer working. We may actually have to produce something. I don't know about you guys, but I'm not up to doing the bidding of some fucking woman. It looks like she has a couple of boys in her corner, though. The college pricks are all over her like they're part of a team out to get us."

"Let's not jump to any conclusions yet," said Sergeant Sherman. "You guys are going to have to look at your caseload pretty closely and come up with a plan of action before your meetings with her. I've told you to get some of your cases cleared. You haven't done much to remedy that. Now is the time."

"You guys? What the fuck are you talking about?" said Grimes. "'You guys' is all of us. You probably need to remember that. I know enough shit to get you demoted or fired, so get off the 'you guys' shit."

Grimes looked like he could kill as he talked to Sherman. His fat, jowly face shook in anger. His eyes were black holes drilling into Sherman's face. Detective Martin showed nothing but fear. If Grimes could get this angry with the sergeant, how angry would he get with him if he knew that he was screwing Clorice? He'd probably kill him if he knew, or so he thought. The booth was tense.

Sergeant Sherman just stared back at Grimes without responding. He knew, or suspected, that Grimes could take him down in a hurry if he wanted to, but it was a standoff. Sherman had a ton of stuff on Grimes that would not only get him fired but would also put him in a prison cell. He'd have to sit on it, though, because Grimes was too threatening for the time being. He'd wait for the right moment.

"What will you guys have this morning?" asked the waitress whose name was Rose, if her name tag was accurate. She wasn't the owner of Rose's Café; at least the three detectives didn't think she was. Rose's smile wasn't returned.

The three detectives recited their orders from memory as if the previous exchange hadn't occurred. They then sat and drank Midwest coffee while directing the occasional glare at the low-life auto theft detectives. Conversation in their booth had died a slow, painful death.

Don and Chuck drove to First and Virginia where the pay phone was located. It was unlikely that it hadn't been used since the call to Don's desk was made, but stranger things had happened. If they didn't dust for prints, some self-important, tennis shoe-wearing, prick defense attorney would bring it up in any potential trial by telling the jury how lazy and incompetent the detectives were. After all, how can you believe detectives who won't even get off their asses to dust a phone for prints?

Don had experienced this from a tennis shoe-wearing asshole who called himself an attorney but smelled like he'd spent the night in a Dumpster, and he had learned that lesson well. The tennis-shoe attorney had looked at the jury while making the statement about Don's incompetence. The jury was made up of your usual geriatric slugs in polyester pants and blue-gray curls. Don had learned the lesson well, but he still held the asshole attorney in high contempt.

They got out the fingerprint kit. Don dusted for prints while Chuck collected some cigarette butts surrounding the booth. DNA had been known to reside in cigarette butts. When they finished, they began a foot canvass of the area surrounding the booth. There were some residential buildings nearby. It was unlikely that anyone had been watching the phone booth at three in the morning, but stranger things had happened. With the defense attorney trick in mind, Don and Chuck picked the nearest building and went inside. They went to the floor where the apartments started and began knocking on the doors of the apartments facing the phone booth. The first apartment they knocked at was occupied by an old man who had problems sleeping. They looked at each other in a way that said *how convenient.*

"I was sitting here in this chair." The old man pointed at an overstuffed chair near a window that offered a great view of the phone booth and the parking lot surrounding it. "At about three this morning, it was. I looked at my clock there on the table. I heard a car door slam and looked out. The car was a boxy looking four-door, maybe a Dodge. It was dark colored. I couldn't see the plates. A man walked from around the car and went into that booth and made a call. He was there about three minutes, maybe less. He then walked back to the car and drove off."

"Did you get a good look at the man? Could you identify him if you saw him again?" asked Don.

"I saw him fairly well, but it was dark with only the yellow streetlights on. When the booth light came on, he was facing away from me, but I saw his clothes and can identify his size. He was a white man, about six feet tall, pretty heavy. He was well groomed with short hair and neat clothes. I do remember that his face was heavy, like he must have been pretty seriously overweight. He was wearing a dark sport coat over what I think was a white shirt, no tie. His pants were dark as well. It looked like he was leaning his left hand against the glass to the left of the phone as he talked."

"Are you a fan of cop shows on TV? Is that why you notice so much detail?" asked Chuck.

"No, I don't watch much TV. I was a Seattle cop before I retired about twenty years ago. I see a lot from this window. I guess I still think like a cop."

"I'd say that you still think like a cop, and we appreciate that," said Don. "How about we get together for lunch real soon? We'd like to hear about the good old days."

"There never were any good old days and never will be," the old cop said. "But lunch would be nice."

They took the old man's information and gave them their cards after telling him to call if he ever needed anything that they could provide.

When they got back to their car, Don and Chuck took the print kit out and returned to the phone booth. With a flashlight at an angle to the glass, Don found a palm print on the glass where the old man said they would find it. The print was smudged, but there might be a small part of it that could be used in comparison with a known print. If only they had a suspect for that comparison. In a matter of three minutes, they had two potential prints that might lead them to a killer and a witness. Life was improving.

While they were at a pay phone, Don called the ID Unit about prints on the ashtray. A print had been found, a good one, one that was put through the Automatic Fingerprint Identification System, or AFIS. A match had been found with one Maurice Williams, a white male, five foot eight, 165 pounds, black hair. His last known address was in Rainier Valley. He had a record for some minor misdemeanors and one gross misdemeanor for assault. The victim of the assault was one Shondra Wilson. He drove a maroon Cadillac when last stopped for a taillight infraction. He failed to pay the fine and had an outstanding municipal court warrant with a one-hundred-dollar bail attached.

"Fanfuckingtastic," shouted Don, who then realized that he was on a city street where John Q. Public was likely to hear him.

"Good news, I take it," said Chuck.

"Better than good. Fanfuckingtastic would be more like it." Don explained what they had while Chuck's smile became almost too big for his face."

"It's not drunks and kids that God looks out for, my man, it's drunks and cops who need a break," said Chuck. "How about we verify that the warrant is good then call Radio to see if they have a car in the area of the address to sneak by and see if the pimpmobile is there?"

"Sounds like a plan, but let's update the bulletin first just in case it's not. Patrol needs this info, and fast."

Don and Chuck drove back to the Public Safety Building where they again left the car but kept the keys. They went to the ID Unit where they explained what they had. The tech they talked to didn't give much hope of a match even if they had a name, but he'd work it up anyway.

Marjorie wasn't at her desk when they got to the fifth floor. Both were disappointed. A shot of Marjorie was like a shot of amphetamines. It was short lived, but while it was in the system, life was much improved, almost orgasmic.

While Chuck updated the bulletin, Don called Radio and verified the warrant for Williams, all one hundred dollars of it. It might as well have been $1,000,000; it was that valuable to their case. They had a hammer on Maurice. After that was completed, they both walked to Sherman's desk to brief him. Sherman didn't look well, and he looked even worse after their briefing. They left out the part about the retired officer who saw the guy at the phone booth. Sherman wasn't yet where they could trust him. Grimes and Martin weren't even close. Sherman's parting comment was something about their having to get their caseloads into presentation form for the captain. "Sure, Sergeant, we'll get right on that" was Don's response. Somehow the comment didn't ring sincere; it wasn't meant to.

The car with plain plates was waiting where they had left it. Don drove out the James Street exit and up the hill toward I-5. It was still raining, but the torrential downpour had reduced to an acceptable shower. The periodic sun breaks that Seattle prided itself in weren't anywhere in the forecast, however. They drove south on I-5 to the off-ramp at Albro Street. This took them to Swift and up the side hill to the top of Beacon Hill. The South Precinct station house was at the top of the hill. They drove into the lot and parked.

The four police precincts had a look all their own. This one was fairly new as those things go. The main building was brick with lots of glass, a serious flaw in the opinion of most cops. Bullets have been known to find their way into precinct houses, so why invite them was the common thought. There was a gas station on the site where many an officer, Don included, had forgotten to remove the hose and drove off with it still attached. Embarrassing at best was Don's thought. Chuck just thought that it was humbling. He would.

They caught an officer going into the station, so they followed him in. They didn't know the officer, but he somehow knew them. Strange how that was, but maybe they were like that when they were new troops. It made Don feel old and a little flattered at the same time. Chuck seemed to know the officer.

They hadn't heard from Radio that anyone had checked the address, so they went to the sector sergeants' desk area and talked to the only one there. Sergeant Morgan was an old-timer who had been there when Don and Chuck worked the South Precinct. Morgan told them that Radio had called him on a landline with the request. He had sent the officer who let them in the building. Officer Grosse had followed them to the sergeant's desk.

Grosse said that he went past the house and saw the pimpmobile in question parked out front. He continued on and returned to the station. His plan was to call Radio when he came in.

Don and Chuck were impressed with the tactical smarts at work. Although it was unlikely anyone was listening to Police Radio who would alert Maurice to what was up, it could happen.

After a short chat with Sergeant Morgan, they decided to park as near the house as possible without calling attention to themselves. They both knew that two white guys in a nondescript car in the area where Maurice parked his car meant one thing: cops. There was no getting around it, so that's what they would do. They again called Radio and logged out to that area. In case the shit hit the fan, Radio could get a marked unit to them quicker if their location was known in advance.

The street where the house Maurice seemed to be calling home was the usual south end street. There were some houses that came complete with mowed lawns and paint on the fences. Mixed in with the showcases were houses with yards that could have been used for grazing cattle. These houses hadn't seen paint since the Korean War and would never have the luxury bestowed again. Maurice's current address was one of the latter. He obviously wasn't into gardening.

Maurice was home; his pimpmobile was at the curb. Don and Chuck noted that the car was highly polished, however, unlike his house. Maurice clearly had his priorities squared away.

Then they waited. Their intent was to catch Maurice in his car with Shondra. They could hope. Stranger things had happened.

After about an hour and the pressure from an earlier coffee began to take effect, Don and Chuck were given the gift of Maurice. He walked from the house and got into his car. Shondra wasn't with him. Maurice drove away from the house, passing the street where Don and Chuck were parked. They slid down when he passed by. After Maurice got about a half block away, Don pulled out onto the street. He stayed back so Maurice might not notice that he was being followed. They had only a short way to go before they got onto Rainier Avenue that had a fair amount of traffic, making it easier to follow Maurice without being noticed. They had to stay close enough so they wouldn't be stuck at a light as Maurice drove into the sunset. Both Don and Chuck were still under some pressure to find a place to relieve themselves; It would have to wait.

Maurice led them over Beacon Hill to an overpass of I-5 and into Georgetown, finally stopping at the door of one of the motels along East Marginal Way that owed its existence to prostitution. It, like the Fairview Hotel, wasn't where you would put Aunt Louise from Duluth up for the week. That is, unless you disliked Aunt Louise. Don parked in the lot of a gas station that gave them a good view of the room Maurice went into. Don updated Radio on the air, and then they waited.

It was Chuck who first offered a solution to the bladder issue. They could go into the station one at a time. They had handheld radios to notify the person inside of any developments that needed immediate attention. Don went along with the plan and agreed to let Chuck go first since his fidgeting was getting embarrassing.

Chuck had been gone for about five minutes when Don saw the door of interest open. Maurice walked out first followed by Shondra, or a woman who looked a lot like her. They walked toward the purple Caddie.

"I would never have believed that Maurice is actually white unless I saw it for myself," Don said to himself.

Maurice had dark hair done in an Afro, but there was no doubt that he was not black. Maurice the pimp and his hooker didn't seem to be in a big hurry, which gave Don time to raise Chuck on the radio. Chuck ran from the station toward their car. He got in just as the Cadillac drove out of the motel onto northbound East Marginal Way. Don got on the radio and asked that a marked unit respond and stop it.

They had almost reached Spokane Street when a marked patrol unit came up behind them. Don got on the radio and asked that the unit pass them and stop the Cadillac. Maurice must have recognized that his chances of escape were pretty slim, because he drove to the side of the street shortly after the marked unit's overheads came on. Don parked behind the patrol unit, and he and Chuck got out, following the officers to the Cadillac.

"What the fuck do you want?" were the first words out of Maurice.

From where Don stood at the driver's door of the Cadillac, he didn't have a clear view of the passenger. Chuck, however, did. "Where the fuck is Shondra?" was Chuck's first utterance after reaching the passenger door.

Don leaned over and looked into the car where he saw a woman who could have been Shondra's twin sister, but she clearly was not Shondra. *How could he have been fooled by this lowlife* was his thought. Then it occurred to him that Maurice was a pimp and pimps often ran a stable of women. This was not good.

"Maurice, you're under arrest on an outstanding warrant," Don said, trying to suppress a smile. "And your little lady will probably have some paper hanging on her, too, if my guess is right. On top of that, we'll have to take the Cadillac as evidence of the suspected crime of pandering."

Don took Maurice from the Cadillac and put handcuffs on him. He patted him down for weapons, and put him in the backseat of their plain car. After the formalities Don got in beside Maurice who had a hostile look on his face. "No, Maurice, I'm not going to abuse you, but I am going to play a little let's make a deal, and if you don't want to play, I'm going to run you and your girlfriend through all the legal hoops at my disposal."

"OK, man, what you want?"

"You know what we want. We want Shondra. Her life is in serious danger. She's a witness who can probably identify a guy we want for two murders. That killer has let us know that he knows where she is and that he is going to kill her. Now are you up to a little cooperation to save your livelihood, or are we back to square one?"

"She's at a motel down on Pacific Avenue," said Maurice. "But she don't want nothin' to do with you guys."

"If she decides to keep up that attitude, she'll be dead before the weekend gets here, and you'll miss that prime weekend business. That wouldn't be good, now would it," Don said with as much sincerity as he could manage. "What we need from you is your chauffeur skills and a little of your time. You're going to drive me down to the motel in your car. My partner is going to follow us with your friend. Are we clear on that?"

"OK," said Maurice with a certain resignation.

"By the way, Maurice, you have great taste in cars and clothes," Don said, checking out Maurice's neon green jacket over a pair of fairly conservative, for a pimp, pants in a dark plum. *Classy* was all Don could come up with.

Don and Chuck agreed how they would carry this off. They raised Radio and logged the address where they would be going. They thanked the patrol officers who then drove off. The hooker in the Cadillac would ride with

Chuck in the pool car. She had an outstanding warrant, so she didn't have much in the way of negotiating options available. At the end of the day, all would be forgiven and Maurice and hooker would be on their way to do business if Shondra was located. If not, Maurice and hooker would be out of business for a few days.

The motel where Shondra was doing business was to an area near SeaTac International Airport known for illicit sexual activities. It was also the strip where the Green River killer was doing business. The motels in the area were, for the most part, not places where Aunt Louise would be staying unless…well, you know.

At Don's direction, Maurice parked near the motel's office. They walked into the office together. Don identified himself to the desk clerk and asked to use the phone; the clerk seemed to know Maurice. Don instructed Maurice to call Shondra's room and tell her to come to the office. He also told Maurice that he had best not tell Shondra to run. The phone rang enough times that it was clear she wasn't there, she was in the bathroom, or she was doing business and wasn't in a position to pick up the phone without destroying the moment.

Don called Chuck on the radio and told him what was up. He suggested that Chuck cuff the hooker to the steering wheel and come to the office. They did this on a tactical channel that didn't get recorded or overheard by any of the local press, which would have sold lots of ads with the story. *Fuck them* was Don's thought. Chuck concurred.

With Shondra's look-alike hooker firmly attached to the steering wheel of their car, where she couldn't escape from nor conduct business, Don, Chuck, and Maurice walked to the room that Shondra was currently calling home. It was on the ground floor well away from the view of the office. This was probably Maurice's doing; he wouldn't want the management to see the frequent visitors that came to the door. But from the motel's appearance, most of its clients traded in one of two things: sex or drugs and probably both.

Maurice had a key to the room. Don told him to knock and tell Shondra, if she was there, that it was him. When Shondra answered, Maurice unlocked the door. As he entered, Don and Chuck were right on his heels. The first thing they saw was Shondra in bed with a man, no great surprise. She was on her hands and knees, apparently having recently engaged in one of the man's fantasies. The man was attempting to recover from the shock of his life. He pulled away from Shondra's ass and grabbed the bedspread to cover his quickly deflating cock. Shondra dropped to her stomach and lay there without attempting to cover what Don assessed as a very attractive butt. He assumed, however, that she didn't acquire it on her bicycle, but the way things were shaping up, who knew?

No one but the john was at all surprised at what they found. The man appeared to be waiting for a thorough beating at best. He ran to where his clothes were piled on a chair and began to dress. He didn't bother with underwear. During the speed-dressing exhibition the man was performing, he was watching the three men who were taking it all in as if this was all in a day's work, which it was for Maurice. Don and Chuck weren't easily shocked, but this was far from a day's work for them.

Don's first words, after he regained his thought process, were, "Hi, Shondra, how much did that act cost the gentleman?"

It was Maurice who answered before Shondra could say anything. "It's a hundred for doggy style. We'll take fifty. I don't think he had the full ride, if you know what I mean."

With business out of the way, and after the man had paid up, Don told Shondra to get dressed. Chuck escorted the john outside where he took his identifying information and car's license number, and then suggested that he just drive away and thank whatever for his luck on this day. There would be no embarrassing explanations to the little Mrs., no court appearances, no attorney's fees, and no absence from church on Sunday because he had been relegated to a motel for the foreseeable future while the Mrs. contemplated her options. The man thanked Chuck and drove off. It was Chuck's guess that the man was thinking that those cops weren't half bad. Only Chuck and Don knew just how bad they could be.

Don told Shondra about the phone call. He suggested that she cooperate from this point forward or the likelihood was that she was going to end up in a black plastic bag under some brush. He then reminded her of the Green River killer who prowled this area for prey. Her life was hanging on a thin thread at this point, and she knew it.

"OK" was her reply as she sat on the bed. She had not yet started dressing and made no attempt to hide her charms as she sat looking at Don. It was all Don could manage to maintain eye contact. He had some experience with hookers and found most of them to be above average in appearance. There was that one time in Juarez, Mexico, however, that came to mind and then went away like a bad dream. "What do you want me to do?"

"How about if my partner and I confer over here and get back to you. While we're doing that, get dressed."

Don and Chuck walked a short distance away, and, with Don still keeping an eye on Maurice and Shondra, they conferred. "How about if we call a prosecutor and ask what the best legal solution is in a case like this," said Don.

"That sounds like a plan. When it comes right down to it, I'd rather not go into the pimp business just yet, although it does appear to have its benefits."

While Chuck kept an eye on Maurice and Shondra, Don went back to the motel office where he asked the deskman if he could use the phone. Although showing a little attitude, the deskman consented. Don called the Homicide Unit. Marjorie answered in her usual upbeat voice. "How's it hanging, Marjorie? I need a phone number."

"Do you finally want mine?"

"Maybe one of these days, but now I need a number to any King County deputy prosecutor who can answer a question."

"That would be Sean Merchant. He pronounces it Marshont like he's French. If you ask me, he's Polish on his mother's side but is ashamed of it. He's full of himself; he won't give me the time of day."

"His loss. What's Monsieur 'Marshont's' number there, Marjorie?"

"Do you speak French? Your accent is perfect."

"No, afraid not. How about that number."

Marjorie gave Don the number and then gave him what sounded like a kiss over the phone as she rang off.

Holy shit, thought Don, as he called the monsieur's number. He answered after two rings, no small miracle. Prosecutors were almost as hard to find at their desks as detectives. The monsieur answered with a voice that dripped with a distinct upper Midwest accent. It may have been from Minnesota. There was a touch of Canadian in it, though. Don knew about Canadian accents since he grew up next door to them. He had even been accused of being Canadian several times because of his accent. The "oot" and "aboot" thing threw most people off. There was more than one day that Don wished he were Canadian so he could escape to their government health care and beer. Then there was the low murder rate.

"Hello, Mr. Merchant," said Don as sort of a test.

"It's Marshont," said Mr. Merchant. *Failed*, thought Don.

"I'm Detective Lake." He almost said that he was Detective Jarvi, but he thought better of it; it would just make the day that much more complicated. Don explained the entire situation in great detail without interruption from the monsieur. At the conclusion of the long and sordid story, Don asked for his thoughts on what to do with Shondra that wouldn't violate more than one of her rights under the Constitution.

"We could make her a material witness. That would require a judge's approval. She would be in King County Jail during the period of custody, which would be set by the court. The city would be billed for it. It could get expensive, assuming the judge approved it. There's another possibility. It would cost the city, but you wouldn't go through the judicial process. There isn't as much, if any, case law on it, though. You could pay for a motel room where she could be kept under some sort of protection and hope that somebody doesn't kill her."

Great! thought Don, *we're going into the pimp business.* There was no way Shondra was going to spend time in a motel room without some of it spent on her back. But he knew that Shondra would not be very cooperative if she was in jail, and the only leverage they had on her was any fear she could muster over the thought that her life was near its end if she was on the street.

"The department may have a budget for such things. You'd have to check with your supervisor," said Merchant.

"That last option sounds like the best approach. Thanks for the suggestions."

Don almost said "thanks, monsieur," but he caught himself in time. He hung up the phone, thanked the deskman who looked at him with a contempt that lay just beneath the surface. *Fuck you,* thought Don. *If we had a little more time, I'd run your skinny ass through the ringer.* The man looked like he had done time and was wanted on several warrants, if not by several states.

"Are you in the habit of running prostitutes out of here, or is this a first?" Don asked, his voice dripping with contempt.

"I don't know what you're talking about," said the now blanched deskman.

"Of course you know what I'm talking about. We just found a john with his dick in a prostitute in one of your rooms. He said that this is where he spends his noon breaks." Don embellished a little for dramatic effect.

"We aren't going to make a big deal of it today, but it'll stay in our note-books, so maybe you need to think about future renters."

"Yes sir" was the best the deskman could manage.

That was enough. Don knew that the man was unlikely to be making any complaints to any police superiors regarding hookers cuffed to steering wheels or johns being allowed to walk. Tactics were what were important in achieving the strategic end, just like he recalled from the 'Nam.

Chuck and Don decided they would take Shondra to a motel where she could be watched as well as be less likely to ply her trade. They also had to talk to Captain Mitchell about the cost. Where was the money coming from?

This time Chuck went to the office and asked to use the phone. The deskman almost fell over in an attempt to kiss Chuck's ass as he showed him the phone. *I think I'm in love* was Chuck's first thought. His second was *on second thought.*

Captain Mitchell was at her desk and didn't sound very happy. Chuck explained what was up and what they wanted to do. Captain Mitchell's first response was to deny anything like the expense of a motel room for a hooker. When Chuck told her about the judicial option, Captain Mitchell agreed. "We can come up with some money for that as long as it doesn't last more than a few days," the captain replied. "Pick a cheap one and one that can be watched by patrol; we aren't going to spring for an around-the-clock guard on her. Let me know what you find."

Chuck hung up and glanced at the deskman who had now regained some of his manhood and was again looking like he didn't much like being treated like somebody's bitch. He was no longer in the joint, after all. *Give it your best shot, asshole,* was Chuck's thought.

Chuck walked by their car on the way back to the room. The hooker was sitting quietly, both hands clasped as though she was in prayer. She looked up and smiled.

Back in the room, they decided that Maurice would leave in his pimp-mobile, the warrant forgiven for the time being. He could take his hooker along. Both got the standard lecture on the evils of their life-style. Don, Chuck, and Shondra left in the pool car.

It took a little more work to persuade Shondra that she would probably die in the next day or two if she didn't go along with the plan. She was not exactly a stranger to fleabag motels, so that was no problem, and she was happy to hear that she was going to a better motel than she was accustomed to. She did, however, demand that they first go to her place to pick up some clean clothes and then to her mother's place to see Raymond.

The motel on Aurora Avenue was midway in quality between the motel she had been in for the past few days and a Holiday Inn Express. There were clean sheets on the beds every day. The toilets had paper sleeves over the seats that guaranteed cleanliness and the glasses had plastic covers over them, all signs of certain hygiene standards. The clientele would be best served, however, by believing these signs of hygiene standards instead of testing them. They could also rest more comfortably by not running a black light over the bedspreads. The bodily fluids that would no doubt illuminate in the dark might be cause for some concern.

The motel's owner, while not solidly on the prostitution-complicit radar, was motivated by a full house, so a prostitute in a room that would otherwise be empty was viewed in a positive light. He could also be intimidated by a badge and the threat of increased future scrutiny, something Don and Chuck were not beneath using should the need arise.

Don explained to the owner/deskman that he wanted Shondra put in a second-floor room near the office and that he wanted to be notified through 911 if any unusual traffic to or from the room was noted. He described Maurice and Maurice's pimpmobile and told the owner that he expected a call if it showed up. The owner was very agreeable to all of Don's demands. He also assured Don that he would get the best rate available. Don was happy about that. The good, God-fearing citizens of Seattle would appreciate that they were getting a bargain for housing a prostitute.

With Shondra settled in her room, Don went back to the office where he asked the owner if he could use the phone. Don called the North Precinct and asked to talk to the watch commander, a lieutenant named Art Driscoll. Art had found a home at the North Precinct; he lived within its borders and was near retirement. He wasn't into any drama this late in his career. Most days the good lieutenant didn't change out of his civilian clothes and into uniform. After roll call he would usually go to the dayroom and watch television until it was time to have his dinner, which he took at home with several glasses of gin. There was a great deal that got past the lieutenant.

Don explained the situation to the lieutenant and asked that a patrol car drive by and check on Shondra as often and with as much visibility as possible. The lieutenant said that he would see what he could do. Don wasn't convinced.

After he hung up, Don again called the North Precinct and asked to talk to the sergeant handling the sector where the motel was located. Sergeant Mary Jones was newly promoted and full of piss and vinegar for the job. She was also slightly in awe of detectives, especially homicide detectives, something that Don picked up on during their short conversation. Sergeant Jones agreed that the job was one she could handle and would type up a memo for all oncoming sector sergeants. Don felt better after their talk.

There was one more thing to do: call Radio. Don called the on-duty sergeant and asked that any calls from the motel be handled in an expeditious manner. When he explained the circumstances to the sergeant, he was assured that the motel would get priority status.

Don went back to Shondra's room where Chuck was waiting. He asked Shondra if she was still on board with what was happening. He gave her an advance on expenses and reminded himself that he would have to get it reimbursed from petty cash. There wasn't much to buy at the motel, but Don thought that she might want to get a soft drink from the machine outside the office. He also told her that he would ask that a patrol officer take her to a nearby café for dinner and breakfast. She seemed to be agreeable or as agreeable as a prostitute could be. Lies and embellishments were part of the business, and Don knew it. Shondra also knew that Don knew it. Don and Chuck tucked Shondra in, figuratively speaking, and left. Don didn't glance in the rearview mirror as he drove out of the lot; he wanted to trust that Shondra wouldn't run as soon as they left.

The ride back to the Public Safety Building was the first time that day that Don and Chuck had the chance to relax. The drive over the Ship Canal Bridge and along the eastern base of Queen Anne Hill could have been through a park if they didn't have to pass one motel that was dug into the hillside and was the drug and prostitution bastion of the city and another that housed only previous occupants of the first motel and now served as "transition housing" for the scum that couldn't work up enough ambition to wipe their butts. *Job security* was Don's thought as they went on their way.

Don and Chuck walked onto the fifth floor and the unit just as Marjorie was leaving for the day.

"How's it hanging, guys?" was Marjorie's preemptive strike.

"That's my line," said Don.

"Yeah, but it seems more appropriate when I use it, don't you think?"

"I suppose it does, but it works both ways if you think about it," said Don.

"By the way, the shit seems to be hitting the fan around here. You should watch out for Grimes and Martin. They probably aren't real happy about now. Sherman isn't exactly brimming with joy either," said Marjorie, who seemed to be pretty cheerful given the news she just broke.

"Thanks for the warning," said Don. "Be careful out there. Don't get blown away. The wind seems to be coming up again."

It's I who does the blowing, but I guess you wouldn't know that," said Marjorie. Then she was off before Don could reply.

Don and Chuck looked at each other and smiled. The girl was always good for a surprise. They both loved her for her honest approach to life. How she stayed single was beyond them.

They walked back to the unit where they found Sergeant Sherman in his cubicle looking like death warmed over. The first words out of Sherman's mouth were "Go see the captain. She's on a major tear. She wants to see everybody by the end of shift. Come see me when you're done with the inquisition to talk about the prostitute thing."

Don and Chuck told Sherman that they would be back to brief him, not mentioning money to pay the motel expenses.

Captain Mitchell was doing some housekeeping when Don knocked on her open door. She was bending over a box of framed pictures and diplomas. Before she had a chance to stand, Don took note of her serious case of bicycle butt. *Could it be?* thought Don. *Is she a bicyclist, too?* This could become more than he could handle. *Let's keep this professional* was Don's second thought.

"Come in, guys," said Captain Mitchell as she stood and turned toward them. As she did, she pulled her skirt down and smoothed it over her very attractive posterior. Don forced himself to look at her face, not a difficult thing to do. Captain Mitchell told Chuck to close the door behind him and motioned both to chairs that were arranged so a desk didn't separate her from the detectives, giving an all-too-perfect view of her legs in a way that didn't separated them by a desk but gave an all too perfect view of her legs.

"You probably know by now that I'm taking a new stance on the way detectives perform their work around here. The people of this city deserve service from their police department. Since I now have some control over how that service is performed, I plan to exercise it."

Don and Chuck both assented by nodding and looking serious. Don made good on his attempt to not stare at her legs that were bare from above her knees to her tasteful shoes.

"I know that you're both hard workers. You didn't get here by being members of the good-old-boys club like most of the detectives assigned here. Come to think of it, I don't quite know how you got around the good-old-boys club to get here. I've looked at your open cases. There aren't any open cases on your dockets that are there because you haven't been working on them. You have been assigned cases out of order because they seemed difficult, maybe cases that the others here didn't want or couldn't handle for one reason or another. I'm not going to ask you the hard questions I asked the others. Just tell me what's going on with your cases."

Don and Chuck began a briefing that lasted for more than an hour. By the time they were done, Captain Mitchell was shaking her head.

"So your suspicions that someone inside the department and maybe inside the unit may be committing murder are becoming more solid? That's a serious issue, one that could destroy the credibility of the department for years," said Captain Mitchell.

"We aren't sure yet," said Chuck. "We have simply seen some things occurring that don't add up. I think it's premature to assume that we have an inside killer on our hands. But, at this time, it would pay to assume that there is a possibility that we do."

With the briefing over, Don again described the motel lodging of the hooker and the reason for it.

"Let's keep the motel name between us. We'll also handle the costs in my office. There is no reason for Sherman to get involved. You can tell him whatever you want, but don't let him see any of the bills from the motel. Lie about where Shondra is located, or better yet, don't tell him anything about her. This has to be confined to my office and you two."

Don had to work to keep from hugging her. He hadn't experienced a person this committed to the job since he arrived in Homicide, Chuck excluded. He still wanted to hug her, however.

"I would suggest that you make up a good story for Sherman just in case, so if he passes it along to anyone else in the unit, it doesn't get Shondra killed."

Don and Chuck got up from their chairs. Don gave Captain Mitchell his best salute, not expecting that it would be returned as it would in the military world he was accustomed to. Captain Mitchell got out of her chair and saluted Don in return. They left the office and went to their cubicle. On the way they noticed that Sherman was still at his desk.

"Well, it looks like the shit has truly hit the fan around here," said Don as they walked into Sherman's cubicle.

"Did you guys get the new bitch's treatment? Strike that last comment. The bitch probably has this place bugged. She learned real well during her time in Internal Investigations. Grimes and Martin are on probation; she told them that if their work standard hadn't improved by the end of the month, they were to find another place to work in the department. She left open the possibility that they would be transferred to patrol. What are the terms of your futures here?"

"She went over our cases and made some suggestions for improvement," said Don. "I think we're OK."

Don had to fight to hide a smirk as he was talking. *Screw Grimes and Martin* was his thought. *They aren't worth a damn and probably never have been. One of them might even be responsible for a couple of murders, and God help patrol.*

"How's the Fairview case coming along?" Sherman asked.

Not wanting to give the impression that they were hiding facts from him, Don said that it was coming along and that they had a person who might be able to shed some light on it.

"Oh, who's that?" Sherman asked in a somewhat surprised tone.

"She's just a hooker who we have on ice." Then Don gave him the name of a motel that was located about a mile north of where she was actually staying: the Cascade Motor Inn.

The Cascade Motor Inn was a true sleaze joint, the go-to motel if you wanted to spend some time with a hooker or send Aunt Louise from Minnesota for a thrill. The deskman was nothing more than a pimp. The cost for a room was reasonable. Sheets weren't changed all that frequently. Photo identification wasn't required unless there happened to be a uniformed officer standing nearby. In short, it was one of the many motels that gave Aurora Avenue its reputation for being a place to get a quick and reasonably priced lay or whatever turned you on.

"Great," said Sherman. "Bring me the bill so I can get it paid."

"OK, Sergeant," said Chuck.

Don and Chuck went to their cubicle and locked up for the day. They walked off the floor and took the elevator down to the first floor. When they walked onto the parking deck, they felt safe to talk without fear of being overheard.

"I don't feel real good about what happened upstairs," said Chuck.

"I don't either," said Don. "Are you up for some off-the-clock time tonight?"

"Sure," said Chuck.

CHAPTER EIGHTEEN

Sergeant Sherman recognized that his career was in serious jeopardy after his meeting with Captain Mitchell and after what Grimes and Martin told him about their meetings. Given what he knew about Captain Mitchell, not only was his career in a world of hurt, but he could even be looking at some prison time if he didn't shape up. He thought that swallowing his revolver's barrel might be an option. *How the fuck does a man drag himself out of this hole* was his thought.

He called a meeting at a nearby watering hole right after his meeting with Mitchell. Grimes and Martin attended; Don and Chuck didn't know about it and wouldn't have been invited if they did. It was a meeting held under a dark cloud and lubricated with liberal amounts of alcohol.

From the first floor, Don and Chuck walked to an elevator that took them to the basement of the Public Safety Building where their car was parked and where they contemplated their next move.

"Is anybody expecting you home at a particular time?" asked Don.

"No, you?"

"Nope. That's one of the blessings of being single."

"I couldn't agree more," said Chuck.

"How about we go up to the North Precinct and see who's available to go to the motel with us? We could make an appearance, see if Shondra is still up for the task ahead, and then go and sit on the Cascade Motor Inn for a while and see who turns up. If somebody in the unit shows up, we know that Sherman is our snitch. That'll narrow the field some."

Chuck agreed but suggested one more thing. "How about we arrange with the artist to meet us at Shondra's room tomorrow?"

"You do have an idea from time to time, don't you? That was a good one, although I thought of it but forgot."

"Screw you," said Chuck.

"In your dreams, my man, in your dreams."

Chuck went to the fleet office where he used the phone to call the artist that they had previously arranged to sketch Shondra's attacker. They agreed on a time to meet the following day at the motel.

Don then drove them to the North Precinct, which was located just north of the North Seattle Community College in a park like setting. A creek ran nearby, a creek that was responsible for flooding the firing range in the precinct's basement when it rained more than usual. Like the South Precinct, the North Precinct was built to satisfy the architect's aesthetic sensibilities, not the practical needs of those who used it. Large windows gave the public great views inside. At night the officers in the building had the feeling that they were in an aquarium.

Don parked the car in the lot with the plain cars assigned to North Burglary. They walked to the locked entrance used by on-duty officers. Don pushed the doorbell to get the attention of whoever was listening. A voice came over the intercom asking who was there. The camera attached to the intercom already told the person at the other end who they were. But maybe that person was new, or maybe he was just exorcizing some past grievance with detectives.

"Detectives Lake and Weinstein, Homicide," answered Don.

The latch buzzed and Don pulled the door open. Just inside the door was an open area that housed computers and workstations that officers used to do criminal histories, warrant checks, and several other things that modern technology offered in the ongoing battle against crime. When they walked into the room, Don glanced toward the workstations that included typewriters for officers to use to write reports. Sitting at one of the desks with her back to them was a familiar figure. Don had seen her before; it was none other than Officer Vickie Morris. *Be still my heart*, thought Don.

"Officer Morris, I presume," said Don as he walked up behind her. Officer Morris turned, gave Don and Chuck a big smile, and got up.

"Hi, Detectives, it's great to see you," she said. "What brings you here?"

"We have a case that brought us here," said Don. "I'm glad it did. We didn't know that you were assigned here."

"I requested the North Precinct out of the FTO program. I also requested to work with Sergeant Jones. I got lucky on both counts."

"Sergeant Jones is the best. You'll learn a lot from her," said Chuck.

"Where are you working up here?" asked Don.

It just so happened that Officer Morris was assigned temporarily to the sector where Shondra was housed. *This is a stroke of luck*, thought Don. *She would bend over backward to be of assistance to them.* Maybe bending over backward wasn't the image he was looking for in this professional relationship, but the image would stick with him during their time together. What a curse.

Don and Chuck walked to the sergeants' desks where they were lucky enough to catch Sergeant Mary Jones before she went on the street. Don's mind was working overtime as he took in Sergeant Jones in her uniform. *I will get on with business no matter what*, thought Don, and he did.

"Hi, guys. It's good to see you both again. It seems that the only time we meet is under less than pleasant circumstances. How may I be of assistance?"

Hold your tongue, be professional, thought Don. "We're going to ask you to lend us Officer Morris for a while." Don reminded Sergeant Jones of their earlier conversation.

"She's new to us, but she shows all the signs of a good officer. Going along with you guys will broaden her experience a little more. I can trust her with you, right? You're not like some of the other snakes in your unit who might view her as a potential lay and nothing more."

Don swallowed and attempted to camouflage the blood rising to his head. *Get a grip.*

"We've had experience with her at the West Precinct when she was still a student officer. She did a great job then," said Chuck.

"OK, you can have her for as long as it takes. Just bring her back in one piece," said Sergeant Jones.

"You know what the situation is with our hooker, right?" said Don. "We'd actually feel better if there were two officers visiting her, or at least another officer in the vicinity, just in case things start going south on us."

"I don't think we have an officer to make up another two-officer car, but I can have another one nearby. Will that satisfy you?"

"We don't want to unnecessarily endanger an officer," said Don.

"OK, understood, and I appreciate the thought."

Don and Chuck went back to the desk where Officer Morris was typing a report. They briefed her on the case and how she could be of assistance.

Officer Morris called Radio and put herself out on a detail that would take her off any call responsibility.

"Follow us to the motel so we can introduce you to Shondra," Don said. "She's really very nice, but she can't be trusted any farther than I could throw her. I guess that goes with the business she's in."

Don and Chuck walked to their car with Officer Morris. Her patrol car was nearby. They drove out of the precinct's lot and turned west toward Aurora Avenue, Officer Morris following.

Aurora was a long avenue running north and south from the city limits on the north to Denny Way to the south. At one time it was the main highway through Seattle, State Highway 99. Interstate 5 replaced it in the sixties as the main way to get through the city, although it still carried its share of traffic during rush hour. Some of the traffic was there to pick up the ever-present hookers who walked the sidewalks along the avenue, both day and night. The many motels on Aurora were mostly there to provide quickie rooms. The remaining rooms were occupied mainly by drug dealers and folks who had fallen on hard times and just needed a place to stay for a few days until they were able to rip somebody off for enough money to get out of town. Don had to admit that there were one or two where he might stash Aunt Louise, provided she was packing a sidearm. He also noticed that a lot of Canadians registered at these.

Don, Chuck, and Officer Morris drove into the motel lot together. Officer Morris parked near the office as Don had requested. He wanted her car to be as visible as possible just in case someone had gotten word that Shondra was actually here and not at the Cascade Motor Inn. They walked up to Shondra's room together. Don knocked and waited for an answer. There was a muffled sound from the room that sounded like a man's voice; it sounded upset.

After about a minute, during which time Don and Chuck had pulled their weapons from their holsters and prepared to stuff the door, it opened just to the end of the security chain. A white male about fifty years of age with little hair growled, "What the fuck do you want?"

Don was nearest the door. His immediate instinct was to kick the door as hard as he could. Before he could manage it, a leg shot past his face, striking the door at about the level of the man's face. The door slammed against the growler's face, knocking him backward onto the bed. "What the fuck do you want, indeed," responded Chuck in an unusually calm voice.

Chuck holstered his karate-trained leg as they all rushed the room. Officer Morris was clearly impressed by the display of bravado. Inside the room they found a scene right out of the best porn movie. Shondra, once again, was on the bed *sans* clothing. As expected, she made no attempt to cover her charms. The john, whose faith in the capitalist system of supply and demand had just been shaken, was sprawled on top of Shondra where he had landed after being hit by the door. His night was shattered. He had been looking for nothing more than a roll in the hay with someone other than the Mrs., and he was smacked in the face by a door. It seemed that Shondra's sex partners were batting zero. Don had to commiserate.

"OK, my man, you might want to find something to cover yourself before you embarrass us all," said Don.

The man got off Shondra, holding his hands over his vital assets to the best of his ability without falling on his face. He looked at Officer Morris who seemed to be taking it all in stride and blanched only slightly. She did a great job of not smirking; she had apparently seen more impressive assets in her short life.

Shondra was slow in getting around to covering herself. Her business had drained any ability to express embarrassment. Her charms were once again not lost on Don. Shondra raised herself from the bed and wrapped herself in a robe that had been thrown over the arm of a nearby chair. The robe, no doubt, came from Frederick's of Hollywood, Don guessed; it left almost nothing to the imagination.

Don walked to the chair where the man's pants lay in a pile. He took the john's wallet from a rear pocket and removed a driver's license. He then removed a small notebook from his jacket pocket and wrote down the man's name, date of birth, and address.

"You realize, of course, that the young lady you were taking advantage of is a prostitute," said Don. "That makes you a john. Both of those are illegal in this city. But, of course, I'm not telling you anything that you're not aware of, am I?"

"No sir," said the man.

"Now I want you to pay the young lady the agreed upon amount, and then you can go."

"Yes sir," said the man.

After the transaction was complete, the man left the room, no doubt pleased that his wife wasn't going to discover that he was banging hookers on Aurora.

"Did you hurt yourself with that heroic kick, Chuck?" asked Don.

"No, I'm fine. That was a training kick. I missed practice yesterday, so that made up for it."

Officer Morris was standing near Shondra from where she had observed the conclusion of the show; that's what it had been. The more dramatic, the better it was in Don's and Chuck's opinions. Visibility counted in matters where the mission was to deter people from a location. This couldn't have worked out better. They weren't even upset with Shondra. After all, fucking for money is what she did, just as they just did what they do: kick doors to impress young female officers. At least that was partially Don's purpose. He hadn't yet gotten inside Chuck's head to find what motivated him other than the desire to get the job done and his love of kicking things.

"Shondra, this is Officer Morris. Officer Morris, Shondra," Don said in a way that belied the facts at hand.

Both women said "Hi" as if they had just been introduced at work. It would appear that that was in fact the case. Shondra sat in the upholstered chair in her see-through Frederick's of Hollywood gown, waiting for the ass chewing that wasn't coming. Don was learning how to act around Shondra in her normal state of undress without being so distracted that he couldn't do the job. Officer Morris seemed to be oblivious to it all.

"We're going to bring a sketch artist by tomorrow so you can describe the guy who assaulted you. Is that going to bite into your business at all?" Don asked.

"You know, Detective Lake, I don't like the tone of your voice. You think that what I do is somehow beneath you for some reason. Why's that? Are you guilty because you've visited a prostitute or two in your life? Do you think that by making a mockery of me that you can atone for your sins? Does Thanksgiving dinner at Mom's house get uncomfortable for you, knowing that you've visited a whorehouse or two while your mom still thinks that you're her sonny boy who goes to church every Sunday? Is that your problem? Or are you really homosexual?"

Holy fuck, she was hitting all the buttons. But there was a ring of truth to what she was saying. Don was raised in a Lutheran household where it was viewed a major sin to say "shit" even though you happened to have a mouth full of it at the moment. Sex was something never to be acknowledged as a natural part of being human; it was an evil means of making new Lutherans. Don thought that he had gotten over that upbringing and become a fully human being. Maybe he still had a piece of that hanging in the shadows. God help him. However, the homosexual reference bit.

"Forgive me if I sound holier than thou," said Don. "I don't mean to. I actually admire you for your honesty. You go about business to provide for Raymond. You're smart, probably smarter than I am in many ways. And you're beautiful. And, yes, I've visited whorehouses in various places in Asia and Mexico. I even found one in North Dakota. Now that's a story worth telling at another time."

Shondra's eyes lit up at this. She probably hadn't thought of herself as beautiful before. Don wasn't even sure that she believed it now. She tucked the robe around her a little tighter. It did nothing but make her body more appealing.

"That's OK," said Shondra. "I'm just a little tired of being interrupted by you every time I'm conducting business. Maybe that will stop once I talk to the artist."

"Have you eaten tonight?" asked Chuck.

"No. I was going to go out as soon as the last customer left."

"Last customer? How many customers have you entertained since we dropped you off?" asked Chuck.

"Three or four. I can't waste time just sitting here doing nothing but watching Oprah, you know."

"Three or four is good, but how about you call it a night and Officer Morris and you go get some dinner," said Don. "And just to satisfy my curiosity, how did you come up with three or four customers in the short time you had?"

"They were old customers. I thought that since the city was paying for the room, it would be pure profit."

The God-fearing citizens of Seattle no doubt would be pleased with the business acumen of Shondra. Don, however, had no intention of advertising the fact to them.

"One more thing, Shondra," Chuck said. "I'm a real live homosexual."

"Sorry if I offended you; you don't look homosexual."

"You didn't. I like who I am and, like you, make no apologies for it. But tell me what a homosexual looks like so I can check out the department for others like me who are hiding behind the badge."

With Officer Morris and Shondra on their way to a nearby restaurant, Don and Chuck drove north on Aurora toward the Cascade Motor Inn.

When they arrived, they found a real sleaze motel, one that they were well aware of but hadn't had the opportunity to visit for a while. The owner/deskman was a Korean who, no doubt, came to the United States thinking that he would get rich by working twenty-three hours a day along with his wife who would clean rooms and fill in when he caught the one hour of sleep that he required. Who rented their rooms and for what purpose was none of their business despite city requirements that they make it their business. Prostitution was a great way of filling rooms, and that's what they did. The Cascade Motor Inn didn't have a view of the Cascades. It did provide space to park in front of each room, however, so the motor part of the name was accurate. But by the appearance of some of the cars, there was some question that they actually motored to their spaces.

Don and Chuck took up a position across from the motel in an unpaved alley that ran between two businesses, both now closed. They suspected that the alley was used to conduct prostitution trade that didn't require a room. They were right; used condoms and empty liquor bottles littered the ground as evidence.

After they waited for about an hour, a car drove into the motel's lot and parked on the blind side of the office. Don and Chuck were alerted by the car because it looked a lot like a department fleet car but wasn't. A lone man got out and walked to the office. The man, though it was dark and the lighting in the driveway poor, looked familiar as well. The lobby of the motel, if you could call a six-by-six box with a dusty plastic plant in one corner and a dirty linoleum floor a lobby, was poorly lit.

The man walked into the lobby and then to a vacant counter where the owner usually sat pouring over his receipts for the day and thinking of legal or illegal ways to boost the bottom line. The owner was in an apartment behind the office where he, by the smell of the place, was cooking dinner. The man rang the bell that sat on the counter and waited.

Don and Chuck got out of their car and did a slow trot across Aurora Avenue. Several people, mostly high on something other than life, met their maker each year trying the same. Don and Chuck were neither high on something nor drunk, so they waited for a clear route before making their move. Once across the avenue and out of harm's way, they walked to the lot where the man had parked and looked around for an escape route in case the man came out. The car was not out of the department fleet pool. It just had the appearance of one that was trying its best to look like an unmarked police unit. There were a lot of cop wannabes in the city. They bought cars that looked as much like cop cars as possible without crossing the line into illegality. This was one of those. The interior of the car was clean; there was nothing on the seats or floor that identified it as belonging to a freak. Sometimes the wannabes carried blue lights that they used to stop cars driven by females. This didn't appear to be one of those, although the light might have been under a seat or in the trunk. The doors were locked, so a search was out of the question for the time being. For that matter, a search of the car would have been illegal, but who was around to keep score?

Satisfied that the car was clear, and after jotting down its license number, Don and Chuck walked quietly along the windowless side of the building then around the side of the building where a wall of dirty windows looked out onto Aurora. There was a bush at the base of the first window. Don walked to the bush and slowly peered around it and into the office. What he saw nearly made him choke and back into Chuck who was standing inches behind him. The familiar-looking man was none other than Sergeant Sherman.

The motel's owner had come from his apartment and was talking to Sherman. The owner had a look of confusion on his face as though he shouldn't say anything, but wasn't sure that he would get away with acting dumb in the face of a police sergeant's questions. Don and Chuck watched the drama unfold, waiting for the conclusion. They didn't want to barge in and damage a possible lead on an assault and possibly two murder investigations. But Sergeant Sherman? This was too coincidental for words.

The owner finally began to talk, denying knowledge of anything Sherman was saying. Although Don and Chuck couldn't clearly hear the conversation, the gestures of both men spoke volumes. The owner shook his head and mouthed a clear "no" while Sherman grew angrier. Finally, Sergeant Sherman slammed his fist down on the counter, knocking over a penholder and startling the owner who backed toward his apartment door. Sergeant Sherman lifted a hinged counter section and walked toward the owner who turned and ran into his apartment, slamming the door just as Sherman reached it. Sherman tried to open the door with the knob, but the owner had managed to lock it. Sergeant Sherman then turned and started for the door that took him onto the drive.

Don and Chuck ran back toward the car in which Sherman had arrived. They found a Dumpster to the side of it and ran behind it. They heard Sherman open the car's door, get in, and start the engine. The car sat idling for a minute or so, and then they heard it accelerate onto southbound

Aurora. They ran back across Aurora, giving the heavy traffic every opportunity to make them the latest statistics. Don had their car's keys out and ready to go before they reached the doors. Don opened the doors without dropping the keys, no small feat given his state of excitement.

Chuck had almost managed to get planted in his seat when Don accelerated, speeding out of the alley and over the sidewalk. There was enough space between cars to get into the center turn lane where Don accelerated up to the speed limit and well beyond before merging into a southbound lane. If Sherman was driving the limit, they probably wouldn't have much trouble catching him before he reached the next motel.

There was one more motel between the Cascade Motor Inn and the motel where Shondra was staying. It was a step down on the sleaze scale from the Cascade Motor Inn. The Aurora Motor Inn was known for its long-term residents, mostly prostitutes and small-time dope dealers. The smell of crack cocaine cooking was known to waft from some of the rooms from time to time. If the Narcotics Unit didn't make this joint a permanent project, it was falling down on the job. The same held for the Vice cops when they weren't engaged in getting lap dances paid for by the God-fearing citizens of Seattle. And where the hell the owners of these motels came up with their names was a mystery to both Don and Chuck; the sleazier the place, the classier the name. It was a subject that they discussed from time to time when cruising Aurora on business or for entertainment on slow evenings.

Don parked about a half block north of the Aurora Motor Inn. He and Chuck hadn't had much time to talk about what they had witnessed, so they started to unravel this growing ball of mystery. "Are we hallucinating here, or do we have a serious murder conspiracy going?" asked Chuck.

"Maybe you're hallucinating, but I'm not. There is more than your average series of coincidences here, and we are in a dangerous dimension. If I have my facts straight, Sergeant Sherman seems to be attempting to locate a witness who can identify a murder suspect and can definitely identify an assault suspect. He could even be and probably is the guy who made the call threatening to kill Shondra. This doesn't look good, Chuck."

"Where do we go from here? If we catch him in the vicinity of Shondra, which it looks like we will, what do we do? If the man is all about killing her, then we will be obligated to stop him. This does not look good under the best of circumstances."

"No, no it does not," Don replied.

CHAPTER NINETEEN

Sergeant Sherman was almost certain that his private life was secure from the scrutiny of anybody in the department, until today. He was at a place in his career where he either left with some dignity or risked giving up all the years he had put in. He thanked the gods that the state would still pay his pension even if his mailing address included his prison inmate number.

During high school Sherman found that he was almost as interested in boys as he was in girls, almost. He tried his best to put on a macho facade for the cheerleaders who threw their assets in his face at every opportunity since he was a football hero. He even obliged a few by dating them, taking them to the local drive-in theater, and checking out what they had to offer under those oversize sweaters that they seemed to like to hide behind. Although he liked what he found under them, and what they offered in the way of sex, he was left wanting a little more. It left him seriously conflicted. Being more interested in his team's tight end than in the tight end of the cheerleading captain was not where a teenage boy should be, he thought.

As life progressed, Sherman found that being a cop was a sure way of proving to the world that he was a real man. He also played with women just enough to prove that he was normal, and he enjoyed the women he played with. He even tried to prove to himself that he was normal by renting a woman from time to time. The women were, for the most part, surprised that he couldn't manage to perform. When he couldn't get it up, Sherman tended to resort to violence, violence that had an almost miraculous effect on his ability to perform. He had assaulted many prostitutes since he began his quest to find normalcy. But there was the periodic "normal" woman who could manage to bring him to a state where he almost believed that he wasn't a freak. One of these women was Clorice Grimes.

After he left the Cascade Motor Inn, Sherman stopped at a pay phone and called Clorice. He hoped that her husband wouldn't answer, but he knew that Grimes spent most of his nights far from home. Clorice answered after two rings.

"Hi, Clorice. Is Bill at home?" asked Sherman.

"Are you kidding? He stops by from time to time to take a shower and change clothes, and that's about all. Are you in the area?"

"I'm on Aurora and thought that you might be up for a meet somewhere. I haven't had dinner yet. Maybe we could catch a bite somewhere."

"Sounds good. How about we meet at the usual place in about a half hour," said Clorice.

"OK, I'll see you there."

The usual place was a small, dimly lit restaurant in Chinatown. The food was pretty good, and the atmosphere was great for their purposes. If you tried, you couldn't see the people at the table three feet from yours. The floor felt a little sticky, but that was part of the charm of the place. It was, however, never a good idea to be seated near the restrooms.

Sherman parked his car on the same street where the Fairview Hotel was located. The restaurant where he was meeting Clorice was two blocks away. He walked slowly uphill to the restaurant thinking about how this part of town had formed his career. There was the famous mass murder that had made international news. He had been a peripheral player in that investigation. The only reason for his involvement in it had been that he was in a secret relationship with a major player in the investigation. That person had attempted to give him points by putting his name on what would be a very important resume-building case; it had worked. A year after the case cleared the court, Sherman was assigned to Homicide. The following year, the Homicide supervisor who had been Sherman's benefactor died. He was given a send-off befitting his rank. There was a rumor afloat that he died of AIDS. Sherman was in a major panic for a while.

Clorice arrived a few minutes after Sherman walked into the restaurant. If Sherman was not bisexual, Clorice would have been his sex partner of choice. She was even capable of making him think that he was normal at times. They went to a table that was as far from the restrooms as they could manage. They sat on opposite sides of the booth.

"You seem a little worried about something," said Clorice. "What's the matter?"

"You've probably heard about the new captain by now, right? She has me in her sights. And I think that your husband is looking at his last days in Homicide, if not the department."

"Let's hope he lasts until his retirement or his death, whichever comes first," said Clorice with a slight smile. "But let's not talk about him. Let's eat and then find a place where we can discuss more pressing issues."

With that, Sherman felt a foot climb its way up his leg. The foot connected to a very attractive leg, a leg that attached to its matching leg at a place where Sherman could feel like something other than a freak. Clorice was giving back a bit of the manhood that he had lost between sessions with her.

Don and Chuck followed Sherman to Chinatown and saw him safely into the custody of Clorice Grimes; then they called it a day, except for one detail: They ran the plate of the car that Sherman was driving. It was registered to Detective Martin.

CHAPTER TWENTY

It had been a longer day than Don had planned. Even though there were issues in the works that needed serious attention, he needed to give some attention to his life. He was, after all, a person who believed that there was life outside the job. Far too many cops thought that the job was their life, that it was not a job but a way of life. Don wasn't one of those. He was in the school of thought that recharging was as important as getting the job done. With that in mind, he got on his office phone and called the ever-lovely, always available Roseanne Vargas. She answered after the third ring.

"Hi, Roseanne, what are you up to this evening?"

"About five foot six and thirty-five, twenty-six, thirty-six, why? What do you have in mind? Like I couldn't guess."

"I had in mind that we get together at my place for a bite and see what develops."

"I'm kind of busy reading a case for a trial that's starting tomorrow. Do you think it would present a conflict if I got into bed with a member of the club of cretins who violated my clients constitutional rights?"

"Only if I was the cretin who made the arrest, otherwise I see no conflict. Besides, I know you have never let that little detail stand in the way of our getting together," said Don.

"OK, Detective, I'll stipulate to that and meet you at your place in about a half hour."

"How about you wait until you see the lights come on at my place; I'm still in the office, and I'm not sure how long it'll take to get home. But knowing what waits, I'll make it as quick as possible."

Don was once again pleased to have a woman like Roseanne Vargas among his closest friends. She was attractive, smart, and funny, all at the same time. She also knew where to place her priorities. What a gal. He only hoped that he would never come up against her in the courtroom; she was also a great attorney.

Before leaving, Don called Radio and asked that either he or Chuck be notified at home if any calls came in from the motel where Shondra was holed up.

With the evening plans in place, Don locked up his files and left with Chuck. The office was empty, so they turned out the lights as they left and locked the office door. Don persuaded Chuck to drive him home since he had taken the water taxi in, and the water taxi had stopped running by the time he left the office. Chuck reluctantly agreed.

The drive to West Seattle was a good time to talk about what they would do tomorrow. They decided that they would call the artist in the morning and arrange to pick her up from her office and take her to Shondra's motel room. The less time Shondra spent around the Homicide office, the better for everyone, mostly for Shondra. If she happened to recognize her assailant among the detectives or other employees, life could get a little complicated. With that out of the way, they drove in silence through a thickening fog.

Don's complex was its usual quiet and orderly place when they arrived. He got out of Chuck's car and said good night. He turned and walked toward the entrance to his townhouse, not noticing the car that was parked about a half block away with a man sitting behind the wheel. Don's powers of observation would need some honing for sure if he was going to survive to see his next birthday.

He opened the door to his townhouse and immediately turned on the lights that would tell Roseanne he was home. He went to the mailbox and collected the day's mail, mostly junk that didn't make it past the recycle bin. His next stop was the refrigerator to explore dinner possibilities. There were leftovers from a meal he had shared with Wyman. The thought occurred that sharing these with Roseanne would somehow be unethical. He quickly dismissed the thought and returned to the practical reality that he was hungry and horny, and since Wyman was not currently present, it was probably OK.

No sooner had he put together the stuff of an acceptable dinner when the doorbell rang. He went to the door, pulled it open, and was greeted by the very attractive Roseanne Vargas. She stood in the doorway long enough for Don to appreciate that she was wearing only a thin pullover, *sans* bra, and shorts that gave new meaning to the word short. The cold night air made the pullover even more attractive.

"Are you going to let me in, or are you going to damage your eyes staring at my chest in this light?" asked Roseanne. Don stood aside with the thought that he might not be as hungry as he thought. His stomach could probably wait until later.

"What's for dinner? I'm starved," said Roseanne. "I've been hard-nosing the trial case since noon without a break. How about if we eat and then find something else to amuse ourselves."

With a sense of disappointment and a certain anatomically embarrassing development, Don led her into the kitchen where the leftovers sat waiting on a counter. He put the food in the microwave and retrieved an already opened bottle of Trader Joe's Chablis from the refrigerator. While they waited the few minutes for the microwave to announce that it had done its job, Don and Roseanne reacquainted themselves with each other's bodies. Don found that her pullover was as thin as he first thought, and Roseanne found that Don was as horny as she first assumed.

"You are aware, Roseanne, that the microwave has a very important feature that allows it to redo what it's already done, aren't you?"

"I know all about the finer points of microwave cooking, and that is the most important one," sighed Roseanne. "So how about we let the food rest a short while and check out a couch or bed, whichever is closer."

With that, they walked to the living room where Don found that Roseanne had already exposed some of her charms and was removing the very short shorts as he turned around. It didn't take long for him to catch up. What followed was a workout that would leave both of them hungry for something other than each other.

The lights in Don's living room, although not bright, were enough to illuminate the show that Don and Roseanne put on. The man who had been in the car down the block enjoyed the show as much as they did starring in it. He enjoyed it in more ways than one. He took several photographs between bouts of giving himself the pleasure that he found in watching others during their sexual encounters. He found watching people he knew to be especially exciting. The photos would be icing on his cake, so to speak. A public defender screwing a homicide detective caught on film might be his ticket to salvation at some point in the future.

"Was that good for you?" asked Roseanne as she put another piece of asparagus salad in her mouth.

"Yes it was. I especially liked the lemon-infused olive oil dressing. It offers the perfect aftertaste to a delicious body." With that, Don raised his glass of Chablis and offered a toast to what they had just enjoyed. Roseanne concurred by slipping an out-of-season strawberry from Mexico between Don's lips.

Fuck, thought Don. *How in the hell have I gotten myself into this menagerie of women?* It also occurred to him that he was attracted to his new boss, a young officer, and a sergeant with whom he had shared the hazards of patrol duty in the south end. Not a good position to be in when there were crimes waiting to be solved. He hadn't forgotten Wyman and Tiffany. Things were getting out of hand. He knew there was a name for it, but he couldn't come up with the name for men who had a serious attraction to women and acted on it. It must be a sickness. Don was at a loss to see how his life was sick, however.

Following dinner, Don and Roseanne retired to Don's bedroom where Roseanne put him under a withering cross-examination. He was left with no way out of the fact that he was nothing more than an extremely horny bastard. Roseanne followed a close second as a horny female who didn't accept second best. The jury was left to decide on the more guilty sex partner.

When the festivities in Don's bedroom came to a satisfactory conclusion, Roseanne told Don that she needed to continue trial preparation. While Don would have preferred waking up beside her, he understood the pressing and unrelenting demands of the job. Roseanne didn't believe in entering the courtroom less than fully prepared. For that she had Don's admiration, that and other more mundane things.

Roseanne got out of Don's bed and put on the revealing clothes in which she had arrived. Don walked with her to the door, gave her a goodnight kiss, opened the door, and watched as she walked toward her nearby townhouse. The path lighting was just bright enough to give Don a show of Roseanne's very well-developed rear end. *Christ, you have to come to grips with this thing you have for butts and the bodies that they're attached to,* thought Don. *Maybe I should strike up a relationship with a shrink and get some free advice concerning my condition. Wouldn't that probably just add one more woman to my already full plate of women, assuming that the therapist was a woman?*

After taking a shower and getting his mind back on the issue at hand, Don called the North Precinct to check on whether Officer Morris was still around. Shift change was in progress for Officer Morris, but she was still in the precinct, although she had changed out of uniform and was on her way to the parking lot when she was paged. She found a phone and picked it up.

"Officer Morris."

"Hi, Vickie."

"How did the night go? Did you put our girl to bed?"

"She was safely in her room when I last saw her about a half hour ago. She promised that she would be a good girl for the rest of the night and not invite any more customers in. I also talked to the third-watch officer who covers the motel and told him what was up. He agreed to keep an eye on her."

"Great, I appreciate your help with this," said Don. "She should only have to stay there until tomorrow when she meets with the artist; then she can go about her merry way plying her trade."

"My, you seem pretty cavalier about the sex trade. Don't you take the typical cop's view that it threatens our mothers and daughters, not to mention the sanctity of marriage?" said Vickie with an audible smirk to her voice.

"Actually, I think that as long as a person isn't forced into the trade, she or he should be given license to do whatever. You can make the argument that there is no choice involved since some are forced for reasons beyond their control to engage in prostitution, and that may be true in some cases. I don't think that prostitution should be criminal, however. If it was made legal, there would be no need for pimps, and the business would be a lot cleaner," said Don.

"Aren't you the liberal detective? I'll bet you even vote Democratic."

"How did you know? I actually think that the last good Republican is long dead, and his name was Eisenhower. As for prostitutes and whether they should be legal, I saw the wisdom of that in Thailand. Not only was it legal, but it was also regulated and the prostitutes had to have a medical certificate that was updated every week. It worked out pretty well as I recall."

"As you recall? It sounds like you have some experience in that area," said Vickie.

"Guilty as charged. When I was stationed in Thailand, there was a standing order that we were to have contact with only those women who had a certificate from a military doc. The base provided medical care for the local prostitutes. I thought that the practice was pretty reasonable and a hell of a lot more civilized than what we see today. The military leadership knew that a bunch of horny GIs were going to get laid anyway, so why not make it work in a way that would keep them healthy? And another thing: Where are the conservatives who think that a free market system is next to godliness? You'd think that they'd be stumbling all over themselves getting a piece of the action. Those same conservatives would have been delighted to know that the practice saved the military the expense of treating the troops for various diseases that would otherwise render them unfit for duty. But, as we know, most of those pricks didn't take part in war because Daddy was getting them deferments, and most of them were screwing their way through college, and most of those were screwing members of their own sex."

"OK, with that out of the way, what else is on your mind?" asked Vickie.

"If you're working tomorrow, how about if we meet for dinner so I can show my appreciation for going the extra mile with Shondra?" asked Don.

"Actually, I'm furloughed tomorrow, but I'll still meet somewhere so you can show your appreciation. How about Ballard? There are some OK restaurants there."

After going over some alternatives, they decided to meet at a place known for its Cajun food, a place that Don and Chuck agreed was great on the few times they ate there. Don didn't recall any talk between Chuck and him about the primacy of vegetarians or the necessity of meat during their main courses or after while they drank chicory and pigged out on bread pudding drowned in brandy sauce.

After hanging up the phone, Don climbed into bed and almost immediately fell into a dreamless sleep.

CHAPTER TWENTY-ONE

Sergeant Sherman and Clorice left the Chinatown restaurant at about midnight. They had both had too much to drink to drive legally, but that didn't deter Sherman. He was above the law and always had been as far as he was concerned. No cop in the city would dare to fuck with the great Sergeant Sherman. The state cops were another matter, so he wouldn't be venturing onto the freeway. Clorice didn't have the same free pass, so Sherman suggested that he drive her home. She could pick up her car the following day; Clorice agreed.

As they drove north toward Ballard, Sherman suggested that they drive to a couple of motels along Aurora so he could check on somebody. Clorice's thought was that Sherman wanted to rent a room; she was wrong.

"Let's stop at the Cascade Motor Inn and see if somebody I've been looking for is there. Maybe you could help me with her. She might trust you more than me."

In her less than coherent state, Clorice agreed to go along with what she would have found to be highly suspect if not under the influence of several drinks. She was also hoping that Sherman would come across with a little sexual activity. She never knew where he was with sex, however, so held her hopes in check for the time being. After all, Detective Martin had paid her a visit that afternoon. *The squad that fucks together...,* thought Clorice.

As they drove north on Aurora Avenue, Clorice pointed out prostitutes standing in various places, usually at bus stops so they would have a reason for being on the street if an officer should enquire. Their dress and stance were dead giveaways, however. Clorice, for some reason, was tuned into both and expressed more interest than the average respectable housewife.

"That wouldn't be such a bad way to earn some extra money," said Clorice.

"Have you been thinking about getting into the business? Maybe we could get together and form a little team. We couldn't lose; I'd know when the Vice stings were happening, and you could provide the rest," said Sherman.

"The thing is, I think there are a bunch of officers in the north end who would recognize me, and then there's the issue of age. I'm not getting any younger, and from what I've noticed, most of the street hookers are youngsters. There is that cougar thing starting to catch on, though."

"Cougar thing? What's that?"

"You know, older gals getting it on with young guys."

"That sounds like fun. Let's leave it open for thought," said Sherman.

When they reached the motel where Shondra was staying, Sherman turned onto a side street and parked. He instructed Clorice to put on her best hooker look and go to the office. He told her to ask for Shondra's room number and identify herself as a friend. If Shondra wasn't registered under that name, Clorice would describe her and say that she went by several names and it was important that she pass along a message. Sherman had spent several gratifying nights at this very motel.

Clorice undid several buttons on her blouse, revealing an impressive cleavage for a woman of her age. Then she applied some more lip gloss, opened the door, and walked toward the motel office.

The owner of the motel was at the desk when Clorice walked in; he was almost always at the desk. Clorice asked about Shondra and was met with a blank stare. Don had briefed this owner about what to do if anything strange happened that involved Shondra. While giving Clorice his best blank stare, he was trying to come up with a response.

"No, no one with that name registered here," said the owner.

Clorice described who she was looking for and gave the owner her most alluring smile. She also said that she had a very important message to deliver. Remembering what Don said about future police attention, the owner denied knowing anything about a Shondra.

Not one who was used to getting around a negative response unlike Sergeant Sherman who might have choked information from the little Korean, Clorice turned and left the office. As she walked toward where Sherman was parked, she saw a marked police car drive into the parking lot. She continued to Sherman's car.

"She's not here," Clorice told Sherman when she got into his car. "But did you see what just drove in?"

"Yeah, let's watch where the officer goes." Sherman backed his car toward Aurora to a spot where he could see where the officer went. The officer, a man, went to the office where he talked to the owner. He checked the register and talked some more. The officer then got on the desk phone and made a call. He talked for about two minutes and left. He returned to his car where he remained.

"I think this little job is over for the night," said Sherman. "How about if we find a place to park and practice your future profession?"

With a slight smirk that left her sincerity in question, Clorice nuzzled against Sherman's right side, her breast flattening against his arm, and whispered, "Fuck you, Sergeant."

"So it's a deal." That just left the decision of where to go to conduct their latest act of cuckoldry.

Don's phone rang three times before he could get to it from his dead-to-the-world position in his bed. He was more than exhausted by the previous day's activities.

"Detective Lake, this is Officer Wilson, North Precinct. Officer Morris asked me to check on Shondra from time to time."

"Thanks for doing that for us. Shondra is in a little bit of a pickle right now as Vickie may have told you."

"It looks like someone was looking for her this evening. A woman came in just before I got here and asked if Shondra was registered. The owner told her that she wasn't there. The woman walked out, but the owner didn't see a car. I'm still here at the motel. What do you want me to do?"

"If you would just do what you're doing and check on her when you can. If you need to write a report, maybe park in the motel's lot to do it. That'll probably spook whoever it is that's looking for her."

"OK, sounds like a plan. I'll keep you posted if anything happens."

"Thanks, I appreciate it."

Hmm, appreciate probably wasn't the most accurate word Don could come up with. His day had been long and diverse. The diversion with Roseanne was what made the day bearable.

When Roseanne opened the door to her townhouse after spending meaningful time with Don Lake, she had a sense that not all was in place.

She thought about calling Don to ask him to come over but thought that she might just be overreacting, and she didn't want to be seen as a weak female. She was anything but a weak female. As she walked toward the living room from the entryway, she got the gut feeling that there was someone beside her in the townhouse. When she reached the living room, she noticed the curtains moving with the slight breeze off Elliot Bay and the sliding door to the deck was open a few inches. Roseanne ran back to the kitchen, turned on the light, and picked up the phone. As she punched in 911, a hand grabbed her dialing hand and began to crush it. The person's other arm came around her neck and pulled back, lifting her off the floor. She dropped the phone; it fell to the floor. She wasn't sure if she had been able to get the last digit dialed. The person's other arm, the one attached to the hand that had done a good job of crushing her hand, came across her chest, covering her breasts and compressing the air from her lungs. The man smelled of old sweat and had a breath that could have been improved with a clove of garlic. Things were not looking good.

The man who was apparently trying his best to crush her was about a foot taller than Roseanne. He leaned into her right ear and said, "If you fight me, I'll not only rape you, I will kill you. Do you understand that?"

Roseanne was just able to get out a gasping, "Yes."

There was a familiar yet difficult-to-place odor that was clearly coming from the man. It wasn't his breath but his clothes. They had an odor that she recognized from somewhere. Then it struck her; it was an odor common to a public toilet. It was Clorox or a cleaning solution that had Clorox in it. She'd have to remember to tell the officer who took her report about that.

"Now we'll walk over to the stove and pull one of your towels off its hook."

Roseanne was pushed slowly across the kitchen toward the stove. Since the initial attack, Roseanne was able to start thinking like a person who might be looking death in the face. She was considering her options. It looked like the man was going to use the towel to blindfold her. That would put him in another position of power. What to do? One of the things she needed to do was to get a look at him, even if it was only his reflection in a window. The man seemed to be able to read her mind.

It wasn't just bicycling and other workouts that kept Roseanne in the obviously great condition that men found so attractive. She was also very much into Tae Kwon Do. She practiced at a small studio a few blocks away. Now was the perfect time to put her months of practice to use. When they had shuffled halfway across the kitchen, where there was the least amount of furniture to get in the way, Roseanne went to work.

First she screamed as loud as she could to distract the goon and, with luck, attract attention. Simultaneously, she threw both arms above her in a wedge. When she reached the top of her reach, she brought her right elbow back with as much force as she could muster, landing in his soft gut. The man let out a huff as though he had lost most of the air in his lungs and might be on the verge of puking. Roseanne wasn't through with him. When she brought her arms up, the man's grip on her had been broken, a sign that he wasn't in very good shape. She then bent over at the waist and grabbed his pant legs near his shoes. She straightened back up, pulling the man's legs out from under him. She noticed, as his feet came off the floor, that he was wearing ankle-high boots: more information for the police report. The man landed on his back on the kitchen floor. The wind was knocked out of him, but he had sense enough left to quickly roll over, hiding his face. Roseanne still wasn't through with him. She landed a kick between his spread legs, connecting with his groin. The man let out a scream that was as good as any a woman could produce.

Roseanne felt as though she had the man in a position where he wouldn't be an immediate threat, so she again picked up the phone and dialed 911 as quickly as she could. As she was doing this, the man got on all fours and crawled like a wounded raccoon until he reached the sliding deck door. He pushed the door so hard that the glass cracked. He then disappeared into the night. Roseanne hoped that the man wasn't familiar with the ground beyond her deck where there was a steep drop into a blackberry bramble. Once in the bramble, the only way out was onto California Way where it came up from Harbor Avenue. If the fuck hadn't tried to rape her, Roseanne might have felt a moment's sympathy. But *screw him*, she thought. A rolling trip through blackberries with their needle-sharp barbs waiting to puncture the bastard all the way down the bluff was what he deserved. He'd also be pretty easily identified if stopped. She hoped that he hadn't made the turn from the deck onto the lawn and walkway that led to the street.

After Roseanne called 911 and was assured that multiple units were on the way, she hung up and called Don, who told her to sit down somewhere and not touch anything.

"You really think that I'm stupid, don't you?"

"Not at all. I just know that you've been through a traumatic situation, that's all."

"I was traumatized enough to kick the ass of the gorilla. That, to me, doesn't mean that I'm going to do something as stupid as destroy evidence."

"I'll be right over," said Don, sensing that further conversation wasn't going to advance the cause.

Before Don left for Roseanne's, he called Radio and asked that a team from Special Assault be sent. Special Assault, or SAU, did all sex crime investigations. They were very good at what they did. In Don's view, SAU was a better investigative unit than Homicide. It didn't require knowing somebody or being a good old boy to get in. Having a track record of good work and results was paramount. But Don was once again at a loss to answer how he got into Homicide.

Patrol arrived in the area in droves. There were two units from the West Precinct that covered the downtown area. Maybe it was a slow night and they needed something to do. Maybe it was that the drive from the West Precinct to West Seattle gave a patrol officer the opportunity to practice high-speed driving skills. Don had taken advantage of situations like this to drive as if he was Mario Andretti. Whatever the reason, the turnout was impressive.

A K-9 attempted to follow the suspect's trail, but when it vanished at the bluff, the handler had to pull it back. They then went to the bottom of the bluff and sniffed at the edge of the blackberry bramble and along California Way. The suspect seemed to have disappeared along with his scent trail. There was always the possibility that he had been killed or seriously injured in the fall into the blackberries. Officers would have to spend the night waiting and listening. In the morning, when the sun came up, the man might be found stuck in a hell of his own making. Or he may have miraculously made his way out and escaped. Stranger things had happened.

CHAPTER TWENTY-TWO

Captain Mitchell was in a good mood when Don and Chuck walked into her office the next morning, although her butt was dragging. Don called her at home earlier and told her about the night's events. He still didn't feel comfortable going through the chain of command to get to her. Chuck was on board with his thinking after their conversation at about 2:00 a.m.

"You're bringing Shondra in this morning to talk to the sketch artist, right?" said Captain Mitchell.

Chuck shook his head and said, "No, we're going to bring the artist to her at the motel. That way nobody here will see her, and she won't see anybody."

"OK, that sounds like a plan. What happens to her after she describes the guy who assaulted her?"

"We don't have anything to hold her on, so she can go wherever she wants," said Don. "I guess we could get chickenshit with her, excuse my language, and charge her with a couple counts of prostitution, but all that would accomplish is to piss her off, excuse my language again, and drive her farther away, like to Las Vegas. My thought is that we try to treat her with kid gloves for the time being and watch her when we can."

"As usual, I agree with Don," said Chuck. "But I think his language needs some work."

"You're both forgiven, Don, for your language, and you, Chuck, for not teaching him better language skills. Now I'm going to bare my chest, so to speak, and tell you something that I probably shouldn't, but the events of the last few days have made me rethink the secrecy I was sworn to before agreeing to take this assignment."

Don and Chuck sat up a little straighter and concentrated on their new boss. Before she began the briefing, she asked Don to close the door and then she turned her radio's volume up so the piece by Schumann coming from KING Classical Music Station would drown out their conversation.

"The chief hasn't been real happy with the clearance rate of murders over the last year or so, and neither has the bureau chief. For that matter, the clearance rate of all cases has reached abysmal levels. Since, as you know, shit rolls downhill, excuse my language, the bureau chief asked me to come on board to see what gives. This isn't a headhunting job that I was given, but if some heads are attached to bodies that aren't performing, then maybe some heads will roll. Both of you have experience with the way I operate. You probably don't know that I was fairly influential in getting you assigned here. It appeared to me for quite a while that the unit was suffering from a chronic case of deadwood syndrome. Most of the complaints that we got in IIS about the unit were for nothing more than failure to perform. Now it looks like we may have gone beyond that to a refusal to perform on the part of some detectives and one sergeant in particular. You two have a fresh approach to solving murders and working some of the less serious cases. Assault cases sometimes lead us to murder suspects, a fact that is lost on most of the people in the unit. From this point on, that will change. I don't want mistrust between detectives and squads to compromise a murder investigation; that too will change. And since it appears that we may have a detective involved in the commission of a crime or crimes, it's paramount that information be held very close to the vest."

"We've already started to lock up our files when we leave the office," said Chuck. "And we're being careful about what we tell Sergeant Sherman."

"Just keep me informed about what you're doing. If you need any overtime on the three cases that seem to be connected, you can have it. I'll talk to Sergeant Sherman and ask that he not give you any more cases until these are either cleared or look like they won't be cleared."

"Do you suppose that's going to make him wonder what's up and give him the idea that all is not well in Homicide land, or just plain piss him off, pardon my language?" said Don.

"If he doesn't already know that something is up, he's a lot dumber than I thought. You guys can go and take care of the sketch artist. I'd like to see the sketch when it's done."

"The artist that we're using is about the best there is. She can draw stuff out of a witness that they didn't know they knew," said Don.

"And by the way," Captain Mitchell said as they were leaving, "the unit is getting computers real soon. You'll be able to lock up your files a lot easier on a computer than in a file drawer."

"Computers? I can barely type," said Don.

"You'll learn," said Captain Mitchell with a slight snicker.

Don and Chuck returned to their cubicle where they gathered the stuff they would need for the day's work. When they walked in, they were surprised to find the night janitor, Wally Fox, with garbage can in hand.

"What's up, Wally? Are you working days now?" Don asked.

"I just got a little behind and thought that I'd get caught up this morning" was, in Don's opinion, Wally's somewhat lame reason.

Wally looked like he might have spent the night in his car, if he had one. His hair was always in need of attention, but this morning it was unusually unkempt. In addition, he hadn't stood nearly close enough to his razor this morning. As for a shower, the concept appeared foreign to Wally.

Poor bastard, thought Don. *His life must be a real pit.*

When Wally walked out of the cubicle with a plastic bag full of garbage, Don noted that his limp of a few days ago had gotten worse.

"Did you hurt your leg, Wally?"

"'Just getting old, I guess" was Wally's reply.

After a quick breakfast of a tofu scramble for both of them in a house-plant-saturated café in Wallingford, a fashionable neighborhood bordering Fremont to the east, Don and Chuck went to the office building where Janet Harniski worked at her day job; she was a graphic artist for a company that did graphics anywhere that ads were seen, but mostly on the sides of trucks. She had an understanding boss who let her do forensic sketches when the requests came in. She was the best in Seattle as far as most detectives in the Investigations Bureau were concerned. Janet could wield a number two pencil like no one else. She was ready to go when they arrived. The case of instruments with which she performed her magic was in her hand as she stood on the steps of the building when they drove up. It consisted of pencils and pad.

"Good morning, guys. How's life treating you this fine day?" was Janet's way of conveying that she was ever the optimist. It didn't seem to damage her positive view of the world that she was again going to listen to a victim/

witness describe some deviant asshole and that she might be instrumental in putting said asshole behind bars for a very long time.

"Good morning, Janet," Chuck and Don said in unison.

Janet climbed into the back of the fleet car and they were on their way to the motel. Traffic was light on northbound I-5, so they took it to the NE Fiftieth Street exit. They drove over I-5 and west on Fiftieth to Aurora and then turned north. The motel was a short drive north on the east side of Aurora.

There was a marked patrol unit in the motel parking lot when they arrived; the officer sitting behind the wheel looked like he could use some sleep. Neither Don nor Chuck recognized him.

Don parked near the patrol unit and got out. The officer eyed him as if he didn't like what he saw. "Good morning," said Don as he walked up to the window with his badge case out.

"Good morning," the officer responded, the suspicion now gone from his face and the weapon in his lap being replaced in its holster.

Don introduced himself and asked how Shondra was behaving.

"She hasn't been out of the room since I arrived at about six this morning. I saw the curtains open a while ago, so I know that she or somebody is in the room."

"OK, thanks for babysitting her. I don't think we'll need any more assistance from you guys, but we really appreciate what you've done."

"No problem, anytime," the officer replied.

As the officer drove out of the lot, Don went back to the car and got Janet. He asked Chuck if he'd mind going to get some breakfast for Shondra at a nearby restaurant. Since this was technically Chuck's case, he knew that he was stretching propriety.

Shondra wasn't in her usual compromising position when Don and Janet walked into the room, which was comforting to Don since he wasn't sure whether Janet had experienced that side of life up close and personal. Shondra was dressed and looked like she might be going to a job interview, if the job was that of a stripper. It occurred to Don that she was interviewed for a "job" several times a day by horny men when she was on the clock.

Janet introduced herself and then took over the scene. Janet may have been the most cheerful person Don knew other than Marjorie, but she became a different person when she went to work to re-create a suspect's likeness. It was almost like watching a hypnotist at work. Shondra was completely under Janet's control. Shondra recalled details about the man who had attacked her that she didn't know she knew. It was magic while retaining admissibility. Nothing Janet did could be described as sugges-tive. The man that Shondra described came from her memory; it wasn't put there by Janet. Don had seen her at work many times in the past but never failed to be amazed and impressed. Whatever the city was paying her wasn't anywhere near enough in Don's opinion.

"Give me a number from one to ten when you look at the drawing," said Janet when she had finished it to her satisfaction. "One will be least like the man who attacked you and ten will be the most like."

Janet then turned the drawing toward Shondra and just held it there, not saying anything. Shondra looked down at the drawing and stared for a few seconds.

"That looks an awful lot like him. That looks like the man who raped me and then beat me up. No doubt in my mind about it."

"How about the numbers?" Janet calmly asked.

"Eight, maybe eight and a half."

"OK" was all that Janet said. She then signed and dated the sketch, tore it from the sketchbook, and handed it to Don.

Don looked at the sketch and had the immediate sense that he knew this guy.

No one had noticed Chuck come into the room with Shondra's break-fast. He had what he thought a prostitute might like: an egg, meat, and potato scramble from the local Denny's. He also had a cup of coffee. Both were now cold. The room's microwave would correct that.

"I don't usually eat like this. The fat and cholesterol aren't good for the body," said Shondra, "but I'm starved." With that, she dug into the food as if she hadn't eaten for days.

The drive to Shondra's mother's house took Don and Chuck by Janet's workplace where they dropped her off. When they arrived at her moth-er's, Shondra almost ran to the house where Raymond met her at the door. Shondra grabbed Raymond and held on to him as if he was going to slip away if she let go. Don and Chuck just stood back and let the scene unfold; they had no role to play in this one.

"You guys gonna keep on screwin' with her, or what?" Maurice asked in his best sneer as he walked out from a back room.

Don had, by this time, pretty much had it with Maurice. He stepped into the house and walked within a millimeter of Maurice's chest. "How about you and I go outside and discuss who is screwing with whom here."

Don didn't give Maurice the opportunity to answer in any meaningful way. He took hold of Maurice's belt and began walking back toward the door. Maurice gave a moment's indication that he might elect to fight with Don but thought better of it when he saw the look in Don's eyes.

Once outside the house, where they weren't as likely to break things, Don let go of Maurice and stepped back within arm's length and slightly to Maurice's right.

"Let's get a few things straight between us so there aren't any gray areas in our future encounters, shall we? First, we are doing our level best to keep Shondra alive. We are also trying very hard to identify the asshole who assaulted her. Maybe that doesn't hold much value with you, but it does with us, and we are going to continue doing it whether you think it's of value or not. You see, your opinion doesn't mean shit to us. You're nothing more than a piece-of-shit pimp. We are sworn to fuck with guys like you in any way we can but mostly legal. If the law gets in our way, we're still going to fuck with you. Am I getting through to you, Maurice?"

"Ye…"

"And furthermore, Maurice"—Don spit about an inch from Maurice's nose—"I don't know if you've noticed, but Shondra happens to be a mother. She has a boy by the name of Raymond. Did you notice that, Maurice, you small-dick piece of shit? What do you suppose he thinks, seeing his mother treated the way she is by the piece of excreta that you represent?" Don was on a roll. He could easily have started to practice his O'Neill on Maurice's face and neck. He was able to retain some composure while dressing down Maurice thus leaving no doubt in his reptilian mind that his very existence was in jeopardy.

"You drive around in that fucking pimpmobile looking like a fool. You know that Shondra is giving it up every night so you can put gas in that joke of a car and dress yourself as if you just stepped out of a fucking sixties pimp museum? At least get some taste, man. Don't leave yourself open for the laughs that you're giving folks. Are you getting all this, Maurice?"

"Yea…"

Don was starting to feel a little sympathy for Maurice as he continued to knock the bluster and bullshit out of him. "Spit it out, Maurice."

"Yeah, man, I get it. But would you step back a little? You musta had some wicked shit for breakfast."

"Sorry about the afterglow of my breakfast," Don said as he moved a few steps back while pulling a breath mint from his pocket. He offered

Maurice and Chuck one before putting the tin back. Maurice declined, but Chuck took one since he had the same breakfast as Don.

"Can I tell you guys something without you getting all up in my face again?"

Don and Chuck nodded, which meant that they wouldn't be going off on him without probable cause.

"Shondra and I are married. I love her and Raymond. Raymond is our kid. I know what we do to support him is all fucked up, but it pays the bills. We been together since high school. I was a serious dope fiend with no ambition to do anything that would get me off the street. That fucked-up attitude got me where I am, nowhere. Pimp doesn't look all that great on the old resume, now does it?"

Don and Chuck were rarely at a loss for words. This was a new one for both of them. They stood there looking at each other and then at Maurice. Don felt a little chagrined by the dressing down he had just given Maurice, but not much; Maurice deserved it. Who knows, it might have shaken him loose and made him confront the fact that he had more than a pimpmobile to support.

Don was the first one to come out of the daze induced by Maurice. "You love them? What does love mean to you? Is it just buying a few groceries? Is it helping with the rent? Is it not hitting Shondra as hard as you would your other whores?" Don felt himself starting to rev into a full-blown rage again, so he backed off and quit talking.

"The 'other whores' is one other woman who happens to be Shondra's cousin. That's probably why you thought she was Shondra; they look like sisters. She's doing this because she wants to. I don't hit either one of them. Fact is, I love them both. I think they love me."

Don was starting to thaw a little from the cold hate he had for Maurice when he first laid eyes on him. He hadn't befriended many pimps in his day, but there could be a first for anything was Don's guess.

Chuck saw an opening, so he wedged his way into the exchange. "Now that Shondra is into this investigation up to her neck and is willing to continue, what do you have planned for her?" Before Maurice could get a word out, Chuck continued with the questions. "She still isn't out of the woods with the creep who threatened her, so she has to be watched and kept off the streets. Are you up to helping us, or are you planning to disappear with her?" Once again, Maurice didn't get his first word out before Chuck was back at it. "If it looks like you're going to disappear with her, we're going to put you in jail for pandering and her in jail for soliciting, and we'll make the case that you are both flight risks, so bail will be set beyond your reach. How's all that sound?"

"I'll help you guys if you'll cut me some slack."

"OK, but those strings are going to stay attached until this is over; then we'll talk about your future and that of Shondra and Raymond. There's one thing that you have to know, so you better start thinking about it. Raymond isn't going to grow up like this. If you and Shondra don't come through for him, I'll personally see to it that you lose him."

"OK, man, you got my promise. I'll help however I can."

Don and Chuck were satisfied that Shondra, Raymond, and Maurice would be staying with Shondra's mother until this whole affair ended. Before they left the house, Raymond walked up to Don and Chuck and shook both of their hands. Don thought that he might be in for a shin kicking, so he was almost brought to tears by the handshake, almost.

"Did you mean all that about taking Raymond away from them?" Don asked after they had driven a few blocks down the street.

"Never more certain of anything in my life," said Chuck. "It seems that letting that little guy turn into another Maurice when I could prevent it should be a criminal offense. It sure as hell is a moral offense in my book."

"You're a good man, Chuck."

"Thanks, I know. So are you."

They hadn't made it halfway to the Public Safety Building before a call came from Radio. A man was going ballistic in a mom-and-pop store in the Central District. He was making threats to the clerk about being ripped off for change from a purchase. The Radio operator made a point of letting responding officers know that the clerk knew that the suspect was a Vietnam veteran, so they should be cautious.

Don felt the hairs on his neck stand up at the description of the suspect. He had heard one too many times that Vietnam vets were all suspect of strange behavior and were not to be trusted. He pulled the microphone from the dash and responded to the call.

"Radio, this is Unit 610. We're close to that last call and can handle it, but have one other unit come along. And you're right, we Vietnam vets are all a little crazy."

The Radio operator didn't answer immediately. She was probably trying to come up with some way of covering her insensitive ass. "Copy, 610."

When Don and Chuck arrived, the suspect was still in the store. He was still running his mouth about being ripped off for change he was due. The store clerk was just standing behind the counter, looking like he wasn't sure whether he should shit or go blind. He was probably used to ripping off the local folk, most of whom didn't have any money other than what was in their pockets.

"Do you mind if I handle this, Chuck?" Don asked.

"Be my guest."

Don got out of the car and walked into the store. He produced his badge for the clerk who showed some relief. "Hey, man, what's up? I'm Detective Lake."

"I don't give a fuck if you're the Queen of England. This fuckin' rip-off artist has fucked over this community for the last time. I bought this beer, gave him a ten, and he gave me change for a five. It happens all the time and it ain't gonna happen again."

The clerk started to say something and Don cut him off. "I want you to go outside and talk to my partner."

When Don and the suspect were alone in the store, Don put his badge away and asked one question: "When were you in the 'Nam?"

The suspect looked at Don and slowly crumbled before his eyes. Black men, in Don's experience, had a serious reluctance to show any weakness in public, especially in front of another man, but this question lowered the man's guard. He turned away and Don watched as his shoulders heaved slowly and his head sank. Don just stood there waiting.

"Welcome home, brother," Don said in a way that only a man who had been there and done that could.

The suspect remained turned away long enough to pull himself together. He then turned toward Don and looked at him for the first time. "I was in the Central Highlands most of my tour with the First Air Cav." He was no longer angry. He was looking back on a time and place that he had never fully left. Don recognized the state; he still relived it from time to time, mostly at night when he was sleeping or trying to.

"That sounds like a place I spent in that summer camp for boys in sixty-seven and sixty-eight."

"We coulda run into each other," the "suspect: said, his focus now on a past he should have let go of long ago and not on the fact that some greedy prick was trying to rip him off.

"Maybe," Don said. "I got into An Khe now and then."

The suspect had returned to the present, so Don walked to him and repeated, while holding his hand out, "Welcome home, brother."

The suspect took Don's hand and held on. As the suspect again lost his composure, Don pulled him slowly toward him and held him in a bear hug while the man wept. There they stood, two victims of the same fucked-up war. Don knew that he hadn't suffered the same way the "suspect" had and still did. He hadn't suffered the indignity of coming home to "the world" where his race still meant that he awoke every day to be reminded that he was a second-class citizen even though he had gone to war for his country. The suspect hadn't gotten past that, and Don knew it.

"Hey, man, what's your name?" Don asked after they were both back to where they could talk.

"George Jefferson, Jr. My daddy was George Jefferson. He died in Korea. He was in the Big Red One."

"It's fucked up, ain't it, George?"

"Yeah, I guess you could say it's fucked up. What's your name?"

"Don, Don Lake."

"It's good to meet you, Don Lake. You know, I think you're the first white guy who ever talked to me like this, and you're the first guy who ever said welcome home, and you're even a fuckin' cop."

"That make's two of us, George. No one has ever said those words to me. But I'm not a fuckin' cop. I'm just a cop."

"Welcome home, Don," George said as he again grasped Don's hand and hung on to it as if it was his lifeline. It was. "I'm sorry about the fuckin' cop shit."

"So what do we have here?" the uniformed officer said as he walked into the store. Don knew by his age that he wouldn't understand what they had there.

"What we have here is a failure to communicate," Don said, remembering the line from one of his favorite movies.

"I thought some threats were made."

"No, no threats were made, and, as I said, it was just a failure on the part of a store clerk to communicate in a respectful manner with one of our nation's heroes."

Don asked the patrol officer to leave while he and the "suspect" talked over a few things. The officer turned and opened the door with a confused look on his face.

"So, George, what should we do here? You aren't going to be on your way to jail or be left with a citation. Have you ever heard about posttraumatic stress syndrome? It's something that guys like you and I seem to be subject to."

"No, never heard of it."

"The Veteran's Administration has finally decided that some of the behavior that you and I have problems with can be blamed on what we saw and did in that fucked-up war. They have programs that can treat it."

"Yeah, like somebody like me is gonna get anything from the man that's been fucking me over his whole life."

"I know that it's hard to trust anybody from where you and I come from, but it's true. You could even get medical care and maybe some kind of pension. I can help you with all this if you'll help me help you."

George Jefferson looked unconvinced, but a look of hope slowly spread across his face. "You ain't just fuckin' with me, are you?"

"I'm your brother, man. I would sooner be run over by a truck than fuck with you."

"OK, I guess I can trust you."

Don and George then walked out of the store to where Chuck and the clerk stood. "This man said that you shorted him in change," Don said to the clerk in a way that the clerk understood.

"Maybe I did but not on purpose."

"You go in and get his right change, and we'll call it even."

The clerk went back in and came out with a handful of change. He handed it to George Jefferson.

"Now apologize to this man for trying to rip him off."

"I'm not going to do anything…"

Don took a step toward the clerk and looked into his eyes with a look that said, *I just might kill you if you don't do as I said.*

"I'm sorry, sir. It will never happen again."

"Now tell this man that you will never shortchange anyone else in this community in the future. And I had better hear sincerity in that statement."

"I will never rip off anyone else in this community in the future."

"Good. Now you can go back in and start lowering your prices so this community can afford what you're selling."

Before Don and Chuck left, Don got all of George Jefferson's information and told him that he would be in touch. George Jefferson walked away with his head up and his beer in hand.

"What was that all about?" Chuck asked as they got into the car.

"It was old home time. A brother just got a welcome home, and I'm that brother."

"I don't get it."

"I don't expect you to."

Don took the microphone from its hook on the dash and cleared the call. "Radio, the disturbance is clear. If I ever hear one more of us Vietnam vets referred to in a derogatory way on the air, there will be some heads rolling." Radio was silent until another radio in another car chimed in with a "roger that." Then there were several more clicks of microphones as more officers registered their approval.

Don and Chuck rode silently for most of the way to the office. "Chuck, I want you to do me a favor. If I ever make reference to PTSD assholes again, I want you to shoot me in the right knee."

"OK, will do."

As they approached the pile of concrete and rebar that was the Public Safety Building, Don recalled that he had a date with Vickie that evening. "How about if you join Officer Morris and me for dinner tonight? I think her work deserves a reward."

"Great. Where are we going?"

"That Cajun place in Ballard, the one with the deadly bread pudding with brandy sauce. Bring a friend if you want."

"It'll just be me if that's OK. Is this a date with Officer Morris? If it is, don't you have your dance book pretty much full?"

"It's not really a date per se, but since we're now on a first-name basis, I guess it has some potential. I'm beginning to think that I should start to examine this thing I have with women and give some thought to settling on one, or maybe two. I just gave Maurice a tongue lashing about how he treats women, and I'm doing somewhat the same."

"You're not thinking of going into the business, are you? Because if you are, I think you'll have to pick your stable from places other than the medical examiner's office and the Seattle Art Museum, not to mention the Public Defender's Office," Chuck said with all the seriousness he could muster.

"I wasn't thinking of it until you brought it up, but now that you have, it deserves some thought. Have you ever noticed the hours that those guys work? Despite what I said about Maurice's ride, I think I'd look pretty good in it."

"True, but have you ever heard of a Finnish pimp?"

"There is that," said Don. They let the subject die as they drove onto the gloomy Public Safety Building's car deck.

CHAPTER TWENTY-THREE

The Cajun restaurant in Ballard that Don had been looking forward to all day was on tree-lined Ballard Avenue. The sidewalk, from the spot where he parked his Subaru to the entrance of the restaurant, was old and cracked. It had seen the boots of many of Don's countrymen who came from Finland to fish or work in the sawmills that lined the water at one time. Ballard still had about it a feel of the old country whether the country was Finland, Norway, or Sweden. For some reason they all found a home here. *But a Cajun restaurant?* That's what Don wondered.

Vickie was waiting for Don just inside the entrance. She was dressed in tasteful slacks and turtleneck with a coat over it, all black. Don's guess was that the coat hid her weapon. She was even more attractive out of uniform, which wasn't a great surprise; it was usually the case.

"I was beginning to think that I had only dreamed that we agreed to meet here," Vickie said with a smile that would make her dentist happy.

"Not a chance. I had a little trouble finding a place to park. This area is known for its little clubs that have great live music, so parking becomes an issue. It's not like the heydays of Ballard when it was populated by working stiffs who went to bed early and only went out for a beer at the local tavern. I guess you could say that Ballard has been discovered."

"Since I started working in the North Precinct, I've been assigned to various districts. I like Ballard best. I'm now in the market for a house or townhouse here. The place I have on Capitol Hill is small and too far from work for my taste," Vickie said. "When the weather permits, I like to bike to work, and the ride from Capitol Hill is a little far and lethal after dark."

"What kind of biking do you do?" asked Don, his interest now distinctly elevated.

"I have both a road and a mountain bike. I prefer road biking, though. The dirt that goes with mountain biking isn't exactly my idea of a good time."

"I couldn't agree more. I have both as well, but I prefer to road bike. There's something about the speed and response of a road bike that just isn't there with a mountain bike. Then there's the running into stumps and driving over cliffs thing with mountain bikes," said Don.

"I haven't broken any bones yet, but I have taken a few headers from my mountain bike that I'm not going to repeat if I can help it. The job seems to frown on folks who try to work on crutches or from wheelchairs."

"True," said Don. "Now where is that partner of mine? I asked him to come along to help pay the tab since this is a thank-you dinner for you."

The words were just out of Don's mouth when Chuck walked in the door. He was especially well turned out, not that he wasn't always a credit to the department in matters of dress. Blue jeans, a pullover in a color hard to describe without a color palette from one of the local art stores, a tasteful cardigan sweater, and loafers were enough to make him a sure bet for membership in the Gay Police Officers Association, if there was such a thing. The slight bulge on the right side of the sweater gave away the fact that he was not only well dressed but was well armed as well.

"Have I kept you waiting?" Chuck asked with only a hint of guilt. Don knew that he liked to be just a little late to most things. Don's suspicion was that it was Chuck's way of showing a little control that he lacked in the rest of his life. Don forgave him for this one flaw, but he was still looking for others he could exploit.

"No, you're just in time because it looks like a table is about to open."

The waiter led them to a table near the back of the dining room overlooking a small courtyard that gave them a good view of the front door. There was always that thing about sitting at tables in restaurants that left one vulnerable and gave cops an uncomfortable feeling. This table was perfect.

The menu was anything but Scandinavian in the dishes it described. The only thing remotely Scandinavian was the fish in almost all of the dishes. Don and Chuck had been here before, but Vickie had not. They helped her decide what to choose: crawfish jambalaya. Don ordered blackened sea bass, and Chuck went with a chef's salad.

"Chef's salad? This is a Cajun restaurant, Chuck," exclaimed Don.

"I'm trying to lose a few pounds."

"OK, you're off the hook," said Don.

"Do you guys usually talk shop when you go out to dinner?" Vickie asked.

"Not always," Chuck said. "We usually talk about Don's love life and my decorating schemes. But it usually ends up being shop talk."

"We aren't usually with an attractive young officer when we have dinner, though, so it's easy to lapse into job," said Don.

"I'll try not to be overly flattered by that. I hope it's not meant in any sexist way. You know, like I'm supposed to gush all over with gratitude for your having noticed that I'm a female when the reality is that I'm also a very capable cop," Vickie said with a slightly darkened look on her face.

"I apologize if I came off as a sexist ass. You must know that you're attractive, though, and we already know that you're very capable. I didn't say that you had a future in the department to get in your pants. I truly believe that you do. I hope that you pursue investigations down the road."

"OK, thanks. I didn't mean to get so defensive, and I hope you know that it comes from having to be defensive when you're a halfway attractive female in a male-dominated world, especially a macho police world. Ever since the academy, I've been hit on by lots of officers. That includes some women. It gets old after a few months. I hope you can see that."

"By this time you might have guessed that I'm gay," said Chuck. "Along with that goes a lot of shit-taking. I've had to put up a shield and toughen my skin to the point that it's hard to feel anything anymore. I wouldn't like to see that happen to you."

"I'm sorry, too, Chuck. I didn't mean to whine; it's so, so female and I've been trying for a more macho image since I was hired. Maybe I should just go for the real Victoria Morris image."

"Speaking of the real Victoria Morris, where do you come from and how did you get here?" asked Don.

"As you already know, I was an army MP. Before that I was a kid from Missoula, Montana, who wanted out but didn't have the money to get beyond the city limits. The army seemed like a way out that might lead to other things."

"That sounds like my story, except for the money part," said Don. "Only my story began in northern Minnesota where options for most were slim to none. I decided that I'd take the poor boy route, although I was far from a poor boy, and go in the military as well. It worked out pretty well for me."

"What brought you to Seattle?" asked Chuck.

"My last posting was Fort Lewis, thank God," said Victoria.

"Why thank God?" Don asked.

"It's close to Seattle. I came to Seattle as often as possible while I was at Fort Lewis and kind of fell in love with the place. When I found that Seattle PD was hiring, I thought I'd died and gone to heaven. Missoula was probably looking for a few good women to fill the ranks of its police department, but the thought of dealing with drunk cowboys for the rest of my professional life was more than I could handle."

"I know what you mean," said Chuck. "Cowboys can be a little over the top."

Both Don and Vickie smiled at Chuck's reference to his love life.

The waiter served their orders in a way that might suggest she had cooked the food herself and had a stake in its presentation and enjoyment. She described each dish and the condiments that would go with it. She excluded Chuck's salad, however. What could be said for or about a chef's salad unless it was a warning about aspirating the egg?

Both the chewing and the enjoyment of the food limited the conversation during the meal. Restaurant reputations were made by word of mouth. This restaurant never seemed to disappoint, nor did the kitchen staff ever seem to lose their enthusiasm for the food. The wait staff carried that enthusiasm to the dining room. Word of mouth had brought Don and Chuck here, and Vickie would probably pass the word along.

They agreed to share one bowl of bread pudding in deference to Chuck's diet. It was plenty, although Don had been looking forward to taking his leftovers home.

By the end of the meal, Don had made a decision about his future: it wouldn't include Officer Morris. She didn't need him in her life. She had a plan for herself that wouldn't be improved by his presence. He would help her career along where he could, but he wouldn't be including her among his female "friends." *What a fucking prince you are*, he thought.

Don and Chuck stood on the sidewalk outside the restaurant with Vickie where they again thanked her for her work and told her that she should keep in touch if she needed anything. She seemed surprised that Don didn't hit on her, or maybe it was his ego-driven imagination. She walked away toward her car while Don and Chuck watched.

"You are to be commended for your behavior tonight, Don. It was my guess that you would have left with her or her with you."

"I've turned over a new leaf, Chuck. There comes a time in every man's life when he has to confront his future. A major part of that future is deciding whether he wants to grow old while still chasing women or grow old with one woman. I think it's time that I made that decision. Of course it doesn't just apply to men and women; it also applies to men and men, etcetera," said Don.

"Are you suggesting that I get my shit together and decide who that special someone is?" asked Chuck.

"I would be the last person to suggest that you do anything to get your fucked-up love life in order."

"Thanks for the sensitive response. I knew I could count on you to be supportive," said Chuck.

With that closing to a very satisfying night, each drove off toward what they considered the more civilized parts of Seattle.

CHAPTER TWENTY-FOUR

Police bulletins can be nothing more than eyewash, a way of showing that an investigation is moving even when it isn't. They can also get an investigation off the ground. Officers who look at bulletins and carry them on patrol tend to be the officers who think of themselves as more than report takers and ticket writers. They really believe that they serve a greater purpose: that of identifying bad guys and taking them out of circulation. Don and Chuck had been among the latter group when they were assigned to Patrol. They knew that there were a lot of officers in Patrol just like they were: full of piss and vinegar and hard chargers who didn't look forward to a day off because they might miss something good.

In Don's and Chuck's humble opinions, the bulletin they had put together, which included the sketch that Janet Harniski had drawn, was a piece of artistry. It should grab the attention of even the most jaded retirement-bound patrol slug. Patrol sergeants would introduce the bulletin to their squads at roll call and give it special attention since a murder or two might be solved with it. Every patrol officer worth a damn wanted the solution to a murder on his or her resume.

When Don and Chuck finished making several hundred copies of the bulletin, they delivered them to each of the precincts rather than send them through department mail. That way the patrol officers would have them as fast as possible. At the end of the day, they passed several of the bulletins out to investigative units on the fifth floor and gave one to Marjorie for posting at the entrance to the floor.

"This guy looks familiar," Marjorie said after she looked at it for a few minutes.

Don had waited for Marjorie to gaze at it while he gazed at her and her wardrobe selection for the day. She had taken the plunging neckline to a new dimension. There was little left to one's imagination in the area of Marjorie's contours. She clearly had no blemishes on her chest or most of her midsection. There was some question left, however, about the issue of whether she had availed herself of enhancement surgery. It was Don's guess that she hadn't and that what he was looking at was a reengineering of existing flesh by way of straps and fabric. *Truly a miracle worker* was Don's opinion.

"What?" asked Don as he tore his eyes from the spectacle before him.

"Yeah, this guy is really familiar looking. But it's a sketch, so it isn't exact. But still, he looks like a guy I've seen recently."

"Keep thinking about who that might be, Marjorie, and let us know when you come up with a name."

"OK, Don," Marjorie said, not taking her eyes from the bulletin. "Oh, I almost forgot to tell you guys that I'll be on vacation for a week starting next Monday."

"Any big plans?" Don asked.

"I'm going up to Vancouver, BC."

"That's a fun town. There's great shopping on Robson Street and lots to see, ay?" Don said in his feeble attempt to mimic a Canadian.

"I've got something to take care of, but I'll get in some of the usual tourist things."

"So you speak the language then, ay?" Don persisted.

"Oh, I get it now," Marjorie said with her humble smile.

"Anything you can share with us: a guy, a major bank heist, an overthrow of the government?"

"It'll be a surprise; I think you'll like it."

"The last time I was there I noticed that every other store on Robson was selling aqua bras," Don said with a hopeful look on his face.

"What I have planned is better than that, but you'll just have to wait."

Chuck looked at Don as they continued on their way to the unit. "You are unhealthily fixated on the female anatomy, aren't you?"

"I don't view it is an abnormal fixation, just a healthy fixation. There are few objects on this planet as perfect as the female body, that's all. Hasn't the entire human race swooned over the face of Mona Lisa and the body of Marilyn Monroe?"

"You forgot Michelangelo's David," Chuck hastened to add.

"I'll give you that, Chuck, but have you noticed that he doesn't appear to be circumcised?"

Captain Mitchell's office was the next stop on their itinerary. Her door was closed, so Don knocked and waited for a response. The wait lasted for about a minute. They were about to return to their cubicle when Captain Mitchell opened her door; she looked a little less confident than she had in Don and Chuck's recent encounters with her.

"What's up, guys? Do you have something on your cases?"

"We just finished the bulletin on the assault suspect, who we think might have something to do with two murders," said Don as he held up the bulletin like a piece of art that he was displaying at an auction. "Good, huh?"

"Come in. Let's look at that."

Captain Mitchell took the bulletin from Don and walked behind her desk where she looked at it a little more closely. "This doesn't really look like any of the people we talked about, does it?"

Don shook his head and said, "No, but Marjorie thinks she's seen the guy before. And we have the added benefit of Shondra giving it an eight and a half. That means a lot. Marjorie is rarely wrong in most things, except possibly in her wardrobe selection, and that isn't all bad."

"I note that you've noticed Marjorie's clothing selection or lack of clothing selection today, Detective."

"Yes, Captain, it's my finely honed observational skills that I get paid for after all," said Don.

"No one has ever considered you anything less than observant, especially when the female body is concerned," Captain Mitchell said with a smile and a look that Don deciphered to mean that she might like to talk about that issue in private. He knew he would.

"But, more to the point, Marjorie said that she would ponder the matter and try to come up with a name. I trust her judgment."

"OK, and keep me informed. Now we have other matters to consider, or at least I do, and I want you guys to lend your thoughts," Captain Mitchell said. "When you knocked, I was on the phone with the bureau chief. He got word via the chief's office that someone in this unit may have lifted money from a scene. It seems that a family member of a victim in a recent suspicious death that turned out to be a suicide thinks that a large amount of cash was taken by one or more of the detectives at the scene."

"Is this some jack-off, pardon my language, who wants to get into the city's deep pockets by any chance?" asked Don.

"No, it looks like the complainant is the guy's mother who happens to be on the board of one of the biggest local corporations. She doesn't need the money. She said that sonny boy, or the decedent, wasn't working with a full deck. He kept his money at home. He was known to have in excess of one hundred thousand dollars in a box in his bedroom. She saw the box less than a week before he killed himself. I looked at the report that was filed on the case. Two of our detectives and a sergeant went to the scene. There was also a fire department unit, a patrol unit and a patrol sergeant there at some point during the investigation. She thinks that it was the detectives and maybe the sergeant who were responsible for the theft."

"Let me join in with Don's suspicion here. How do we know that the money was there at the time sonny boy killed himself? Maybe a member of the family thought up another way to fuck over the city, pardon my language, and collect some big bucks to add to their already big bucks," said Chuck. "And if it was there at the time sonny boy killed himself, what makes her think that Patrol or Fire aren't responsible or that sonny boy gave it away before he ended his sorry life?"

"Good questions. The short answer is that we don't know. But we do know that Fire doesn't have much to do at a scene other than determine whether someone is dead or alive. If dead, end of story, they split. If alive, they work on him or her to get him or her stabilized to the degree possible. They don't wander around looking in closets. The same is true for Patrol, although there have been cases of patrol officers taking things from a scene or a body that don't belong to them. But a box of cash would be tough to conceal, get to the officer's car, and then to his or her personal car. If there actually was cash at the scene and it was taken by someone, I'd have to guess it was a detective or detectives who were responsible."

"Is this going to be another case for us to work?" asked Don.

"No, this is an IIS case, but the detectives who were at this particular scene are in your squad, and they were there with one Sergeant Sherman. What I want you guys to do is lend IIS a hand where they want one. You know that most IIS investigators have never seen the inside of an investigative unit other than IIS. I want you to meet with the IIS investigator in his office in the near future. Don't call him; he'll call you. In addition, keep this not only under your hats but also sit on your hats. If this reaches the press, the shit will hit the fan, pardon my language."

Fuck, thought Don. He had already pardoned his thought. *This is all we need.*

"OK, guys. Keep your heads up for anything that might lend something to this, and keep me informed day or night."

"We'll do that," said Chuck.

There were times when Don found it hard to forgive himself for some of the things that crept into his life, for thoughts he harbored, and for the way he conducted himself with women, but he had never stolen from the dead. That was a new low.

Chuck pulled Don from his dark thoughts when he came up with one of his brilliant but obvious suggestions. "How about we get a jump on the IIS guys and do a little background? We probably shouldn't be snooping in and around Sherman's, Grimes's, or Martin's desks for follow-up reports, but there is going to be an incident report in Records that we can get our hands on without raising too many questions. Sonny boy's name will get us the case number."

"Brilliant, Chuck. If we know who the patrol officer and sergeant at the scene were, we could probably pretty well guess whether they had any hand in the theft, if there was a theft. However, I think we should be focusing on the cases we have on our plates without getting too involved in an IIS job. Besides, IIS has been known to get pretty possessive of their cases."

"Good point, and I don't really want to get my fingerprints on a case that could land whoever's involved in prison. But I want to know how the guys involved, if anyone is involved, are going about their business so they don't touch us. That is, assuming there has been a theft, if our guys did it."

"Sonny boy comes from a seriously influential family with a serious bank account and serious political influence in this city," said Don. "I don't doubt that sonny boy's mom knew where he kept his cash and about how much he had. She probably gave him most if not all of it."

"Are you coming down to Records with me?" Chuck asked as he got up from his desk.

"Sure, but after this we need to stop and give everything that's happened a chance to settle before we start with the assumptions. I think that should be done over a sandwich and coffee."

"Food and sex, it's always food and sex with you. You really need to talk to the department shrink about that. I'm sure he'd find some oral fixation and lack of maternal affection thing. Or it might be as simple as being too closely attached to your need for immediate gratification."

"Thanks, Sigmund, the check will be in the mail. Now let's go before you start getting all analytical about my dreams of kicking your ass from time to time."

"In your dreams," Chuck said with his almost smile.

Chuck and Don walked past the back door to the lineup room on their way to the stairs that would take them to the fourth floor and the Records Unit. As they passed the lineup room door, it opened and the night janitor, Wally Fox, walked out. He was pushing a mop bucket by the mop handle. The lights were still on in the lineup room. Don noted that the floor in the room was dry. It hadn't experienced the attention of a mop in all the time that Don had been assigned to the fifth floor. *Maybe he was taking a nap. He's been working long hours lately,* thought Don.

There was something a little different about Fox since Don last saw him. He had cleaned up just a little. He had a fresh haircut and was sporting a short and rather stylish beard, or what would be a beard when it grew out a little. The shapeless work uniform that Fox was known for had been replaced by a pair of clean blue jeans and a clean, tan, long-sleeved shirt. *What the...* was Don's thought.

"Got yourself a new girlfriend, Wally?" Don asked as they walked past him.

Wally grunted in a barely audible response, "No, why?"

"You're looking good, and you seem to be spending more time here during the day. I can see that nights would cramp your dating life a little."

"Yeah, I suppose so," Wally grunted.

Don's immediate thought was *If it's a woman that's influencing Wally to dress better and pay some attention to his appearance, she must be a serious piece of work.*

The suicide report was on file in Records, so Don and Chuck had the clerk burn them a copy. There was no follow-up report attached to it, which meant that the detective or detectives were still working on it. That was unusual since it appeared to have been determined to be suicide at the scene. The only loose string would be the autopsy report. Don and Chuck took the report with the intent of reading it over lunch.

Lunch was a sandwich at a dive in Georgetown, a mostly industrial area near Boeing Field. The few people who called Georgetown home were a mix of homeowners who mostly took pride in their working-class roots and the truly down-and-out who found affordable rooms to rent and generally lived off the community, giving nothing back but a bad reputation.

"It looks like there was no evidence of foul play," Don said through a mouth half full of pastrami on rye with hot mustard and sauerkraut.

"Your mother obviously failed to tell you about talking with your mouth full," said Chuck.

"Yes, yes she did. That among many other things she failed to tell me. Her most serious failure was not warning me against working with a smart-ass. Now, as I was saying, this looks like a straight-up suicide. And if it was a straight-up suicide, why was anybody from Homicide called out? One other item comes to mind: there is no mention of money being found on the body or in the house, but there is mention that Sergeant Sherman, Grimes, and Martin responded to the scene."

"If it was an obvious suicide, why would anyone search the house?" Chuck asked. "Maybe the money was in plain view, so anyone would have seen it, in which case it would be difficult to take it without being noticed. And even if whoever might have taken it did take it, there would have to be an entry in the report and the money would have to be placed into evidence. So assuming the money was there as sonny boy's mom said, it would probably have been where it required a search to locate. And if a search was required, it would obviously cast some suspicion on someone who happened to be at the scene and who might have had some legitimate reason to do a search. Would a cop be stupid enough to cast suspicion on himself? I don't think the department has a lot of stupid people on board, maybe some very thoughtless and greedy people but few stupid people."

"Given who sonny boy was and who Mom is and who Mom happens to be married to, I guess we can assume that Mom knows what she's talking about," Don mused. "Given all that, I'm guessing that the way to get a handle on whether Grimes, Martin, and Sherman are responsible for the theft of the money is to look at how they happen to be spending money. If Grimes actually has his clothes cleaned, that would be a sure indication that he has come into some extra cash. If Martin gets a new gadget for that cop car lookalike he drives around, we can be pretty sure that he is drawing on a new source of income. Who knows what Sherman would be spending money on to make his life complete."

"I think we should just sit on this for the time being," said Chuck.

"I think you're right," said Don through a mouth full of pastrami and sauerkraut. "Besides, I think two murders trump a theft."

"We go on nights next month. There might be a little more spare time then to devote to this latest kettle of worms," Chuck added.

After the pastrami and sauerkraut had taken care of the hunger pangs he had been suffering, Don came up with another brilliant idea. "How about if we stop by Radio and listen to the suicide call on tape? That might give us some idea of how Sherman and his boys found themselves there."

It took the on-duty Radio sergeant all of five minutes to pull up the call. The recorded call was classified a death, probable suicide, at a very posh address on Lake Washington. The patrol officer assigned responded, and a few seconds later Sergeant Sherman came on the air. He, Grimes, and Martin were on the street and offered to back the officer on the call.

Chuck and Don looked at each other with an understanding that didn't require words.

"Can we get a copy of that tape, Sarge?" Don asked.

As they left Radio, Don and Chuck felt a lot more confident that Mom was telling the truth about sonny boy and his box full of money.

CHAPTER TWENTY-FIVE

Don's trip home on the water taxi was an opportunity to think once more about where his life was going, an all-too-frequent occurrence. He had already concluded that bringing one more woman in the form of the very attractive Officer Victoria Morris into his life was not the smartest move he could make. He congratulated himself on his restraint. Mixing job and romance wasn't a good idea under the best of circumstances. That would have to be applied to his apparently blossoming relationship with Dr. J. Wyman Mills, pathologist and assistant medical examiner. She, like him, seemed to be committed to being a loner at home surrounded by fair to good artworks and great food. The periodic sexual encounter was about all she was looking for, if he read her right. Roseanne Vargas was sort of in that gray area. She wasn't exactly in his line of work, but she had some strings attached to him in a legal sense. He could find himself in a conflict of interest if she was defending one of the dirt bags he happened to put in jail. But she was so damn attractive and available. Those features could cover a lot of the negatives.

Then there was Tiffany Winslow. She wasn't on the water taxi with Don, leaving him with a short time to review his life. He missed being with her on the taxi and walking up the hill by her side. Her only connection to law enforcement that he was aware of was him. She liked cats and art and had a great sense of humor, all serious pluses in his opinion. She was good to look at with or without clothes. *Careful, Don, you're coming off like some kind of Sherlock Holmes, but you're thinking about women, not solving crimes*, thought Don.

When he reached the water taxi pier in West Seattle, Don was thinking more clearly about how he wanted to proceed, romantically speaking. Instead of walking up the hill as he usually did when Tiffany was with him, he took the shuttle to the top and got off. He turned west instead of east toward his townhouse.

When he reached Tiffany's door, he had it all worked out about what he would tell her. He knocked at the door and waited. There was no answer after a minute, so he pulled a note pad from his jacket pocket and wrote a note asking her to call him when she got home. After he tucked the note behind the door knocker, Don turned to leave and saw movement at the window beside the door. It was George and Martha with their paws on the windowsill. Both were looking at him as if they were old buddies. Don thought for a moment that they might wave, but they didn't. *I'm even falling for her cats,* Don thought as he began the walk toward home.

After checking his mail and throwing most of it into the recycle bin, Don walked to his door. He noticed a piece of paper rolled up and shoved between the door handle and the door. He took it out, catching a slight whiff of a familiar scent: Tiffany's. "Don, I left work early and thought I'd stop by to see if you were home, but no luck. Call me when you read this and maybe we can get together this evening for a bite somewhere." It was signed "Tiffany."

Don thought about what had just happened for a few moments. They must have passed somewhere on the street between his townhouse and her house, strange.

When he tossed the mail on the kitchen counter, Don noticed that he had a phone message. Rather than listen to it, he called Tiffany. She answered after two rings. This was getting serious.

"We're like ships passing in the night," Tiffany said, apparently assuming that it was him.

"Yeah, we must have taken different routes. Massachusetts is the shortest, so that's what I took."

"If I was walking, that's what I'd have taken, but I rode my bike today. That's why you didn't see me on the water taxi this morning; I've got to keep the old bicycle butt thing going. Besides, it was a perfect day for a bike ride."

"I'm going to have to get on the stick and start riding to work again now that the weather is more agreeable. Then there's that bicycle butt thing that I have to maintain as well. Is that something that women notice?"

"Yes we do, and yours is a specimen worthy of a cover of *Bicycling* magazine. But let's get on another subject; I think George and Martha are getting a little uncomfortable. How about tonight, where would you like to have dinner?"

Don thought for a second and said, "How about here at my place? You haven't been here. You can check out my taste in art and decide whether we have a future and check out my cooking. I'm not a great cook, but I'm OK. It's mostly vegetarian stuff that I put together, but a little meat sneaks in now and then."

"That's a great idea. I'll have to take George and Martha on a short walk and feed them; then I'll be over. I'll ride my bike."

"OK, see you when you get here."

Don took pride in his skill in the kitchen; it didn't take him much time to come up with a dish or two that were not only good but were also appealing to the eye and body. Pasta was not only easy but it was tasty as well, in Don's opinion. It sometimes got a bad rap because it was high in carbohydrates, but Don knew that only people who never got off their asses needed to be concerned about carbohydrates.

Don just happened to have fresh tomatoes, basil, and Parmesan cheese in the refrigerator. He would need to make a quick trip to the market just up the street to get some bread and a bottle of so-so wine. He was out Trader Joe's Two Buck Chuck. Trader Joe's was too far away at such short notice. A nice little "House Red" or "Big House Red" would have to make do.

Don went to his garage via the inside entrance. He opened the garage door and drove out, closing the door behind him. The Subaru hadn't been out of the garage for a few days; it could use some gas and an oil change. He'd have to fit those things in. As he drove away, he didn't notice that there was a car parked down the block with a man behind the wheel. The man was just sitting there. He had been there for quite a while.

Don hadn't returned from the market when Tiffany rode her bicycle into his driveway. She had a bottle of wine stuck down one of the pockets in her jersey. It was Two Buck Chuck Shiraz, Don's favorite. She got off her bike and pushed it along the path leading to his front door where she propped it against a wall and rang the bell. There was no answer.

The man in the car took notice of the woman, got out of his car, and walked across the street to the sidewalk that would lead to Don's townhouse.

He was careful not to be noticed, however, and walked by as if he had a reason for being there that wouldn't raise suspicion. He wanted to get a good look at the woman and find out where she lived. As he was about to turn and go back toward Don's townhouse, he saw Don's car coming toward him. He quickly turned to cross the street; Don would recognize him. He could sit in his car a little longer and watch for the woman to leave and follow her.

As Don's garage door opened, Tiffany was pushing her bike toward the street with the intention of going home. She was confused about finding Don gone when he had told her to come over. She saw his car drive into the garage just as she came around the side of the garage. When Don got out of his car and bent over to retrieve a bag of groceries, Tiffany walked up behind him and yelled, "Stick 'em up, mister."

"OK, but please don't take my virtue, that's all I ask."

"I'm afraid that your virtue was taken long ago, pardner."

Don turned around with the bag of groceries in his hand and confronted the robber.

"On second thought, you can have my virtue, such as it is."

Tiffany took the bag from Don's hands and kissed him.

"Why thank you, ma'am; that was mighty nice."

"Yes it was," said Tiffany. Then she kissed him again.

This was the first time that Don had seen Tiffany in a biking jersey. By their nature, biking jerseys were tight—on the female body, a serious asset. The jersey was pulled tighter by the bottle in one of the pockets. None of this was lost on Don who was thinking that he was very happy to have decided that Tiffany was a woman worthy of serious consideration. Now the question was did she think he was worthy of the same consideration? He could only hope.

"What say we take this show inside so I can make dinner?"

They walked in through the interior door. Don closed the garage door with the button on the wall as they entered his townhouse.

"Nice. I thought that men, especially cops, were slobs. The exceptions are always gay or weird in some unhealthy way," Tiffany said as they walked into the kitchen.

"Guilty on all counts; I'm a weird gay guy who gets off on a clean and tastefully decorated home. Actually, I shouldn't make light of the fact that I just like to live in a clean and artfully decorated home. There's nothing like looking forward to coming home to a great place that contains art to admire and good ingredients in the refrigerator with which to make a tasty meal. That's what gives life meaning. Not to make too fine a point of it or become too preachy, but my partner, Chuck, has added a lot more to my life than just being a good partner; he's gay. He has a beautiful condo on Capitol Hill that he takes great pride in. His life is worthy of anyone's admiration. But there is his messy love life."

"Well said. Now let's make dinner; I'm starved."

It didn't take long for Don and Tiffany, working side by side, to put together a meal worthy of any Italian restaurant. While they were making the meal, they drank from Don's bottle of House Red, saving the Two Buck Chuck for another time.

Following the meal, which both agreed was just short of fantabulous, Don asked Tiffany if she wanted a tour of his art collection. Since his taste in art was eclectic, he didn't have any doubts that they could get along on that basis.

"Lead on," Tiffany said. They walked along the entry hall where he had almost every available space on the wall covered by a piece of art. Some were prints, but most were originals. A lot of it was by local artists whose style Don liked. There were brooding watercolors of mountains and water. There were cityscapes that showed off Seattle at its best and its worst. One of Don's favorite watercolors depicted an alley in Pioneer Square. It was almost possible to smell the urine-saturated brick when standing in front of it.

"It looks like you may pass muster. I haven't seen anything yet that would lead to an immediate separation."

When they reached the living room, the ceiling soared above them. It went from eight feet in the hallway to sixteen feet in a step. To maintain the scale of the room, Don had placed one large painting on the wall that faced the windows overlooking Elliot Bay. It was a Jackson Pollock, and it was big like most work by Pollock. It was surrounded by several smaller pieces, leaving it the center of attention.

"Is that for real?" was all that Tiffany could say as she stood with her mouth slightly open in a way that Don found very sexy. "You must know what you have there, don't you?"

"Yes, as a matter of fact, I do. My grandparents, then my parents owned it. They gave it to me when they felt I had become responsible enough to appreciate and take proper care of it. They made the gift on one condition, however. If I can no longer care for it, I have to give it to the Walker Art Museum in Minneapolis. They were aware of my interest in art even though I was always a little rough around the edges."

Tiffany looked critically at the work's location. She looked at the window wall that faced the bay and at the glass. She glanced at the work from the side, apparently looking at how it was hung.

"What glass is the window made of?"

"It won't let any UV in, and the hanger was professionally installed. It will not fall in an earthquake. And the townhouse is alarmed."

"I can only make an educated guess at its value. Is it insured?"

"Snoopy little bugger, aren't you?"

"Art is my life. Now that I know that this is here, I'll worry about it. You have enormous responsibility to care for it."

"I know all that, and I'm very happy that you know what it is; most don't or don't particularly care. I made the mistake of talking about it around some detectives one day, and one of them asked why I would hang a fish on my wall."

"I like the fish, but I like the painting even more. Now, if I can regain control of my legs, let's continue the tour."

The tour took them to the second floor and along a hallway that led to two bedrooms and a study. An eclectic array of prints, posters, photographs, and original oils and acrylics covered the hallway. The final stop on the tour was Don's bedroom overlooking Elliot Bay and downtown Seattle. It, too, made Tiffany weak in the knees. There was a small deck separated from the bedroom by French doors. An iron spiral stairway led to a fenced-in garden. Don had the impression that Tiffany would have said yes to a proposal of marriage at that moment even though they had known each for a short time. Then he figuratively slapped himself, pulling his ego back in check.

It was no accident that Don ended the tour in his bedroom. Tiffany's butt had been enticing him since she arrived. It was covered in black Lycra that enhanced every curve and valley. Not only were Lycra shorts functional on a bike, they were a great conversation starter.

"Did I ever tell you that you have the greatest case of bicycle butt I have ever seen?"

"Why yes, yes you have. You can see it without the Lycra if you play your cards right."

Don took that as an invitation to explore the contours under the Lycra and went to work. Under the many and varied artworks that covered the walls of Don's bedroom, they did their best to massage the day's kinks from each other's bodies. Sex and art were high on both of their lists of things that made life worth living.

It was almost midnight when Tiffany sat up in Don's bed and told him that she had to go home to the cats. She had to work in the morning, and George and Martha had to be wondering where she was.

"I'll drive you; it's too late to be riding your bike."

"I'll be OK; it's a short ride on deserted streets."

Tiffany got out of bed, quickly dressed in her biking kit, and walked downstairs with Don close behind. They went through the living room where Tiffany took another long look at the Pollock, now cast in the dim light filtering through the window wall. Reluctantly, she left the Pollock and walked to the garage to get her bicycle. Don opened the garage door, letting Tiffany push her bike onto the drive. She threw a leg over the top tube and locked into one pedal. They performed a little more tongue gymnastics, and then Tiffany rolled away, clipping into the other pedal.

After Don watched her ride away and fade into the dark, he closed the garage door and returned to his bed. He didn't notice the car that had been parked up the street slowly leave its parking space and follow Tiffany with its lights out.

It was about thirty minutes later that Don's phone rang; it was Tiffany.

"Someone tried to kill me, Don!"

"What? Is this you? What happened? Where are you?"

"Don, a man drove up behind me with no lights and ran his car into me! He forced me into the curb! I fell off my bike and rolled onto the sidewalk! I have a few scratches, but my bike is a wreck! What's going on?"

Don's thoughts returned to the night that Roseanne was attacked after leaving his townhouse, where they had spent time exploring each other's anatomy. What was the connection?

"I don't know, but I'll be right there. Are you at home?"

"Yes, I pushed my bike."

Don called the dispatcher and asked that a patrol car be sent to Tiffany's so she could file a report, then he got dressed, making sure that he had his service weapon.

When he got to Tiffany's, she was in the kitchen cleaning a scraped knee and elbow. He pitched in by finding a hand brush so he could do a thorough job.

"If you think you're going to work on me with that, you've got another think coming, mister."

"If you were at Harborview or if I was a fire medic, you would get a scrubbing. There are all sorts of nasty things that can infect scrapes like those; they need to be scrubbed."

Tiffany whimpered only slightly as Don went to work. George and Martha did not take it as well, however. They watched the whole process as though their mom was being tortured.

"Did you see the car that hit you?"

"I heard it coming from behind me. The next thing I knew, it was beside me, very close beside me. It slowed to my speed, and then the driver turned into me. I didn't have time to swerve to the right before it hit me with the right front door. The glancing blow saved me. If it had hit me from behind, I would still be lying on the street."

"Could you describe the car?"

"It happened too fast, but I know that it was a full-size American make, probably a Dodge or Ford, and it was dark. The streetlights weren't much help, but I think it was dark green or brown, maybe blue."

"It would be asking too much that you identify the driver."

"All I know is that he was white. I was going to holler at him when he turned into me, so I saw that much."

"Is your bike in the garage? When the officer gets here, I'm going to check to see if there was any paint transfer."

"The officer? You called an officer?"

"This has to be reported so that it might be possible to develop some sort of pattern. This was no accident. He probably followed you from my place with the idea that he might find you on a lonely street where he could rape you. Then he lost his nerve when you crashed."

"Rape me? Why on earth would anyone want to rape me?"

"People are raped, and not all are as pretty as you. He might have been an opportunist who saw you leave my place, or he saw you cross California. Who knows? But one thing I do know, this is the second time that a female friend of mine has been attacked. It might just be coincidental, or it might be something else."

"Are you saying that any woman who gets involved with you is at risk?"

"In your case, you're at risk of being lavished with my attention that borders on love. Maybe it's even love."

"OK, you can continue scrubbing if you feel that way. By the way, I have the same feelings for you, bordering on love and maybe love, and the lavish part fits as well."

Don kissed her lightly as he scrubbed her scrapes until they bled a little more. Then he dried them, applied some first-aid ointment, and bandaged them.

The officer arrived as Don was finishing bandaging Tiffany's wounds. He was an officer whom Don knew only by name. He had read several of his reports and was impressed with the way he went about his initial investigations. He was not one of the report takers whom Don disliked almost as much as he disliked Bainbridge Islanders and others too numerous to name. *Worthless fucks*, he thought.

"Would you like to have Fire look at you? You might have a concussion and not be aware of it," the officer said with concern that might have been motivated by Tiffany's looks or by very real concern for her welfare. Don thought it was the latter, given what he knew of the officer's reputation, but he couldn't be sure. Who could blame him if it was the former?

"I didn't hit my head on anything. Here's my helmet. See, no scratches or dents."

As the officer took Tiffany's report, Don went to the garage where Tiffany's bike lay like a wounded animal on the floor. The front wheel would never again serve its purpose, but it still turned in the fork. The handlebars were twisted in the stem and bent up on one side. But the death knell for the bike was the frame where it had suffered an irreparable bend in one chain stay. If there was any paint transfer, Don could not find it. He would ask the officer to take it to the Evidence Unit so people who knew about such things could examine it a little more thoroughly and under better lighting.

By the time Don was finished and had walked back to the kitchen, the officer had taken all the necessary notes for his report. "Your bike is toast, I'm sorry to report. I'm going to send it with the officer as evidence."

"But what am I going to use for a bike?"

"Your bike is no longer road worthy, so we can talk about what we'll do about replacing it."

After the officer collected the bike, loaded it, and was on his way, Don started talking about what they could do about her biking future.

"I feel that I owe you a bike. Let's think about what you want, and we'll go and find it on our next day off."

"The bike I want I'm not sure you can afford."

"I can afford a Pollock for my wall; why wouldn't I be able to afford a bicycle of your choosing?"

"The Pollock was a gift from your grandparents and parents."

"Along with the gift of the Pollock was a seriously sizable inheritance. Most detectives don't live in a place like mine or indulge in things that I have or things that I do. Believe me, I can afford anything in the way of a bike that you might want."

"If I may be so bold, tell me how your grandparents got so rich. They weren't from Sicily, were they?"

Don considered her question for a while and decided that filling her in on his past, at least part of it, would be a good way of getting her mind off the trauma she had just experienced.

"It seems that my grandfather arrived on Minnesota's Iron Range at a time when iron mining was taking off with a vengeance. He was fresh off a boat from Finland and a train from New York. When he landed in a small town called Hibbing, he had only a few dollars in his pocket. However, what he lacked in money, he more than made up for in foresight. He saw iron miners flooding into a town with very few places to stay or eat. With the few dollars he had, he bought the items necessary to make lunches that he sold on the street. They were so good that his reputation grew until he was the go-to guy for a lunch pail full of food. As his profits grew, he was able to swing a loan for a boarding house where he continued his lunch business and boarded several miners. As time progressed, he bought another building and added another boarding house, then a laundry to wash the miners' clothes. Before his empire was complete, he had the market on boarding houses on the Iron Range. Then he built the finest hotel the Iron Range had ever seen. That's when he and my grandmother started to look at art as a way of giving something back to the community. When they died, they had artworks and property that were worth several million. I was the only grandchild, so I benefited from their foresight. The Pollock was the last painting they added to their collection before they died. Pollock was new on the art scene, but they saw something in him that others may not have."

"A Colnago isn't out of the question? Is that what you're saying?"

"Yes, a Colnago, a Gitane, a Bianchi, a Masi, or whatever else you think would fit between your legs is definitely in the question. I hear that a fairly new company called Trek is making a good bike."

"How about this weekend? Should we start the search this weekend?"

"OK, we'll start looking this weekend."

"Do you mind if I stay with you tonight?" Don asked.

"I thought you'd never ask," Tiffany said, apparently forgetting her scrapes and bruises.

CHAPTER TWENTY-SIX

Night shift in the Homicide Unit wasn't really nights in the usual sense; it started at four and ended at midnight or until the job was done. Sometimes the night shift ended long after the sun came up the following day. The night shift wasn't on Don's list of favorite things, but there were a few benefits. Among them was the absence of the brass. Most of them left at or near four. It wasn't that Don disliked most of the brass, but not having them around had a liberating effect.

Then there was the dress code. While it didn't go out the window, it did drift toward the casual and, in some cases, the sloppy. Then there was Marjorie who seemed to get even more creative in her dress on nights. *God bless her* was Don's thought and that of most of the others on the squad. Some of the brass would have found her costumes—they couldn't be called anything but—unacceptable on the day shift. Don couldn't walk past her on this, the first night shift, without a congratulatory comment on her taste. This, the first night shift, was special.

"Marjorie, is there something different about you today? Have you re-arranged your anatomy in some way?"

"Yes I have. You recall that I went to Vancouver on my vacation, don't you? There's this great plastic surgeon up there who does outstanding breast enhancement surgery. I went from a thirty-four A to a thirty-six C in no time."

"He did nice work; you're a new woman. It must have cost you an arm and a leg, so to speak."

"It was a gift from my admirers. Now there's more for them to admire."

"They are truly beautiful."

"Thank you. You're welcome to explore them anytime you like."

"I'll have to give that some thought," Don gulped. *Get a grip,* he thought. "Am I the first one in?" Don asked the very alluring Marjorie while trying unsuccessfully to pry his eyes away from her over-exposed and very attractive chest.

"No, Chuck came in about fifteen minutes ago, and then he left a few minutes later. He said that he'd be back shortly."

"Thanks, see you later," Don said as he turned to walk back to his cubicle.

"We can only hope," said Marjorie.

Man, this is going to be a long month was Don's thought as he continued on.

Although not anywhere near the show that Marjorie put on, there was the parking benefit. Parking around the Public Safety Building during the day was a royal pain. The night-shift detectives parked in the building wherever space was available. Don liked to park between motor pool cars since they were less likely to be used on nights, which reduced the chance that his doors would be dinged. His Subaru wasn't exactly new and pristine, but it was in good condition, and he wanted to keep it that way.

Don walked into the Homicide Unit, which was void of detectives, not unusual when he worked nights. He and Chuck tended to be the first to arrive and the last to leave. It also occurred to him that the others didn't do much in the way of casework during the month that they spent on nights. But they didn't do much on day shift either, come to think of it.

What caught Don's eye when he walked into his cubicle were the new computers on his and Chuck's desks. On the desk in front of his computer was a stack of instructions on the use of the thing. Don's thought was that he would need more than a stack of paper to make him proficient on it.

Beside the computer was a pile of the usual mail that asked for the usual stuff. The prosecutor's office wanted more information on this or that case. The crime lab finally came through with something he needed to get a case out of a rut. There were phone messages to answer or not, depending on their source. Just when he was about to open the files on the two murders that Chuck and he were working, Chuck walked in with a smile on his face that might indicate he had just taken in the feast that Marjorie offered to the male eye, gay or straight.

"Say, Chuck, did you notice anything different about Marjorie today?"

"Yeah, quite the chest reconstruction; I'd like to feel them just to get a sense of whether or not they retained their natural suppleness."

"I know what you mean. There's nothing like that malleable nature of the female breast. I get goose bumps just thinking about it, academically speaking, of course."

"Of course, professor," Chuck said.

"If we can get beyond Marjorie's breasts for a second, I have something that might interest you."

"Shoot."

"There was a phone message from Maurice, our pimp in residence, on my desk when I came in. He said that Shondra saw the guy who assaulted her. She was plying her trade on Aurora last Saturday night when the guy stopped and got out of his car. When he saw her, he got back in and drove away."

"Did she get a license number?"

"A partial. The first three were BMP, or that's what she thinks they were; she's not certain. She knows that the first letter was B and that the car was a dark, full-size American make. It was not a Cadillac. Maurice made a point of that. It was dark in color and a four-door. She said that the guy seemed a little better groomed than the night he assaulted her."

"OK, how many full-size American-made cars that are dark in color and have a B as the first letter on the plate are there in Seattle? Just a guess."

"Quite a few."

"I would guess that you're right. But, in Shondra's defense, this along with the sketch and where she saw him, we have more to add to the bulletin."

"Right, let's get that out and hand-deliver some to the North Precinct since he seems to be prowling there," said Chuck.

"OK, and we can have dinner up there while we're at it."

"Why we don't weigh about three hundred pounds is what I don't get," Chuck said.

On their way to check out a car, Don and Chuck stopped at Marjorie's desk to reassess her new chest. They both agreed, after they left her hearing range, that she had been correct in selecting the size she now displayed. Anything bigger would have been tasteless. The cleavage possibilities, given her current size, were endless.

Pool cars were located on three floors in the Public Safety Building. They weren't assigned spaces; the last person to use one was supposed to write its location in grease pencil on the fob. The car that they were assigned was on the bottom floor, the floor that was truly in the bowels of the building. Even Don found the place creepy at night when he had to go there alone. It was not a floor you wanted to be on when the next seven-point earthquake struck.

Their assigned car was squeezed among several other pool cars and a few employees' personal cars. When Don unlocked the driver's door, he looked at the car next to it. It was an older four-door Dodge. It had a few dings on the right side along with a long scratch that extended from the front door post to the middle of the back door. The scratch was at about bicycle handlebar height.

Don closed the pool car's door and looked more closely at the scratch. There was no paint transfer as he had hoped for, but there was something as interesting: a smudged fabric pattern stamped in the dirt that coated the front door and the rest of the car.

"Chuck, look at this and tell me what you think."

Chuck came around from the passenger side of the pool car and squeezed between the two cars.

"It's my guess that the car hit something or someone, don't you agree?"

"That would be my guess."

They walked to the front of the Dodge and checked the plate. It was Washington BNR626.

"Shondra's rapist was driving BMP, or that's what she thought, right?" Don asked.

"Let's check with Data and see who the registered owner of this piece of shit is. I can't see a cop driving something like this, can you?" was Chuck's response.

Chuck pulled his radio from his briefcase and was about to key the mike when Don stopped him.

"Let's not advertise what we're doing. If this does belong to a cop, he might get wind that we're interested in his car. Let's walk up to Radio and keep it quiet."

Don and Chuck went to the second floor where Radio was located. All of the 911 calls in the city came to that darkened room. Several operators, one for each precinct and one to handle data calls, were spread around the room. Given the number and types of calls that came in, Don was always amazed at how calm and quiet the room was.

They went to the supervising sergeant's desk and told her what they wanted. The supervisor didn't hesitate to get on her commuter and run the plate.

Don's and Chuck's mouths dropped just slightly when they looked at the Department of Licensing response on the screen. The car was registered to Wally Fox, janitor on the fifth floor. The address under his name was in West Seattle but in the White Center neighborhood, aka "Rat City," well south of Don's townhouse and in another social stratum.

When the supervisor printed the information on the screen and gave the printout to Don, he asked her to keep it under her hat; she agreed. Next they asked her to run a criminal history and arrest record on Fox. He had neither.

"That means no mug shot to show Shondra," Don said as they walked back down to their car. Then he had an idea. "Let's go back to the office, get the Polaroid, and take a couple pictures of the car. We can show Shondra those and get some idea where to go from there. We should take a look at our bulletin, too. Wally might just be the match that Marjorie was trying to come up with."

Don drove the city car out of its stall to give them more room to take pictures of Fox's car. As Don took the last picture of the right side where the scratch and smudge were located, a light bulb came on over his head.

"I need to make a call before we go. Wait here in case Wally shows up."

"OK, but make it quick; I'm getting hungry," Chuck said with a slight whine.

Don went back to his cubicle and called Tiffany who just happened to be home and who just happened to answer on the second ring.

"Do you recall if you touched the car that ran you into the curb?"

"What, no 'Hi, how are you' or 'I really miss you?'"

"Hi, Tiffany, how are you, and I really do miss you. This month is going to be tough because I miss checking out your butt on the water taxi."

"That's better. Yes, I think I pushed myself off the car with my left hand. Why do you ask?"

"We just came across a car that may, I repeat, may have been involved in another incident. It has some interesting marks on it that may have resulted from coming into contact with a bicycle. It's a serious long shot, but it's all we have."

"Thank you for thinking of me. I miss you, too. It will be a long month. What do think this means?"

"I think it means that we really like each other. What's the area between really like and love? Is it live?"

The phone was silent for a short time, and then Tiffany said, "My guess is that it's very simple. You found me because you admire my butt. I enjoyed your appreciation of my butt. We finally acknowledged that we had something in common, and the commonalities started a life that's turned into something pretty nifty. I think that's what brings two people together, just those small things that grow into bigger things. You go from anatomy to bigger things. Oh, by the way, it's not 'live,' it's love. I love you, Don Lake."

The phone went silent for a few seconds while Don sat down.

"I get off at midnight. Are you going to be home then?"

"I'll be in bed but nudge me."

"OK," Don said with a slightly raspy voice. "I'll try not to wake George and Martha."

Don was almost out of his cubicle when he remembered that he needed to pull the bulletins out of their file. He unlocked the drawer, found the file, and pulled the bulletins from it. He gave the top one a quick once-over. It did not look like Fox. He kept the bulletins and locked the drawer.

He walked from his cubicle and past Marjorie without checking her new breasts. He didn't fully wake up until he was on the lower parking deck. Chuck had his hands cupped against a rear window of Fox's car when Don walked onto the deck.

"See anything that might be good enough for a search warrant?"

"There's a pair of boots without laces on the back floor, a couple of well-used towels on the backseat, and a lot of just plain junk scattered around. There's nothing to give us probable cause for a warrant," Chuck said.

"I just talked to Tiffany. She said that she pushed herself off the side of the car that ran her off the street. Let's check for a palm print."

They looked at the area where the fabric smudge and scratch were and found what might have been the imprint of a palm, but it was so smudged that it couldn't be of any comparison value. They photographed the smudge anyway.

"If we show Shondra the pictures and she says that this is definitely the car that her rapist was driving when she saw him on Aurora, then what? Do we go with that? One letter in a license plate is pretty thin for a warrant. Any defense attorney who has been out of law school longer than a week will pick that warrant apart with both hands tied behind his or her back."

Chuck thought for a second and then said, "She gave the sketch an eight and a half, right? Does the sketch resemble Fox? I don't think it does, but if we had a photo of Fox to put in a montage, it would get even better if she picked him. We need to get a photo from DOL. But let's not get carried away until we eat. I'm so hungry I could eat the ass out of a skunk."

"Now that's a great image to carry into a restaurant. Where did you come up with that one?"

"From you."

"Oh yeah, I recall now. That was when I was trying to reform you from the refined lad I found when we became partners in the south end. I'm pleased to know that my efforts weren't wasted," Don said.

"I hope you're proud of what you've created," Chuck said in an exaggerated whine.

"I still have work to do, but you've come a long way." Then Don handed the bulletin to Chuck who confirmed what he already knew.

As they drove north on I-5, Don began his usual thinking aloud. Chuck got concerned when Don got into this mode while he was behind the wheel. On I-5 it was important to devote full attention to driving was Chuck's opinion.

"If Marjorie comes out of nowhere with a new pair of boobs, what does that mean?"

"It means that...," Chuck started to respond.

"We know that she couldn't afford the boob job. We also know that the suspicion is that someone in the unit pilfered money from a suicide scene. We also know that we don't tend to go to suicides unless the circumstances look questionable. What do you think?" Don asked pretty much to himself.

"I think that you need to attend to traffic and getting us to a restaurant in one piece. Where are you taking us, by the way?" Chuck said.

"I hadn't thought of that. Where would you like to go?" Don asked.

"How about that Denny's on Fifteenth in Ballard?"

"You're not talking about squalling kid central?"

"That was only one time. I'm sure that there aren't squalling kids there every night."

"OK, but if you're wrong, you pay," Don said.

"How someone with as much money as you have can be so cheap is beyond me," Chuck said.

"How do you suppose I got so much money?"

"You inherited it, like most rich assholes."

"There is that, but I keep it by being cheap."

Don parked in the lot behind the restaurant. The only available space was between two minivans, one with a child's seat visible.

"Looks like you're going to be paying, Chuck." Don said, pointing with a thumb at the van's seat.

"Always the pessimist, aren't you?"

The Denny's they walked into wasn't the greatest one around, but the food was predictable. That was the great thing about Denny's in Don's opinion: its food in Seattle was indistinguishable from that in Paducah, Illinois, not that Don had been in Paducah. It was all pretty good. However, there were the kids.

The waitress, whose name tag over her very ample left breast, which matched her right breast, identified her as Kelly, showed them to a booth toward the back of the dining room. She gave them a smile and menus and said that she would be back. Chuck could only hope; skunk's ass was looking better all the time.

"No squalling kids, Don. I guess you'll have to get off that wallet for a change."

"It's early. Just wait."

When Kelly came back to take their orders, Chuck ordered chicken-fried steak. It came with mashed potatoes, green beans, and a roll. He decided to go with coffee since it was early in the shift. Don ordered a veggie burger, side salad, and Diet Coke.

"Veggie burger? Why would someone even think up such a thing?" Chuck asked with a certain amount of honest disdain. "That sounds like something that's trying to be meat but isn't. Why not just call it beans on a bun or peas where they shouldn't be? Something like that?"

"I'll try to forget that you're ridiculing my diet. I try my best to avoid comments about your wardrobe," Don said in his best hurt feelings mode.

"Sorry, Don," Chuck said just as a young kid started squalling about four booths away.

"Guess I'll be sitting on my wallet tonight. I hope you don't have a problem paying for my travesty of a meal."

After listening to thirty minutes of pretty much nonstop squall, Don and Chuck left, wondering how such a small critter could produce so much misery.

With brat central in the rearview mirror, their first stop was the North Precinct where they dropped off a stack of bulletins. They then drove back along Fifteenth Avenue to Western, up Denny to Second Avenue that took them to Cherry and into the Public Safety Building. Don maneuvered the car down to the lower deck in hopes of finding Fox's car still parked there. It wasn't.

"Do you think old Wally goes out for lunch, or maybe he's out chasing hookers?" Don asked rhetorically.

"I suppose he does. Both, that is."

"That question was rhetorical, Chuck."

"You forget that I don't have all the fancy degrees that you do, so you'll have to explain the meaning of rhetorical."

"Well, you see, Chuck, a rhetorical question is one..."

"I was being facetious, Don."

"You'll have to enlighten me on the meaning of facetious, Chuck."

"Screw you, Don."

"That I understand."

"Thank you. I thought for a moment that I'd have to shoot you in the leg. Can we get on with what the taxpayers of this city pay us for?"

Don and Chuck returned to their cubicle via Marjorie's desk. Don was disappointed that she wasn't there. He looked forward to her as if she was the dessert he didn't have after their meal at brat central.

They walked into the office to find that they were alone, not all that unusual on night shift. It wasn't unusual during days, come to think of it.

"I'll call DOL for a picture of Wally," Chuck said. "Give Shondra a call. Ask if she can get out of bed long enough to look at the Polaroids."

Don took out his keys to unlock his file drawer where he kept the case file. He unlocked the drawer with some difficulty and looked at his files. They seemed to have been moved around. He was neat about his files, and these weren't neat. He pulled out the file on Shondra that he kept separate from Chuck's and noticed another change: the last two pages of his follow-up report were upside down. That was something he never did.

"Chuck, someone has been in my file drawer. Look at this."

Chuck hadn't had time to call DOL when Don called his attention to his files.

"Yeah, I think we have a new concern. Locking up our files hasn't quite gotten the point across, but I can't see why any of the detectives would leave files in that condition. He would have to be drunk or stupid to do that."

"That pretty much covers the rest of the squad," Don said.

"Agreed," Chuck said as he opened his file drawer. "I'm guessing that someone has been in mine as well. I line them up along this side, and they're now lined along this side."

"Being the tight-assed housekeepers that we are serves some purpose, doesn't it?"

"Is that a rhetorical question, Don?"

"You learn fast for a puke from Capitol Hill."

"Shall we start again? You call Shondra and I'll call DOL. When we finish with that, let's get out the powder and dust our file drawers. If this fuck is as careless as he appears to be, he probably left some prints behind," Chuck said in a less whiny voice.

Shondra was at her apartment and said that she'd be available to look at the Polaroids anytime during the evening. She did have an appointment at around ten, probably with a steady customer who was also on the mayor's staff; just a guess on Don's part.

Don and Chuck did some work on their files, which they were now entering on the newly acquired computers, computers that would make it more difficult for anyone with criminal intent to get into. The person who was pilfering their files was clearly not the brightest bulb on the tree, so his computer skills probably stopped with the exclamation, "What the fuck?"

When it came time to leave for the meeting with Shondra, Don and Chuck locked their files and polished the surfaces of their file drawers with window cleaner. They made doubly sure to place every item of furniture and desk paraphernalia in exactly the right place. Then they took Polaroid pictures of the cubicle.

Both Don and Chuck looked forward to checking out Marjorie once again as they left, but she wasn't at her desk. She hadn't left for the night because her computer was on and her desk was strewn with stuff that she used during her shift: magazines covering the latest movie star drama, fingernail polish, and an open can of Coke beside a hairbrush.

They walked through the door to the foyer toward the elevator that would take them to the lower car deck. As they passed the lineup room, they heard a muffled sound coming from inside and saw a dim light casting a slight glow under the door and onto the gray tile. Thinking that they might find Wally Fox up to no good inside, Don slowly opened the door just a crack and looked in. He wasn't entirely prepared for what he saw, but not much surprised him anymore. In the light that was at its lowest level without going dark, Don saw what he had been hoping for every time he passed Marjorie's desk. She was nude to the waist, her new breasts standing firmly as though suspended by invisible wires; there was no droop, no imperfections, just two perfectly round globes with nipples that extended from light brown areolas. They looked like they belonged on a Barbie doll.

Don closed the door as slowly as possible and then whispered to Chuck, describing what he saw.

With as much finesse as he could muster, Don eased the door open a few inches so both Chuck and he could see what was unfolding on the other side. Marjorie was standing in front of Detective Grimes who now had both hands on her breasts. As they watched, Grimes not only fondled Marjorie's breasts but he bent down and sucked her nipples as well. Don felt a certain amount of guilt, but he didn't back away and close the door. A detective, after all, was by nature first and foremost a voyeur.

Grimes lifted his head from Marjorie's breast and gave her a kiss on the lips. "See what a little money can buy? They're perfect. Just one more little favor and they'll be paid for," Grimes told Marjorie as she began to place her very skimpy bra over her new breasts. Marjorie didn't look like she was having much fun, but she was cooperating with Grimes.

"What's the favor this time?" Marjorie asked in a voice that might have been that of a hooker talking to her pimp.

"You know. These didn't come cheap, so there has to be a little payback, don't you think? You and I are going to take a ride up north after shift tonight."

"Where are we going this time?"

"The usual place; I reserved a room at our favorite motel."

"OK, but this is the last time. The boob job is paid for after this."

"We'll see how it goes."

Don closed the door, and he and Chuck walked away as quietly as possible.

When they reached the elevators, they waited until they heard Grimes and Marjorie leave the lineup room. They waited for a few minutes longer and then walked back to Marjorie's desk.

"Hi, Marjorie," Don said to a now less exuberant Marjorie. "We just overheard something interesting. We couldn't help but notice that there was light coming from under the lineup room door as we were on our way out. Being the snoopy bastards that we are, we looked through a crack in the door and saw what went on between you and Grimes."

Marjorie was looking down as Don was talking. Her new breasts seemed to be giving her less pleasure than she anticipated.

"It looked like Grimes wants some payback for buying your new breasts. Is that true?"

"Yeah, he said that if I wanted them he would pay for them, but that I had to let him play with them whenever he wanted and that I had to have sex with him one more time."

"That's the deal for tonight? You're going to have sex with him as payment for the boobs?"

"Right."

"You do know that what Grimes wants is extortion, don't you? We also have reason to believe that he stole the money he gave you to have the surgery."

"I wondered how he came up with the money. It wasn't inexpensive, and I had to stay in Vancouver for a week following the surgery, which he also paid for."

"How do you feel about his demands on you?"

"I hate it. His hands on me are the creepiest thing you can imagine."

"Would you like to help us get him on the theft and stop him from making any further demands on you or anyone else?"

"Yeah, I guess, but I don't trust him. I think he's capable of almost anything."

"Put him off for tonight but promise him that you'll go with him on another night. We have to have time to get a court order to put a wire on you before you meet him. Will you do that?" Don asked.

"I guess, but what would the other people in the unit think if I snitched on him?"

"We'll do our best to keep it a secret. But if anyone gives you any grief, we'll put a stop to it. Do you trust us?"

"You two are the only people I trust in the unit except for our new captain."

"That's great because we'll be going through her to get the wire. We have something else to do for a while, but we'll be back. In the meantime, think up a reason to skip the motel meet with Grimes."

"No problem, I'll tell him that my period just started."

"If that doesn't work on him, let us know, but don't go with him tonight. He told you that he made reservations at the usual motel. What motel is that?" Don asked, knowing full well what it was.

"The Cascade Motor Inn. He's a big spender when it comes to motels."

"Have you gone there with him before?" Chuck asked.

"Back when he and his wife were still in the life, they would conduct business there."

"The life? What's the life?" asked Chuck.

"You know, the life: swinging and threesomes, that sort of thing. That's how I got this job. Grimes and his wife liked me, so he promised that he would get me into the department if I would go along with his wife and him."

"Real fucking hero, isn't he?" said Don.

"How about we just catch him on a car deck and practice on him for a few hours," Chuck snarled, only half joking.

"No, I think we ought to put the fuck in prison if possible. Now you keep this real quiet. Don't tell anybody what's up," Don said. "And, by the way, your breasts came out very nice. They're stunning."

"Thanks, Don. Anytime you want a tour, just let me know."

Don gave Marjorie a smile, turned, and walked with Chuck to the elevators.

"A tour?"

"I would seriously consider it under different circumstances, but given what we have planned, I better keep my hands off that particular terrain," Don said.

"How about after we get the asshole behind bars?" said Chuck.

"Then I'll have to reconsider."

"OK, but I still want to know firsthand what they feel like."

"There's still hope for you, Chuck."

CHAPTER TWENTY-SEVEN

The drive to Shondra's apartment wasn't wasted time. By the time they arrived, Don and Chuck had formulated a plan for handling the wire on Marjorie. It wouldn't be a real brilliant idea to put her in a situation where she couldn't hide the wire. Granted, her breasts were now big enough to conceal a small dog in their cleavage, but they couldn't take that chance. Besides, it wouldn't look real good in court if it appeared that she was offering sex in exchange for a confession. Don and Chuck were very aware of case law on entrapment and the negative impact it tended to have in a courtroom. But if there were pictures offered as evidence to a jury of old guys...

As they approached Shondra's apartment building, they noticed Maurice's pimpmobile parked outside. That could be a good thing because it would give Maurice less incentive to leave town with Shondra if he knew they were diligently working on her case. But how could he have any doubt by this time, given all he had witnessed?

Raymond answered the door a few seconds after Don knocked. Don's first impulse was to prepare for a kick to his shins, but it didn't come.

"Hi, Detectives," Raymond gushed. They might have thought that he was a nephew whom they were picking up for a special occasion, like a birthday party.

Don reached down and took Raymond's hands in his. He shook them and then tussled his hair. Chuck patted Raymond on the back and asked how kindergarten was going. Raymond, they both thought, really liked them. The feeling was mutual.

"Is your mom here? We have something for her to look at," Chuck asked Raymond.

Just then Shondra and Maurice walked out of a hallway that no doubt led to a bathroom and bedrooms.

"Hi, guys," Shondra said with a genuine cheerfulness that neither detective had seen before in her. "You have a picture to show me?"

"Yes, but we have to show you without anyone else around, so do you mind either coming to our car or asking Maurice and Raymond to go in back?" Don said.

"We'll go in back," Maurice said as he took Raymond's hand and walked him out of the room.

All three went into the kitchen where the dining table was located. The kitchen, like the rest of the apartment, was clean and well furnished. Clean dishes were stacked in a rack over the sink.

"I've got to tell you, Shondra, that you don't fit my image of a prostitute," Don said.

"Oh, why? Is it because I take care of myself and my son whom I love with all my heart? Or is it that I know the difference between who and whom? Or could it be because our home is clean and warm with the rent paid on time? Maybe it's because I also love my pimp who is the father of my son. We're a middle-class family that just happens to be supported by my body. And that isn't all that bad. Don't you guys like sex? Just imagine having sex with a different partner every day and being paid for it as well. Some of my customers are very attractive, you know. I treat them well, so they come back. If I start to hate fucking for a living, I'll stop, but until then bring 'em on."

"Well said, and I can only imagine having a new sex partner every day," Don said.

"Let me know when you can afford an hour with me."

"I'll keep that in mind, but now let's look at some pictures."

Don took the Polaroids of Wally Fox's car and laid them on the table. Shondra looked at all of them for about thirty seconds.

"That's the car I saw on Aurora," she said as she thrust a finger at Wally's car.

"That's not the first three letters of the license number that you gave us, is it?" Chuck asked.

"No, but the letters are similar and it was a fast look, but the car is the one that the guy who assaulted me was driving."

"Can you tell us anything else about the driver? His hair, was it short or long, light or dark?" Don asked.

"I think it was short and dark. But, again, it was a fast look and it was night."

"How can you be sure that it was the suspect's car if it all happened so fast and it was so dark?" was Chuck's skeptical reply.

"Put it together, Detective. The guy was looking for a prostitute, and when he saw me, he hit the gas because he recognized me as the woman he assaulted. This car is the one because that's part of being a hooker: you remember cars and faces. You remember cop's faces because one of them might just be the next john I pick up. You might be surprised at how smart a lot of us are. At least those of us who don't end up on a slab at the morgue or in jail are smart. The others have bad teeth at thirty-five and turn tricks against a brick wall in a piss-drenched alley in Pioneer Square."

Don found himself getting a little emotional as Shondra enlightened him. He thought of Yvonne Gillespie and that she never had the opportunity afforded a smart hooker like Shondra. Yvonne was alone in the world without the brains to keep her from the clutches of a killer. If she hadn't died in the Fairview Hotel, she would have ended up in that piss-drenched alley. And although her teeth were still beautiful, she did end up on a slab. Don had to excuse himself for a while to walk to the sink where he found a glass and got a drink. *I wish Shondra had been around to teach her a few things about the life,* Don thought.

"That's the car. There is no doubt," Shondra said.

"OK," Don said as he turned back to the table. "Would you just sign the back of that photo and then we'll be on our way.

Don and Chuck watched Shondra sign the photo of Wally's car with a flourish that would have done credit to an author signing his latest book.

"Thank you, Shondra," Don said as he put the photos back in their envelope. Don turned toward the door, took a few steps, stopped, and turned back to Shondra. "I would have liked to have had you as a sister."

Shondra got the sense that if she didn't hug Don, he would burst into tears, so she did. "Thank you, Don. Do you mind if I call you Don?"

"I would be honored if you did," Don said as he hugged her, smelling her intoxicating scent and feeling her firm breasts against his chest. *Should I?* Don thought. *No, better not.*

Chuck and Don went to the door as Raymond and Maurice came out of the back. "Are you going?" Raymond asked with disappointment in his voice. Both detectives shook Raymond's hand, turned, and walked to their car.

"Fuck, man, I'm getting too soft for this job," Don said as he drove away from the curb. The streetlights had a halo around them that hadn't been there when they arrived.

Chuck patted his shoulder and said, "I think you're just letting yourself become a little more human than you have been for a while, and that's good. Just try to stay a little soft but not so soft that we stop hammering the assholes who kill people like Yvonne, assault people like Shondra, and victimize women like Marjorie."

"Deal."

The drive to the Public Safety Building was a good time to reflect on what remained to be done. It was almost a given that when things started to break in a case or cases, they did so in a hurry, and the work started to increase accordingly. This was no exception.

"Do we try to talk to Fox now or not?" Don asked, knowing the answer.

"No, not yet. We don't have probable cause for an arrest until we can get a positive ID on him, and that's going to have to wait until we have the DOL photo. We don't want to get him all panicky and start cleaning things up. After Shondra positively IDs him, assuming she does, then we can seize his car and get a warrant for it, his locker here in the building, and his house if we push it. Then there's the bulletin sketch that doesn't look like him."

"I'm not so sure we can get his house in a warrant, if we can get a warrant for anything. What have we got that we might be looking for in his house?" Don asked.

"You're the guy whose brain is in overdrive most of the time. You tell me, or was that one of your rhetorical questions?" Chuck replied.

"Maybe Shondra can describe some clothes for us. He had to be wearing clothes before he assaulted her. That should be specific enough for an affidavit of probable cause. And, no, it wasn't a rhetorical question."

"See, I told you that you were the warrant go-to guy."

"Now that we have that out of the way, what do we put in an affidavit to get a wire on Marjorie?" Chuck asked.

"That should be easier. The prosecutor's office has a whiz kid in getting wire requests past a judge. We'll talk to him after running the whole thing past the captain."

Don drove the car down to the same deck where it had been parked and found that all of the spots were occupied. Fox's car was back where it had been when they photographed it. Don put a hand on the hood; it was warm. He looked into the car again, this time with a flashlight that he always carried in his briefcase.

"It sometimes takes me a while to put two and two together," Don said as he continued looking through the windows of Fox's car. "You can slap me if you think I'm going overboard here with assumptions and premature conclusions, but look at these and see if anything comes to mind."

Chuck gazed through the window where Don was standing, following the beam of the flashlight. The beam landed on the pair of work boots without laces that Chuck saw the last time he looked through the window.

"What kind of laces do you think those boots might have had?" Don asked.

"Probably leather ones about two feet long."

"How long was the leather lace that was wrapped around Yvonne Gillespie's neck?" Don asked in his best non-rhetorical manner.

"About two feet, as I recall."

"Exactly two feet. We measured it; it was exactly two feet. Holy shit, Chuck, I think we may have our first serious break in Yvonne's murder."

It was no surprise to either Don or Chuck that they walked into a mostly vacant office. Marjorie was at her desk, but she was reading a glamour magazine for new wardrobe ideas, no doubt.

"Hi, guys. I told Grimes that I couldn't make the meeting tonight. He was seriously disappointed, but he accepted it. I told him that I'd let him know when it would work."

Pulling his eyes away from where they naturally settled when he was talking to Marjorie, Don said, "We'll work on getting the legal stuff done tomorrow. In the meantime, keep it under your hat. And one more thing, I'm getting to like the new you."

"Thanks, Don, but I hope you liked the old me, too."

"I did, very much, but now there's more to like."

Don and Chuck walked to their cubicle and updated reports on the new computer system. "Whoever thought this up should be given some sort of medal," Chuck said as he typed.

"I couldn't agree more," Don replied. "I went through too many correction tapes on the typewriter."

When they finished the secretarial stuff, they started work on an affidavit of probable cause for the wire on Marjorie. It took about an hour to finish during which time Sergeant Sherman, Grimes, and Martin returned from wherever it was they had been. It was Don's guess that it was a bar.

Sergeant Sherman walked with a slight wobble into Don and Chuck's cubicle, confirming Don's earlier assumption.

"What are you guys up to? Getting any leads on the Gillespie and Barber murders?"

Both Don and Chuck did a quick once-over of their desks to check for anything that might tip him off about the wire. There was nothing.

"No, we're pretty much waiting for DNA from the lab. We're hoping for a match between the fingernail scrapings and the ligature in the Gillespie case. Since we think they're from the same person, we'll use that in the Barber case, too." Don was giving Sherman just enough information to let him think that they were doing something but not so much that word of what they were doing got into the wrong hands.

"I know you guys will do a good job," Sherman said. Then he walked away, taking the slightly sour smell of a gut full of booze with him.

Don gave Sherman the finger as he walked away.

"That was a little more juvenile than I expected from you, Don," Chuck said with a somewhat haughty smile.

Don flipped Chuck the finger and opened his desk where he kept his paper files. They again had that gone-through look about them that only a person as meticulous as Don would detect.

"Open your desk and let me know if you think someone has been going through your files again."

Chuck opened his file drawer, gave it a quick look, and then looked at Don with a concerned expression.

"Looks like you're right. My file on Shondra has been moved, and the suspect sketch is misaligned with the rest of the pages."

"Your neatness pays dividends at times. This is the third time that we've had our files gone through, and two times the drawers were locked. How do you suppose this fuck is getting into them?"

Chuck was looking at his desk key as Don was talking. "It's my guess that these keys have been around for a long time. During that time a lot of people have had access to them, so it shouldn't be any big surprise that more than one key is floating around."

"How about if we ask that our locks be changed? Who manages that sort of thing?"

Chuck thought for a minute and then said, "Let's ask Marjorie; she knows everything about the management of the unit, and if she doesn't, she knows who does." Then he pulled the sketch out of the file that had been tampered with. He looked at it for a while and then took a piece of paper from a file and covered part of the sketch.

"This is too weird, Don. I know this guy but without the scruffy beard."

Don got up and looked at the sketch that Chuck had altered with the piece of paper. "That's Wally, our friendly janitor? Is that what you're thinking? But when you look at the entire sketch, it doesn't resemble Wally. Did you notice that little flaw in your idea?"

"Bingo. I don't know how I missed it before. Now that Wally is clean-shaven, he looks a little different but not that much. Man, are we dumb or what?"

"You aren't listening, Chuck," Don said with a certain exasperation. "Even you agree that the sketch doesn't look like Wally."

"This is getting too fucking weird. Within a matter of less than a shift, we link Wally to the case on Shondra and the murder of Yvonne. Before the night is done, we may just link him to JFK's assassination. But seriously, I'm thinking that he might have had something to do with Tiffany being forced off the road and Roseanne's attempted rape."

"Let's get to work on finding some DNA from Wally," Don said.

"That might be pretty easy if we could get into his janitor's closet. Who knows what he might be pack-ratting in there," Chuck responded. "But we don't have much time until the end of shift, and we don't know where he is right now. He may be in his closet beating off as we speak. Let's go and check, just in case."

Don and Chuck left their cubicle after locking their file drawers and walked down a darkened hallway toward the area where Pawn Shop Detail, West Burglary, and Sex Crimes had their offices. They didn't cover their offices at night, so the area wasn't very well lit. They approached Wally's closet where he kept all of his cleaning supplies, and stopped. A light shone from under the door. That didn't mean that Wally was inside, but it did mean that he could be. They walked away from the door to talk over their next move. They decided that it wouldn't be out of the ordinary to ask for something with which to clean their desktops. Before Don tried the door, he listened for any noise coming from inside; there was none.

Don knocked but got no answer. He tried the knob and, to his surprise, it opened. This was the first time that either Don or Chuck had seen the janitor's sanctum. It contained the usual stuff that a janitor might use to accomplish his job, but it also contained some other things that went beyond the job, merging into personal gratification supplies. There were several neatly hung photographs of nude women. They weren't the usual nudes that littered the pages of *Playboy* or *Hustler*. These were right out of magazines for those with some specific and weird sexual interests. The woman on all fours with a man on her back who had a rope around her neck was especially interesting.

"I think we better call the captain and tell her what we have here. This guy has serious issues," Don said. "While we're at it, let's photograph this so we'll have it if he decides to clean it out. I'll stay here if you'll get the camera."

Chuck walked back to the unit and opened the cabinet where the camera equipment was stored. He took the 35mm and a roll of film and walked back to the janitor's closet. Don had gone into the closet to look for anything that might contain some of Wally's DNA. There wasn't anything obvious like a used condom, but he did take a used latex glove, thinking that there might be some of his skin cells inside.

When Don stepped out of the cramped closet, Chuck took several photographs of the sexually explicit pictures as well as a wide shot of the entire closet. They finished and closed the door just in time.

"You guys need something?" Wally asked as he walked down the hall toward them. He had a suspicious look about him. He wasn't the friendliest guy under most circumstances.

Don looked Wally up and down and then said, "Yeah, we need some desk cleaner. Do you have any?"

"If you're talking about the stuff that is meant for desktops, no I don't."

"I guess we'll have to use plain old soap and water then."

"I guess you will."

Don and Chuck left Wally standing in front of his closet; he didn't seem to be in a big hurry to open it. When they got back to their cubicle, Don turned to Chuck and said, "I wonder why he would lie about not having desk cleaner. There were two cans of it in there, maybe more."

"We need to put this in the Gillespie and Shondra follow-ups. But what we really need to do is put a tail on this asshole to see where he goes at night."

"Why, Chuck, I think your word choices have been negatively influenced by your crass partner," Don said, his eyebrows slightly raised.

While Don called Captain Mitchell at home, Chuck added the latest to the follow-ups. When Don hung up, he turned toward Chuck, who was pounding away at the keys of his computer, and said, "Did you know you no longer have to pound on the keys to accomplish the job?"

"What did she say?" Chuck said, ignoring Don's critique.

"She'll come in after midnight when Sherman and his goons are gone. But she wants us to tail Wally tonight."

"Great, like I don't have a life outside the job!" Chuck exclaimed.

"If you will recall, Chuck, my lad, I had a date tonight with the very beautiful Tiffany who is probably at this very moment anointing herself with sensual oils in anticipation of my arrival."

"You are so full of yourself. The only oil Tiffany might anoint herself with for you is ten-thirty Pennzoil."

"That hurt, but the fact remains that we have to wait for the captain."

When Don had finished with Chuck, he called Tiffany. She answered after five rings. "Hi there, I have some bad news and some good news. Which would you like first?"

"Who is this?" Tiffany responded.

"It's your poorer neighbor on the east side of Duwamish Head. You know, the guy who has the Pollock, the painting, not the fish. That guy."

"Ooooohhh, that guy. So what's the good news?"

"We may have a handle on the guy who ran you off the road. I have some photos I need to show you."

"And the bad news?"

"I can't make it tonight. We have business that needs attention."

"But I need attention."

"This is one of the perks of the job: it always comes first."

"That kind of sucks, doesn't it?"

"Yes it does," Don commiserated, "but it's one of those sad facts of life that one must adjust to when one gets involved with a cop."

"How about you? Don't you have to adjust to this art major as well? One of the characteristics of this art major is that she has gotten accustomed to you, and she likes some of things that you do for her."

"Just make sure that your doors are locked before you go to bed. I'll stop by when I get off and maybe we can take care of that part. That is, if you haven't already left for work. It looks like we may be here for a while."

"OK, I guess. By the way, Don, did you know that this is my first exposure to a cop, and I kind of like it. And on top of that, I kind of like you."

"That's mutual, and I have never been exposed to a very attractive woman with a serious case of bicycle butt and who rides a water taxi to work at an art museum. See, we're even. Say 'Good night, Don.'"

"Good night, Don."

Don hung the phone on its cradle feeling a little more pleased with his world.

CHAPTER TWENTY-EIGHT

Since a very young age, Wally Fox was considered a strange duck to almost everyone he encountered. He was a loner during the two years he spent in high school in a small town in the mountains of northern Idaho, where his primary activity was hunting anything with four legs and gazing at women through a spotting scope from a distance. He quit high school after his sophomore year when he was the prime suspect in the rape of a ten-year-old girl who was attacked from behind as she walked along a river path after dark. She wasn't able to identify her attacker, and he had worn a condom. Wally came up with a plausible alibi, so he was never charged. The incident didn't go on any arrest record since he was sixteen at the time. He and his parents moved away from the town a short time later. They went to Hayden Lake, Idaho, the center of the universe for neo-Nazis and racists of all stripes. It seems that Wally's father harbored some very unsavory views of people who were not of the Aryan race. It rubbed off on Wally.

Over the years that Wally worked on the fifth floor of the Public Safety Building, he became more enthralled with some of the people who worked there and with some of the crooks these people came in contact with as a part of their job. Wally knew that he could never be a cop, but he wanted to experience some of the authority that cops seemed to enjoy. His size, power, and willingness to use them were what Wally had to access this authority. Women were his favorite targets.

Wally found that he could vicariously experience some of the detectives' professional lives by reading their reports. Most detectives filed their reports on their desks thinking that no one would tamper with them. Those who locked their files were of special interest to Wally. He had gained access to keys to most of the detectives' desks, and he used these whenever the floor was vacant for the night.

The person he paid closest attention to ever since she started work as a secretary was Marjorie. His apparent invisibility to her made him come to hate her, that is, until he was introduced to her by Detective Grimes and his wife, Clorice. He hadn't had access to her since Grimes and Clorice stopped their swinging life. Her new breasts entrenched his rage with her even more. She threw them at him without so much as an acknowledgment of his existence. He swore that he would have his hands on her breasts before long.

Captain Mitchell arrived at the Public Safety Building at about twelve thirty. She parked her car in her assigned spot and came up on the elevator from the ground floor. As usual she found the building, at that time of night, creepy and slightly threatening. She was reassured by the 9mm Glock on her left hip.

The Glock was an innovation in small arms, but it was a proven piece of hardware. The Israelis had been using it for a while, so it couldn't have too many faults, was Captain Mitchell's thought. The $450 price tag was not unreasonable when it could pull one's ass out of a serious jam.

Don and Chuck were working on polishing the affidavit for the warrant for the wire when Captain Mitchell walked in. She was not in her usual professional garb: a black suit. This night she had on a tight pair of black Levis and a tight, black, long-sleeve pullover turtleneck. A waist-length denim jacket covered the ensemble.

"Good morning, Captain," Don said as he attempted with no success to pull his eyes from the great visual image that she presented. "We think we have the affidavit ready to go on the warrant for the wire on Marjorie. Wally's car was still here when we came back a while ago. He works until after midnight, so he's probably still here."

"Let's hope that he's still here. You two have to keep tabs on him tonight. Now, as for the warrant on his car and apartment, we have to get a consult from the prosecutor's office on the admissibility of the plain view of the boots. But there is the sketch that might cover the issue of the assault on the prostitute. The prostitute identified the car, right? You put that all into an affidavit and it should fly. There is one problem that I can see in the search related to the assault on the prostitute: what are you looking for? The boots are related to the murders. How about if we put the two cases together and write the affidavit accordingly?"

"I always knew that you were the smartest captain in the whole fucking department; pardon the language," Don said.

"Thank you, Don, but I'll bet that you and Chuck are about two steps ahead of me."

"Only one," said Don.

Don and Chuck briefed Captain Mitchell on what they had instructed Marjorie to do. After she read the affidavit for the warrant for the body wire that might make the theft case on Grimes, the captain agreed that they should bring it to the wire wiz the next day.

"Are we fitting any sack time into this plan?" Don asked Captain Mitchell.

"Are you suggesting something highly inappropriate, Don?"

"No, nothing like that; I'm just wondering when Chuck and I can fit sleep into this schedule. I know that Chuck starts getting foul tempered if he hasn't had his eight every few days." That's not to say that he didn't harbor inappropriate thoughts about his boss from time to time, and this time was no different.

"You guys can trade off napping when you're following Fox tonight, which should be enough to hold you."

"I suppose you're right," Don said, yawning.

"I called Narcotics after you called me and got one of their plain seized cars for your tail. They parked it on Fourth Avenue. The keys are in the gas cap panel. It's a black Dodge Charger with British Columbia plates. They assured me that the tank would be full. Try not to burn it so the crooks know that it's a cop car, and don't wreck it. And one other thing: give me your overtime requests, and don't let anyone else see them."

"I'll drive," Don said, "otherwise we'll probably be paying Narcotics for damage to their Charger."

"Screw you, Don," Chuck said, "and pardon my language, Captain."

"You beat me to it, Chuck. I was about to say the same thing."

Captain Mitchell read the affidavit for the body wire warrant, made a few suggestions, and then bid them good-night with the order that they keep her informed if "the shit hit the fan" no matter the time. Then she asked to be excused for her language. She was.

Before they left the office, Don called Radio and gave the supervisor a description of what they were up to and what their car would look like in case someone reported a suspicious car being driven recklessly or parked in a suspicious place with two questionable-looking white guys on board.

They locked their desks, took the elevator to the first floor, and walked by the spot where they last saw Wally's car to make sure it was still there; it was.

Fourth Avenue was dead at that time of night. A cab might pass from time to time with a couple of drunks on board, but it was mostly a street left to cops, crooks, and bums. The Charger was parked where it was supposed to be, and it was, in Don's opinion, a beauty. It no doubt had been ridden hard and put away wet on many occasions, but it screamed power even sitting still. It was a shade of purple under the yellow/orange streetlights, which meant that it was probably anything from dark blue to green in the sunlight.

"This should be fun," Don said as he opened the access door to the gas tank and found the key that would get it on the road. "I hope it's as fast as it looks."

Don climbed behind the wheel as though he owned the car. It brought him back to high school when a car like this would almost guarantee a date with the prettiest girl in school and the possibility of some side benefits to go with it. He put the key in the ignition, turned it, and the engine came to life. It let out a growl that meant that they might be in for a fun night.

Don drove to a point on the street where they could watch for Wally's car as it came out of the Public Safety Building. Chuck promptly slid down in his seat and closed his eyes. Don kept an eye on the exit and waited.

"I'm hungry," Chuck said, his eyes still closed.

There was a bar/restaurant about a half block from where they waited. It was none other than the infamous Crazy 8. Don had fond memories associated with it, not the least of which was his introduction to Marjorie and her naked foot. He, however, did have some misgivings about the quality and purity of the food. But Chuck was hungry, and, come to think of it, so was he.

"I'll get a little closer to the Crazy 8, and you can run in while I watch for Wally."

Don drove nearer the Crazy 8 and parked facing the Public Safety Building's garage exit onto Cherry Street. The bar closed at two and it was only one thirty, giving plenty of time to get something from the kitchen. Chuck went into the dive carrying his radio. Don had requested a mushroom burger, fries, and coffee. Chuck wanted to ask him about the order but thought better of it. He wasn't as concerned about the meat issue as with the challenge of eating a mushroom burger in a car. You add ketchup to that, and you had the potential for a serious stain on clothes and car seats. He decided to let Don live with the consequence of his decision. He wasn't going to touch the vegetarian thing.

Twenty minutes after Chuck walked into the Crazy 8, he walked out, loaded down with two grease-stained paper bags of food and two cups of coffee. Don opened the door for him and took one of the bags and one cup.

"This smells so good that I think I could just eat it," Don said under the quizzical gaze of Chuck.

"You're supposed to eat it; it's food."

When Chuck had settled himself in his seat and had taken the first bite of his burger in order to stave off starvation, he began to talk, his mouth still full.

"Dayanwho'sn."

"Don't talk with your mouth full, Chuck. How many times do I have to tell you that?"

Chuck chewed thoroughly and then swallowed. "Do you know who's in there?"

"No, why don't you tell me."

"Sherman and his brothers in crime: Grimes, Martin, Hase, and Monson."

"Did they see you?"

"I think they must have since I sat at the bar while I waited for our order, but they didn't acknowledge me."

"No surprise there. But let's move this thing so they won't see us when they come out."

Don started the Charger and drove it around the block to an alley that gave a good view of Cherry Street and the exit from the Public Safety Building. The spot hid them from the view of anyone leaving the Crazy 8. It was there that they polished off their burgers, fries, and coffee. Don lost a few mushrooms, but they didn't land on his pants as Chuck predicted.

"That was the best burger I've ever eaten," Chuck said with nothing in his mouth. He took the last remaining sip of coffee and said, "Now I have to piss."

Don rolled his eyes while rolling up the bag his burger and fries came in with more force than was required. "There's a big vacant alley just for you right outside the car door."

Chuck got out, walked to the back of the car, and added to the already urine stink of the alley, giving the Bainbridge residents added reason to harbor superior attitudes toward Seattle. The suggestion of peeing gave Don the urge, so he got out and added to the stream that was now running down the alley toward Cherry Street and on to and past the Public Safety Building. As he was zipping, Don saw a car stop at the sidewalk before coming out of the Public Safety Building and proceeding uphill toward them; it was Wally's. Don got into the Charger, started the engine, and waited to see which way Wally would turn. When Wally turned left onto Fourth Avenue, a one-way going north, Don put the Charger in gear, turned the lights on, and turned right out of the alley, then onto Fourth Avenue. When Don reached the next one-way downhill toward Elliot Bay, he turned left and then right onto Third. This might prevent Wally from noticing that he had company, that is, if he was smart enough to figure it out. Wally had worked around cops long enough to know that at this time of night there were only drunks, street slugs, crooks, and cops on the streets of downtown Seattle. There was the odd cab taking drunks home and a stray dog or two, but damn few others.

With Chuck as his eyes, Don continued to parallel Wally, checking on his progress at every intersection. When they reached Pike Street, Don turned right toward Fourth Avenue, thinking that Wally was planning to get onto Aurora at Denny. He was right.

Aurora was where the prostitutes were in abundance at this time of night. It was possible to find one hanging out on a street corner in downtown or several in various bars around town and near the airport, but most street whores hung on Aurora. It's where the cheap motels were, so it was where they went.

Once Wally got on Aurora, it was easier to follow him without being made. The traffic increased with Boeing workers going home and bars closing. Don or Chuck gave Wally no credit for brains enough to recognize a tail when he saw one, but he might. They hung back about four cars from Wally and one lane to his right. Just in case the shit hit the fan, Chuck gave Radio an update on their location and what they were up to. He used a channel that wasn't monitored by the local news folks, and only those patrol officers who happened to be monitoring it would hear the news. The last thing they wanted was a nosy patrol officer driving up beside them and waving a cheerful hello.

When they passed Green Lake, the true Aurora sex market opened up. The speed limit reduced from forty to thirty miles an hour, and there were no further barriers on the sides of the roadway. Seedy motels with pretentious names sprouted like weeds along both sides of the avenue. A popular cemetery with dark roads gave those whores who didn't want the light bright enough to illuminate wrinkles and scars from their years on the street a place to practice their trade. The further north Aurora progressed toward Everett, the more prostitute-friendly it became. Wally clearly knew where to troll.

Wally drove north without slowing except for lights; he seemed to have a destination in mind. Anyone who was looking for a street whore would slow when one came into view, and Don saw several as they drove. Wally didn't appear to take interest in any of them.

Wally's brake lights came on when he approached the Cascade Motor Inn. He turned left, crossed southbound Aurora, and drove into the entrance to the motel. Don drove through the next intersection, continuing on to where he could do a U-turn on a red light, and drove back to the Cascade Motor Inn. Wally was getting out of his car as Don and Chuck drove past. Don hit the brakes and turned into a lot on the south side of the motel's office. The Charger had barely stopped before Don and Chuck were out and running to the drive where Wally parked. They made it in time to see which room he went into: number thirteen.

"How about we see if any of the 'Lap Dance Crew' are on the air," Chuck said. The "Lap Dance Crew" worked prostitution, gambling, and crimes that both Don and Chuck thought were a stretch and little more than demands made by the holier-than-thou gang who lived in the city and who exercised their rights to be busybodies. These detectives were actually paid to spend shifts in strip clubs buying lap dances from beautiful women in hopes that the women would solicit them for a blow job in the back room. They were also interested in things like the women's pubic hair and nipples: they couldn't show.

"They could stop Wally if he comes out so we don't get burned."

"Sounds like a plan," Don responded.

Don called Radio on the same channel that they used earlier so they wouldn't alert the world to what they were up to. There just happened to be a car in the area that was out trolling for street whores. They agreed to meet behind the Cascade Motor Inn.

Detectives Gary Means and Kirby Benton had been around for many years. They both fit right in with the people they dealt with on the job. They could pass for Boeing line workers or, if cleaned up a little, as high-stakes gamblers. They were good at what they did, but Don and Chuck knew that both enjoyed the benefits of working Vice, aka the "Lap Dance Crew."

Means and Benton drove into the lot and parked beside the Dodge Charger. They were in a new and very red Chevrolet Z28. Don was immediately envious because he knew, but had forgotten, that these guys came up with a new car about every other month, courtesy of the taxpayer. He was feeling a little less pleased with the hotrod that he and Chuck had weaseled out of Narcotics.

All four detectives renewed acquaintances before getting down to business. Means and Benton were familiar with the motel/whorehouse, so they didn't register surprise that there was some more of the same going on. Don told them that they had to keep quiet about what they were up to. Vice cops lived in a shady world every day of their working lives, so they had no issues with being secretive. They thought that the best approach would be to watch Wally for a while, and if he came out with a woman, Means and Benton would stop him on suspicion that he was engaging a prostitute, although engaging wasn't the word that described what Wally would be doing with her. If they could find probable cause, Means and Benton would arrest Wally and the woman and tow the car. That would give Don and Chuck the opportunity to search it incident to the arrest and see if there was any good reason to get a warrant on it. They might even find some DNA in the car. Any prosecutor who got such a case might holler foul because such a stop might be viewed as a ruse, but all agreed that "fuck him or her" was the operative term.

While they waited for Wally to conduct his business, Don and Chuck decided to go into the motel office to try to identify the prostitute who Wally was sticking it to. The man at the desk was Korean, which was anything but unusual on Aurora. He knew the drill since police probably paid him regular visits. Don asked to see the register after identifying himself. The clerk/owner lifted a book from under the desk and opened it to the last page of registrants. Most of the rooms had been rented more than once during the day, which gave even the most naïve person the sense that this was a brothel and not an actual motel. Room thirteen had been rented three times during the previous day. Don wondered if the sheets had been changed.

"How many times have you changed the sheets in room thirteen today, Mr. Park?" Don asked the clerk/owner.

"I no know what you mean," the clerk/owner/pimp replied.

"I mean, do you change the sheets between prostitutes? They probably get the sheets a little spotted, don't they?"

"I not understand."

"You do understand prostitute and whore and changing sheets since you own this place, don't you?"

"Maybe I need to call attorney."

"Maybe you will tell us who rented room thirteen before I close your place down for the night."

The clerk/owner/pimp pointed to room thirteen in the register. It was in the name of W. Grimes who had used a Washington State driver's license to register. Don and Chuck looked at each other and then looked at the register to confirm what they saw. W. Grimes was Bill Grimes, homicide detective.

"Did this man register in person, Mr. Park?"

The clerk said that he had registered that morning for an arrival after midnight. "And how you know my name?"

"We have our ways," Don said in his most sinister voice.

It now became a little clearer: Grimes had planned to take Marjorie to the room after their shift, but when Marjorie told him that she couldn't make it, Grimes let Wally use it. But why did Wally drive right to the room unless there was a woman waiting for him? He should have picked up a prostitute along the way if he didn't have someone waiting.

"I think we made a mistake bringing the 'Lap Dance' boys here," Don said after they left the desk. "If they get wind that Grimes rented the room, even they won't keep it under wraps."

"Yeah, and we don't know who's in there with Wally, which makes the problem even bigger," Chuck said.

"Let's tell the boys that we changed our minds and don't need them after all. Then we can find out what gives between Grimes and Wally," Don said.

Both walked outside to the shadow that hid Means and Benton, who were both savoring cigars. *These guys aren't really up on surveillance* was Don's immediate thought. The cigars, however, smelled like top of the line.

"You guys want to try a real Cuban?" Means asked.

"Yeah, but where the hell do you get Cubans?" Chuck asked.

"You don't want to know because if I told you I'd have to kill you," Means said as if he was only half joking.

Don told Means and Benton that they decided against trying to arrest Wally and that they could leave if they wanted to get on with their business.

Means and Benton looked a little skeptical but didn't ask any questions. In their work they knew that it was best not to get too inquisitive; it might lead to a trip into a dark alley with less than pleasant results. They walked to their new Chevy Z28, Cubans glowing in the dark, and drove away. There might be enough time to get a lap dance or a grope from a street whore. Life was good.

After a short conference in the parking lot of the motel/whorehouse, Don and Chuck decided that the best course of action was the most obvious: they would try to get a look at the room through the drapes. If the drapes were anything like the rest of the place, they weren't exactly quality. They were right.

Being as quiet as possible, they walked to the window on the parking lot side of room thirteen. Wally's car was parked directly in front of it. They first went to the door and listened. Sounds usually associated with whorehouses were what they heard. Wally was obviously going to town on some unfortunate prostitute. The bed was squeaking and the woman seemed to be enjoying whatever Wally was doing for her. The question for Don was this: were prostitutes supposed to enjoy the sex act as much as this woman seemed to be? Maybe it was all a show for Wally.

They tried to find a crack in the drapes covering the large window that gave the occupants of room thirteen a great view of an asphalt parking lot or, if they were lucky, a view of the grille of a Ford F-150 owned by some cowboy poseur from Ellensburg. The crack wasn't much, but it was enough to give one person intent on being a voyeur a view of a part of the room. That part was the bed and its occupants.

Don was the first lucky voyeur of the activities in room thirteen. He saw Wally's naked profile. He hadn't seen Wally naked before—why would he?—but he recognized the profile of his head as he worked away at the woman who lay under him. The woman under Wally was not a prostitute, at least not in the common meaning of the word, but someone with whom Don and Chuck were familiar if not well acquainted. She was Mrs. Bill Grimes, aka Clorice. In Don's opinion, Mrs. Grimes appeared to be enjoying the work performed by Wally the janitor.

Don drew back from the window and motioned for Chuck to look. Chuck leaned into the window to get his bearings; he then stiffened a little and settled in. He said nothing until he drew back and walked a short distance from the window so he wouldn't be heard.

"I would never have thought that Wally was so well equipped. Mrs. Grimes seems to be enjoying that tool of his."

"Yes she does, but why Wally and her? That's what I'd like to know. Wally isn't exactly the greatest catch on the block."

"Did you see his Johnson?" Chuck asked.

"I guess that might explain it."

"Yeah, I think that more than explains it, but why would Bill rent this room so his wife could screw Wally?"

"That's a strange twist."

The sounds from room thirteen became louder as Don and Chuck conferred on the sidewalk. A loud slap was followed by a louder moan, then another slap. Don slipped slowly to the crack in the curtain to check whether they needed to kick in the door to rescue Clorice. What he saw belonged in an S-and-M film.

Wally had repositioned Clorice on the bed so he could ram his monster into her and slap her ass, squeeze her breasts, and apparently make every effort to beat and screw her at the same time. Clorice's moans could be translated through the glass now that Don had his face pressed to it. She was asking to be slapped around in graphic ways and screwed in even more graphic ways. Don's thought was that the beds at this motel/whorehouse must be fairly sturdy.

"Check this out," Don whispered to Chuck after stepping away from the window.

Chuck quietly approached the window and looked in. He seemed, in Don's opinion, to be viewing the porn show more academically than voyeuristically. Whereas Don found himself mildly stimulated by the show, Chuck might well have been taking notes in a class on the various ways in which the human genus performed the sex act.

When Chuck had his fill of the show, he stepped away from the window, motioning Don to follow him to a dark spot behind a car where they wouldn't be heard. "You recall what the guy who assaulted Shondra did, right?"

"Yeah, he screwed her and then he beat her up. She didn't enjoy it, however, not like Clorice seems to be."

"Right, but if you get two people together who both get into that sort of thing, it can be pretty enjoyable. Or so I've heard," Chuck was quick to add.

"This is one more paragraph for our warrant for his car and house."

Chuck nodded and said, "It could be the central part of the warrant. Shondra was both screwed and beaten by a guy who kinda looks a little like

Wally but not much; Wally drives a car that Shondra is sure about being the one her assailant was driving. Yvonne Gillespie was beaten and killed by a guy who screwed her violently with an object, not his cock. He used a leather cord to kill her. Wally has a pair of boots in his car absent the leather laces. John Barber was shackled by something, probably handcuffs, when he was dragged to the roof of the Fairview. He was dragged by a guy bigger and stronger than him. Wally is big and strong. Wally had a limp the day after Barber was killed, and Wally has access to our desks and therefore has access to someone's cuffs. Now we witness Wally brutally screwing and beating Clorice."

"Do you think the powers will go along with our identifying the wife of one of Seattle's finest in such a degrading way?" Chuck asked. "Then there's the issue of unlawful search. I don't think what we're doing here will pass muster with a judge."

"It's my guess that some of them, judge included, will make copies of the affidavit for late-night reading. Grimes, no doubt, gave her the green light tonight, and he's probably getting off thinking about what Wally is doing with his wife."

"Agreed, but let's go somewhere so we can watch what they do when they come out of the room. We may have more for the affidavit before the night is over," Chuck said.

They walked to the car, got in, drove south on Aurora, made an illegal U-turn, then another, and parked about a half block north of the motel. Traffic on Aurora had dwindled to a few late-night drunks coming home or trolling for hookers while keeping an eye out for cops. They settled back and waited. They were propositioned only once by a hooker looking for one more customer before calling it a night. As she walked away after being turned down, they heard her say, "Faggots."

About forty-five minutes passed before a car came out of the motel lot; it was Wally's. He was alone. He turned south on Aurora and disappeared into the early morning gloom.

"Should we follow him?" Chuck asked.

"There's so little traffic that even he might pick up on us. Besides, if we spook him, he might start getting rid of things that we want to find later. I think we should wait to see what Clorice is up to."

They waited thirty minutes with no movement from the motel lot. "Do you suppose he killed her?" Don asked.

"If he did, we are in deep shit, but why would he kill her when Grimes obviously knew he was here with her? And, besides, we saw him assaulting her and did nothing to stop him. That would not look good on our next evaluations."

"How could you think of your next evaluation at a time like this? Here the wife of a fellow cop has been violated, consensually of course, and you think of yourself and your future. This won't look good on your resume after we get the ax," Don said with just a touch of irony.

They drove the car closer to the motel lot, parked, and got out. Lights in the office were still on, but the No Vacancy sign was lit. The "ca" in vacancy was burned out. It struck Don that the motel was anything but "vancy." They walked toward the back where number thirteen was located and saw the glow of a light through the thin curtains. Don walked to the crack in the drapes and peered in. Clorice wasn't on the bed with a leather lace around her neck; so far so good. He was just able to get a sliver of a view into the open door of the bathroom where the light over the sink cast a dim glow. Clorice was standing in front of the mirror, examining her face. Her hair was wet and she was still nude. *Not bad* was Don's first thought. He backed away from the window and let Chuck have a look, although Chuck probably wouldn't enjoy it as much as he had, but who knows about these things?

When Chuck took Don's place, he found Clorice sooner than Don had. This time, however, she was looking directly at him. Chuck jumped back and whispered that she had seen him. Before they had time to work on a plan of action, the door opened.

"What the fuck are you two sick pricks doing here peeping at me?" Clorice asked while clutching a towel that she had barely wrapped around her torso. The towel covered it for the most part, but there was still a lot of skin exposed.

Both Don and Chuck were at a loss for words. Don recovered first and, trying his best to keep his eyes locked on hers, said, "We're conducting an investigation that involves Wally."

"Does your investigation include peeping on me in the nude and Wally and me fucking?"

"Clorice, do you mind if we go inside? The whole world is getting a pretty good view of you standing out here," Don pleaded.

Clorice turned and walked back into the room with Don and Chuck close behind. Don caught a scent of sex in the air, which probably came from the bedding that had been twisted by Wally and Clorice's acrobatics a short time ago. Then there was the couple before them, etc.

Clorice sat down very carefully on a desk chair, doing her best to keep the towel in place. Don and Chuck stood since the only other place available was the bed that probably harbored several as yet unidentified diseases. "Would you mind telling me what you were doing here besides copping a look at me? Maybe you'd like a feel, too, or are you both gay?"

Don thought that her choice of words was ironic, but he didn't say so. "As I said, we're conducting an investigation that involves Wally. We can't go into any details." Don then found his old confidence and turned the interrogation around. "Maybe you could tell us what you were doing here with Wally and how that came about."

"I don't think I'll be telling you anything tonight or any other night."

Don sighed and looked at Chuck who was trying his best to stay composed. "Actually I think you might want to talk to us after what I tell you about what your future might look like if you don't. You see, your husband rented this room. Does that mean that he's pimping for you? And if he is, the newspapers are going to have a lot of fun with that. If he merely let you use it with Wally because he knows that you like to be slapped around during sex and he can live vicariously through you, well, that will go well with the mayor's morning coffee. On the other hand, there is the possibility that he doesn't know that you came here to screw Wally and that he gave Wally use of the room because he couldn't use it tonight for whatever reason. Your choice where we go from here."

Clorice lost some of her attitude after Don finished. She even lost some of the control she had of the towel covering her upper body. One of her breasts slipped into full view as her towel fell away; she didn't seem to notice nor care if she did. Don, however, did notice.

"You might want to cover up, Clorice; we've already seen you, remember?"

Clorice looked down and pulled the towel slowly over her breast as though she was performing a reverse striptease, something not lost on Don.

"Wally and I have been getting together for a while. You now know what we both like, and he has a certain ability that not many men have, if you know what I mean. He called me tonight after Bill told him that he could use the room since his date had evaporated. Bill was going to take some woman there, but she backed out. I drove up before the end of Wally's shift and parked on a side street south of here. You know the rest since you were no doubt watching us."

"We saw enough to get the idea. We also saw Wally leave, and when you didn't follow him, we thought that we might find you dead," Chuck added.

"Dead? Why would you think Wally killed me? Is this what the investigation is about? Did Wally kill someone?"

"We aren't going into any details with you on that. Now let's talk about how we should word our report. Do we use your name or just refer to you as an unidentified hooker Wally picked up on the street?"

Clorice was defeated, although she didn't flinch at being referred to as a hooker. She got up from the chair and walked into the bathroom. Don followed her to prevent any more unpleasant incidents like suicide or retrieval of a gun from a bag followed by the unpleasant sensations of being hit by a poorly aimed bullet. She walked into the bathroom, dropped the towel, and started to dress. Don's thought was that she could do a lot better than Bill or Wally. For an older woman, she was damned attractive. When she finished dressing, Clorice combed her hair and checked her face in the mirror, apparently for bruises; there weren't any that Don saw, much to his amazement. She then walked back to the bedroom and sat on the chair.

"As you can guess, I don't lead the most stellar life. In addition to Wally and a few others I won't name, I'm screwing Jack Martin pretty often and Will Sherman from time to time. Then there was that one time with your former boss, Captain Black. I did him to make sure Bill didn't lose his job before retirement. He wasn't the most exciting guy in bed. I would have attempted to seduce you, Don, but you seemed too straight. And as for you, Chuck, well. I got onto Wally one night when I came to pick up Bill because his car was in the garage. I was waiting at Marjorie's desk when Wally came to empty the garbage. He gave me a look that sort of told me he was interested. Maybe he knew about my sex life by then. You see, Bill and I were swingers at one time, and it was no great secret. Wally decided to get brave and sat down near me. He made a point of showing me a bulge in his pants that extended well down one pant leg. It didn't look like he had taped a sausage to his leg. It got my attention, so I told him that he should meet me sometime and show me what that thing was. He did, and the rest is history. I really don't have much to hide anymore, but I'd rather keep this little episode out of any legal documents or newspapers. I'll do almost anything you want, and that includes asking for a change of sheets."

"We aren't interested in making your life or ours any more difficult, but what we have to insist upon is that you keep this very quiet. Don't tell anyone about what happened tonight, and I mean anyone," Don said.

"OK, I don't have any friends whom I confide in anyway. There are just sex partners; that's it."

"One last thing before we go," Don said with more reluctance than he usually felt. "Did Wally use a condom tonight?"

"No he didn't; he never does. He says that he can't have an orgasm with one."

"What did he use to clean himself?"

"Nothing. He didn't clean up after; he never does."

Don looked at Chuck as though he wanted him to ask the next question. "Would you mind if we got a semen sample from you?"

"I already cleaned myself pretty well, but I suppose there might be some left." Clorice stood, walked into the bathroom, and closed the door. She came out after about a minute and handed Don a tissue. Don opened the bedside table, found an envelope next to a pristine Gideon's Bible, and handed it to Clorice who placed the tissue in it.

"I suppose that if this proves whatever murder you're investigating, I'll have to be identified as the source," she said.

"Probably, but it's a little early in the game for any speculation," Chuck said in his most convincing voice.

Don added, "Let's check the sheets for stains; maybe we can attribute it to the sheet and leave you out of it."

It didn't take much searching to find a wet spot on the bottom sheet just about where Wally would have discharged his DNA. Don took out his pocketknife, cut the stain out, and placed it in another envelope that he found under the unused Gideon Bible. Don thought that he might be forgiven for damaging the property of this motel/whorehouse, but he really didn't care one way or the other.

Don, Chuck, and Clorice left the scene of the crime and walked to the Dodge Charger. They drove the three blocks to where Clorice had parked her car under a tree in front of a small bungalow. To any night-owl neighbors looking out their windows, they were just two guys returning a hooker to her car after a night of debauchery at a nearby motel. In a way, it was.

As Don and Chuck drove back toward the Public Safety Building, Chuck asked, "How did you know his name was Park?"

"They're either Park or Kim. I just got lucky."

"You are a real piece of work, Don. You left out Lee and several others," Chuck said over the rumble of the Charger's exhaust.

"Thank you," Don mumbled. Then he pushed the Charger's accelerator to the floor in an attempt to relive a part of his youth.

CHAPTER TWENTY-NINE

Don parked in front of Tiffany's house just as the sun came over the Cascade Range, casting a rose-colored hue on the clouds above the Olympic Mountains to the west. He was surprised to see George and Martha sitting on the living room window ledge as he started up the walk. They seemed to recognize him.

Tiffany opened the door before he had a chance to ring the bell. She had just climbed out of bed if her state of dress, or lack of it, was any indication. Before Don had a chance to say "good morning" or "you're looking great," Tiffany threw her arms around him and gave him a seriously impassioned kiss. Don hadn't experienced a kiss like that in a long time. It told him more than anything that she might have said. He hoped that the effect on his breath from the mushroom burger he consumed many hours before didn't turn her off. It didn't.

When Tiffany let go, she stood at arm's length and looked at him and his somewhat exhausted face. "I had a night to remember. There are insights that I get from time to time that let me know when something is real and probably lasting. I had one of those last night."

"What are you talk..."

"Don't interrupt me when I'm attempting to express what I think I'm feeling. I know that you're a cop, and I know that that means certain things, some not so good. It means that you are subject to things that most of us aren't. You see things that most of us only experience in nightmares or novels and other things that we see only in porn magazines."

"Can we go in and close the door before the neighbors start to talk?" Don said.

Tiffany turned and walked to the couch and sat down, her short gown sliding up her legs. George and Martha jumped from the window ledge and walked onto her lap in turns. Don closed the door and joined her. Martha stepped onto his lap and started to purr. Now the cat was in love with him.

"What I found last night after you called was that I am seriously in love, Don. I was afraid for you and worried about you and what you might be mixed up in. That's not something I've ever felt for another person. What that tells me is that I am a very self-sufficient woman who hasn't needed anyone for a long time but who now needs to know that you are part of me and my life."

Don was looking at Tiffany as she spoke, and Martha purred on his lap. His mind was a little muddled from lack of sleep, but he knew that what she said was as true for him as it was for her.

"I love you, too, Tiffany. I love what you love: art and cats. I guess that means that we are an item."

Tiffany gave Don a kiss on the cheek, got up, and walked to the kitchen, Don following close behind with Martha cradled in his arms and George following.

"You look hungry. Let's have breakfast and then get on to other more urgent things, shall we?" And they did.

Don was semi-awake at noon. Tiffany had called in to take a day off. She was up long before and was in the kitchen making lunch when he pulled his still tired ass out of bed.

"Good morning, or afternoon, Tiffany," Don said as he grabbed her around the middle from behind. "May I use your shower before lunch? I must smell like I spent the night in an alley in Pioneer Square."

"You smell like someone whom I love and whom I want to feed as soon as he gets out of the shower."

Don felt a certain pressure that, if he exercised it, would make lunch a cold one and seriously piss off George and Martha as they waited outside the bedroom door.

Lunch was simple and good. Don was happy and full, full of good food and a feeling that he had never experienced, not ever during his previous marriage.

"I have to call the office. We're on the tail end of a couple of cases. The captain expects updates on both."

Don called Captain Mitchell's desk directly; she answered on the second ring.

"Good afternoon, detective, are you coming in anytime soon? We have a meeting with the assistant prosecutor who does the body wire warrants. You or Chuck will have to appear before the judge who reads the affidavit. This shouldn't take too long; then you and Chuck can talk to Marjorie who can make a date with our guy. Sound like a plan?"

Captain Mitchell was the very definition of efficiency; she didn't waste time or effort by spinning wheels. That was what Don admired about her, that and the fact that she found everyone in his squad except Chuck and him to be wastes of perfectly good oxygen.

"Sounds good. I got my requisite three hours of sack time, so I'm good to go. Chuck's probably a little grouchy, though."

"Call Chuck and tell him to get over the grouches and get his ass in here; pardon my language. I want this to get off the ground as fast as possible. The other thing: how's that going?"

Don briefed her on what they had found that morning at the Cascade Motor Inn and that they had DNA samples in the mill with a "get this done immediately if not sooner" request attached.

"Wally is looking better all the time, isn't he?" she said.

"If I had to bet on him, I'd make a small fortune if I placed him to win. We have an affidavit ready to go but waiting for the DNA findings."

"How about if when we're at the prosecutor's office this afternoon, we bring that along and get a call on whether it would fly as is? I'd hate very much for Wally to go out and kill someone while we're waiting for the lab results."

"OK, let's do that. But I've got to tell you that Chuck and I are getting a little short on manpower since we need to cover both of these cases at the same time."

"What do you suggest? If we call in someone to give you a hand, we make the other guys in the squad wonder what's up."

"The other guys don't spend much time wondering about anything except where the next drink or piece of ass is coming from; pardon my language."

"I'd be shocked if you didn't throw in something totally obscene and very unprofessional every time we talk," Captain Mitchell said in an exasperated tone.

"What I would like to suggest is that we ask Sergeant Jones up north to give us Officer Morris for a while. She's got a future in investigations, and I'd like to give her a little more opportunity. I know that she's new, but from what I've seen, she's a better cop than most and a hell of a lot smarter than any of the guys in this unit."

"Smarter than you? That's going a little far, isn't it?" Captain Mitchell said with just a hint of sarcasm.

"Nope, she's a damn sight smarter than I am. She's smart enough to know that she didn't get here by kissing ass and that she isn't going to kiss any to get anywhere now that she's here."

"I've seen Officer Morris; she's not too hard on the eyes, is she? Does that have anything to do with your suggestion?"

"She's very attractive, but so is the woman I'm committed to and who I spent my time with since leaving the office this morning." I'm still attached to her as we speak, figuratively speaking, that is."

"Of course and OK, I'll talk to Mary and her commander this morning. Maybe we can get her by this evening."

"Thanks, Captain. I'll call Chuck, and we'll be in as soon as possible."

When he hung up, Don recalled that the second reason he went to Tiffany's house was to show her the photos of Wally's car. She said that she couldn't be sure but that it looked a lot like the one that ran her off the street. That was good enough for Don and would add to the long list of crimes he thought Wally was good for. Now if only they had the DNA test results back on the bootlace and Yvonne's fingernail scrapings.

After a long good-bye, ending in more than a kiss, Don made a trip home to shave, change clothes, and bring in the mail. He ran into Roseanne Vargas at the mailboxes. She was her usual smoldering self. She had taken the day off from defending the assholes of the world and was dressed accordingly: Levis (tight), pullover (tight and white), no bra, hair pulled back, and no makeup except for light eyeliner. Don could smell that very familiar scent that was unique to Roseanne and immediately questioned his new commitment to Tiffany.

"Hi, Don, I haven't seen you around for a while."

"The job has been kicking my ass lately, and I'm on nights."

"Do you have plans for after work tonight?"

"I'm afraid I have a case that's taking almost every hour of the day."

"OK, but don't forget where I live."

Roseanne then turned and walked toward her townhouse, leaving Don tongue-tied and his judgment clouded. What an ass for even thinking what he was thinking was the best Don could come up with.

Chuck wasn't exactly delighted to hear the news from Captain Mitchell when Don called him. He said that he'd be in ASAP, but he wouldn't be happy.

"If you wanted happy, Chuck, you should have stayed with that carnival job."

Chuck didn't dignify the comment with a response. The click in his ear told Don that Chuck might be hell to live with for the rest of the day.

When Don got in, Chuck was already at his desk applying the final touches to the affidavit for a body wire; they had decided to keep the warrants separate. He ignored Don until he was done, and then he turned in his chair.

"Glad you could make it today."

"Traffic was a bitch. You know how that West Seattle Freeway can be this time of day."

"The captain wants to see us immediately if not sooner," Chuck said as he hit the print button and closed down his computer with a touch of expertise that Don had to admire.

Chuck and Don walked into the captain's office without knocking. Don closed the door behind them and sat on the only vacant chair. Chuck took one of the others, and Officer Vickie Morris was in the third.

Vickie was in civvies that brought out the best in her. Don had thought of her as very attractive and sexy in a different sort of way. He had seen her in an asexual uniform and conservative civvies; she had morphed into a style of dress that might be described as "Aurora Avenue Whore." Her hair was pulled back in a tight knot, and her face was done up in a slightly over-the-top way that suggested one thing: she could be had for the right price. Her blouse exposed what Don only imagined before this, and her skirt, what there was of it, would have mortified her mother. All very much approved of by Don.

"I'm over here, Don," Captain Mitchell said. "We were lucky enough to get Vickie this afternoon. You know both of these characters, right?" Captain Mitchell asked Vickie.

"Yes, ma'am, we have done some work together."

The "ma'am" didn't quite meet with Captain Mitchell's view of herself, but she let it slide since she knew that Vickie was military and new.

"I thought Vickie should be along on the warrant stuff so she gets a look at how this is done. But I asked that she dress like she is so she won't stand out around the Cascade Motor Inn if we get lucky and put Marjorie and Grimes there sometime today or tonight. Now let me see the affidavit."

"That's all good, but we have to keep her out of sight around here, don't we?" Don asked. "She isn't exactly an unknown around these parts."

"Sure, but you knew that when you asked for her, so we just have to be careful. We'll keep her away from the office when Sherman and his boys are here, which shouldn't be until well after four. When we leave, she'll wear that long coat hanging on the rack. With a scarf over her head, she'll look like a suspect or witness that you had in for an interview. OK, let's go over to the courthouse and visit the prosecutor, but let me look at this before we go."

The deputy prosecuting attorney was a man considerably older than most DPAs in the office. The specialized area of wire warrants was one that was best handled by someone who did little else but. Magistrates weren't so eager to approve wire warrants in a state where recording conversations requires the approval of both parties. Washington, unfortunately, was one of those states. DPA Pearson had long since stopped being impressed by the mystique of homicide detectives. His speech was littered with as many or more profanities than that of most detectives, and he didn't bother making excuses for them.

"So what the fuck do you have for me today, Captain?" DPA Pearson asked while chewing on a sandwich of questionable origin and vintage. After a loud sip of coffee from a Styrofoam cup, Pearson said, "Oh yeah, it's the cop wire thing. Did you know that the big guy was very interested in this? I guess everybody of any significance in your shop is on board with this? The shit will, no doubt, hit the fan in the press and the mayor's office when this sees the light of day."

"We're all good to go on our end. We have the chief's blessing. He's more interested than most in getting the rot out in the open so we can move on."

"Good, let's see the affidavit."

After Pearson read through the affidavit with suggestions for one change, he nodded and gave his approval. "Now let's find a judge who isn't fucking his bailiff and get this signed."

Don noticed that during his monologue, DPA Pearson had his eyes on Vickie who gave right back with an expressionless glare. Could Pearson be one of the johns that trolled Aurora? Probably.

After the minor changes to the affidavit, DPA Pearson, Captain Mitchell, Vickie, Don, and Chuck walked upstairs where they found a superior court judge who had some time in his schedule to review their affidavit. Don presented the affidavit to the judge who sat very quietly and read, and then he read it once more. When he looked up from the paper in his hands, the judge said, "This is unlike any warrant I have ever had my name attached to. It will probably make the police department a little uncomfortable for quite a while if anything comes of it. OK, Detective Weinstein, raise your right hand and swear that the facts stated in this affidavit are true."

Chuck swore to the facts and signed the affidavit before the judge. The judge then signed the warrant.

"Good luck, and be very careful with this. You all recall the last time the department was on the hot seat in this city, don't you? It wasn't pretty."

Captain Mitchell thanked the judge, and then they all turned and walked out. The cat was now beyond out of the bag.

Captain Mitchell, with the concurrence of DPA Pearson, told Chuck and Don to skip filing the warrant after it was served. They would attempt to have it sealed from the eyes of the press after the tape was safely in evidence.

Captain Mitchell suggested that they not return to the office with Vickie and that she would spring for lunch at any restaurant so long as it didn't serve tofu. Chuck said that he had missed lunch since he was rudely pulled from bed by a phone call. Don said that he wasn't hungry but could always eat something.

They were near Chinatown, so they all agreed on a small, dark place where it was unlikely that anyone from the department would eat. "Dong Chow" didn't strike either Don or Chuck as the most appropriate name for a restaurant, but they went in anyway, placing irony aside.

"Don, no comments about the name, please," Captain Mitchell pleaded.

"I had no such thoughts, Captain. I think that 'chow' and 'dong' are perfect when used to name a restaurant. They're the same as 'cock food,' which are words I might well use if naming a restaurant; how about you, Chuck?"

"Let's order, shall we, before Don takes us down another very rude and unappetizing road," Chuck said, his face buried in the menu. Sadly, it was in Mandarin. There were, however, pictures beside the Mandarin characters.

They all found something that looked good and ordered by pointing at the pictures while a small and very old Chinese woman who spoke no English wrote the appropriate characters on a piece of paper. To everyone's amazement, when the old woman served it, the food looked precisely like the pictures on the menu, and it was as good as it looked.

After eating, Captain Mitchell walked back to her office, leaving Don, Chuck, and Vickie on the street in front of the Dong Chow. Vickie got several riveted stares from the "suits" who worked at the nearby city offices and who were perfectly willing to spend their lunch hours in bed with a hooker.

"Shall we get on with the business at hand, or should I turn a couple tricks before we do?" Vickie said with a slightly flirtatious smile.

"Only if we, or I, get the first crack," Don said.

"We have work to do, guys, so how about if we get the car and get hold of Marjorie to arrange tonight's activities?" Chuck said with less patience than he usually expressed toward Don and his high school antics.

The city's vehicle maintenance shop where the Dodge Charger sat waiting was within walking distance of the Dong Chow. After passing up several opportunities to pimp out Vickie, they arrived. They had parked it in the city's lot because they didn't want any of the other homicide detectives or Wally to see it parked in the Public Safety Building. Don drove the Charger to the gas pumps and filled it with low test, the only grade available through the city. Don had the sense that the engine in this car suffered with every stroke under the anguish of eighty-two-octane gas.

With Vickie in the backseat, hidden from prying eyes behind the smoked glass windows, they drove north on I-5 to the first University District off-ramp. Don parked near a low-life bar on Forty-fifth Avenue where he was almost sure he would find a pay phone on the wall near a nasty restroom. He was right.

As Marjorie's phone rang, Don checked out the messages on the wall around the phone. "Jersey sucks big ones, call 873-SCREW." "For a good time, 682-4276." Don was wondering whether "Jersey" was a man or woman when Marjorie answered.

"Oh hi, Don, I'm just getting ready for work. As a matter of fact, you'll be pleased to know that I just got out of the shower and am nude. My new breasts look very good. Do you want me to describe them for you?"

While Don would have liked that a lot, he kept the conversation professional. "Maybe some other time, Marjorie. Now I want to ask if you would be up to getting Grimes alone with you tonight. We have that thing that we talked about."

"Yeah, but I'm not sure if we can use the motel tonight."

"That's OK, but it would be good if you could get him to rent the Cascade Motor Inn room again, but if he doesn't want to, we'll work with it. The only thing we have to be certain of is your safety."

"How about if I call him now and get back to you?"

Don gave her the number of the pay phone and hung up. He walked toward the front door through a haze of cigarette smoke and the smell of stale beer and out into a bright and fresh afternoon. He told Chuck and Vickie what was up and then walked back into the lung-killing atmosphere of the bar.

"You gonna use that phone or jush look at it?"

Don looked up from where he was concentrating on the tip of his shoe as he waited for the phone to ring. What he saw was the face of a man who didn't appear to care if the sun was shining or that the smoke he was breathing would kill him long before he had time to enjoy many more Millers on tap.

"I'm actually waiting for a call, so you'll have to wait awhile," Don said to the guy who didn't look like he was willing to wait for much of anything, especially when told to do so by a guy who was considerably smaller than he was.

"Then howsh about I shove the phone up yer ash while yer waiting?" the man said in his best barfly voice.

"Oh, OK, that sounds like fun. Why don't you do that while I'm waiting? And in the meantime, I'll remove what is left of your teeth. Does that work for you, asshole?"

"Asshole" then took a beer-induced swing at Don who caught it with his left forearm and raised it while delivering a fist to "asshole's" midsection. "Asshole" expelled what Don thought was breath that hadn't benefited from mouthwash in several days and then crumpled to his knees.

The phone rang as "asshole" was struggling to get to his feet. Don picked it up while holding a finger out toward "asshole" as though to say, *One moment, please.*

Marjorie said that she had managed to catch Grimes at home. He, rather than Clorice, answered the phone. She was out with someone doing something. Don could imagine what she was doing and probably with whom. "He said that he's got a room at the Cascade Motor Inn for later this evening."

"We need to meet you before you go and get you set up with the gear. We won't be in the office tonight, so how about you leave early and meet us at the Denny's lot in Ballard at about ten."

"OK, I think I can swing that. Grimes will probably want to get into my pants earlier than midnight anyway."

"Are you planning on going the whole route with him?"

"If that's what it takes, sure. It's not that I haven't screwed the guy before, you know."

"I want to be aware that we won't be far off and that we'll be listening to everything that's said and everything else that goes on."

"I'm OK with that."

"See you at ten, and thanks."

Don hung up and looked into the eyes of "asshole" who was now on his feet and about to say something that would have done nothing but cause him more pain when Don said, "Thanks for your patience. The phone's all yours." Don then walked away, leaving "asshole" standing there at a loss for words from his limited vocabulary and wondering what had just happened. He followed Don out and saw him get into the Charger, not quite up to remembering the British Columbia plates. "Fucking Canadians" was all he said as he turned and walked back to his next beer, forgetting that he needed to make a call.

"We have a lot of time to waste before we meet Marjorie at ten. Let's pick up the gear and get a quick training session on how to use it."

Don drove the Charger from Forty-fifth Avenue to the Montlake Bridge and south to the East Precinct where the Technical Services Unit was located. They parked the Charger in the precinct's garage so it wouldn't be seen on the street and then went to the second floor and into Technical Services.

Vickie saw a fellow academy classmate on the first floor when they were waiting for the elevator and asked if it would be OK if she talked to her for a while. Chuck told her to go ahead but that she couldn't tell her what she was doing there. The way she was dressed, any officer could guess that she was doing a hooker detail with Vice. That was a good thing for them to think.

The guys in Technical Services were very good at what they did. If there was a "spook" unit in the department, they were it. Anybody who needed advice or equipment to conduct undercover work went to them. When Don and Chuck left, they were sure that they could get the job done and that no one in the Technical Services Unit was going to spill the beans.

From the East Precinct, Don drove to Aurora Avenue where he found another bar with a pay phone hanging on a wall near the men's room. He wondered why using a pay phone in a bar came complete with the odor of stale urine. He called Radio and told the supervisor what was on for later that night. Radio would be monitoring them on an alternative channel and would attempt to keep Patrol out of the motel/whorehouse's parking lot.

"Well, what to do until ten tonight?" Don asked. It was only five-fifteen.

"Let's drive north, find a place to park, and take a nap; this could be a long night," Chuck said.

"If it's OK with you, Vickie, let's do that," Don said.

With all three on board with the idea, Don drove to Everett on Highway 99, aka Aurora Avenue. He drove the speed limit so the Charger wouldn't be pulled over by some overzealous cop who also hated Canadians. Don found a secluded spot and parked. Chuck was already sleeping when they parked. If Don hadn't already committed to living a cleaner life, he would have suggested to Vickie that he climb in back with her. *What a fucking Boy Scout,* he thought.

It had just turned seven thirty when Don woke up. He had to pee in a serious way, which meant one thing: find a restaurant so they could both eat and take care of that problem before they went to work.

"Do you think you guys could find a toilet before I soil the seat of this warrant wagon?" Vickie asked from the backseat.

"Sorry about that, Vickie," said Don, now reaching the point where he might have to step out and pee on the pavement. He knew that Vickie didn't enjoy that option.

They drove to a Denny's about ten minutes after the declaration of the state of emergency. Vickie pushed past Don and Chuck and ran into the restaurant with the detectives close behind. Don gave his name to the cashier so they would be called when a table was open. Both then walked with some measure of urgency to the men's room.

Dinner didn't include tofu, vegetarian, or vegan dishes. Don had a hamburger and fries with a vanilla malt chaser. Chuck thought it best not to comment as he enjoyed his liver and onions. Vickie had a salad of some sort while ignoring the stares of most of the men surrounding them.

During the drive back to Seattle, they went over their plan for what was going to take place. Don told Vickie that she would be in the shadows near the room where Marjorie was recording Grimes. In case the shit hit the fan, she would be first into the room. Although she looked like a hooker, she had her .38 and radio in her purse. Don and Chuck would be parked behind the motel and watching her from the shadows. The one thing Vickie wouldn't have on was her body armor; it wouldn't go with her ensemble. Don and Chuck left their vests in the office, so they were all on the same page if the shit did hit the fan. They also talked about the best-laid plans turning to shit.

Don drove the Charger into the Ballard Denny's at exactly nine fifteen. He parked in a spot where they could see Marjorie's car when she drove in. She arrived at exactly ten. As she walked toward the restaurant's entrance, Don called to her and she turned and walked to where he was standing in a shadow. He could have been summoning a hooker for a night of fun and games instead of a night of "Fuck you, Bill Grimes." He was impressed with the dress, or lack of it, that she had decided on.

Marjorie climbed into the back of the Charger with Vickie. *They could easily have made a thousand bucks between them on Aurora on any night* was Don's thought.

Don briefed Marjorie on what was going to happen and where the recorder and transmitter would be. They all decided that she should not wear the wire on her body since Grimes was going to want to check out her breasts again, and he would probably expect that she get naked. She would put the wire in her oversize handbag and keep it near her and Grimes. Don and Chuck assured her that Vickie would be right outside the room and that they would be nearby if anything unexpected happened; everything that was going to take place could be placed in the category of "unexpected."

Marjorie told them that Grimes had made a reservation at the Cascade Motor Inn, room eight, and that he would meet her there at about eleven thirty.

"One last thing, Marjorie," Chuck said. "If it comes down to it, are you still planning to have sex with Grimes? We don't want this to look like we entrapped him into anything."

"That's what he expects, otherwise he wouldn't have rented the room. As I said before, it's not like we haven't done it before."

"OK, but we don't want you to do something that you feel forced into."

"Don't, because I'm not."

After Don and Chuck had placed the wire in Marjorie's purse and tested it, Marjorie got out and walked back to her car. They all drove north on Fifteenth Avenue, then east on Eighty-fifth to Aurora.

Aurora became hooker central at about this time every night, and this night was no exception. At least one woman who wasn't waiting for a bus occupied every stop. Don and Chuck kept their eyes peeled for Shondra. They didn't see her.

When Don, Chuck, and Marjorie got near the Cascade Motor Inn, they got into their hyper-vigilant mode. The lot wasn't full, but it contained enough cars so Vickie wouldn't stand out. Don did an illegal U-turn and drove back to the Cascade Motor Inn and into the dark lot behind it where they waited.

Marjorie drove in shortly after and parked in front of the office. The same Mr. Park who had tried to give Don a ration of shit the day before was behind the desk. *Did these guys ever take a day off?* entered Don's mind. They watched as the man gave Marjorie a key, adding ammunition to Don's case that this was nothing more than a whorehouse. Marjorie left the office, turned, and looked toward the lot where the Charger was parked and then walked out of sight toward room eight.

Grimes wasn't supposed to be there until eleven thirty, but just in case, Don and Chuck decided that it would be best if Vickie took a walk past the room to check. Vickie got out, pulled her inadequate skirt down, and walked away into the night. Don called Radio on a tactical channel and told the operator that they were in place. He used a call sign that he and Radio had agreed on. His actual radio call sign could be recognized by anyone in Homicide. Then they waited.

Grimes wasn't the best detective known to man, but he was punctual when the reason was a piece of ass with someone other than Clorice. He drove in at eleven thirty and parked in front of room eight. Vickie knew his car's description and walked in the opposite direction when it slid in beside Marjorie's car. She wouldn't be out of place in the lot, just another hooker looking for work.

When Grimes got out of his car, he gave Vickie's rear a long and hard look, closed his car door, and walked toward room eight. He was staggering.

Don and Chuck opened their doors, dome light unscrewed, and walked slowly to the corner of the office from where they could see the door to room eight.

"Hi, Bill," Marjorie said in a static-garbled voice. Grimes responded. The transmitter was working. Don and Chuck could hope that the recorder was doing as well.

"Well, what are you waiting for? I didn't buy those tits so you could hide them from me," Grimes said in his usual gentlemanly manner, mixed with a booze-induced slur. Then came the sound of something heavy landing on something. Don and Chuck knew that it was Marjorie's purse hitting the bed or somewhere close. Then they heard the unmistakable sound of shoes landing on the floor and a zipper coming down. Marjorie had worn a jacket with a zipper that ran diagonal across her chest in an alluring way. When it was partially unzipped and allowed to flap open, it gave a great view of the top of one of Marjorie's new breasts. Earlier both Don and Chuck had been beneficiaries of her good taste in clothes for this occasion. Then they heard what they knew was the jacket as it was tossed on a chair or maybe the bed.

"Very nice, Marjorie. Now how about if you get to the most important stuff? I didn't give you all that money so I could look at your bra."

"Let's not be in such a hurry, Bill," Marjorie said in a way that might have come from the mouth of a hooker. Don could imagine her licking her lips and smiling in her best Marylyn Monroe imitation as she teased Grimes. "You know that I'm very appreciative of all that you did for me. No one else would think to give me enough money to do this."

"You can thank Sherman and Martin, too. They threw in some money. They may come calling sometime."

"Where did you guys get all this money?"

"We have sources that you don't need to know about."

"It's clean money, I hope. I don't want my boob job to be illegal in some way."

"Don't worry. Now take off that bra."

The next sound that Don and Chuck heard was Grimes telling Marjorie that she was beautiful and that he wanted to see all of her, not just her tits.

"If I have to show you mine, you have to show me yours," Marjorie giggled.

There was a distinct rustling of clothes for the next minute as Grimes and, apparently, Marjorie undressed.

"Holy shit, you got your money's worth in Canada, didn't you? Do you remember the last time you, Clorice, and I got together? That was a great time, wasn't it?"

"Yeah, those were the days. I didn't have the build I have now, but you still thought I was something special. Now come over here and let's see if we can get that thing working."

There was the sound of a mattress compressing, a cheap mattress, and then a sound that both Don and Chuck recognized as a man getting some very personal attention from someone else, man or woman.

"Bill, do you guys have any more money? I'm thinking about getting some other things done that will require a lot of money that I don't have."

"You're just about perfect the way you are," Grimes gasped. "But we have as much as you need to do anything you want. Just let me know how much. I think that you'll owe us some more attention, though."

"Don't worry, I'll give you attention just like this anytime you want if you give me what I want."

"Oh yeah, oh yeah, that would be great. Now just lie back and we can talk about that later."

"No, let's talk about it first, and then you can do whatever you want. I'll need about twenty thousand dollars to do all of the stuff I have in mind. Do you have that much?"

"We have that much if that's what you need. We have a lot more than that," Grimes boasted. "But your body doesn't need any improvement."

"Thank you, Bill, but how do you get that much money together?"

"We're the police; we find that much lying around from time to time, but you need to lie down before I lose this."

"Don't be in such a hurry; we have the room for the night. What do you mean 'lying around'? That kind of money doesn't grow on trees."

Don and Chuck could hear the bed squeak as Marjorie talked to Grimes. This wasn't the Four Seasons where the mattresses didn't squeak under the thousand-dollar hookers that operated there.

"Oh fuck, Marjorie, we need to just get this on."

"Just tell me what you mean by 'lying around,' and we'll get it on."

"OK, we find it lying around at some crime scenes. It's just there, and nobody would suspect that a cop would take anything from a scene, especially not from a suicide."

"You, Sherman, and Martin took money from a suicide scene? Which one?"

Don thought that Marjorie should get an Academy Award for this act. She was a natural. Maybe she should have been a cop. Then it occurred to him that cops didn't have the luxury of enticing a crook with the promise of sex. Come to think of it, they did; that's what Vice did for a living.

"You remember the faggot who died about a month ago? He came from a high-roller family that kept him in everything he needed as long as he lived somewhere other than their house. They provided him with a lot of spending money, all in cash. Then he killed himself, and because of his family name, we went to the scene. He had a box full of money. We took it."

"Was that the first time you did something like that?"

"Marjorie, are you going to fuck me or talk me to orgasm?"

"Just tell me about this money you have. Did you take some other money? I think I like the idea; it's easy money and who would suspect?"

"Yeah, we've taken quite a bit over the years. I suppose Sherman will retire in Mexico a wealthy man. As for Martin, his disappears somewhere from time to time. Who knows where he spends it."

"How about you, Bill, what do you have planned for all the money you've accumulated?"

"When I retire, I plan to divorce Clorice, give her half of my retirement, and then go somewhere where the women are young and real willing, maybe Thailand."

"You are a pervert, aren't you, Bill?"

"I suppose I am; now let's get down to business."

"One more thing before we get to that, where do you keep all this money? You probably can't put it in the bank because the IRS might want to know about it."

"I keep it in various places. Some is at home in boxes, some is in a safety deposit box, but some is in my desk at work. I even have some in my car's trunk. Do you need some tonight?"

Don and Chuck couldn't quite believe their luck. They wrapped up all three of their targets in one fell swoop. There might be the promise of a roll in the hay with Marjorie that motivated Grimes to spill his guts, but the department wouldn't care about that. Entrapment wasn't an issue with Internal Affairs. That was a matter that the courts might have a problem with, but the fact remained that Grimes, Sherman, and Martin were history as far as the department was concerned.

"If you keep that up, I'm not going to have anything left for you," Grimes said with more than a little suggestion that he was very near adding to the stain pattern on the bedspread. Then, if the noises coming from him were any indication, he was done for the night. Marjorie wouldn't have to perform what she had expected would be demanded of her.

"Oh, I'm sorry, Bill. That was unexpected."

"That's OK, it felt great, just like old times."

Grimes was both drunk and sexually satisfied, so he did the expected under the circumstances: he rolled over and went to sleep; his face sunk into a pillow of questionable cleanliness. Before she got up to get dressed, Marjorie pulled a blanket over Grimes's naked body. The last thing that Don and Chuck heard from the room was Marjorie saying, "And that's a wrap."

CHAPTER THIRTY

Marjorie opened the door to room eight, walked out, and then slowly and quietly closed it. Vickie walked with her to where Don and Chuck were waiting. Mr. Park came out of the office as Marjorie and Vickie passed his window on his very narrow and very sordid world.

"Is room vacant?" he asked with hope in his voice.

"No, it's still occupied. We're just going out to pick up another john, but we'll be right back. Keep the No Vacancy sign lit," Vickie said.

"OK, but tell me when you go."

That's all Don and Chuck needed to hear. Here was an admission that the man was running a "disorderly house." They came out of the shadows and into Mr. Park's view, and he got that "oh shit" look on his face as they approached.

"Even you must realize what you just said and how we have to take it, don't you?" Don asked.

"I no know what you talk about. Maybe I should call attorney."

"Yes, you probably should. You might want to talk about how you're going to support yourself and pay his fee when we close you down," Chuck said in his best Marlin Brando imitation.

"OK, we make an arrangement, right? I can have room for you when you like."

"Now you're trying to bribe us. It gets worse all the time. But you may have hope yet," Don said.

"Anysing you want."

"You will change sheets between customers or we will close up your shop."

"But I no have people who do that."

"We'll be back tomorrow night to watch from a distance. If you don't have the sheets changed between hookers, we will close your place right then," Don said.

"How I do this? I no have housekeeping at night."

"That's an issue that you want to resolve by tomorrow at the latest. Maybe you could hire two women who need the work. You have to pay them a fair wage, of course," Chuck said. "If it comes to our attention that you're cheating your housekeeping staff out of wages, we'll be back with any number of city inspectors."

"OK, I hire two housekeepers for night shift. They will clean between hook...customers."

"We wish you a long and prosperous life here, Mr. Park," Don said.

Don, Chuck, Vickie, and Marjorie walked to the Charger. When they were seated in the car, Marjorie took the wire equipment from her purse and gave it to Chuck.

After a short debriefing, Marjorie got out of the Charger and walked to her car. After he saw Marjorie drive out of the motel lot, Don started the Charger and drove onto southbound Aurora, looking for a pay phone and finding one near a filthy toilet in an even filthier bar. Captain Mitchell sounded a little groggy when Don woke her, but she became fully alert when he told her what they had just recorded. They decided between them to let Grimes drive away and not put him in cuffs until they had talked to IIS whose case this really was.

When Don, Chuck, and Vickie arrived downtown and closed in on the Public Safety Building, they started looking for a place to park the Charger where it wouldn't be associated with the department. Don found a spot under the Yesler Street overpass on Fourth Avenue, about two blocks from the Public Safety Building. If it happened to be ticketed and towed, so much the better.

So she wouldn't be propositioned on the way, Don and Chuck walked with Vickie to where her car was parked. During the short walk, Don had to struggle with his new resolution to remain faithful to Tiffany. Vickie's skirt was the ultimate test, and he passed with flying colors. *What a fucking Boy Scout.*

"Good night, Officer Morris," Don said as she climbed behind the wheel of a car that made his look like it belonged in a wrecking yard. "If you're up to it, come in at about noon. We'll have a talk with Captain Mitchell and decide what to do next. And wear something a little less provocative, maybe something that you would wear to court."

"OK. I'll see you guys tomorrow…today then."

"Welcome to Investigations. The hours are a little unpredictable," Chuck said.

"If I wanted predictable, I would have taken a job at Boeing."

"Good point," Chuck said with a wink before Don could say anything smart assed.

Bill Grimes woke up with a headache, sprawled nude across the bed in room eight at the Cascade Motor Inn. After he got past the smell of the pillow and the dried substance on the bedspread that had been covering him, his mind wandered back to the night with Marjorie; it was enjoyable but troubling. What had he said to her? He had a way about him, one that he didn't exactly like, that led him to run his mouth when under the influence of intoxicating beverages and in the presence of a woman who might just tend to his needs. He liked to brag to women, generally about things that he shouldn't. Had he spilled his guts about where he got the money for her boob job? Probably.

He got out of bed, covered in a tangle of very thin sheets, thread count about two hundred, if that. He staggered into the bathroom, turned on the shower, and stood under it, trying to recall the night and clear his brain. Marjorie was still on his side after all these years, wasn't she? After all, hadn't she taken part in some pretty kinky and incriminating stuff with him, Clorice, and a few others? He felt better after stepping out of the shower and drying off with a towel that probably wouldn't meet Fairmount Hotel standards.

Grimes's mind drifted back to a night at the Fairmount with one of his "victims," a woman who had reported a burglary. What she was really reporting was a need to have her sexual needs satisfied. Grimes, then a burglary detective, gave her the full measure of service that the department had to offer. It didn't hurt that she was rich and lived on the shores of Lake Washington with her very rich husband. *How did I sink into this hole?* was his last thought as he closed the door behind him, climbed into his car, and drove away. It was nine o'clock on a rainy Seattle morning.

Don didn't go back to Tiffany's after the night's events. He needed to sleep a few hours before starting all over again. He and Chuck still had another warrant to write. What they really needed was quick DNA results, but that wasn't going to be sped up by wishing. Science had to run its course, no matter that another body might turn up while they waited. They could only hope that it wouldn't.

Don woke up at ten in his own bed with eight-hundred-thread-count sheets and goose down pillows. He rolled over, put his hands behind his head, and gazed out over the mist that shrouded Elliot Bay. The tops of the downtown buildings were lost in the clouds, all but the Smith Tower, which managed to stand out except for the very top. Rain ran down his bedroom window, bending the otherwise straight lines of the Smith Tower that weren't lost in the clouds. *What a great city* was Don's first thought. Then his phone rang.

"Good morning, Detective. You had a good night's sleep, I hope?" Captain Mitchell chirped in her most cheerful voice.

"Yes, ma'am, I had a great night's sleep. It was made even better with the knowledge that you would fuck it up with this call; pardon my language."

"No pardon required. What is required is your presence in my office within the hour. I'll call your partner and Officer Morris and get them moving as soon as I'm sure that you have both feet on the floor."

"Yes, ma'am, I'm now upright and well on my way. A quick shower and I'll be out the door. Can you tell me what's up?"

"I'd rather leave that until you arrive. See you by eleven."

Don heard a click as Captain Mitchell hung up. He got up, started a pot of coffee, and then did the usual bathroom stuff. When he was dressed and ready to face the day, Don poured a cup of coffee into a travel mug and walked to the garage. The water taxi would have to leave without him.

The day-shift receptionist was at her desk when Don walked in. She didn't quite meet the sexpot standards that Marjorie had set over the years, but she must have been hired by someone with standards similar to those of the person who thought Marjorie was the girl for the job. The final interview was probably conducted on a couch was Don's guess. She smiled and bid Don a good morning as he walked past her, eyes firmly glued to the floor in front of him.

As usual Chuck had beaten him in. Don had the excuse that Chuck lived closer and without the bottleneck created by the West Seattle Bridge to negotiate. But how to explain that Officer Vickie Morris was also there, sitting at his desk when he walked in?

"Good of you to show up, Don," Chuck said.

Don ignored Chuck and told Officer Morris to stay where she was as she started to get out of his chair. "Is the captain in her office?" Don asked Chuck.

"Yes she is, along with the IIS commander and our bureau chief. I'm surprised that the big chief isn't there as well, but it's early."

"Does she want us to come in or what?"

"She hasn't said anything yet; we just got here."

As the clock on his desk turned to eleven, Don's phone rang. It was Captain Mitchell. "You made it? Bring everybody into my office."

Don walked into the office, followed closely by Chuck and then Officer Morris. All three commanders sat with faces that might be found on someone en route to the gallows. The bureau chief had the longest face. He was, after all, the person who could have fingers pointed at him if the shit hit the fan on any given day. Why was he not aware of the thievery in his most prestigious unit? This would not look good on his resume when he retired and needed a job with some university or company that wanted a well-known name in the business of investigations to add to their letterhead. No, it would not look good at all. The commander of IIS appeared to be licking his chops with the anticipation of taking over the Investigations Bureau. Captain Mitchell was clearly in charge among this crew of high rollers. She didn't give the impression of caring about her future, just so long as the job at hand was done and done right.

"Come in guys, Officer Morris. We all know each other, so we'll get right to it. Oh, you may not know Officer Morris," Captain Mitchell said to the brass. "She is assigned the North Precinct, but she has some expertise that we thought would be useful to us."

Both commanders got up and shook Vickie's hand and sat back down, not offering her their chairs. *Rude fucks* was Don's thought.

"Don and Chuck, would you find three more chairs and bring them in?" Captain Mitchell asked.

When everyone was settled, Captain Mitchell started to go over what Don, Chuck, and Vickie already knew. Then she went into the question of what to do next.

"As I see it, we can't really let the three that are now implicated continue in the department. We also have to make every effort to recover as much of the money as possible. They can't be allowed to spend it when we know that they have it. But that brings about the issue of Sergeant Sherman and Detective Martin. We haven't yet determined that they're involved except from what Grimes told Marjorie. I would suggest that we search their desks before they come in this afternoon to see if they have any money stashed. Grimes already said that he has money in his, so let's assume that he does. Based on the tape we have from the little escapade at the Cascade Motor Inn, we should have no problem getting a warrant for all of their desks, cars, houses, and bank records. It should be a fairly straightforward warrant."

Don looked at Chuck and both did a subtle eye roll. They could be almost sure that none of these high rollers had done an affidavit of probable cause pursuant to a search warrant, so they probably didn't know what it took to put one together. Probable cause, to them, was an academic concept, not something you tried to manufacture out of sometimes limited facts. Maybe the same judge that signed the wire warrant could be enticed to approve this one. He would be considering suspected dirty cops here, after all, not some schmuck who received stolen goods for a living.

"If I may be permitted a question, Captain," Don said.

"Of course, Detective," Captain Mitchell said. "You three and Marjorie made this all happen, so ask away."

"Where does Marjorie stand in this? I mean we can't very well take back what she bought with the stolen money. Then there is her safety to consider. I personally wouldn't trust any one of these fucks, pardon my language, when they find out what and who brought them down. I would feel better if all three were arrested this afternoon and put in jail."

"If I may say something," Chuck said. "All three of them have to be interviewed to see if they will give statements before they are carted off to jail."

"I agree, Chuck," Don said. "But we can't be the ones who do the interviewing."

The Internal Affairs commander raised his hand as if he was a student asking permission to talk. "I think that my guys should do the interviews. They don't have the personal relationships with them that you two have."

"That's a good idea," Captain Mitchell said. "But let's first get the warrant going. We have to have it before they arrive for work."

Based on what had happened during the early morning hours at the Cascade Motor Inn, what they had witnessed in the lineup room, and what the complainant had said about sonny boy and his box of cash, Don and Chuck did the fastest affidavit of probable cause in memory. They, along with Vickie, took it across the street to an available deputy prosecuting attorney who wasn't too pleased with the facts as stated.

"I wish I'd have taken a long lunch. This is information that needs to be kept under wraps, you know," the DPA said. Then he signed the affidavit.

No shit Sherlock was Don's thought.

Don, Chuck, and Vickie walked up a few flights of stairs to the courtroom where the judge who had signed the wire warrant was located. He was in trial but in recess when they arrived. The judge invited them into his chambers where he sat and read the affidavit. His eyebrows rose from time to time as he read. Don, Chuck, and Vickie glanced at each other, knowing that he was enjoying the story. Judges had to live a cop's life vicariously through trials, and by reading the explicit stories contained in affidavits of probable cause, this was probably the closest to an erotic novel he had ever seen.

When the judge finished reading, he asked Don to raise his hand and swear to the facts in the document. Don did so, and then he signed the affidavit. While the judge was signing the warrant, he smiled and said, "I thought that I'd seen everything until now. Do you suppose the young lady will have to bring her breasts in as evidence if this goes to trial?" He appeared to be only half joking.

The thought hadn't occurred to Don and Chuck, but they could be assured that some defense attorney would demand it if only to get at Marjorie for what she had done to his client, and maybe to further demand that she expose the fruits of the crime to the jury.

"You can be assured, Your Honor, that there will be standing room only during that trial," Don said.

"Good luck. I don't envy you having to arrest your colleagues."

Chuck said in leaving, "Your Honor, these guys are just members of the same squad; they aren't our colleagues."

The warrant covered the desks of Sherman, Grimes, and Martin as well as their lockers and cars. Their houses and any other places they might have stashed money would be added as evidence unfolded.

"Let's do their desks first, then their lockers, and then go to lunch; I'm starved," said Don.

"You're always starved," Chuck said. "I could use some lunch, though, but if you tell me that we should give that Chow Dong or Dong Chow another try, I'll have to kneecap you."

"We wouldn't want that now would we," Don gasped. "How about if Vickie picks the place this time?"

"OK, but if you insist on vegetarian, I'll have to kneecap you," Chuck said to Vickie who stood there with a puzzled look on her face.

They changed the order of business to start with lunch and then go to work serving the warrant. There was a place in an old hotel turned low-rent housing near the Public Safety Building. It had attached to it a Japanese restaurant that served mostly cops and attorneys. That's where they had lunch. Nobody got kneecapped, and all left full.

With warrant in hand, the three walked into the unit and into Captain Mitchell's office. They agreed that the desk and locker searches would be done immediately and that the day squads should be out of the office when they did them. Captain Mitchell went out long enough to talk to the two day-watch sergeants and then came back in.

"They're going to make some excuse to get their guys out of the office for an hour or two."

Captain Mitchell gave the squads fifteen minutes and then went out. She turned and said that all was clear and told Don, Chuck, and Vickie to follow her.

They first went to Sergeant Sherman's cubicle. His desk was strewn with paper, the trash can was full, and there were several empty paper coffee cups sitting here and there. Captain Mitchell tried his desk and found it locked. That was no surprise; that's why she had two detectives and one officer along. Don put the head of a screwdriver that he just happened to have on hand into the drawer lock. He hit the handle of the screwdriver with the hammer that he also just happened to have handy. The lock required five solid whacks from the hammer before the screwdriver turned and the drawer was unlocked.

Don pulled the drawer out as far as it would go. It was about as much of a mess as the rest of the cubicle. He and Chuck went through every piece of paper and every object; they found no money. The other drawers unlocked along with the top drawer, so Don didn't have to do more damage to the desk. Chuck searched the right drawer and Don the left.

"Holy shit" were the first words out of Chuck's mouth as he started going through the drawer. "These are magazines that I would expect to find in your desk," he said, handing one to Don.

Don turned the pages of the magazine that Chuck handed him. When he came to a page that was inexplicably sticking to its neighboring page, he closed it and let it drop in a wastebasket. Most of the magazines were those that gay men might get a charge out of. They certainly weren't purchased for the quality of the stories, what there were of them. These were photo magazines that gave well-endowed men the opportunity to make a living by showing the public what they had and how they utilized what they had. Chuck appeared to be appalled, but it might have been an act.

"These are the guys that give us a bad name. But you have to admit that they are well endowed, don't you?" Chuck said to no one in particular.

"Yes, you do," Vickie agreed.

Among the magazines were a few that could be referred to as straight, but they all had one thing in common: the women depicted were all being used in humiliating ways by men with multiple prison tattoos.

Near the back of the drawer was the most interesting piece of evidence. It was a plain manila folder containing several Polaroid photographs. They were primarily of two women whom Don and Chuck knew and one whom Vickie knew: Marjorie and Clorice. Both women were in various states of undress. Marjorie was photographed before and after breast enhancement surgery. She was standing in the lineup room against the wall where lineup subjects stood. She did both full-face and profile poses as the photographer snapped the shots. She had no top on in any of them.

Clorice was photographed in what could only be described as pornographic poses. They confirmed to Don that she looked good in the nude, like he didn't already know. One of the photographs included Sherman. He was getting some serious oral attention from Clorice. Don thought that he could use some gym time.

"Does your unit Polaroid have a remote shutter?" Vickie asked.

"I don't think so, why?" Chuck said.

"How could that photo have been taken of Clorice and Sherman if there wasn't a remote shutter? There must have been a third person taking it."

"Marjorie was part of this little group, so she was probably the photographer," Chuck said.

Captain Mitchell, who had been standing back and watching this drama unfold, said in a somewhat strained voice, "Are we working with a bunch of perverts or what?"

While Chuck was listing the items found and seized on the warrant return, Don went to work on the next drawer. There were some work-related files, but most were not. There were travel folders and more gay and straight porn magazines. In the back of the drawer were two items of great interest: a Polaroid camera with remote shutter and an eight-by-eleven envelope filled with a large amount of cash, mostly twenty, fifty, and one-hundred-dollar bills. The unofficial count was $13,150.

"We have two questions answered," Don said. "A third party probably did not take the picture of Sherman's blow job, and he probably got this money from someplace other than his work for the city. And I use the word 'work' reluctantly."

"The answer to the first question is certainly comforting," Captain Mitchell said. "As for the second, he put this money here for a reason that is certainly suspect. Most people put that amount of cash in a bank or in an investment of some sort. It will lead to some interesting questions for him this afternoon."

Don and Chuck continued to search until they were satisfied that they wouldn't find anything that would further incriminate Sherman. Then they moved on to Martin's and Grimes's desks.

Either these guys were stupid or they were arrogant beyond belief. Both of their desks were unlocked. Neither of them contained money. Both were a mess.

The locker room was off a hallway near the elevator. It was dark, dirty, and rarely used for anything but riot gear and a uniform for those rare times when everybody had to suit up. Don had borrowed a bolt cutter from maintenance and did quick work of the padlocks on all three lockers.

Sherman's was the first locker they looked at. It, like his desk, was a mess. The uniform hanging in it hadn't seen the light of day in many years. Sitting on the floor of the locker was a pair of dusty, high-top boots that were in serious need of a shine. Both were without laces. Dust had accumulated on the eight-point cap that sat on the top shelf. And there was an envelope pushed toward the back of the shelf. It contained several bundles of cash wrapped with rubber bands. Don and Chuck verified the amount before putting it into evidence: $27,660.

Grimes's locker was the next to get their attention. If it was possible, it was even grubbier than Sherman's. There were socks jammed into a pair of boots that, if pulled out, would reveal a green something resembling a high school experiment. They didn't touch them. Grimes, however, had been truthful to Marjorie to the extent that he was storing a large amount of money. In a small box, Don found what he and Chuck would verify as $56,427. Why he put a five and two ones in the box would remain a mystery.

Martin's locker contained his uniform and some other things that were work-related but no cash. One item caught Don and Chuck's attention, however. Lying next to his cap on the top shelf was an address book. While they were looking for money, they decided that the book might contain information that would lead to the discovery of money, so Don took it out and opened it. It was an address book, but it contained addresses only as an afterthought to the real content.

"I would never have guessed that Martin was such a lady's man, would you?" Don asked to no one in particular.

It seems that Martin liked to take pictures of his women in various states of undress and kept them with their addresses and phone numbers. These photos weren't Polaroid, however. They were high-quality 35mm. Among the women photographed was Clorice, which wasn't too surprising given what Don and Chuck already knew about her. They had to admit that Martin was a more creative photographer than Sherman, assuming Martin took the photos.

One photo caught Don's eye: it was taken through a window and included not only a man and woman who were clearly engaged in consensual sexual activity, but it also included the bottom half of a Jackson Pollock, There was only one original Pollock like it, and Don owned it. The two people in the photo were not identifiable unless one was very familiar with their anatomies from the waist down.

"Don, isn't that..." Chuck started to say before Don interrupted him.

"Let's take these and the book and look at them up in Evidence," Don said.

"Just a second, guys," Captain Mitchell said. "I think I recognize that guy in the picture."

Chuck looked at Don as if to say, *So you and the Captain had a fling, too.*

Don looked back at Chuck in a way that could only be described as menacing. The look meant *If you continue that thought, I'll have to remove your walking privileges.*

"Let's talk about that photo before you put it into Evidence. Maybe we can pin a peeping charge on Martin if we don't find any money that ties him to the thefts," Captain Mitchell said with a big smile directed at Don.

"That's a thought," Don replied with a grimace. Of course, he knew that Captain Mitchell had never been in his townhouse, nor did she know about his Pollock. At least he thought that she didn't.

Don and Chuck locked the results of their searches in Don's desk, and then they and Vickie went for coffee while Captain Mitchell briefed her bosses.

By the time they returned to the office, Captain Mitchell's conference was over. They walked into her office without knocking.

Captain Mitchell decided that a quick addendum to the warrant, which included Sherman's house, was now in order, so Don wrote the addendum and took it across to the courthouse where the same judge called a recess while he read it and added it to the warrant. As Don was about to leave the judge's chambers, the judge asked Don a question that gave them both a chuckle: "Do you think you'll be able to sell movie rights to the book that you have planned after this is concluded?"

"Thank you for the suggestion, Your Honor. I hadn't thought of that."

Marjorie took the night off, which was unusual. If she wasn't on vacation, she very rarely took a day off. It was as if the job was her only life; it probably was. If the captain hadn't called her and given her an order to stay home, she would have been there to witness the carnage that resulted from her boob job.

Three members of Internal Investigations were waiting in the bureau chief's office when shift change arrived. Don and Chuck were going to be given the dubious honor of arresting the three other members of their squad and reading them their rights. The potential ramifications of such a thing weren't lost on either of them. They would then deliver them to separate interview rooms where the Internal Investigations guys would take over. No matter the outcome of the interviews, all three were history as members of the department.

Sherman was the first to arrive as was usually the case. He walked into his cubicle and was met with his file drawers open and Don and Chuck standing behind him.

"What the fuck happened here?" Sherman bellowed. "Is this some kind of fucking joke?"

"No, Sergeant Sherman, this is no joke," Don said. "You are under arrest for theft and possession of stolen property." Don read him his rights from a card that he kept in his pocket for just such occasions.

Sergeant Sherman turned red and sat back onto his chair like he had been pushed. Don and Chuck thought that he might have a heart attack. He was still wearing his gun, which Don reached down and grabbed so it wouldn't get Sherman into any deeper trouble.

"Stand up, Sergeant; we'll have to pat you down," Chuck said.

"I'm not going to be frisked by any fucking faggot."

Chuck placed a pain compliance hold on Sherman's right hand and pulled him from his chair, swiveled him so his face was against one of the half walls of his cubicle, and whispered something in his ear. Sherman went limp and put his one free arm to his side in complete surrender. Chuck then did a thorough pat-down of Sherman before putting cuffs on him. With Chuck's assistance, Sherman was put in his chair: he was a broken man. Don's thought was that he would be spilling his guts to IIS.

After Don, Chuck, and Vickie delivered Sherman to one of the interview rooms and turned him over to an IIS investigator, they walked back to the unit.

"What did you tell Sherman that got his attention?" Don asked a now very angry Chuck.

"I asked him how it felt to be put in jail by a faggot and said I hoped he got fucked by some big bubba in the prison that he was going to."

"Good job, Chuck. I couldn't have put it any better."

"Of course you couldn't; you're not a faggot."

Amazingly, Grimes and Martin arrived only about a half hour late for the start of shift. They parked near each other on the bottom floor and walked together to the elevator. By this time, word of what had happened to Sherman had spread to most of the department's units. Rumors had a way of spreading around the department as if it was a little old ladies knitting circle.

When the elevator doors opened, they got in and rode it to the first floor where it stopped and a burglary detective they both knew got in.

"Did you guys hear what happened to Sherman today?" Being the first to spread bad news about anybody in the department was a form of sport. The burglary detective was the first to give Grimes and Martin the news about their boss; ten points for him.

As the burglary detective told the story and the elevator got closer to the fifth floor, the more aggravated Grimes and Martin became. They were going to their doom if they couldn't stop before the door opened on the fifth floor.

When the elevator stopped on the fifth floor, the burglary detective got off. Grimes and Martin waited for the doors to close so they could consider their next move. The doors closed and the elevator continued up to the next floor where the Evidence Unit was located. They wished at that point that they were on the public elevator, which went to the fifteenth floor.

Don and Chuck hadn't been detectives and officers for the years that they had without learning one thing: don't trust anybody any farther than

STILL LIFE WITH BADGE

you could throw them. Vickie was quick to catch on. That little maxim led them to wait for Grimes and Martin in the parking garage. They saw them arrive and get on the elevator. They would wait for them to return to the garage after the burglary detective told them that they were walking into an ambush. They told the detective to inform them what awaited them; he was only too happy to comply. Anxiety had a way of causing poor decision-making.

It took only about five minutes from the time that Grimes and Martin got on the elevator until the doors opened on the bottom floor and they got out and walked toward their cars.

"Hi, guys, you're leaving work a little earlier than usual," Chuck said as they approached their cars.

As Grimes started to pull his jacket away from where his weapon rested on his hip, Don did his best imitation of Jackie Chan and kicked him in the right kneecap. Grimes groaned and fell onto the oil-stained floor. With his foot firmly attached to Grimes's neck, Don bent down and pulled Grimes's weapon from its holster. Don was sure that the weapon hadn't been fired or cleaned in several years and that he was probably one of the good old boys who had only to make a call to the right person at the range and tell him to give him a passing score on the latest qualifications. It turned out that Don's guess was correct. When he unloaded the rounds from the weapon, all were tarnished from not having seen the light of day since being loaded several years before.

While Don handcuffed Grimes with the cuffs he had taken from Grimes's own belt, he advised him of his rights from memory. This wasn't what Don usually did since he knew that any defense attorney with half a brain would ask him how he had advised his client. If Don said that he did it by memory, the attorney would tell him to recite the warnings. In front of a jury, that could cause problems if he misspoke one word. Don's thought was *Bring it on. I'll review Miranda if I have to testify at this vermin's trial.*

Martin just stood there while Grimes lay on the oily floor, cuffs on, his face on cold concrete.

"Wait, guys, I'll tell you anything you want to know," Martin choked out, Grimes glaring at him.

"You better not tell this faggot crew anything, you fuck. You have been fucking my wife for how long, and now you're gonna fuck me?"

At that point Don practiced some O'Neill measures on Grimes as he brought him to his feet. There was a department policy about the use of force after the cuffs were on, but Don could easily explain the use of pain compliance if the suspect was a further threat to him or someone else. He used it liberally.

While Don delivered Grimes to the next IIS Investigator, Chuck and Vickie kept Martin company in the garage. Grimes made several incriminating comments during the ride to the fifth floor, among them that he was going to kill whoever snitched him off as well as Don and Chuck for arresting him. Don thanked him when he took off the cuffs and sat him down, none too gently, on the interview room chair.

By the time Don returned to the garage, Chuck and Vickie had Martin crapping his pants in anticipation of what life in prison was going to be like for a cop.

"You do understand that you have the right to an attorney and all the other stuff that goes with it, don't you?" Don asked Martin in a very calm but menacing voice.

"Of course I know about that stuff. But you guys have to understand that none of this was my idea."

"What wasn't your idea, Jack?" Chuck asked.

"I knew that we shouldn't be taking money from scenes. It was Sherman's idea. He said that it was easy money and that no one would ever find out. He even told us to look for expensive jewelry. He took a ring from the finger of a woman who died under suspicious circumstances. It must have been worth a small fortune."

Then Don reached into his shirt pocket and removed a photo, the one that they found in the search of Martin's desk. It hadn't yet found its way into evidence.

"Do you recognize this picture, Jack?"

"I've never seen it before."

"If I showed you a picture of you and Clorice Grimes in a very intimate situation, would you recognize that?"

"Yeah, I took a picture of us with my 35mm with a timed shutter. I took a few of us, why?"

"We found those in your locker along with this one," Don said. "Why would this one be in your locker?"

"I have no idea, but I just know that I didn't take it or put it in my locker. Why don't you dust it for prints? That might tell you something."

"You're smarter than you look, Jack, did you know that?" Chuck said. Then Chuck glanced at Don who was slowly shaking his head. Amazingly, neither Don nor Chuck thought to check the photo for prints. One point for the other side.

Over the next half hour, Martin told Don and Chuck the whole story about taking money from various scenes and how he, Grimes, and Sherman split the takes. He identified as many of the cases as he could recall and said that the biggest haul was about $100,000 at some "faggot's" house. The guy committed suicide and had a lot of cash just stashed in the house. They split it three ways and chipped in for Marjorie's boob job. Marjorie had been so grateful that she put on a little show in the lineup room before and after the surgery. According to him, she had offered lap dances to each of them after the surgery. He hadn't yet collected on the promise, but he had made plans to. He seemed disappointed when Don told him that it was unlikely to happen anytime soon, if ever.

"You guys have been scaring the shit out of Sherman and Grimes for a long time, you know. They thought that you couldn't be pulled into the theft thing, so they've tried their best to fuck with you. Sherman has been downright spooky, he's so paranoid."

"What do you mean by spooky?" Don asked.

"He makes comments like he might be planning to get you one way or another. It might be directly or indirectly."

"You mean that he might try to get to us through someone else?"

"Yeah, that could be."

"And by 'get us,' what do you think he meant?"

"I mean get you as in get you!"

"You think he might have been planning to kill us?"

"Yeah, I think he might be capable of that."

"Why do you think that he might be capable of killing us?" Chuck asked.

"Well, we were at dinner a few days ago and he said that you guys wouldn't learn to leave things alone until you were both dead. That was at the Crazy 8. He saw you," pointing at Chuck, "come in and commented that you were alone for a change and that you could be taken out back and shot in the alley without too much trouble."

"OK, Jack, where did you stash your money from the thefts?" Don asked.

"I put all of it in a safety deposit box except for some I spent on the kids, Clorice, and my car. I'll go with you tomorrow and get it out."

"Do you have the key to the box with you?" asked Chuck.

"Yeah, it's on my key ring."

"You can sign a consent to search and we'll do it tomorrow, if that'll work for you."

"Yeah, OK, I guess that means I'll be in jail tomorrow, right?"

"Right," Don said.

Don, Chuck, and Vickie delivered Martin to the fifth floor where an IIS sergeant waited. They briefed the sergeant on what they had gotten from Martin, turned, and walked away. All three had smiles on their very tired faces.

They walked the short distance to Captain Mitchell's office where they found her sitting behind her desk looking more than pleased. Chuck looked at her in a completely new light, assuming that she and his partner had swapped bodily fluids. That assumption would give him greater advantage in making crucial choices in the future. Which restaurant to eat at, for example.

"It looks like we'll be looking for some new detectives and one new sergeant in the near future."

"True enough," said Chuck. "Now if we could find a way to get rid of Monson and Hase, we'd be sitting pretty."

"Guys like that have a way of getting rid of themselves," Captain Mitchell responded." Now let's search Sherman's house before calling it a day."

"Food, we need food before we barge off to anything that's going to take as long as searching a house might take," said Don. "Besides, we need to impound their cars so we can go through them tomorrow. How about the Chow Dong, or was it the Dong Chow?"

"You are very close to having to walk with a crutch for a very long time," Chuck said. "We haven't been on Broadway for a while. How about that for a change?"

"Yeah, there's a great International Pancake House up there where you can almost find the pancakes under a hill of chemically manufactured stuff. My kidneys need a wake-up call; they get way too complacent with their diet of healthy food," Don shot back.

"OK, Broadway it is. You joining us, Captain?"

"No, I have too much here. You guys stay in touch and let me know when you plan to do Sherman's house, and don't forget to tow their cars before you go anywhere."

The National House of Pancakes wasn't a bad choice as long as you steered clear of the pancakes. Don swore that the corporation couldn't possibly stay in business unless they continued serving pancakes that could be used as doormats to people who judged the quality of a restaurant by the size of the plate they served their questionable food on; they were that big. He had an omelet filled with stuff that was unidentifiable and a side of a pancake that covered the plate. Chuck had eggs over easy and hash browns with toast. Vickie had coffee.

Before they left the restaurant, Don called the office and talked to Captain Mitchell. Sergeant Sherman, Grimes, and Martin had all been interviewed and booked into the county jail to wait for charges. IIS was going to file the cases. Don had doubts about the wisdom of letting those guys do the business of filing a case with the prosecutor. He doubted that any of them had ever done it. He was right.

Sherman's house was a small bungalow on a narrow street in Ballard. The lawn was in serious need of attention. A narrow dirt drive ran along the side and led to a garage that might have accommodated a 1930s car but had stopped being a garage in about 1949. It looked as though it might be full of the detritus of a life full of nothing but meaningless crap. A Ford pickup with nearly flat tires and a box full of garbage sat in the drive; it appeared as though it might have potential as a project. Its roof was green with mildew.

Chuck walked around to the back of the house while Don, Vickie, and Captain Mitchell walked onto the covered porch. A current *Seattle Times* lay on the floor along with discarded items that Sherman no longer needed.

The front door was locked, but Don had no problem prying it with a bar that they brought along for the job. Given what they'd seen in the yard, the house was surprisingly clean and orderly; Sherman must have used the services of a housekeeper. She was probably hired out of the "topless maids" section of the *Seattle Weekly* if Don's guess was accurate.

Don walked through the house to the back door and let Chuck in. The house consisted of two bedrooms, a kitchen, living room, and one bath. The door to the basement was off the kitchen. The whole place was in serious need of a paint job.

Don suggested that they split up the house with one person responsible for searching one room. He would do Sherman's bedroom, Don the other bedroom, and Captain Mitchell and Vickie would do the living room and kitchen together. The basement would be last.

Sherman's bed was neatly made, and his clothes were hung in the narrow closet. There were several pairs of shoes and a pair of boots on the floor of the closet. They were lace boots. Neither had laces. There was a neat row of pants, shirts, and three sport coats. There was also a rack of ties on the door. Among them was a club tie with diagonal maroon, gray, and royal-blue stripes.

"Chuck, come here." When Chuck came in, he asked him if he recalled the tie that Shondra described during their first interview.

"Yeah, I'd say that pretty much matches the tie she described."

Don was as orderly as he could be in searching so he didn't make a mess of the place. He went through every drawer, under and between the mattresses, through every pocket in every piece of clothing. He found nothing that would further link Sherman to thefts of money. Then he looked up to the ceiling of the closet.

A small trap door, opened by pushing up and back, was located in the ceiling. Don dragged an end table into the closet and climbed onto it. He pushed the trap door up and slid it back and out of the way, then pulled himself up on the ledge of the hatch and peered into the dark space. There wasn't enough light to see beyond a few feet.

He climbed off the table and retrieved the flashlight that he kept in his briefcase and then climbed back onto the table. He shined the light around the dark space, expecting the usual Christmas decorations. What he saw was a box measuring about eighteen inches by twelve inches and about twelve inches in height. It was taped shut. He reached in and slid the box out of the gloom, pulled it through the trap door, and jumped with it to the floor.

"Chuck, come here," Don called.

Chuck, Captain Mitchell, and Vickie all walked into the bedroom. Don put the box on the bed and took his jackknife from his pocket.

"I wanted you guys to witness this just in case it is what I think it is."

Don slit the tape holding the box closed, refolded the knife, put it in his pocket, and then opened the box.

"Holy shit! Excuse my language," said Don.

"Holy fuck," said Captain Mitchell.

"You're excused," said Chuck.

The box was full to the top with neat stacks of cash. There didn't appear to be any small bills among them. All of the top bills were twenties, fifties, or hundreds.

"I think we might have hit the mother lode here," Don said. "This will take us a while to count."

"We'll do it back at the office," Captain Mitchell said. "Now let's finish searching the place."

They didn't find anything else in either bedroom, but Vickie did find a key to a safe-deposit box in a desk drawer in the living room. There were bank statements in the desk that would probably take them to the box where they hoped to find more cash, or maybe more photographs that would further incriminate Sherman and embarrass Don.

Don and Chuck went into the basement together. It was a dark, damp, and thoroughly creepy hole that contained the usual furnace, water heater, washer and dryer, and workbench. Above the workbench were pictures stapled to the wall. They all depicted nude women in poses that could only be described as torturous. They were eight-by-ten glossies, the kind that led one to conclude that they didn't come out of a magazine. Sherman had probably taken them himself.

Don opened a drawer located under the workbench and found more pictures. These were voyeuristic; each one of them was taken from outside a window and showed either a nude woman or a man and woman engaged in sex acts of various sorts. One caught Don's eye: it was a duplicate of the one they found in Martin's locker. Don thought that his ass hadn't improved in this one.

"This explains the picture in Martin's locker," Don said. "Now we need to find the camera and developing stuff. I doubt that he took this film to the local One Hour Photo shop."

They found the darkroom in a corner behind the furnace. There were more pictures hanging from clothespins. All of them would make great exhibits at Sherman's trial or in a very creepy porn magazine. One depicted a woman, a nude woman, who was engaged in a sex act with a man. The man was holding the camera. The woman was Clorice. Then they saw an item hanging from a nail that caught both their eyes at the same time.

The item was a wooden nightstick, or baton, but an unusual baton. It was made of a polished wood with ornate turnings separating the handle from the business end. At the tip was what appeared to be the head of an erect penis.

"Didn't Dr. Mills say that she determined that Yvonne Gillespie was raped with a wood object?" Chuck said.

"Yes she did," Don replied. "I think we need to take our own pictures before we take this stuff down."

The camera they were looking for, an expensive 35mm with long lens was in a case in the hall closet.

The detectives minds were working overtime as they drove back to the Public Safety Building. They were both exhausted, but the day was far from over.

Clorice was not pleased when Don, Chuck, and Vickie showed up with a search warrant later that same night. They explained what was happening and that they wouldn't make a mess, and she settled down. They found nothing that would tie Grimes any further into the theft of money. They did find several envelopes containing photographs that linked him, Clorice, Sherman, Martin, and Marjorie to a very interesting ring of sexual perversion. The only person missing was Martin's wife. What surprised them was the fact that Wally Fox was in most of them. It seemed that he had a serious way with the women.

After a discussion with Clorice, they decided that they would leave the pictures with her and not make her life any more difficult than it had already become. Besides, she was now one of the good guys.

When Don, Chuck, and Vickie reached Martin's house, it was near midnight. Martha met them at the door with a look of acceptance on her face. Martin had called her from jail and given her the complete story. She in turn had given him the complete story of her life with the assistant principal at her school. Their marriage was at an end.

They did a cursory search of the house and took another key to Martin's safe-deposit box, along with the bank's address, and account and box numbers. They left after thanking Martha.

"What the fuck was Martin thinking?" said Don as they drove away. "He has a nice wife and good kids and he hooks up with Clorice?"

"Men think with their cocks. It's as simple as that," Victoria interjected from the backseat.

"I think you have something there, Officer Morris," Don said in his most sincere voice.

CHAPTER THIRTY-ONE

When Don, Chuck, and Vickie drove into the Public Safety Building, the only people still there were a few janitors. The Homicide Unit was dark. They hadn't had time to count the money that they recovered from Sherman's house, so they locked it in a safe that the unit had just for that purpose. They bid Vickie good-night, or good-morning, and they all went home for a shower and a few hours' sleep before the start of another eighteen-hour day.

Don went directly home and fell into bed. Things were looking up for his chosen profession: the bad guys were losing, something that he had believed impossible a few days before.

The phone beside Don's bed awoke him at a little after nine. He had slept longer than he had planned. It was Captain Mitchell.

"Did I wake you, sleeping beauty? I'm sorry, but we have some stuff to accomplish today, so pull your ass—pardon my language—out of bed and come in. I'll get Chuck out as well. Do you want Vickie to come in?"

Don had to think about what she just said; she had a way of speaking in paragraphs, a good share of which were questions. "OK, I'm getting up. Yes, I want Vickie to come in. Please give Chuck a call. Do you mind if I shower and shave and have a bite to eat first?"

"Of course I don't mind. We can't have a less than well-groomed and nourished detective running this show, now can we?"

"Running the show? Me? I'm just a lowly grunt doing the bidding of the law and my superiors."

"We both know that there are no others superior to you and Chuck when it comes to putting cases together."

"Thanks, Captain, I'll be in forthwith. By the way, may we park our personal cars in the building today?"

"I think that will be OK, but just today."

"Thanks."

As Don stepped out of the shower, his phone rang. It was Chuck asking for a ride since his current partner was using his car.

Don drove across the West Seattle Freeway past the First Avenue exit. Traffic was light since rush hour had ended about an hour earlier. The sun was shining for a change and all seemed right with his world. Traffic on I-5 was even bearable, which was rare on a freeway where rush hour seemed to last all day and well into the night.

The area of Capitol Hill where Chuck's condominium was located was home to the city's oldest and most elegant residents. Chuck's condo was in a converted brick mansion on a narrow elm-lined street. Don had to admit that Chuck's taste was equal or superior to his, but he wouldn't be admitting that to Chuck anytime soon.

Chuck wasn't waiting outside as he promised, so Don parked and walked up the brick walkway to the ornate front door. He rang Chuck's unit and waited a few seconds. Chuck answered and told him to come up since he wasn't quite ready. The door buzzed and Don walked into the foyer.

Although he had been there before, Don never ceased to be impressed. There were original artworks hanging on three walls and a working fountain in the center. The floor was polished terra-cotta. Antique sconces on the walls and a chandelier over the fountain produced a soft glow. Although there was an elevator, Don enjoyed the curved terra-cotta stair that took him to the second floor.

The second floor consisted of two condos: Chuck's and one owned by a mysterious musician whom Chuck said he saw only once and whom he never spoke to, but he thought he was famous for something. Chuck's door was heavily polished oak with a small brass door at eye level in the center. Don knocked, and the brass door opened almost immediately. Chuck's eye was all that was visible.

"I gave at the office, so go away."

"Just exactly what did you give at the office?"

"That will be my secret," Chuck said as he opened the door.

Don had to admit that Chuck's art collection eclipsed his in several ways, but it didn't include a Pollock. As he walked into the living room, Don was certain that Chuck was at least catching up.

"That, Chuck, has to be your best work yet."

The new piece that hung over the working fireplace was an original Jacob Lawrence. The brilliant colors of the painting fit the room. With a little concentration, Don was certain he could hear the musicians that were the subject of the painting.

"Are you planning to build a fire under that painting?" Don asked.

"That sounds like a question an insurance underwriter might ask."

"It's a question that somebody who is attached to an art curator might ask."

"No, we don't plan on any fire, that's why the plant is in the hearth. But it's not a Jackson Pollock, so we don't have to be quite as protective."

Chuck picked up his briefcase, and they walked to Don's car and drove away.

Parking in the Public Safety Building during the day was restricted to brass and fleet cars. It was a rare privilege to park a private car there if it wasn't a weekend or night shift.

Don found a vacant spot on the basement floor, the darkest and creepiest floor in this creepy building. He thought on many occasions that it would make a great horror movie set. They climbed out of Don's Subaru and started to walk to the elevator that would take them to the fifth floor, provided it didn't malfunction en route.

"Hi, assholes. So you and your faggot friend put Sherman, Grimes, and Martin in jail last night."

The voice was that of Detective Roland Hase. Standing beside him was his partner, Detective Brian Monson: the incompetent twins, in Don's opinion.

Both of the detectives worked the day shift and were just about to get into a pool car to go to a breakfast spot; they rarely did anything resembling police work. They stood in a menacing stance and waited for Don and Chuck to reply or walk around.

"Yes, my faggot partner and I did put your asshole buddies in jail last night. Maybe you would like to join them."

"How would you like to visit Harborview ER this morning?" Hase sneered.

Don had been waiting for some time to practice his O'Neill techniques on somebody, and this looked like the time. Chuck, however, got in his way.

"You know, of course, that you just scare the crap out of me, don't you? I can just see you and your fat fuck partner beating me to a pulp in your dreams," Chuck replied.

Chuck started to walk to where the two detectives stood side by side in the shadows of the garage. He noticed that Monson didn't look all that sure of the wisdom of the remarks Hase had made. Chuck continued toward them, deciding which one he would drop first. He decided that Hase should be first since Monson was clearly a coward who would only act with a gun in his hand.

As Hase reached for his gun, Chuck kicked him as hard as he had ever kicked anyone. His foot made contact with Hase's right thigh, very near his only claim to manhood. Hase lost his will to fight as he crumbled to the floor, clutching his leg and moaning in pain. Chuck reached under Hase's coat and removed his weapon from its shoulder holster while keeping an eye on Monson.

"You may want to take your partner to Harborview for a checkup," Chuck told Monson. "Or do you think both of you should go by ambulance? You know I may have cracked a bone, don't you? If I didn't, it wasn't for lack of trying. If I hear another disparaging word out of his mouth, I'll neuter him."

"No, I'll take him."

"Good. That's good," Chuck said. "And one more thing: if I hear about a complaint being made about my assaulting this piece of shit, I'll come for you. Are we clear on that? And one more thing: I don't think either of you will feel very welcome on the fifth floor in the future. I plan to kick your asses every time I hear you make a disrespectful comment about either of us, the captain, Officer Morris, or Marjorie. And I may think of some others, so maybe you should both start looking for a new place to screw the department and the taxpayers."

"Yes sir, I mean, yes, Chuck," Monson choked out.

"Tell this piece of shit that he can get his gun from me after he apologizes for being an asshole."

"Yes sir."

Don and Chuck walked to the elevator feeling refreshed. They had the sense that the era of the scum running the show was over. Good old boys were finally on their way out. Officers like Vickie could now find an honest way into investigations without fucking somebody who held the keys to the gate.

Captain Mitchell was behind her desk working on something when Don and Chuck walked in. She looked up and smiled her most sincere smile.

"Good morning, Detectives. You both look like cats that just swallowed the canary."

Don and Chuck told her what happened in the basement. They didn't want her to hear it from someone who had ulterior motives, like Hase's and Monson's attorneys or IIS.

"Good for you, Chuck. Let's start to work on getting those two out of the unit and the department, but not before this case is wrapped up. The guys in IIS are doing a good job with the paper as far as I can see. I read their affidavits that went with the arrest reports, and I think they will hold them until they can get the cases to the prosecutor."

As Don and Chuck walked out of Captain Mitchell's office and toward their cubicle, they both felt a certain threat in the air associated with dark alleys and smoky bars. Hase and Monson weren't the only remnants of the good-old-boy culture that would need to be filtered out before the office air was breathable.

Neither Chuck nor Vickie had time to eat breakfast before coming to the office, so they demanded that they eat before serving any more search warrants. They went to a place in West Seattle that Don recommended. It had been a chain restaurant until the chain rusted and broke. It was now a locally owned place that hired waitresses who were interviewed by a man with a tape measure. Not only was the food good, but the cleavage was excellent as well. Vickie was not impressed.

The first stop after breakfast was a bank in Fremont where Martin kept his money. They served the warrant on a manager who seemed reluctant to accept the validity of it. Don and Chuck finally persuaded the manager to accept the warrant by asking him if he had time in his busy schedule to tell a judge why he wouldn't give them access to the safe-deposit box identified on the warrant. He decided to provide the bank's key at that point.

The box was the biggest that the bank had. When Don opened it, Chuck, Vickie, and he just looked at it for a while. Martin had been meticulous in his storing of cash for a rainy day. He had used cash wrappers with amounts printed on them as a bank would. There were no wrappers identified holding less than $1,000. There were many bundles. Before they counted each bill, which they had to do, Don, Chuck, and Vickie added the amounts on the bundles and came up with more than $225,000, the largest amount yet. When they left the bank, the thought crossed Don's mind that they might soon need an armored car to transport their finds.

The next stop was the department's impound lot. It was a secure garage tucked behind a set of gas pumps in what appeared from the street to be a service station and auto repair shop. They found the three cars belonging to Sherman, Grimes, and Martin parked side by side.

They each took a car so the searches could be wrapped up as fast as possible. Don took Sherman's car. He first went through the passenger compartment where he found the usual junk accumulated by a slob: empty coffee cups, cans, and newspapers. The trunk, however, became more interesting. In the well that normally held a spare tire, Don found that the tire had been replaced by a flat metal box. He lifted the lid and was not surprised to find that it contained cash, a lot of cash.

Don closed the lid and continued to search. Two paper shopping bags gave off a musty smell in the back of the trunk. Don reached in and pulled one of them toward him. It was full of clothing, women's clothing, lingerie, to be more precise. On top of the clothes was a brassiere.

"Chuck and Vickie, come over here."

Both Chuck and Vickie looked into the bag. Chuck exclaimed, "Holy shit, on top of being a thief and peeping Tom, he's a fucking pervert."

"That's not your everyday brassiere," Vickie said as she looked more closely. "That looks like something out of Frederick's of Hollywood."

Don gave Vickie a sideways look without saying anything. Vickie noticed the look and said "Yes, I know what Frederick's of Hollywood is, and yes, I have some stuff from them, and yes, I wear them from time to time, not that you will be verifying that anytime soon."

OK, thought Don.

"Let's get some gloves to handle this stuff before we go any further," Chuck said.

With latex gloves in place, Don started to lay the contents of the bag out on a table covered with clean butcher paper. All of the items were similar in that they were female undergarments that looked like they must have come from Frederick's. Then Don came to the bottom of the bag.

One leather lace similar to the one that they found wrapped around Yvonne Gillespie's neck lay there. Next to it was a clear plastic bag containing a dildo that looked almost like the real thing except that it was perpetually hard.

Don and Chuck looked at each other. The proverbial lightbulbs seemed to come on.

"I think we might have here what is commonly called a 'clue,' Chuck."

"I think you may be right, Don. But which of the dildos was used on Yvonne? The nightstick or this?"

"Given the amount of underwear here, I think he's good for other perverted acts," Vickie said.

"You are one perceptive officer, Vickie. I think we need to start looking at any other unsolved murders of prostitutes in the region. But let's prove this one first before we get too greedy," said Don.

The search of Grimes's car was less impressive, but Chuck found an envelope that contained enough cash to fund a lavish vacation in any number of the world's great vacation spots. Then he saw something that struck his eye: a maroon, gray, and royal-blue necktie stuffed between the front seats. That was two matching ties. They must have a club going. But who was wearing it when he assaulted Shondra?

Martin's car was another story. Vickie found a box of cash in the trunk that Martin had clearly failed to mention when he gave his statement. She called Don and Chuck over so they could verify the find.

Don looked at the cash and then at Chuck. He asked Chuck to join him for a short conference out of Vickie's hearing.

"Do you recall our conversation about how we could help Raymond get a start in this world?"

"Of course I remember. I still think about how I'll go about accomplishing that."

"How about we start right now? Some of this is money that will end up being returned to a woman who doesn't need it. A lot of the rest of it will go to the Narcotics Unit, the state, or to a fund that provides counseling to criminals like Sherman. Let's use this for Raymond's scholarship fund. Just look at it as redistribution of wealth."

"But that's illegal," Chuck said with a slight smirk. "Let's do it."

After a short conference, Don called Vickie to join them. He explained what they planned to do and that they did not want her to be a part of it, so she should deny any knowledge of what happened. She thought the idea a great one.

Chuck then held up a finger as though to stop everything. "I think that part of this should be used to give Yvonne Gillespie a decent burial with a nice headstone. I think that would be poetic justice, don't you?"

"Brilliant, Chuck. If Sherman knew that he was going to be part of paying for the burial of the woman we think he might have murdered, he would shit," Don said. Vickie concurred.

The first order of business, after securing $50,000 in an undisclosed location, was sending the bootlace they found in Sherman's trunk to the state crime lab with a request that it be processed as soon as possible if not sooner. The lace found wrapped around Yvonne Gillespie's neck was to be the comparison along with a DNA sample from Sherman. They also sent the wooden dildo in hopes that Gillespie's DNA was on it. The baton had already been submitted for DNA.

While Chuck was writing another affidavit of probable cause for the collection of saliva from Sherman, and Don was adding to their follow-up reports, Captain Mitchell walked into their cubicle, her face less than cheerful.

"Sherman and his boys have bailed out. The judge felt that high bail wasn't warranted under the circumstances and let them go on one thousand dollars cash bail each."

Don looked at Chuck and then at Captain Mitchell. "We fucked up, gang. As soon as we left Sherman's last night, we should have rebooked him on everything we could. We had photos that clearly showed that he is into some very kinky peeping."

"We didn't have DNA and that's the only thing that's going to prove anything in court," Chuck said. "With what we found in his car, we have a shot at him that will put him away for a very long time."

"And John Barber, how do we tie Sherman to Barber? There is no doubt that the person who killed Gillespie also killed Barber," Don said.

"Barber was in cuffs before he was pushed, right?" Chuck added. "Who carries handcuffs? Cops, that's who. We need to ship Sherman's cuffs off with the other stuff with a request that it all be processed yesterday. We just happened to get lucky because Sherman's cuffs, gun, and badge stayed here when he marched off to jail. They're all in the evidence room. Then there's the nightstick we found in his house. I bet that we'll find Barber's blood on it."

Don, Chuck, and Vickie spent the next two hours collecting the items that the crime lab needed to examine. Then they delivered them in person. When Don and Chuck were through explaining to the lab supervisor what was at stake, she agreed to drop everything to work on this case.

There's one unfortunate thing about fingerprints and DNA that cause problems in court: if the defendant had a legitimate reason for being at a crime scene, it's often tough for a jury to accept them as boilerplate evidence. That is, unless the DNA is found on an object used to rape or murder the victim, or the DNA of the victim is found on the handcuffs of a cop, or if fingerprints of the same cop are found in places that he couldn't have been without being involved in the crime. Don and Chuck worked around these facts to the best of their abilities.

Jim Shuller, SPD identification technician extraordinaire, was at his desk when Don called. He agreed to stay put until Don, Chuck, and Vickie arrived.

Shuller was generally unflappable. Both Don and Chuck had been forced out of stinker crime scenes by odors that saturated clothes and sinus cavities, leaving Shuller behind to search for and find prints. This time, however, Shuller was definitely flapped. He had known Sherman for a long time, although he hadn't much liked him during all that time. He agreed to give all of his attention to comparing prints from both the Gillespie and Barber murder scenes with Sherman's prints, which were on file along with those of every officer in the department. Sherman's palm print had already been found on a table in the room where Gillespie was murdered, but it could be explained away. After swearing Shuller to secrecy, Don, Chuck, and Vickie returned to the fifth floor and their cubicle.

"Good morning, Detectives, Officer," Marjorie virtually sang as they approached her desk. Marjorie had been away from work since the night at the Cascade Motor Inn and was clearly happy to be back.

"Good morning," all three responded.

"You look stunning today, Marjorie," Don said. She was wearing a pullover that was clearly meant to call attention to her chest's recently renovated contours. Stunning was the only word to describe the appearance. When used to describe anyone but Marjorie, the word would have been excessive and possibly insincere. Marjorie had a way of showing the world her newly acquired charms that only she could pull off, so to speak.

"Thank you, Don. You don't think that this top is a bit much?"

"No, I think it's just what's needed to showcase your new self."

"Thanks, and remember that anytime you want to check them out, just let me know."

"OK, I'll remember that. And why are you in now? Shouldn't you be on nights?"

"The captain told me to come on days and hang around you guys as much as possible until this all ends."

All three then walked away from Marjorie's desk. Don was walking beside Vickie with Chuck slightly ahead.

"Check them out?" Vickie asked Don as they walked. "I think we all just checked them out. There wasn't much left for the imagination."

"I think she was offering a more tactile tour, if you know what I mean."

"Yes, I know what you mean, and I can't believe that you would actually take her up on the offer."

"You're right, I wouldn't take her up on the offer, but there is the question about how fake boobs feel."

"Why don't you pick up a prostitute and find out?"

"Hey, gang, I think we have a murder suspect to find and an arrest to make, so let's get off the boob fixation, shall we?" Chuck said as they walked into their cubicle.

CHAPTER THIRTY-TWO

Speaking of fixations, Don had become so fixated on the job at hand that he almost forgot that he had a new mission in life: keeping healthy his relationship with Tiffany Winslow and her cats. The job had a way of doing that to Don. He had to admit from time to time that he was partially responsible for the disintegration of his first marriage. Granted, his first wife had found solace in another man's or men's beds, but he had contributed by spending too much time in the library during graduate school. Books were not fulfilling her needs, so she found something that would. That something just happened to be more than one of his fellow students and probably a professor or two. Don wasn't about to let that happen again.

Tiffany was walking to the water taxi on her way home from the Seattle Art Museum when Don caught up with her. She had a colorful canvas bag in her right hand, one that she had purchased from the museum store during an exhibit of Impressionist painters. One of Monet's best-known paintings decorated the canvas. The water lilies, however, were faded.

Don followed from a few steps behind, keeping step with her. "Say, lady, what ya got in the bag?"

Tiffany stopped and turned. "Are you harassing me, sir?"

"Yes, and that's not the only thing I would like to do to you."

Don planted a kiss on Tiffany as she stood in the middle of the sidewalk, other passengers rushing past. "Would you take exception to me following you home?" Don said.

"I would take exception if you did not follow me home," Tiffany said with great enthusiasm.

The trip across Elliot Bay was like a first date. Both Don and Tiffany were engrossed in each other to the point that the taxi was tying up on the West Seattle side before they realized that the trip had ended. Then it struck Don that his car was in the Public Safety Building garage.

To make the trip from the taxi to Tiffany's house shorter, they took the bus as far as possible. They were left with a five-block walk that they spent discussing nothing in particular. By the time they reached Tiffany's door, they had talked themselves into a state that left George and Martha on their own without their usual walk and locked out of the bedroom.

About an hour after their arrival, Tiffany suggested that they get a grip and attend to things other than demands of the flesh. She suggested this to Don as she straddled him, her breasts presenting an appealing view from where Don lay on his back.

"You know that this must be love, don't you?" Don said as he tried to make eye contact with Tiffany, failing miserably.

"Oh, why?"

"I was so intent on catching you on the pier before the taxi left that I forgot my car. It's on the other side. I'm stuck here unless I take a bus or ride my bike."

"Is there something urgent waiting downtown that you have to get back to?"

"I think we have a major lead on a murder suspect, and I have to go back to work as soon as we're through here."

"By 'through' do you mean through with this liaison or through with this sexual interaction?"

"The sex. The sex was and is great. It's better than I think I've ever known, and I believe that's because I love you."

With that, Tiffany again began to perform magic with her body while George and Martha made beckoning calls from outside the door.

It was almost eight when Tiffany dropped Don at the Third Avenue entrance to the Public Safety Building. The six-hundred block of Third Avenue was empty except for the down-and-out crowd who spent days sleeping in alleys and under bridges, coming out at night to be less vulnerable to the violence and threats of violence that the true scum of the earth heaped on them.

Don walked up to the locked door and knocked. The guard opened the door and asked for identification. Don had never laid eyes on the guard, so he took out his ID card and badge, holding them up for the guard to examine. He did a thorough job of it before telling Don to enter. Don was appreciative of someone who took his job seriously, introduced himself, and then went to the bank of elevators that would take him to the fifth floor.

The Public Safety Building at eight in the evening had to be the spookiest building in town, in Don's opinion. This was added reason to identify, find, and drown its architect.

Chuck and Vickie had agreed that they all needed to take part of the afternoon to recharge before resuming work. They had, however, agreed to meet on the fifth floor. Don was first to arrive.

When Don walked into the Homicide Unit office, the only light came from desk lamps left on. His squad was on night shift and half of it was now out of commission, so it was understandable. However, it was eerie. Don rarely found himself afraid of anything or anyone, but this was frightening. Then the ceiling lights came on.

"Why are you working in the dark?" Chuck said as he walked into their cubicle.

"I look better under subdued light."

"No argument there."

"Vickie said that she would be a little late, so we should wait before finding some place to eat," Chuck said.

"Have you had any thoughts where we might start our search-and-destroy mission?" Don asked.

"Where would a lowlife like Sherman, who knows that he's being pursued, go?"

Don pondered the question for a short time and said, "I think he might be on Aurora looking for new prey. Or maybe he's made contact with Clorice Grimes, and who knows what she might do for him."

Before they left that afternoon, they put out a department bulletin and a "BOLO," or be-on-the- lookout notice. Every officer in the state would be on Sherman's tail by now.

"Do you really think he'd be stupid enough to hang on Aurora?" Chuck said.

"He seems to like Aurora. He could even be hanging out at the Cascade Motor Inn. Let's check it after we stop by his house. But first we have to eat."

"Vickie hasn't arrived, so let's clean up some paper before she gets here," Chuck said.

As Chuck was booting up his computer while Don watched him, Wally Fox walked in, pushing a vacuum cleaner with all the enthusiasm of a man going for a prostate exam.

"I heard that you guys arrested Sherman and his boys," Fox said in his usual down-in-the-dumps manner. "I just thought that you should know something."

"What's that, Wally?" Don said.

"I know that you think that I'm some kind of a pervert. That may be true in some ways, but I don't go around beating up prostitutes or crap like that."

"How do you know what we're doing here?" Chuck asked, turning away from his computer.

"Believe me, there ain't no secrets around here. All a person needs to do is keep his ears open and he knows pretty much everything that's going on."

"What do you want us to know, Wally?" Don asked.

"Sergeant Sherman, Grimes, and Martin have asked to use my car more than once during the last four or five months. They told me that they liked it and were thinking about getting their own just like it. One time when Sherman brought it back, I found a used condom on the back floor. He also took laces from some boots I had in back. I just didn't want you guys looking at me for any crimes that I didn't do. Oh, and one more thing: Grimes gave me some panties and bras and some pictures that he said he took. They were of women in some interesting poses. Two were of Marjorie before and after her boob job. He just said that he thought I would appreciate them. Now it looks like he might have wanted me to be caught with them."

"Marjorie said that you look at her in a way that makes her very uncomfortable," Chuck said.

"Who doesn't look at Marjorie? Now that she had a boob job, everybody looks at her even more. Don't tell me that you guys aren't looking at her in a way that might make her uncomfortable."

"You've got me there, Wally," Don said. "She is pretty easy on the eyes."

"Something else you probably don't know, but before you got here, I was a part of the group that Marjorie was in. She can't be too uncomfortable around me since she and I have done some stuff together that she hasn't told you about. I didn't always look like I do now. She used to think I was good enough to take to bed, but that was when she was new here and would do anything with anybody to get ahead. I never did figure out how she thought a fucking low-life janitor could get her anything but a venereal disease."

"OK, Wally, would you be willing to put what you just told us on tape? Not the part about Marjorie, but the other stuff," Don asked, recalling the pictures that included Wally.

"Sure, I never liked Sherman. He always thought that he was so much better than me because I was just a janitor and he was a big-shot detective."

"You probably shouldn't go into that in the statement. Just stick to what you said about your car," Don said. "By the way, you wouldn't have that condom you found in your car sitting around somewhere, would you?"

"You really do think I'm a pervert, don't you?"

"No, just asking. How about the panties, bras, and pictures; do you still have them?"

"Yeah, they're in my locker. I'll get them."

While Don was taking Wally's statement in an interview room, Hase walked into Don and Chuck's cubicle with a significant limp. Monson was walking slightly behind him and looking sheepish.

"Brian tells me that you have my gun and that I should apologize to you before I get it back," Hase said in his best bullying voice.

"Yes, that's true. I have your gun," said Chuck. "You can have it when I hear an apology from you about your disparaging remarks about my lifestyle."

"Fuck you. I'll apologize to you when hell freezes over."

Hase just about had the "over" out of his mouth when he again hit the floor. He was moaning and clutching his right knee. It was only Chuck's momentary compassion that prevented him from dislocating it at the very minimum. Hase would have been in a cast for six months if Chuck had unleashed his full force.

"I didn't hear that apology there, Detective Hase. Did you not hear me?"

"I'll fucking kill you before I apologize to you, you fucking faggot asshole."

The next blow hit Hase in the crotch. He screamed and doubled up in pain that must have radiated throughout his entire body.

"Was that an apology that I heard?" Chuck asked. "Did you hear that, Detective Monson?"

Monson stood in the same spot apparently expecting the next strike to land on him.

"I'm going to offer you one more opportunity, and then I'm going to make you a eunuch and even more ugly than you already are. Now what's it going to be?"

"I'm sorry that I insulted you," Hase whispered.

"What do you plan to do about that little personality disorder that you have?" Chuck said in his calmest voice.

"I don't know what you're talking about."

"You like to bully people you think are weaker than you, that one."

"I won't bully them anymore," Hase said as he held his crotch with both hands.

"There's one more thing I want you to do."

"What's that?"

"After you get up, go to your desk and start to clean it out. You and your chickenshit partner no longer work here. If I find you here tomorrow, I'll finish what I started. I'm sure there's a spot for you in Parking Enforcement or shoveling horseshit at the stables."

"You can't fire us."

Chuck took a stance that told Hase he was about to be the recipient of a blow that could well end his life as a useful male member of the human race, if he had ever been one.

"OK, you can. I'll leave, but can I have my gun?"

"No, you won't need it writing parking tickets, and it would just get dirty in the horse barns."

"One more thing before you go: where can we find Sherman? And just to give you fair warning, if I suspect that your answer isn't completely truthful, I'm going to drill my fist between your eyes and let you try again. We'll continue like that until I believe you."

Hase had managed to stand but was covering his crotch with both hands. It was obvious that he wasn't sure if he should put his hands closer to his face. "When he got out of jail last night, he asked us to give him a ride home. Munson and I took a pool car, drove him home, and dropped him off. I saw him walk toward the front door and that's the last I saw him."

Hase stared intently at Chuck's face, not certain whether Chuck believed him. After about ten seconds, he relaxed; Chuck hadn't thrown a punch, so he probably wouldn't.

"You fucking criminals had the gall to come back here and check out a pool car? Is there no fucking limit to your arrogance?" Chuck then turned and walked away, letting Hase off the hook.

After Don finished taking a statement from Wally, they walked to Wally's locker. Vickie followed close behind. It was a mess, but there was a neatly displayed array of pictures taped to the inside of the door. One that was immediately recognizable was of a couple performing a common sex act. The man's ass was clearly visible: Don's.

"The SOB made sure that he spread this around for the world to see," Don exclaimed.

"What do you mean?" Wally asked.

"Never mind, you wouldn't understand."

There were two of Marjorie posing nude, one before and one after her breast enhancement surgery. The after shot was definitely an improvement in Don's opinion. There were two others, one of Clorice and one of an Asian woman neither Don nor Chuck recognized.

"Who's this woman?" Chuck asked, pointing at the stranger.

"She's a prostitute Sherman takes to one of the motels on Aurora from time to time. I don't know her name, but she's a regular at the Cascade Motor Inn. I saw her in the parking lot a while back."

Wally then leaned down and picked up a pile of silky clothes from the floor of his locker. There were some slinky and apparently very expensive undergarments among them. Vickie gave her assessment of what they might cost, and it was impressive.

"What did you have in mind for this stuff, Wally?" Don asked." And where did you get it?"

"You know, some women are impressed by these things. I thought I'd use them in trade. I got some from Sherman and some from Grimes."

"In trade for what, Wally?" Vickie asked, surprising both the two detectives and her. She had fixated on the bartering part of Wally's answer.

"You know, things. Sometimes women will take stuff like these in trade."

"In trade for what, Wally?" Vickie persisted.

"You know, sex."

"Oh, so you're not only a pervert, you're a cheap pervert."

"Do you recall when Grimes and Sherman gave you these?" Don asked.

"No, but they would give me pieces from time to time in exchange for my car."

Vickie was working herself into a righteous lather, so Don told Wally to put the stuff in a paper bag and give it to him. Neither he nor Chuck would be handling the items without latex gloves. Then the three of them walked away toward an elevator and a ride to a car that would take them to a restaurant.

CHAPTER THIRTY-THREE

G od, I hate playing the bully," Chuck said as they waited for their food. Vickie had decided that they should try a Mexican place on Rainier Avenue in the South Precinct. It didn't exist when Don and Chuck worked there, but Vickie had gone there several times with her field training officer.

"You did good, Chuck. A bully understands one thing, and that's a lightning-fast fist to the nose or a kick to the balls," Don told him in commiseration. "But I'm not sure you can actually fire someone. Isn't that best left to the chief or at least the captain?"

"You're probably right, but they seemed to think I could, so it might have worked. But I still feel bad."

Vickie chimed in with a "You'll get over it. Now let's eat."

Their food had arrived. One thing was immediately apparent: the servings were monstrous. A lot of what covered their plates was refried beans, rice, and cheese, but the other stuff did a great job of taking what room remained.

"Who was your field training officer down here?" Don asked.

Vickie named the officer, making it clear why he brought her here on a regular basis. Clearly, the officer had weight issues that would not be corrected anytime soon.

After they paid and walked outside, they realized that they hadn't really arrived at a plan to find Sherman. By the time they reached the car, they had agreed that they were dealing with a very dangerous man, made even more so by having been backed into a corner with nowhere to go. That sort of man was capable of almost anything. They needed to focus on what they knew and not drive around on guesses. They would function better on full stomachs.

Clorice was home when Don called. She was hostile at first and became less so when Don told her what he suspected Sherman of.

"OK, here's what I know. He called Bill last night after he got home from the jail. He wanted to meet Bill somewhere on Aurora. That was about eleven or a little after. Bill left and I haven't seen him since."

"Did he take a gun?" Don asked.

"Probably, but I'm not sure."

"Is there any way you can verify whether he did or didn't?"

"Hang on, I know where he keeps his off-duty gun. You guys have his other one."

The phone went dead for a short time, and then Clorice came back on. "Yes, he took a gun. It's a five-shot revolver, a Smith & Wesson."

"Did he take extra ammo?"

"He had a speed loader that's gone, so I guess he has five extra rounds."

"Where would Sherman go on Aurora?"

"When he and I went to a motel it was always the Cascade Motor Inn. The owner there was always accommodating to him no matter how full he was."

"What car is Bill driving?" Don asked.

"Mine since you guys still have his. It's a gold-colored Dodge four-door sedan. I don't know my plate number."

"One more thing, Clorice," Don said with as much sincerity as he could muster. "Would you withhold anything from us to save either of these guys from prison time? You know that they both have less than stellar characters, and they wouldn't hesitate to destroy you or anyone else to save their asses, don't you?"

"I know, and I'm not holding anything back. I'll even go with you to try to find them if that's what you want."

"No, you don't have to do that, but you do have to let us know if you get a call from either of them. You just call nine-one-one after you get off the line and the operator will let us know that you have something for us."

"I guess there is one more thing before you go: are you missing any underwear? I'm talking about the kind you might buy at Frederick's of Hollywood or Victoria's Secret."

"No. I'd know if I was because I don't have much of that and the things I do have are still here."

"OK, thanks, Clorice. I'll be in touch."

The underwear question gave Don an idea that he was surprised hadn't already occurred to him. Roseanne Vargas had a visit from a man who was not yet identified. The man's motivation for burglarizing her townhouse and attacking her was sexual, but he didn't know if she was missing underwear since the Sex Crimes Unit was handling the case.

With the frilly underwear in a bag on the car's seat, Don, Chuck, and Vickie drove across the West Seattle Bridge, which was wide open, rush hour long over. When they drove into Don's driveway, rain was falling steadily. They walked to Roseanne Vargas's townhouse along a dimly lit brick pathway.

"So Roseanne Vargas is one of your many girlfriends?" Vickie asked in a non-judgmental way. At least Don took it as non-judgmental.

"I guess you could say that she was, but I've since come to my senses about women and how many are enough."

"Oh, and how many are enough?"

"I've narrowed the field to one, and I think she will be it."

"Congratulations," she said with what Don took as disappointment. Or it might have been a return to his past way of thinking.

"Thank you."

They continued walking past Don's townhouse and on to Roseanne's, stopping at one point for Vickie to exclaimed about the view.

"If I had known you lived in a place like this, I may have made a more serious play for you, Don."

"Yes, real estate has a way to a woman's heart. But I would rather a woman love me for myself and not my address."

Chuck chimed in, "How about your Jackson Pollock? Could you blame a woman for falling in love with it rather than you?"

"You own a Jackson Pollock?" Vickie again exclaimed.

"The painter, not the fish."

"I may be from Missoula, Montana, but I'm not a complete Neanderthal. I know that a Jackson Pollock is a premium make of drift boat," Vickie said with a smirk.

"When we get done at Roseanne's, I'll let you see my Jackson Pollock."

"If I'll show you what?" Vickie said with genuine delight.

"No *quid pro quo*," Don said with some reluctance.

Roseanne answered the door in a pair of short shorts and white T-shirt shirt *sans* bra. Don was impressed and for a split second sorry for his new-found ethics regarding women. Vickie was also impressed, since the last time she saw her was in a courtroom where Roseanne was defending a crook that Vickie had arrested. Roseanne was wearing a suit at the time.

"Hi, Officer Morris, it's good to see you outside the courtroom," Roseanne said. "It's unfortunate that you made such an airtight case against my client."

"I was just doing my job."

"That's what they all say. You did a great one on that guy. I hope I don't have to go to court on any of your cases in the future."

"Thanks, I guess," Vickie said.

"What brings you here, Don?"

"We have some stuff to show you. But first, was any of your underwear taken the night that you were attacked?"

"Yes, but I already described that to the officer who took the report and again to the detective who is handling the case."

"Describe it again for us, will you?"

Roseanne gave a detailed description of the items taken. Her description would be offered in evidence at trial if there ever was a trial.

"We have some items with us that we want you to look at."

Don threw caution to the wind and reached into the paper bag, pulling the underwear out one item at a time. When he had removed all of the items and spread them on the floor, Roseanne confirmed that some were items taken from her bedroom.

Chuck took a statement form from his briefcase and asked Roseanne to describe having identified the items as hers and that they were stolen from her bedroom on the same night that she was attacked.

Although Don, Chuck, and Vickie wanted to resume the hunt for Sherman as soon as possible, the Jackson Pollock took priority. They listened to Vickie exclaim about Don's townhouse as they entered and walked through the kitchen, along the art-strewn hallway and into the living room where the Pollock hung.

"Holy cow, you really do own a Pollock," Vickie again exclaimed. Then she went on to identify it and the year it was painted. "Are you sure you're really committed to just one woman?"

"Yes, sorry. You may, however, come over and look at it from time to time. You might also want to visit Chuck and check out his recent Jacob Lawrence acquisition."

"You guys are unbelievable. How did two art collectors find their way into the police department?"

"In addition to a love of art, we like to put assholes away," Chuck said. "Now can we go and find one more asshole and put him away?"

The drive from West Seattle to the Cascade Motor Inn was less jammed than usual. Nighttime traffic flowing from downtown along the Alaska Way Viaduct and north along Aurora was moving at a brisk pace although a light rain was falling. The drive gave Don, Chuck, and Vickie time to talk about what they would do if they found Sherman at the motel, knowing that once the shit hit the fan, the plan would go out the window. It also gave them time to stop long enough to put their body armor on. Don and Chuck decided against calling in the North Precinct cavalry so no alarm would register in Sherman's mind on the slim chance that he had a police radio. They did make one more stop at a pay phone to call Radio and give an update on where they were and what they were up to. That could pay dividends if the shit did hit the fan and the cavalry was required. The pay phone, not unlike all the others, was next to a restroom that needed some attention.

Don parked the pool car in the shadows behind the Cascade Motor Inn. All three of them got out and walked to the side of the office that faced Aurora Avenue. The motel's sign that told the public that there were rooms available flashed on and off in red. It could well have doubled as the mark of a whorehouse. Don, Chuck, and Vickie knew that it did exactly that. They looked down the parking lot that ended at a graffiti-strewn cement block wall. The rooms seemed to be pretty much occupied if the parking lot was any indication. A car that looked like Clorice's was parked in front of number eight. The lights in the room were on and the curtains closed.

Mr. Park, the owner, was standing behind the counter entering something in a ledger when Don walked into the office. Chuck and Vickie kept watch on the lot. "Good evening. You remember me, don't you?"

"Of course, how you? How I be of service?"

"Are Sergeant Sherman or Detective Grimes here?"

"I no see them today," Mr. Park said without looking at Don.

"Let me see your register," Don said.

Mr. Park pulled the register from under the counter and handed it to Don. All of the rooms were full except eight and fifteen.

"You show eight as vacant. Why's that?"

"It vacant."

"The lights are on and a car is parked in front of it."

Mr. Park stammered and said that he must have forgotten to enter the name of the person who rented it.

"Do you recall what I told you not too long ago about lying to me and renting to prostitutes? I might just close you down if it looks like you're still insisting on lying to me. Now, who's in eight?"

"Sergeant Sherman. He say that I no tell anybody that he here."

"How about Detective Grimes, is he in room eight as well?"

"Yes, he come after Sergeant Sherman."

"Is anyone else in room eight?"

"Yes, I see woman go in after Detective Grimes."

Don took the picture of the woman whom Wally couldn't identify out of his pocket and showed it to Mr. Park.

"That look like woman who go into room eight."

"Have you seen her here before?"

"No."

"You're lying to me again," Don said.

"Yes I am. I very sorry. She here most nights. She go into many rooms."

"You're telling me that she's a prostitute, right?"

"Yes, must be."

"What's her name?"

"I no know."

"Yes you do."

"OK, her name Mrs. Park. She my wife."

"Now we're getting somewhere. Your wife is a prostitute and you rent her out to whoever happens to be renting a room here."

"Yes, that true, but she clean rooms, too."

"Oh, she cleans rooms as well as putting out for customers? She's versatile and quite a bargain for you. Where did you find such a bargain?"

"She come to this country illegally, so I marry her and give her job."

"You are a real prince, Mr. Park," Don smiled. Then he motioned for Vickie to come into the office.

"Keep an eye on Mr. Park. If he attempts to leave or pick up a phone, shoot him."

"You no can shoot me!" yelled Mr. Park.

"You're right. I can't shoot you because I will be down in room eight, but she can and will because she will be here with you."

Vickie smiled at Mr. Park who seemed to think he might just never see his home country again.

Leaving Vickie with Mr. Park, Don went out and around the building where he and Chuck made their plans.

They agreed that there were not many things that really scared them in their work; going after an armed cop who probably murdered two people and maybe more was definitely on that short list. They both checked their weapons before walking to room eight. There was a round in the chamber of both and two magazines ready to go on their belts. Maybe if they were smarter, they might have considered calling out SWAT to remove Sherman. Smart had nothing to do with it. They just wanted the pleasure of again putting the cuffs on Sherman but this time for murder.

Don, weapon in hand, walked slowly toward room eight. Chuck was at his back. When he reached the window of the room that they had recently visited and witnessed some sordid behavior, Don stopped. The same gap in the curtains was conveniently there. Mr. Park was missing a great business opportunity to charge admission to watch his wife in action through that gap. Maybe he did.

Mrs. Park was providing great customer service as Don looked through the gap. Both Sherman and Grimes were receiving her skilled attention. She wasn't exactly cleaning their room.

Don slowly back stepped from the window and then stopped and told Chuck what he saw. Chuck didn't feel a need to catch the act. They decided in very hushed voices that the best approach would be to kick the door and rush the room. Granted, there was no crime occurring in the room. Neither Don nor Chuck cared about the act being performed by Mrs. Park; however, it was distracting.

Since Chuck was better at kicking things around with his very lethal feet, he would do the honors at the door. Don would be directly behind him with weapon out and ready.

Chuck concentrated as he stood four feet from the door to room eight. His hands were by his side, his feet spread shoulder width apart, his weapon in his right hand. When he uncoiled and hit the door near the knob with his right foot, Chuck brought his weapon up to his left hand, assuming the two-hand firing technique used by anyone who knew anything about semiautomatic handguns. When the door lock disintegrated and the door flew open, Chuck stepped aside, replaced by Don who ran into the room.

Unfortunately, Sherman had a gun within his reach when Chuck kicked the door. He had just enough time to bring it to the side of Mrs. Park's head who, a few seconds before, had been working on his reluctant cock.

Sherman was on the bed with Mrs. Park lying on him. His left arm was around her neck; his gun was drilled into her right ear. Both were nude. It was right out of the most pornographic crime novel. Grimes now had both hands covering his groin while sitting on the one chair in the room. Don's immediate thought was, *gross.*

"Sergeant Sherman, you are under arrest for the murders of Yvonne Gillespie and John Barber and who knows how many others," Don said, his weapon aimed at the portion of Sherman's head that wasn't covered by Mrs. Park's. Everyone in the room, including Chuck, knew that Don would cheerfully put a bullet in Sherman's brain.

"You must be shitting me. I seem to be holding the cards here. If you so much as twitch, I'll blow this gook bitch's brains all over the wall."

Don then lowered his weapon to a very exposed part of Sherman that he couldn't cover with Mrs. Park's body. "How about I blow a hole in your balls and watch you bleed to death? You can do what you want to this whore, I don't particularly care, but I will take you in one way or another."

Mrs. Park began to holler and squirm, knowing that her options were looking grim. Sherman had little to hold onto since both of them were nude. Just as it looked like Sherman may have figured he had nothing to lose, he took his gun out of Mrs. Park's ear and just started to bring it toward Don. A shot rang out, then one more. Sherman's head took on a new appearance; half of it was gone, now decorating the wall above the bed and Mrs. Park's face.

Sherman's gun fell, and Mrs. Park, now covered in blood and brain matter, screamed and pulled loose of the dead man's loosening grip. The sheets would definitely require changing after this.

"Thanks, Chuck. Your timing was exquisite as usual."

"You're welcome, Don. The second round probably wasn't necessary, however."

"Training kicked in. The review board will be impressed."

"You're right, thanks," Chuck said as he calmly turned toward Grimes, weapon in hand. Grimes sat on the chair from where he had been watching the real-life porn flick before him, exposed and thinking that he might be next. He had apparently forgotten that he was *sans* clothes. "I didn't know, guys. I swear, I didn't know."

"Didn't know what, Grimes?" Don asked with full knowledge that he probably should not question him at this point.

"I didn't know that he killed anyone. I thought that this was about the money."

"It was about the money, but it was about killing people, too."

While Chuck put cuffs on Grimes, not bothering to cover him, Don threw a sheet around Mrs. Park who was hysterical, babbling in Korean. Vickie ran into the room, gun in hand, and stopped. "Looks like you didn't need me."

"No, we needed you to do what you did," Don said. "Would you take Mrs. Park to the office and keep her there for the medic unit? Don't let Mr. Park go nuts on you."

Just as Don got the last out of his mouth, Mr. Park stormed into the room. "What you do to my room? You have to pay!"

"Mr. Park, if you don't leave this room and return to the office in two seconds where you will wait for us, I will shoot you," Chuck said.

Mr. Park looked first at Chuck, who was still holding his weapon, and then at the ruined head of Sergeant Sherman whose blood, mixed with brain matter, was making its way down his chest and into the thick hair covering his chest. He then turned and walked away.

When Don and Chuck led Grimes from the room, closing the door behind them, it started to rain. The neon lights in the office and those in businesses across Aurora reflected on the wet and uneven surface of the parking lot. People who occupied other rooms in the motel were coming out to see what was happening. Most were only partially clothed. Most were women. The lights from their rooms added to the reflections on the pavement, which had taken on the appearance of an Impressionist painting. The image wasn't lost on Don, nor was the image of Sherman's collapsed face: a face that was reminiscent of one he recalled seeing in Vietnam, a face that had collapsed after suffering the therapy offered by an M-16, the face of a teen Don had just killed.

The motel parking lot looked like a country carnival by the time Captain Mitchell arrived. Officers from three precincts had responded when they heard the call of shots fired on Radio. Three fire department aid units as well as one medic unit added to the traffic jam. There was nothing like a police shooting to bring out everybody and his uncle. The chief hadn't yet arrived, but he would unless the rain, now falling more steadily, persuaded him otherwise, and it was late. The painting on the pavement changed with each new emergency light.

After they parked Grimes's naked ass in the back of a patrol car, Don and Chuck cordoned off the scene and identified witnesses who would be interviewed by Homicide day squad. All of Homicide knew Sherman well, so they didn't know quite what to make of what they found. They did their usual professional job, however, except for Hase and Monson whom Chuck had fired.

The medical examiner who responded to examine the body and take it for autopsy was none other than Dr. J. Wyman Mills. Her technician was the very competent Mike Griswold. Dr. Mills appeared to be pleased to see Don and just managed to hold back her desire to congratulate Chuck for killing the fuck who murdered Yvonne Gillespie. She would delight in slicing Sherman apart even without the proof that would come from DNA testing.

"There is something you might like to know, Don," Dr. Mills said as she zipped and sealed the bag containing Sherman's body. "We didn't find any of Gillespie's family who would take her body for burial. It seems that the entire family is too busy to transport her back to Iowa. Are you and Chuck still interested in kicking in to the fund to give her a respectful burial and headstone?"

"We just happen to have come into a bit of cash that should cover the whole burial. Let's talk next week over lunch. One other point of fact comes to mind: who the fuck would want to be buried in Iowa?"

"Ditto on Iowa, but if you and Chuck take me out for brazed tofu, I'll have to cut you, you know that, don't you?"

"Chuck and Vickie have done a great job of reeducating me. No more tofu, only bean curd will pass my lips from here on," Don said with the best smirk he could manage under the circumstances.

"OK, bean curd it is, but what the fuck is bean curd? Pardon my language."

Before Don, Chuck, and Vickie climbed into the pool car for the drive back to the office and all of the paperwork that awaited them, they stopped at the motel's office to have one more word with Mr. Park.

He was sitting on one of the chairs meant for customers. He had his head in his hands, his life, as he knew it, clearly over.

"Mr. Park, we'll be taking all of your registers for at least the last year. Where are they?" Don asked.

"In back, but you need warrant first."

"I need you to get up and give them to us before I make good on that last threat," Don said.

Mr. Park got up and walked toward a back room with Don, Chuck, and Vickie following. The room was a cluttered mess, but Mr. Park called it home. Along one wall was a cabinet filled with videotapes. Above the cabinet was a video monitor that was on. It showed room eight where detectives from the Homicide Unit day squad were busy photographing, measuring, and collecting evidence that would never see a criminal courtroom. There was a bank of switches near a video recorder that was apparently wired to every room in the motel. Mr. Park was recording activities in the rooms for later viewing or sale or both.

"Chuck, what day was Shondra raped and beaten?"

Chuck had to think for a while, and then he came up with not only a date but a time as well.

"I think Mr. Park just solved that rape as well."

Don found a consent to search form in his briefcase and asked that Mr. Park sign it, which he did. They then found a box in which to place all of the tapes, even those that didn't include the date on which Shondra was raped. They would make for interesting viewing at a later date when things were slow in the office.

CHAPTER THIRTY-FOUR

Two weeks to the day after Chuck put Sherman down, Don, Vickie, and he walked into the chief's office with Captain Mitchell. The ceremony took only fifteen minutes, but it capped all four of their careers in the Seattle Police Department. They were each awarded commendations for the work they had done in stopping a budding serial murderer among the ranks and bringing about a start to the rebuilding of the reputation of the Homicide Unit.

"Do you suppose the rest of the unit will balk at Vickie being given a detective's badge and assigned to the unit this early in her career?" Captain Mitchell asked of no one in particular as they waited for the elevator down to the fifth floor.

"Fuck the motherfuckers if they do," Don said. "Pardon my language."

"That was new, Don, and quite creative. Do you mind if I use it from time to time?"

"No, Captain. I would be honored if you did."

"Great, I will. Now where should we go for lunch? I'm buying."

Vickie, not quite comfortable in her new station in life as a detective, piped in, "Let's go to that Chow Dong or Dong Chow place. I really liked it."

"Have you been shot in the knee recently, Detective?" Chuck asked.

After the media frenzy, plea deals and firings, the department and the Homicide Unit settled down. All of the deadwood either found other places in the department to hide until retirement or retired knowing that the alternative was probably a very public firing. Things were looking up. Vickie even had a partner new to the unit but with lots of experience in violent crimes investigations. She had time on Vickie but didn't have the stuff on her resume that legends are made of. She made a great partner for Vickie. Sergeant Mary Jones, formerly of the North Precinct, took supervision of the squad. As Don told anybody who would listen, "Life was good."

Things don't usually have happy endings in the world of policing, especially where murder is involved, but there was an exception in this case. Raymond, his mother, Shondra, and father, Maurice, with some reluctance, met with Don, Chuck, and Vickie and her new partner at a restaurant in Chinatown. Raymond was excited because he rarely had the chance to eat in a real restaurant; McDonalds didn't count.

After they finished a meal that contained not a hint of tofu, they drove to Shondra's mother's house. While Raymond was with his grandmother, Don, Chuck, Vickie, Shondra, and Maurice gathered around the kitchen table.

"Are you going to tell me to get my life together?" Shondra said.

"How did you know?" Don responded. "We have an idea that might be of some interest to you and Maurice. We have come into some money that we would like to apply to Raymond's education if certain things happen."

"Here it comes."

"Yes, here it comes. What's coming is a plan that will help Raymond have a life that doesn't guarantee that he will end up in a gang or dead. That's the plan. If you and Maurice are so self-absorbed that you aren't willing to go along with it, then we will be leaving. But the first stop we'll make after leaving is at Child Protective Services. I think they may have a place for Raymond." Don was now on a roll.

"I'm listening," Maurice said.

"As I said, we have come into a large sum of money. We want to apply it to Raymond's education and nothing else. It won't buy a car or travel. It will be managed by a person you will never meet. The other condition is that you two get jobs other than what you're now doing. That is not negotiable. If you slide back into your current lives, the money will no longer be available and Raymond will be on his way to a better home where your lifestyles won't ruin him."

Shondra and Maurice sat in silence, both looking at Don and waiting for the next condition. It didn't come.

Shondra looked at the floor and her shoulders began to shake. Raymond's mother was sobbing, something she thought she had forgotten how to do.

Vickie got up and put her arms around Shondra's shoulders, and then both wept.

About five minutes passed before Don dared to say anything. He was damned if he was going to put his arms around Maurice as he joined in the pity party.

"OK, we've been talking about getting out anyway," Maurice said. "We have a bundle of money put away. We even have an IRA."

"The next thing you're going to tell us is that you take a tax deduction for oil changes on your pimpmobile," Chuck said.

"Can I do that?" Maurice asked as if he thought it possible.

"Do we have the start of a plan here?" Don asked. "And, no, you cannot expense your pimpmobile."

Both Shondra and Maurice nodded and said that they did.

Before the trio left the house, a visitation schedule was arranged. Chuck and Don would come by periodically to check on Raymond. They would take him to events and places they thought might advance his early education and be just plain fun. Vickie thought that her presence would be good for Raymond, so she inserted herself into the plan. It was hugs all around when they left. Even Maurice joined in. Don had never hugged a pimp. He found that this former pimp didn't feel or smell any different than Chuck or he did, although Chuck's cologne was a bit much on some days.

CHAPTER THIRTY-FIVE

The next days were full of the post police shooting stuff for which Don and Chuck were ready. It was new to Vickie, so her learning curve was steep. The tapes that they had confiscated from Mr. Park were critical to everything.

Chuck found the tape that corresponded to the date that Shondra was raped and put it into the VCR player. He fast-forwarded until he found what appeared to be Shondra standing in all her natural glory in front of a bed. On the bed was none other than Detective Grimes wearing nothing but a sneer. He was mouthing something to Shondra, but there was no audio in the rooms. Don thought that he might have to talk to Mr. Park about that.

Grimes didn't appear to be overly impressed with the charms in front of him. Then he motioned for Shondra to get on the bed. As he began his assault on her, Grime's erection grew to monstrous proportions. Well, maybe that was a slight exaggeration on Chuck's part, but he was clearly capable of taking care of business at hand as he hit Shondra. As she fought back, Grimes overpowered Shondra and then raped her. At that point Shondra gave up the struggle and went along with him. As she stopped struggling, Grimes also gave up and slid off her, once again in a less than impressive state.

"It would be great if Wilbur Olson had wired the Fairview for video. It would have made our job a lot easier," Chuck said.

The tape of the shooting in room eight was enough for the Shooting Review Board to give Don and Chuck a clean bill of health. Don, Chuck, and Vickie talked over several meals about how the tape must be making the rounds in the department. Another subject came up from time to time: how could three detectives sink to such depths?

"I've come to realize that arrogance and greed trump common sense and smarts every time," Don said. "I saw it in the civilian world and in the military. I've even seen it in myself from time to time. Sherman, Grimes, and Martin just forgot what they were about."

As Don drove over the West Seattle Bridge toward Tiffany, George, and Martha, he realized that he had grown more in the last few weeks than in all of his previous years.

Tiffany opened the door, letting out the rich smell of something good to eat. George and Martha rubbed against his pants legs, leaving cat hairs behind. Then Tiffany gave him a kiss that said it all.

Following the meal that Tiffany had put her heart into preparing, and after they had made history of a bottle of Two Buck Chuck, Don and Tiffany went to the living room and just sat. It felt right.

"What would you say to giving a small boy an introduction to the SAM, starting with the Impressionists and moving on to the lesser works of the Abstract Expressionists?"

"I think I can do that," Tiffany said as George and Martha jostled for spots on Don's lap.

CHAPTER THIRTY-SIX

Like kayaking to work across Elliot Bay, assuming that people change for the better belongs only in romance novels and schmaltzy movies. Don held the notion throughout his life that people don't change in any real sense. If they were born assholes, they died assholes. He was, of course, pleasantly surprised when he was mistaken, which rarely happened.

Maurice, it turned out, was a born pimp. He just could not get the purple Cadillac and neon suit thing out of his self-image. He tried working at a metal recycling yard on Harbor Island, but the hours and dirt didn't agree with him. He ended up back in the life with Shondra's cousin, who was as good at her job as Shondra had been or better.

Don, Chuck, and Vickie forgave Maurice and let him go on his way only because Shondra had taken to heart her new role as mother to Raymond. She divorced Maurice and took a job as a nursing assistant at Harborview Medical Center. It seems that she had somehow never been charged with anything in her former profession, so she thought that she might start to work on an RN degree because she liked the way that the nurses at HMC carried themselves. That and the fact that some of the new doctors were cute.

Raymond did well in his new private school where he was required to wear a uniform. Once a month, Tiffany and Don took him to a different museum or park where he learned stuff that a television tuned to a cartoon channel didn't teach. Chuck and Vickie pitched in with trips to places around Puget Sound that extended Raymond's world. They made sure to include places that showed him how his race had influenced the area. He was a happy and challenged little boy.

Then there was Marjorie, the perennially happy Marjorie. A fairly new officer who worked the South Precinct happened to come up to the Homicide Unit on a day when Marjorie was dressed in a way that was impossible to go unnoticed by any other than the most obtuse. The officer was not in that group. Their conversation led to a lunch date and then to a meaningful relationship. After three months had passed, the unit received invitations to Marjorie's wedding. Sadly, her dress toned down after the announcement.

Lab work has a way of lagging behind the conclusion of an investigation. The DNA that Don and Chuck submitted in the murders of Yvonne Gillespie and John Barber arrived a week after Sherman's untimely death. The scrapings from Gillespie's fingernails matched the DNA collected from Sherman. Barber's DNA also matched the DNA found on the handcuffs recovered from Sherman's desk and the nightstick recovered in Sherman's darkroom. No doubt remained about who was responsible for Yvonne Gillespie's and John Barber's deaths. Both cases were closed and put on shelves to collect dust.

Then there was the happy occasion of the sentencing of former Detectives Grimes and Martin for theft of several thousand dollars taken from crime scenes. It came as a serious shock to Grimes to learn that the rape of Shondra was taped and that he was the star actor. He was sure that he would skate on that crime because, after all, she was a fucking hooker. He was going to do some serious time for that "freebie." Clorice heaved a sigh of relief when he was sentenced. They were both sent off to a special place out of state where they weren't as likely to run up against a guy named Bubba.

As time progressed, Don's spare time was dwindling. He had managed to persuade George Jefferson to go to the Veteran's Hospital in Seattle to get some treatment for PTSD and to register for medical treatment on the government's dime. George would consent to go on one condition: Don had to go along. The Kumbaya sessions that Don and George attended gave Don new insight into his view of the world in general and his fellow man in particular. George and Don became fast friends as only fellow combat vets could be.

The day that Yvonne Gillespie was laid to rest in a cemetery over-looking Aurora Avenue, the stretch of asphalt where she would have been earning her living if Sergeant Wilton Sherman hadn't cut her life short, Don, Chuck, Vickie, Dr. J. Wyman Mills, and Tiffany all stood, heads bowed, as the Seattle Police Department chaplain sent Yvonne on her way. None of them had known Yvonne in life, only that she was a fellow human. The chaplain made no mention of her life as a hooker. She was one of God's children, according to him, worthy and valued in His eyes. There were no dry eyes on the lawn on that bright day. Yvonne had finally found a respectful address beside some of Seattle's most respected citizens.

It was a few weeks later and after things had returned to a state of some normalcy that Don and Tiffany arrived at Chuck's condo for dinner. When Chuck opened the door, Vickie and a man whom Don didn't know stood beside Chuck. An older man, much older, stood behind them.

"Come in. You're late as usual. Thankfully, the meal isn't time sensitive," Chuck said.

"I would return the sentiment, but since we're not at work, I won't." Don said.

"I'd like you to meet Randle. You can call him Officer Matthews if you wish, but Randle is his first name. And you remember Officer Charles M. Brown to whom we promised lunch a while back."

Officer Brown, retired, was the man who sat at the window of his apartment at First and Virginia at all hours. He was pleased to have been invited to dinner. It just so happened the Officer Brown was the life of the party with stories about "the good old days."

Don recognized Officer Matthews as an officer whose reports he had read on many occasions and was impressed with each one.

"Good to meet you, Randle. I've been noticing your work; it's great. Maybe you would like to come to Investigations some day."

"No, I like Patrol," Randle said.

"Let's leave work behind for the evening, shall we?" Chuck said as he led them into his living room. Don noticed that Randle seemed right at home.

"Oh my God, is that a Jacob Lawrence?" Tiffany exclaimed. "I hope you aren't using the fireplace with it hanging there."

Don and Tiffany found that they shared more than enough on which to base a long-term relationship. Tiffany wouldn't, however, budge on the issue of moving George and Martha into Don's condo until it occurred to her that the Jackson Pollock wouldn't fit in her house. It turned out that George and Martha loved Don's condo. The view from the master bedroom out onto Elliot Bay was very much to their liking; they had never seen the Cascades.

EPILOGUE

Sitting cross-legged on the living room floor of an old bungalow situated along a tree-lined street about a half mile from the Seattle Veterans Medical Center, an Oriental rug and an ornately patterned pillow separating his ass from the hardwood beneath, wouldn't have been a scene that Don could have imagined himself a part of just six months before. It would not have gotten him high marks from most of the people with whom he worked. There was the faint scent of incense that Don recalled from his days at San Francisco State University. He couldn't put a name to it, however. Soft music, perhaps a Gregorian chant, added to the atmosphere. The two additional but missing elements that would have transported Don to an earlier time would have been a hint of marijuana and "Kumbaya."

Six months earlier Don would not have imagined in his most bizarre dream that he would be sitting in a circle of men, holding hands and meditating on the question: who am I? What men were, outside the narrow confines of their heads, was a question best left to the "PTSD assholes" whom Don had made all manner of evil assumptions about. He was now one of them. He wasn't even gaming the Veterans Affairs system for money and sympathy, nor were the other six men in the room holding hands and contemplating who they were, six men who now referred to themselves as members of the "PTSD Assholes Club."

"OK, guys, let's examine what we've learned," said Ms. Constance, a woman of about fifty-five with long gray hair, tied into a ponytail with a purple ribbon. She appeared as though she might have run a marathon that morning. Her faded blue jeans fit as if they were custom made for her. Her peasant blouse placed her in a time that Don was sure she felt more comfortable in: the sixties. "You can let go of the hands of the men to your left and right, but try to feel what that connection lent to this short period of self-reflection."

As Don released the hand of George Jefferson on his left and the man's hand to his right, which belonged to a gray-haired biker who wore his "Vietnam Vet" cap like a medal, he had to reflect on what the fuck had become of him. He was required to check his attitude at the door before the start of the weekly session that he and George took part in without fail. Before the start of this session, he found that he had no attitude to check; he was now attitude deficient.

"Don, would you share with the others what you discovered during this period of reflection?" Ms. Constance said in her most somnolent voice.

Don wasn't all that into "sharing" with strangers when he started the PTSD therapy that the VA offered. He felt exposed in a way that he had never been before, even when he was engaged in the most intimate "sharing" sessions with Tiffany. Cops had to wear a mask against the emotions thrown at them. Homicide cops had to wear full-body armor against them. "Sharing" was for the fire department heroes.

"It wasn't too long ago that I thought this was all bullshit, pardon my language, but I've had second thoughts about that. The best therapy I've ever been exposed to was in a convenience store in the Central District. A man said something to me that I didn't know I had been waiting to hear since my return from Vietnam. He said these simple words: 'Welcome home, brother.'"

George reached over and touched Don's hand as he spoke. Don was just able to continue, now that his emotion shield was lowered. "Before that day in a cluttered corner store, I never had a brother. Now I do. In my arrogance, I thought I was helping a man get out of a trench that he had no part in digging. In fact, he was pulling me out. He was my therapist. So who am I as revealed by my short period of reflection? I don't know. But I think I at least know this much: whereas I was a piece of work, I'm now a work in progress."

The room was silent for several minutes, the music just above the level of consciousness. Don had been allergic to silence but no more. The group had learned, with the guiding hand of Ms. Constance, the value of silence. It was now natural to just sit without filling the silence with noise.

"It may be fair to go around the circle and ask the same question of each of you, but I don't want what Don just shared to be left behind. Those may have been the most powerful words I as a therapist have ever heard. Enlightenment is an elusive thing. When we try to achieve it, it slips away. When we don't, it sometimes comes toward us on cat's feet and curls up on our laps. As the masters have taught us, 'Chop wood, carry water.' To attempt to explain those words is to lose them. We each carry within us the answers to our own questions. I can't answer for you; only you can do that. But I do know this: by hearing what Don just shared, we know that we can take something from it. Even if it's not ours, we can look for those moments that may just lead us to our own enlightenment. I only hope that I am as fortunate as Don in achieving what he has. Now let's help each other up from the floor and share tea and cookies."

George was up before Don. He stood before him and held his hand out. Don took it and George pulled him to his feet; he put his arms around Don and gave him a hug. "Thank you, brother."

"I don't think it would be very professional of me to ask who this brother is you found in that store in the CD," Ms. Constance said as she approached Don and George with a cup of tea in hand. "But I'm not feeling exactly professional at the moment."

"Ms. Constance, meet my brother, George."

Ms. Constance had become very familiar with everyone in the group over the past six months. She knew George as well as she knew Don. "Brother George, it's great to know you and an honor. It's not often in our walk along life's path that we are met with the perfect answer. What I heard today was that, the perfect answer."

"We now refer to each other as PTSD assholes," said George. "That's my piece of enlightenment. I didn't think that my enlightenment would come by way of a fucking cop, pardon my language. This fucking cop is now my brother."

George dropped Don off at his condo following the session. Don wasn't exactly pleased with the car that George bought with the money he was earning from his job in the Seattle Police Department's fleet office. A Subaru Outback would have served George's transportation needs better than the five-year-old Olds Cutlass. Don hadn't yet asked George to park down the street when he and his girlfriend came over for dinner. *What a fucking prince.*

When Don walked in the door, George and Martha met him. They were now of the opinion that they owned him. He was also met by some great odors that could mean only one thing: Tiffany was at work in the kitchen.

"Hi, Mr. Kumbaya. How did the session go?" Tiffany asked as she held out a glass filled halfway with a red wine of questionable vintage.

"I think we had a breakthrough today. Ms. Constance admitted that she has not yet achieved enlightenment."

"Bless her soul. That's the mark of a true professional. If she can admit a failure, she is the person to go to for therapy. It's the people with all of the answers you want to steer clear of."

"Does that apply to art as well?"

"Yes it does. You may have noticed that George and Martha sit in front of the Pollock for hours on end. They never gave Abstract Expressionists a second look before they arrived here."

"I thought that they were just attempting to get up the latest hair ball."

Then they sat down and ate.

The End

Made in the USA
Charleston, SC
12 October 2013